SHE WANTS HER TOO

....

THE SEQUEL

TASHA C. MILLER

CREATIVE AFFLICTIONS PRESS
BROOKLYN, NEW YORK

Copyright © 2015 Tasha C. Miller
All rights reserved.
ISBN-10: 0985477830
ISBN-13: 978-0-9854778-3-7

Author photograph: © Tasha C. Miller
Editing: Carrie White
Book Layout: Tasha C. Miller
Jacket design: Tasha C. Miller
Jacket photography: Javier Sánchez

For mommy

"let 'em know I'm like a Icee. For the best effect you gotta use your tongue."

–INGA "FOXY BROWN" MARCHAND

She Wants Her

A NOVEL BY
TASHA C.
MILLER

SERIES DISCLAIMER

The following is part two of a series. If you have not read *She Wants Her Part One*, please read it before continuing on to read *She Wants Her Too*, the sequel. The reading of *She Wants Her* prior to reading the sequel will significantly increase your understanding of the characters and storylines and maximize your entertainment and enjoyment. *She Wants Her* is available for purchase at Amazon.com.

PRAISE FOR *SHE WANTS HER*

PART 1

"I absolutely LOVED this damn book. I swear I didn't put this book back till 5 am. The romance, the drama, and of course the sex, can you say whew? I laughed over this one, found myself getting hot and bothered on more than one occasion, and I'm straight. This is a GREAT read for anyone lesbian or straight." **—Wani**

"I absolutely fell in love with this book from just reading the first page. The book was well written, the characters were well developed. I love the fact that the book had so many layers to it: Love, lust, desire, betrayal, family, friendship and so much more. If you are a lesbian you should definitely pick this up and add it to your collection." **—Becky**

"I really love that Tasha C. Miller is an incredible story teller. Yes, there is awesome erotica here, absolutely. BUT more incredible is the story! This world can certainly use more "love" stories and this one is beyond good. Ms. Miller handles all these with such depth of awareness and feeling that reading this book is an incredible experience." **—Jean N. "MaggieJ"**

"Tasha C. Miller has done an outstanding job with her first novel. There were so many twists and turns that you couldn't help but to want more and more. I can easily see Jacqueline and Cleo coming back in a sequel." **—K. Rogers**

"Wonderfully written. I could not put the ereader down. It had me hooked after the first three chapters, the buildup of each character and their relationship was excellent leaving you yearning for more. One minute you are feeling the heat build between them and the next you are left with a broken heart. Wonderful read, saucy, sensual, hot and fulfilling—a must for any library!" —**Nikstar21**

"This book blew me away. I could not put it down. Ended up staying up late one night to get to the ending. The author's detailed storytelling draws you in and makes you fall in love with Jacqueline and Cleo's relationship. There's also plenty of humor, drama, and plot twists to keep things interesting. Highly recommended." —**D.D.**

"This book is a rare find indeed. Most of the books about lesbian relationships do not go into depth as this book did. I could not stop reading this book from the moment I got it, to the final chapter. This book was so GOOD that I used a sick day from work so that I could finish it. I am waiting anxiously for the next book because I know Cleopatra and Jacqueline's story is only the beginning. For anyone thinking about getting this book, mark my words, you WILL NOT regret it." —**Dagoodnmore**

"This book is definitely a page turner, I couldn't put it down. You get so wrapped up with the characters and the story that I lost sleep finishing it then was mad I finished so quick...so I read it again. Great job hopefully there is another soon!!!!" —**Wife&Wife+3 4eva**

PART ONE

MAYHEM

ONE

SET IT OFF

There was no possibility now that Mandisa would not die screaming. The trouble had begun long before Alexis stood at her front door on that frigid February night, and this would be an epic end to their decade-long battle. It had been written in the stars. That, Alexis was certain of.

"So why am I here, bitch?"

Mandisa had only invited Alexis over to tell her that she'd been sleeping with her husband. But now she was more interested in why she'd just seen Alexis sneaking out of her ex-girlfriend's house across the street. How did Alexis even know Cleopatra? And what was she doing tiptoeing out of her house after dark? Peeking out her window at Cleopatra's had become Mandisa's hobby ... or a bad habit. She hadn't decided yet which sounded better.

Now Mandisa and Alexis sat across from each other in the living room of her townhouse, and Mandisa was ready to set it off.

"You said there was something important I should know?" Alexis flipped her long black hair out of her face and clutched her midnight blue fur coat, pressing it close to her bare skin underneath.

It hadn't been a surprise to get Mandisa's call. The former college rivals checked in occasionally, if only to ensure that they were better off than the other. It was a twisted, ongoing competition that Mandisa always instigated but never won. She hadn't liked that pretty bitch Alexis from the first moment she set eyes on her during freshman-year orientation.

"Are you sure I can't take your coat?" Mandisa asked.

"No need to take the chinchilla, sweetheart. I won't be staying long," Alexis answered.

Interesting, Mandisa thought to herself. Alexis was never usually covered up. Back in college she wore her clothes too tight and too short. She was confrontational, loud, and often inappropriate. Mandisa, the 'pampered African princess,' was a prim, proper, and rich bully. Though many considered her attractive, she was no Alexis. Mandisa was lean, with chocolate skin and medium-length black hair that she kept bone straight. Her prayers to grow into a B-cup had remained unanswered, and the comparisons to Alexis only fueled her hate and insecurities. She would become a chronic over dresser to compensate, wearing a white pantsuit to a BBQ, or full makeup just to workout.

Back then, Mandisa's jealousy toward Alexis's hazel eyes, coke-bottle shape, and ability to draw everyone's attention and admiration took her on a mission to make Alexis's life miserable. It was only then that Alexis set out to give Mandisa a real reason to hate her. She went after Mandisa's man and got him—a popular business major who, after graduation, started a multimillion-dollar conglomerate with a supposedly pregnant Alexis by his side.

"Anyway, let's get on with this. You look like you're ready for bed." Alexis examined Mandisa, who sat across the glass coffee table with no makeup on, and in pink loungewear that looked to be of a low-end cashmere blend that Alexis wouldn't be caught dead wearing.

Mandisa remained silent and studied her, still curious as to what the situation was underneath the ridiculous fur coat.

Alexis broke her gaze and scanned the large living room. Even with its high ceiling, the room felt small, due to all the furniture and crystal knick-knacks Mandisa crammed in to the space. Light from the crystal floor lamps reflected off the gold chandelier, threatening to blind her.

"Hmm ... it's awful quiet in here. Still alone?" Alexis leaned back on the white leather sofa. "When are you going to get married and push out some little crumb snatchers?"

With that remark, Mandisa momentarily forgot why she'd asked Alexis over in the first place.

"That life is not for me." Mandisa stuck her non-existent chest out. "Not like some people. Get into college, steal my man, and marry him because of a fake pregnancy scheme. Never wanted to lift a finger like your mama huh? What was your mama again? A maid? And your daddy a preacher? Never heard of him. Guess his pimping for the Lord wasn't good enough for TV?" Mandisa raised her eyebrows and waited for clarification.

"My mother cleaned offices," Alexis said.

"Guess she couldn't be trusted in someone's home or hotel room. She didn't make beds, but she still cleaned toilets, right?"

"Thank you." Alexis said to Mandisa's housekeeper who had entered the room to serve them water. "My mother doesn't clean toilets anymore." She sipped Perrier from the champagne flute while she watched the housekeeper—an elderly African woman—add logs to the simmering fire in Mandisa's fireplace. "Not everyone was fortunate enough to be born with a diamond-encrusted bone in her nose." Alexis laughed. "Tell me, where do you keep your elephant? The kitchen?"

The housekeeper, whose ill-fitting wig seemed to rotate on an axis all its own, scowled at Alexis.

"I'm going to steal your maid," Alexis said, winking at the woman. "I haven't seen one fly since I've been here. Oops, spoke too soon." She pretended to swat one away from her face. The housekeeper jostled her wig nearly 45 degrees as she hurried out of the room in a desperate effort to get away from Alexis.

"African jokes? Ignorant. She's the caregiver to my home." Mandisa pursed her lips.

"Bullshit!" Alexis glared. "You're not even paying that woman enough to buy a proper wig. I thought it was going to fall into the fireplace and melt."

"Have any regrets about stealing Christopher from me?" Mandisa abruptly returned to the purpose of the meeting—informing her nemesis that she was going to take her husband away from her for good.

"Sweetheart, I can't take my husband away from anywhere he wants to be. My pussy is lined with honey, and it leads to a pool of cream, but you are giving me way too much credit. You're sweet, though. Still mad, are you?"

"You stole him a long time ago. My college sweetheart left me for a country chick who they only let on campus because of a generous financial aid policy and—probably—affirmative action. But your husband is all over the media, and rarely seen with you." Mandisa pointed a finger at Alexis. "So why would I be mad that you supposedly got him?"

"Anyway," Mandisa continued, "did your husband ever tell you that I liked women just a little too much? We'd have three-somes and I always paid more attention to the girls. He likes lesbians in his porn, but not in his bed. That's why he picked you, not because you told him you were pregnant." Mandisa smiled. Christopher had been so traumatized by Mandisa's les-bian affairs in college that he put a stringent lifestyle clause in his and Alexis's prenuptial agreement. If Alexis violated it, she would leave the marriage exactly how she entered it: with noth-ing.

"You're gay?" Alexis tried to recall if there were any signs she'd missed. "I had no idea. So why are you so mad? He would have left you anyway."

"That's not the point," Mandisa snapped. "He's a man, he was bound to cheat. The point is, he cheated on me with you, and then dumped me for you. You, of all people. The one chick he knew for a fact that I couldn't stand. And everyone on cam-pus knew you were sneaking around and shoved it in my face, every chance they got."

"Yeah. That was a very long time ago." Alexis dismissed her little tirade. She was more interested in Mandisa's announce-ment. "So, you have a girlfriend? If not, you better hurry up. Better find someone before it dries up down there."

"Speaking of dry, I know your husband isn't putting it down … at least not on you." Mandisa ran her hand across her face; his cologne was still on her skin from their morning rendez-vous. "I'm curious, when was the last time—"

"So do you have a woman or not?" Alexis interrupted her. She took a delicate sip from the gold-stemmed flute.

"I broke up with someone very special not too long ago."

It was the first time Alexis had ever seen any vulnerability in Mandisa, and she liked it. She tried to force her facial expression to one of sadness, but failed.

"She was still in love with her ex," Mandisa continued. "She went back to her and married her. What's even worse—" Mandisa was now in the mood to share. "We work together, and she lives right across the street." She studied Alexis to see if her reaction would betray her.

"What?" Perrier dribbled down Alexis's chin. She leaned over and grabbed a cloth napkin and dried her mouth, careful to dab around her red matte lipstick.

"She lives across the street with her wife and kids," Mandisa repeated, confident that Alexis had just outted herself. "You sure you don't want to take off your coat?" Mandisa still needed to know if she was naked underneath the fur. Then she would know exactly why she'd been sneaking out of Cleopatra's.

Alexis struggled to control her anger. How was it that she didn't know anything about Cleopatra and Mandisa? She had private investigators monitoring Cleopatra sporadically, but knew nothing of this relationship. It couldn't have been more than a short fling, she convinced herself. "You don't say." She regained her composure. "That must make you quite miserable."

"It does. The things she put my mind and my body through…" Mandisa lied, knowing full well that Cleopatra had never touched her.

6

But Alexis knew of Cleopatra's abilities. She had been her sugar mama many years before, and had proclaimed herself Cleopatra's guardian angel. She had done and would continue to do the unmentionable for her, all the while knowing she could never have her. Now Alexis only emerged when she sensed trouble in Cleopatra's midst.

"She sounds amazing." Alexis fidgeted in her chair, reminiscing about when Cleopatra was in her bed. "Too bad you weren't good enough to hold on to that," she smirked.

"Really?" Mandisa slammed her champagne flute down on the glass coffee table. "Why were you coming out of Cleopatra's house?" She couldn't contain her anger any longer. Telling Alexis that she was doing her husband would have to wait. "How do you even know her?"

"I don't know anyone by that name."

"Liar." Mandisa sprang to her feet. "What's underneath your coat?"

"I'm leaving." Alexis stood up. "This was a tremendous waste of time. My pilot is waiting." She clutched her coat tight, even though it was already securely buttoned.

"Why did you get so upset when I told you I dated her?" Mandisa pressured her to answer.

"I told you, I don't know her."

"You're going to tell me I didn't see something I know I saw? Ok…" Mandisa thought for a moment. "So you don't know anything about Cleopatra's tongue? They call it the 'snake.'"

"Ooh" slipped from Alexis's lips, her body jerking just enough for Mandisa to notice. "I don't know her." Alexis struggled to control the fluttering of her eyelids.

"Right. Whatever." Mandisa tapped her chin as she paced back and forth. "I wonder what she would say if I asked her if she knew you?"

"Cleopatra would deny—" Alexis caught herself before she could finish. She had never been this close to being outted, and her finesse for slipping out of situations didn't always work so well with Mandisa. "I'm warning you."

"I'll keep your little secret." Mandisa sucked her teeth. For a moment, Alexis felt a bit of relief, and her shoulders relaxed. "But if it'll make you feel better, I'll tell you a secret of mine." Mandisa pointed to herself.

Alexis couldn't hide the eagerness on her face. "Go ahead," she said enthusiastically, all the while wondering who she would tell Mandisa's secret to first.

Mandisa leaned in and whispered in Alexis's ear. "I had your husband first, I have him now—had him this morning, as a matter of fact—and I'll continue to have him when, where, and how I want." Mandisa walked back around the coffee table and stood in front of her armchair with her arms folded across her chest, defiant.

Alexis stared at her, studying her before she spoke. She enunciated her words slowly. "I don't believe you."

"We ran into each other a while back, and he's been, how do you say? Running up in it ever since." Mandisa laughed. "Still fits like a glove. I'm the one lesbian that he actually wants in his bed. He still can't resist me."

Alexis's body shook. "No. Anybody but you."

Mandisa grabbed her cell phone from the coffee table. She held it up and flashed a picture on her screen. Alexis glanced at the phone and quickly averted her eyes. "What type of fucking lesbian are you? That's not how it works. I think you're doing it wrong. Must not be a very good one if you're fucking my husband."

"Oh I'm good at what I do no matter who is in the sheets." She waved the phone around, forcing Alexis to look at it. "Wait, do you not recognize it? Maybe not ... when was the last time you saw it when it was actually hard?" Mandisa laughed.

Inside her head, Alexis was screaming at the top of her lungs. She and her husband had an understanding as far as his activities outside of their marriage, but this was an outright violation of that. He had to know that carrying on with Mandisa would incite a war between them. Her eyes were tortured as she studied the malicious smirk on Mandisa's face.

Mandisa's chair scrapped aggressively against the hardwood floor as she stepped back. She watched for Alexis's eyes to broadcast her intended direction, no stranger to being jumped; her narcissistic and elitist tendencies, along with her fresh mouth, had often been more than people could tolerate. So she knew when a blow was coming, and from what direction, but that was where her fighting skills ended. She had yet to win a scuffle in her life, and she was now in her late twenties.

Alexis stared straight ahead at Mandisa's throat. Then she hurdled the coffee table, five-inch Tom Ford heels, blue chinchilla, and all, and tackled her. Mandisa fell to the floor with the thud of a dead body. Alexis's 24K gold gel manicure was securely clenched around Mandisa's throat as she slammed Mandisa's skull onto the hardwood floor. Mandisa struggled and finally pried Alexis's fingers from her neck, only to have

Alexis right hook her in the face. Stunned by the spine-chilling sound of what she believed to be her own jaw cracking, Mandisa stopped putting up a fight. She just lay there, praying that not fighting back would turn Alexis down. But it only enraged her and allowed Alexis to completely trap Mandisa by straddling her, with her arms pinned to her sides. She squeezed Mandisa tight between her thighs, grabbing a wrought iron fireplace poker with her right hand and holding Mandisa by her throat with her left. She stuck the poker in the fireplace, heating it to her satisfaction, and brought it up close to Mandisa's temple.

Mandisa's bloodied face started to sweat as she quivered, terrified that the slightest jerk would cause Alexis to burn her.

"Stay away from my husband." Alexis waved the poker back and forth across her face. "You understand? Or I will finish you."

Mandisa gritted her teeth and clinched her restrained fists, but refused to agree. "You don't even want him."

Alexis brought the hot poker closer to Mandisa's face and squeezed her hand tighter around her throat, choking her now. "I don't give a fuck." She released her chokehold and pulled Mandisa closer to the poker by the collar of her pink pajama top. "Last time. I don't like repeating myself. Stay away from my husband."

"Ok. Ok."

"Ok. What?" Alexis demanded.

"I'll stay away from Christopher," Mandisa surrendered.

Alexis used the poker to push herself up to her feet, scorching a hole in the hardwood floor as she stood erect. She looked back down at Mandisa.

"Like I said, my pilot is waiting."

Mandisa rolled over on her side, grabbed a fistful of ashes from the floor in front of the fireplace, and threw them up in Alexis's face.

Alexis stumbled backward and coughed as she fanned the air. "I didn't know you had it in you," she laughed as she spat. "That's much better." She wiped her face with the sleeve of her coat. "I won't feel so much like the bully when I end you." She picked a white cloth napkin up from the coffee table and dusted off her fur. Then she checked her makeup by looking at her reflection in the belly of a crystal unicorn prominently displayed on the fireplace mantel.

Mandisa pulled herself up to her feet. She touched the back of her head and put her hand to her face, surveying her busted lip as the pain streaked through her jaw. She clutched her left side with her hand and practiced taking shallow breaths.

Alexis walked to the front door and opened it, then motioned her bodyguard to proceed to the car. "I'm fine. Just go," she demanded. "Give me a minute." As she turned around, she saw Mandisa's housekeeper peek from the kitchen. Had Mandisa paid the woman a living wage, she might have been inclined to come to her aid, but that was obviously not the case.

Mandisa shuffled slowly to the door behind her. "I'll tell Cleopatra you said goodbye." She struggled to smile.

Alexis stepped outside onto the front step and looked down at her hands. Her manicure was still immaculate, but she had bruised her knuckles. The harsh winter air gusted around her legs and whipped up into her coat. Mandisa saw her red lace panties, and her bloodied mouth fell open in shock and desire. Alexis put two fingers to Mandisa's lips, pulled her bottom lip down and kissed her. She smacked her lips as she swallowed Mandisa's blood. "Keep fucking with me and you'll die screaming.

....

TWO

ALLOW ME TO INTRODUCE MYSELF

Architect Supriti Khan had an early morning presentation scheduled at Midtown Properties in Times Square. She and her client Mandisa Botha were set to present their plans for a residential project on Manhattan's Upper West Side. Supriti, a native of California who was new to the East Coast, was nervous; she had never dealt with NYC executives before. She arrived early for the late-morning meeting, entered the lobby of the glass tower, and headed toward the security desk. That's when Supriti first laid eyes on her.

The woman looked to be at least 6 feet tall. She was muscular and lean, with milk chocolate skin, high, chiseled cheekbones, and large, dark brown eyes. She had black locs down to her waist and wore large diamond studs in her ears. Nice taste, Supriti thought. She wore all black everything. Black jacket, jeans, John Varvatos boots, and a leather backpack on her shoulders. And she had a habit of licking her full lips.

Supriti sniffed the air, wondering if she smelled a hint of her cologne. Yes, she thought to herself. Fine-ass stud. With that cologne alone, she could get it. This woman was handsome, and confident. She was chatting up a security guard like they were at a family reunion, and he appeared to be enamored by her, as if her attention had made his day. Who was she? And what was she doing there at 8 in the morning?

"Ma'am … excuse me, Ms. Khan." The young security guard at the desk held out her building pass. "Just take one of those elevators up to the fifty-fifth floor." He pointed to the elevator bank directly behind her.

"Thank you," she said, not taking her eyes off of the stud, who was now busy laughing with another security guard seated at the guard's station. She caught Supriti staring at her, and they made eye contact. The woman smiled and continued her conversation with the guards.

The polite smile and immediate dismissal of her presence would never do for Supriti.

As she walked toward the elevators, it hit her. This was New York City. Eight million people lived here, and she may never see that woman again. She didn't know who she was, but she wanted to. She must do something, she thought. She hadn't encountered a woman yet in the city that had commanded her undivided attention without uttering a word in her direction. This woman pulled her in, and she didn't even know why.

Supriti contemplated fainting, but there was no need to get security or EMS involved. She just needed her attention. She wanted her eyes on her. So she dropped everything in her hands.

"Can I help you with that?" The stud immediately sprang into action, bowing at Supriti's feet to pick up her belongings. Supriti loved seeing her down there; she could get used to that vantage point. She covered her mouth, feigning helplessness as she watched the stud pick up her purse, portfolio case, and architectural drawing transport tube.

"Thank you so much." Supriti looked at her as she allowed herself to be rescued. She had even dropped her cell phone, which had popped apart when it hit the ground. All in an attempt to get the fine woman's attention.

"I think you need an assistant." The woman smiled at Supriti as she tucked the portfolio case and storage tube under her arm. She handed Supriti her purse and the pieces of her cell phone. Supriti caressed her hands as she took the parts from her. Soft hands, too.

"Later, fellas." The stud turned around and waved to the guards as she walked toward the elevators.

"Later, Cleopatra." The three guards waved from behind their station.

Supriti followed close behind the woman named Cleopatra as she carried her belongings to the elevator. She gazed into Cleopatra's eyes and her lips appeared to be moving, but she didn't respond, just smiled at her.

"Are you ok?" Cleopatra waved her hand in her face.

"Yes, why?" She blushed and smiled.

"I asked you what floor you were going to, and you just kind of stared at me."

"I'm sorry. I must have been daydreaming." Supriti licked her lips and tossed her jet black hair back, showing off her slender neck.

"So, what floor do you need?" Cleopatra asked again as she pointed to the elevator.

Supriti drew a blank. "Oh, it's on my cell phone." She

scrambled to put it back together, forgetting that the security guard had told her to go to the fifty-fifth floor, and that it was printed on the guest pass she was still holding in her hand.

"Ok, what company and department are you visiting?" Cleopatra shuffled Supriti's belongings from one arm to the other.

Supriti snapped back into reality. "I need the executive boardroom for Midtown Properties."

"Please." Cleopatra smiled as she held out her hand, allowing Supriti to get on the elevator first. She entered behind her and pushed the button to the top floor. The executive express elevator ascended quickly toward the fifty-fifth floor.

"I hope you don't mind," Supriti said as she began to unbutton her trench coat. She took it off and threw it over her arm.

They stood a few feet apart and Cleopatra could feel the woman's eyes running up and down her body, but remained silent. She knew this type of woman well. Men wanted her, while women either hated her or wanted to be her. She needed all eyes on her at all times, but Cleopatra thought, the red suit, really? It was stunning, as was the ivory silk blouse that she wore underneath it. The suit flaunted her curvaceous body, and looked like Prada or something, but was not the best choice for the good 'ole boys club that she was about to present to in a meeting that could make or break her career.

Cleopatra's wife Jacqueline was gorgeous, too. She thought she was the most beautiful woman on the planet. But Jacqueline only wanted to be the center of Cleopatra's world, and could care less what anyone else thought. This woman was nothing like her wife; she was the kind that lived for the world's attention, while Cleopatra's wife only lived for hers.

Cleopatra glanced at the woman as she often did with females, not even aware she was doing it. The glance was quick, a non-offensive gaze, her need to check out a woman's body inbred into her. Cleopatra was a breast and ass woman. Her gaze rose to the woman's face, but slowly enough that Cleopatra caught the way her eyes widened with sexual tension and anticipation.

The woman was particularly attractive, Cleopatra thought. She was showing way too much cleavage for the daytime. But Cleopatra would never complain about breasts in her face. She always did have a thing for Indian women. One of her first loves had been Indian.

The woman reminded Cleopatra of her, and she wondered where the girl was now.

As the elevator neared its destination, it came to an abrupt stop in between floors, knocking Cleopatra out of her daydream.

"What was that?" The woman braced herself by grabbing a hold of Cleopatra's arm and clutching it tightly.

Cleopatra exhaled. "Damn. We're stuck." She looked up at the elevator display panel.

"No. No. No." The woman went into panic mode and gripped Cleopatra's arm tighter.

Cleopatra pried the woman's fingers from her bicep, and watched as the woman paced the small elevator and slapped herself on the cheek. Cleopatra tried to ignore her, laying the drawing tube down in the corner of the elevator and picking up the emergency phone to dial the security desk.

"Not today, not now," the woman mumbled. "This can't happen."

Cleopatra watched her for a moment; she knew she needed to get her off the elevator before she drove both of them crazy.

"I'm sorry. I'm kind of a claustrophobic," she admitted.

"Kind of?" Cleopatra smiled. "That's funny. I wouldn't have known if you didn't tell me." She laughed. "Hi, we're in elevator number six, and it's stuck in between the fiftieth and fifty-first floors. Just me and one other passenger. Thank you." She hung up.

"Don't worry." Cleopatra made eye contact with the woman. "They're working on it, but it might be a few minutes. Ok?" Her eyes were soothing, her voice warm.

"Ok." The woman deflated right in front of Cleopatra and went from 10 to 0 on the panic scale. "I'm good." The woman licked her lips as her chest heaved. "I'm at ease." She smiled. She couldn't keep her eyes from running back and forth across Cleopatra's body.

"So tell me about yourself. I'm guessing you're an architect?" Cleopatra pointed to the drawing tube. She knew exactly who Supriti was, but saw her examining her body again and decided to break her focus.

"My name is Supriti Khan. I'm the architect to Mandisa Leratho Botha." She beamed proudly, but didn't invite Cleopatra to introduce herself.

Cleopatra smiled as she looked down at her watch; 8:15AM. The woman was ridiculously early for the 11AM board meeting, she thought. So this was the architect whose resume she'd read. Her education and experience were impressive on paper. But she was a close personal friend of Mandisa's. Cleopatra would have to forgive her for that, since her designs were extraordinary. She wondered how many times the woman had practiced that introduction in her bathroom mirror.

"I'm sorry, you've probably never heard of Ms. Botha," Supriti apologized.

"The name sounds familiar." Cleopatra nodded, loving the fact that the woman had no idea that she was Vice President of Acquisitions and Asset Management, and knew her BFF Mandisa very well. Maybe Supriti wasn't expecting a lesbian, and certainly not a stud. Cleopatra's attire certainly could not have helped—her jeans, boots, leather jacket, and backpack didn't scream executive that could make or break her life. But that was the power she held at Midtown. She let Supriti continue; she would never deny her the opportunity to practice her self-aggrandizing monologue.

"So Ms. Botha is an African princess fairly new to the city, and is commencing several real estate projects in Manhattan. I'm here to give a presentation on some of our ideas."

"Sounds like an important meeting." Cleopatra took special note that she used the word 'commencing' in everyday conversation. Supriti was trying way too hard, she thought.

"It is. This is a huge deal. I'm excited. I'm nervous, all of that."

"I'm sure you'll be amazing," Cleopatra encouraged her. "So how is your morning going so far? Besides dropping all of your belongings and getting stuck on an elevator with a perfect stranger?" She tried to help calm Supriti's nerves.

"You are no longer a stranger, but you are definitely perfect."

Supriti gazed at Cleopatra, who froze momentarily. She couldn't remember the last time she'd heard something so corny.

"I was kind of a discombobulated until a few minutes ago," Supriti continued. "With this presentation being so important. But I'm getting more and more relaxed." She smiled, continuing to study Cleopatra's body. "Do you work out?"

"Why do you ask?" Cleopatra raised her left eyebrow.

"I can tell." Supriti sucked her bottom lip into her mouth.

"Ooh. Under my leather jacket, you can tell?"

"I squeezed your bicep."

"I noticed that," Cleopatra smirked.

"Your clothes fit you perfectly." Supriti perused Cleopatra from head to toe again. "You must work out like every day. You're pretty cut." Supriti lowered her head and put her hand over her face. "Sorry, that was a horrible line."

"That was pretty bad." Cleopatra laughed as she nodded in agreement.

Supriti stepped toward her, inhaling. Cleopatra's cologne had wafted around Supriti's nose, and it was intoxicating. "What is that you're wearing?" She closed her eyes.

"Um … did you just step into that inhale? You just sniffed me?" Cleopatra laughed.

"I'm so sorry."

"You're a good time." Cleopatra smiled. "No need to apologize."

Supriti laughed and immediately felt comfortable with Cleopatra. "Any advice on how to deal with these stuffy executives? Are they really all grumpy old white men?"

"Just about all of them. And they all think they're a whole lot more important and special than they actually are. Most of them are quite dull and could use a spanking and a coffee enema, if you ask me."

Supriti laughed. "You're funny. I like that." She bit her lip again.

"Even though this opportunity may be once in a lifetime, don't take it too seriously," Cleopatra continued. "Just have a good time. Be yourself. No matter what happens, life goes on. I doubt you would have come this far if you weren't intelligent and ambitious. So try not to worry too much."

"Thank you. I appreciate that. You're a straight shooter. I like that too." Supriti zoned out. This woman was handsome, she smelled good, her voice was raspy and just deep enough, and her hands were soft when they grazed Supriti's. And she obviously had a job that she knew how to show up on time for. "So, you're here pretty early this morning."

"I like to get here in time to relax my mind and change into my work clothes."

"Do you have a uniform or something you need to get into?"

"Something like that," Cleopatra smirked. "It's not very comfortable, and I'm much more at ease like this." She looked down at her jeans and boots.

"I can't imagine you being any sexier than you are right now, but a uniform just might do it." Supriti tried to imagine what service job afforded her the luxury of the slick thousand-dollar Italian boots she wore.

Then the elevator jolted and jerked back up until it arrived at the fifty-fifth floor. Cleopatra motioned to the woman. "After you." She stepped back and allowed Supriti to get off the elevator first.

"Executive boardroom," Supriti said, scanning the directory.

"I'll take you there."

Supriti had no doubt that Cleopatra could take her there, and followed her down the long corridor. Cleopatra walked with confidence and power, posture immaculate. Like she could have anything and anyone she wanted. But she somehow managed to come across as ultra-charming and without an arrogant bone in her body.

"I don't know how I'm going to repay you for taking such good care of me." Supriti touched Cleopatra's shoulder and her locs brushed across her hand, sending a shiver down her spine. "Umm..." She tried to keep her eyes from rolling back. "But I'd like to try."

"Not necessary." Cleopatra smiled at her.

They passed a woman from the overnight cleaning crew. "Good morning, Mavis. How are the grandbabies?" Cleopatra asked the gray afro-wearing woman.

"Loves of my life. Don't tell my husband." She beamed.

"No ma'am." Cleopatra laughed. "But you killing the kids with that high top fade. They ain't ready." Cleopatra swooped her hand around her head like Dougie Fresh. The woman's high top was actually immaculate, and Cleopatra was its biggest fan.

Cleopatra waved goodbye to the woman as she and Supriti continued to walk down the long hallway. A tall, white-haired, gray-eyed executive passed Cleopatra as they approached the reception area in the lobby.

"Morning. Ready for today?"

"I stay ready." Cleopatra winked at him as they approached the reception desk, where two executive assistants sat. Sonia, a Puerto Rican chain-smoker, fifteen years Cleopatra's senior, was not impressed by Cleopatra and didn't jump through hoops for her like her overeager coworkers. She thought Cleopatra was attractive but too masculine, and she didn't do studs.

"Good morning, Ms. Giovanni." Sonia's counterpart and fresh-faced assistant, Nikki, a young twenty-something brown-haired beauty with long legs, hopped up from behind her desk to tend to Cleopatra. She addressed her as 'Ms. Giovanni,' knowing full well that she had called Cleopatra every name in the book when they had dated years before. Daddy, damn Cleopatra, fuck Cleopatra, shit Cleopatra, it's yours Cleopatra. But this morning it was Ms. Giovanni. Nikki cocked her head to her good side, ensuring that Cleopatra could see her dimple, pivoted on her not-appropriate-for-work stilettos, and prepared to hang on her every word.

Supriti was taken aback by the attention that Cleopatra commanded from the moment she stepped off of the elevator. *Who is she?* she wondered.

"Good morning, Nikki. Could you please help Ms. Khan? Supriti? If I'm not mistaken, that means true love, doesn't it?" Cleopatra asked.

"Yes, it does." Supriti smiled at Cleopatra in appreciation.

Nikki rolled her eyes and chicken popped, making a clucking sound loud enough for Cleopatra to hear.

"Nik." Cleopatra raised her eyebrows at her. "It's early, but could you help Ms. Khan get set up for her presentation, and make her comfortable, whatever she wants." Cleopatra looked at Supriti. "Anything in particular? Coffee, tea, breakfast? Have you eaten?" She looked at her watch.

"No." Supriti shook her head, still wondering who the hell

Cleopatra was.

"Order her a full breakfast, please." Cleopatra studied Supriti as she rattled off a menu to Nikki. "Egg white veggie omelet, twelve-grain toast, fresh fruit cup, freshly squeezed orange juice, no pulp, and a masala chai."

Supriti looked at Cleopatra in amazement.

"Good?" Cleopatra asked for confirmation.

"So good. Perfect." Supriti smiled as she clinched every part of her body; Cleopatra made her throb.

"Excellent," Cleopatra said to Nikki. "Please send the bill to Racquel. She'll charge my account. You and Sonia order yourselves breakfast if you haven't eaten yet."

Sonia looked up from her computer after pretending she wasn't listening the whole time. A free breakfast had piqued her interest. She got up and came from around the reception desk.

"Feel free to tack on anything else Ms. Khan wants," Cleopatra said.

But Cleopatra was what Supriti wanted—she had already decided. Her destiny had just been determined. Her fate sealed.

"Of course. Whatever she wants." Nikki nodded and took Supriti's materials from Cleopatra.

"Thank you." Cleopatra touched Nikki lightly on her shoulder in appreciation.

But Supriti interrupted them. "I'm sorry, I actually never got your name." She held out her hand to Cleopatra.

"Cleopatra Giovanni." Cleopatra took her hand and shook it. Her grasp made Supriti clench her thighs tight together as her panties dampened. The rush that shot through her skin only deepened her want. Then it struck her.

"Vice President of Acquisitions and Asset Management Giovanni?" Supriti covered her face and bowed her head.

Cleopatra dropped her hand, but her touch remained on Supriti's skin.

"Oh my God," Supriti said, embarrassed by the high pitch in her own voice. It made sense now. She'd known who Supriti was all along. The thought made chills go up and down her spine. She had practically thrown herself at one of the top executives in the company. Freaking out at the moment was not an option.

"That would be me." Cleopatra winked at her. "But don't worry—I'm not one of those grumpy old executives you referred to on the elevator. I'm looking forward to your presentation later." Cleopatra smiled. She paused, then moved her gaze over Supriti's body. "Since you did ask me for advice earlier, you might want to come up a good two buttons on your blouse. That is, if you want them to actually listen to what you have to say. And as mind-altering as your perfume is, you might consider washing it off and putting your hair up in a bun."

Supriti felt flush, and her face grew warm. She wasn't sure what Cleopatra meant, but from her tone, she felt judged. "Excuse me?" Supriti asked stunned by her candor.

"I'm sorry. I must not have been clear. You're not appropriately dressed for this meeting."

Supriti had felt an immediate rush of desire before, but now she was embarrassed, and anxious. And moments away from panicking and being angry. Ok, her suit was a bold red and form fitting. And her blouse was half-open, but Cleopatra sure didn't appear to mind during their extended elevator ride. Or had her imagination made a cursory glance a much longer, lust-filled stare?

Cleopatra's firm tone resonated through Supriti's head and rung in her ears. "Do you want you and your work to be taken seriously, Ms. Khan? Because right or wrong, fair or not, you'll be giving the men in that meeting a reason not to."

Supriti bit her lip and clenched her fists. She was always down for a debate—but now she found herself at a loss for words. Cleopatra was right, and Supriti exhaled in defeat. "I'm so sorry. I apologize if I sounded combative or in any way disrespectful."

"No need to apologize. I hope I didn't offend you. But you are a very attractive woman and the men that you'll be meeting today don't have the ability to focus as well as I do." Cleopatra deadpanned her. "Welcome to the big leagues. Have a great morning, ladies." Cleopatra waved to Nikki and Sonia before she walked away, strolling down the corridor and disappearing into her corner office.

"I need that in my life," Supriti said out loud. Then she realized that Nikki was staring at her. "She's fascinating," Supriti whispered as she buttoned up her blouse.

"You have no idea." Nikki shook her head, reminiscing on her short time with Cleopatra. After Cleopatra was promoted to the Times Square headquarters from the Rockefeller Center office, Nikki transferred right along with her, just to stay on Cleopatra's radar, in the hopes that they would rekindle the office romance they once had. But Cleopatra never jumped off twice with her jump offs.

"Follow me, I'll show you to the conference room." Nikki wiggled in front of Supriti in a tight black pencil skirt. They entered the all-glass meeting space, and Nikki waited for the reaction she always got when a nervous newcomer realized they would be presenting for their lives out in the open. "This is the fishbowl."

"Are there any privacy shades?" Supriti asked, stunned by how exposed she felt inside the glass walls.

"Of course, but they won't be used for this meeting. There are a lot of interested parties that don't have a seat at the table." Nikki enjoyed the traumatized look on Supriti's face.

"Great." Supriti felt nauseous. "If I throw up from nerves, everyone will see it."

"Pretty much," Nikki laughed as she helped Supriti set up for her meeting.

"So tell me more about Cleopatra."

"Aren't you supposed to be focusing on this presentation?" Nikki pointed to the clock on the wall.

"I'll get to that. Tell me about her."

"I'm sorry. How do you say your name again?" Nikki asked.

"Supriti." She enunciated slowly. "It's easy to remember if you think, 'so pretty.' Or sue pretty like sue me for being pretty."

Nikki rolled her eyes. "Uh yeah, so pretty, stay away from her. Few women leave relationships with her unscathed. Lust after her from afar, like everyone else. Don't look directly into her eyes or inhale her cologne. She will put you in a trance and have you doing stupid shit. Sh—" Nikki caught herself and snapped out of her flashback.

"I'm sorry. What does that even mean?" Supriti asked, confused.

"It means, you in danger girl." Nikki looked in her eyes. "Just don't. Just don't." She waved her hands in the air as she

27

walked out of the conference room.

✿✿✿

A short time later, after Cleopatra changed out of her street clothes and into her office attire, she stood at the desk of her assistant and gatekeeper, Racquel, going over her agenda for the day.

Supriti, meanwhile, had been wandering around the executive floor until she found the Mergers and Asset Management department. Now she stopped in front of Cleopatra. "Wow. You clean up very well," she interrupted, studying Cleopatra's body in the tailor-made black business suit. She wore a black plaid gingham button-down shirt with black titanium cufflinks.

"Is this your uniform?" She chewed the inside of her lip as she studied the curves in Cleopatra's frame.

"It is." Cleopatra smiled.

"I must say, the jeans and boots are just as sexy on you."

"Hmmph…" Racquel grunted at Supriti and rolled her eyes at Cleopatra. She patted her tiny fro and the gold bangles on her wrist chimed loudly. Cleopatra saw it coming—Racquel was emerging from what she deemed her silent fury. Whenever Racquel patted her head, she was about to read someone and needed to ensure that no hair was out of place before her head and neck got to rolling.

Cleopatra smiled. "Be good, Racquel," she whispered, resting her hand on her shoulder.

"May I speak with you for a moment in private?" Supriti asked.

"Sure, come inside my office."

Supriti followed her into the grand corner office, where Cleopatra sat down behind her desk. "What can I do for you?"

Supriti was seduced by the office the moment she set foot inside. "Office big enough?" she joked.

"It is roomy isn't it?" Cleopatra smiled. "Bigger than my home, growing up. Have a seat."

"I wanted to thank you for everything." Supriti sat down in one of the two black leather modular chairs that faced Cleopatra's bevel-edged glass desk. "Thank you for breakfast and for the advice. And I wanted to apologize," she said shyly as she looked around and studied the modern space, which was decorated in black with red and white accents and bold-colored abstract art.

"For what?" Cleopatra leaned back in her chair and laced her fingers behind her head. Supriti thought Cleopatra looked especially sexy with the bustling view of Midtown Manhattan behind her. "I wanted to apologize for not knowing who you were and calling executives here stuffy and uptight. I'm usually more put together."

"Don't worry about it. Most of the executives here are exactly that. Stuffy and uptight." Cleopatra smiled. "Excuse me." She grabbed the television remote, pointed it toward the lounge area of her office, and turned off the flat screen TV that was tuned to MSNBC. Supriti made a mental note of the large black leather sectional couch, and the kitchenette. She wondered if Cleopatra had spent any nights there.

"You like?" she patted her hair. "I put my virgin Indian Remy up in a bun."

"Much better..." Cleopatra caught herself. "I'm sorry what

did you just say?"

"My Indian Remy." Supriti laughed as she patted her bun again. "Get it? It's like the best quality hair weave you can buy, but this is my real hair, my being Indian." She laughed nervously.

"Ugh." Cleopatra crossed her eyes. "That was horrible. Listen, I'm full of advice today. Don't make jokes that are potentially offensive. Don't make jokes in an attempt to become familiar too quickly. And lastly, don't make jokes that aren't funny. Having said that, if you knew me like that it would have been hilarious. But since you don't, be careful."

"I'm so sorry. Won't happen again. I take direction very well." Supriti opened up her red suit jacket and ran her hand over the ivory blouse that now covered her bosom. "I washed off the perfume. You would have to get very close to smell it now."

"I'll take your word for it."

"Is it particularly cold in here? Or is it me?" Supriti asked.

"It's how I keep people from getting too comfortable in my office. There's only one thing I hate more than wasting people's time."

"And what's that?"

"Wasting mine." The corner of Cleopatra's mouth turned up in a slight smile. "The temperature encourages people to get to the point of their visit. It's quite efficient."

"Gotcha. I guess I will get to the point, then. I'd like to treat you to dinner and maybe dessert sometime soon, really soon … like tonight?"

"Dinner and dessert is reserved for my wife."

"Of course." Supriti's heart sank into her stomach. "I

should have known. Lucky woman." She leaned back in her chair, thankful for the emergency support it offered her, because in that moment she wanted to die.

"I'm the lucky one." Cleopatra pointed to her wedding photo, prominently displayed on her desk.

Supriti ignored the photograph. "How about lunch or coffee then?"

Cleopatra's phone rang. "Excuse me." Cleopatra said, picking up the handset. "Yes, Racquel?"

"Do you need me to come in there and Captain-Save-You-From-A-Ho?"

Cleopatra cleared her throat. "Umm..." She tried hard not to laugh, and snorted instead. "What did you say?"

"Do you need me to come in and rescue you, dial THOT-11? Do you need me to save you?"

Cleopatra could tell that Racquel was outside, pacing and getting hyped. She looked up at Supriti, wanting to laugh so bad that her body shook and her eyes began to tear, then she leaned over and covered her face. She exhaled hard. "No ma'am, we're wrapping up now. But thank you." She hung up the phone.

"I should probably let you get back to work." Supriti stood up and smoothed out her skirt, and Cleopatra escorted her out of her office.

Racquel stood by her desk and watched Supriti disappear down the hallway. She waited until the coast was clear, and grabbed Cleopatra by her arm once Supriti was out of sight. She patted her hair again and Cleopatra held her breath, awaiting her wrath.

"That woman was creaming all over you." Racquel's Ethiopian accent was even more prominent when she was upset. "I don't like her. How do you say?" She looked up at the ceiling as she always did when she was trying to concentrate. "Her energy is stank."

"What did you just say?" Cleopatra struggled to hold back her laughter. "Creaming? And her energy is stank? Where are you learning these phrases?"

"From you! She was creaming in her panties, the whole time."

Since Cleopatra had gotten married, her exchanges with women had been platonic—as they should be. But she seemed to have lost the ability to detect when women were throwing themselves at her now, or maybe she didn't care. The only woman that mattered was her wife, Jacqueline.

"I'm so not having this conversation with you, Racquel. You ever say creaming or THOT-11 to me again and you're fired," Cleopatra laughed.

Racquel and Cleopatra had first crossed paths many years before, as they both navigated the city's social service system, Cleopatra as a teenager and Racquel as a new immigrant. Racquel watched after Cleopatra when her mother couldn't, and had stepped up even more in the years since her mother's death. After graduating from business school, Cleopatra was courted by the city's largest firms. And she presented herself as a package; she required a position somewhere in the company for her childhood friend Shawn, and Racquel was to be hired as her personal assistant. Now, years later, Racquel was Cleopatra's mother figure, so talking about sex with Racquel made her uncomfortable as hell.

"Does she know you're married?" Racquel inquired.

Cleopatra stuck out her ring finger with the two large pave diamond bands. "Yes. Doesn't everyone?"

"Yeah." Racquel put her hand on her hip. "Well, I guess the question is, does she care?"

✿✿✿

A short while later, Supriti was in the executive boardroom, preparing for her presentation and reading over her notes. Mandisa arrived and air kissed Supriti hello, careful not to touch and get makeup on her heather gray pants suit.

"Are you nervous? You look beautiful, as usual." Mandisa ogled her friend's scarlet business suit and cupped her bun in her hand.

Supriti studied Mandisa's face. "You look puffy as hell. A little heavy with the makeup today, huh?"

Mandisa cowered a bit; she'd been hoping that Supriti wouldn't see the pounding her face had taken during her fight with Alexis a few days before.

"Anyway," Supriti continued, "I was nervous when I arrived. Flustered and anxious, but someone gave me a little pep talk and some advice that calmed me down. Now she has every other part of my body riled up."

"What?" Mandisa asked. "She? Who are you talking about?"

"I don't see her yet," Supriti said as she watched executives trickle into the boardroom and take their seats. Then Cleopatra walked in with a group of men. Supriti lit up when she saw her. "There she is." She pointed to her like an excited schoolgirl.

She definitely had it, Supriti thought. Men even realized it, and were captivated by her charisma and confidence. She smiled when she spoke, the dimples in her cheeks digging deeper as if screaming for acknowledgment. Men with no gaydar were enchanted. And those men who were confident that they would never have her were still inexplicably intrigued by this woman, who emasculated them just by standing next to them. She was taller than most, leaner, her muscles harder, her features soft but well defined.

"Oh, hell no." Mandisa shook her head and waved her hands, trying to snap Supriti out of her trance. "Not going to happen, ever."

Supriti ignored her. "Is she really married? Please tell me she was joking." They both studied Cleopatra from across the conference room before the call to order.

"She got married on New Year's Eve in Maui," Mandisa said, annoyed. "You didn't see those diamond bands on her ring finger? I can see them from here. You do realize her wife got them that huge so they can be seen from afar. She's taken. Believe me, I've tried."

"What do you mean you've tried?" Supriti asked, surprised.

"Shouldn't you be getting your head wrapped around this presentation? This is your career," Mandisa reprimanded her. "She is in love with someone else, always will be. That's all you need to know."

"You let her get away?"

"Presentation. Now. Focus." Mandisa snapped her fingers in Supriti's face.

They presented their proposal to Midtown's top executives and board members that morning. From all appearances, the key players and decision makers were impressed and excited about moving forward with their plans. Cleopatra ran the meeting from start to finish. Supriti thought she was sexy, commanding, intelligent, and funny. Most of all, she thought she was powerful. She struck Supriti as the type of woman who could have whatever she wanted with little effort. She struggled to maintain her professionalism rather than melting when Cleopatra addressed her directly. But she was the consummate business pro and both she and Mandisa dazzled all those in attendance.

Mandisa pulled Cleopatra to the side after the meeting.

"Hi, Disa." Cleopatra kissed her lightly on the cheek.

"How is life being a newlywed?" Mandisa cringed, not really wanting to hear how good she was doing with her new wife.

Cleopatra knew Mandisa didn't want explicit details. "It's amazing. How are you?"

"Good. Let me ask you something." Mandisa nodded her head toward the corner and Cleopatra followed her. "How do you know Alexis?"

"I don't know anyone by that name," Cleopatra said without hesitation.

"I saw her sneak out of your townhouse the other evening, and when I told her that we dated, she nearly had a heart attack. Now, how do you know her?" Mandisa folded her arms across her chest and shifted her weight to one high-heeled leg. "We're friends from college," she lied. "And she's never mentioned you before."

"Uh-huh." Cleopatra didn't believe a word Mandisa said, and remained silent. She assumed that Alexis was the cause of the bruising under Mandisa's caked-on makeup and that whatever Mandisa was fishing for was better left alone. Alexis had never mentioned Mandisa to her before, and Mandisa had said the magic word that confirmed she was lying. Friends. Alexis didn't have any.

"I thought I knew her pretty well," Mandisa continued. "But now I'm not so sure. So she never mentioned me over any pillow talk or anything, huh?"

Supriti interrupted them, clearing her throat to draw attention to herself.

"You met Supriti earlier, right?" Mandisa asked.

"Ms. Khan and I met this morning. It is Ms., isn't it?"

"Yes, I'm very single." Supriti smiled as she flipped her hair. "And please, call me Supriti."

"You can call me Cleopatra."

Supriti touched Cleopatra's forearm lightly. "That is a beautiful watch." She leaned in close and lowered her voice slightly. "I love your style, Cleopatra." Supriti fluttered her eyelids and smiled. Mandisa marveled at how hard her friend was flirting with her married ex, right in front of her.

"Thanks." Cleopatra smiled. "If you'll both excuse me, I have another meeting to get to." She kissed Mandisa on the cheek and ran off to her next appointment.

"What do her lips feel like?" Supriti asked.

Mandisa rolled her eyes. "You'll never know."

Supriti whispered, "How did you let her get away?" She licked her lips.

"I never had her in the first place. She wouldn't touch me."

"And you work with her?"

"It's not every day, all day, but I see her often enough."

Mandisa consciously chose not to mention that she and Cleopatra were neighbors.

"So this is the woman you never wanted to talk about, isn't it? You don't sound like you're over her." Supriti folded her arms.

"We dated a while ago; of course, I'm over her." Mandisa lowered her head. "She's off limits to you, though; she's my ex, and she's married and very much in love with her wife."

"How long has she been married?"

"A few weeks. You want to know what her wedding gift was to her wife? She let her quit her job. She's paying her way through graduate school, and loves Jacqueline's kids as if they were her own. That's how much she loves her wife. Even after everything Jacqueline's put her through. No one can compete with that. Certainly not you."

"What do you mean, 'put her through'?"

Mandisa shook her head. "It's not important. You are a beautiful woman," she continued. "You can have whoever else you want. So you—"

"I just want to get to know her better," Supriti blurted out.

"You can go after whoever else you want, but not Cleopatra. Is that clear?"

THREE

....

MRS. CLEOPATRA GIOVANNI A.K.A
THAT BITCH

Over the course of the next few days, Supriti did nothing but fantasize about Cleopatra … whenever she wasn't stalking her. She was everywhere Cleopatra was. The elevator, the building lobby, the executive floor lobby and reception areas. The building cafeteria. Even outside on the street in front of the building. They were there when Supriti became convinced that she had finally gotten Cleopatra alone.

Supriti was on her way home after work on a bitter cold Friday evening when she spotted Cleopatra. Despite Mandisa's stern warning, she walked in her direction. They made eye contact and a smile spread across Cleopatra's lips, her eyes dancing as she looked up and down Supriti's body. Supriti moved in closer to her. Cleopatra extended her arms and Supriti was about to reach out to her when someone else swooped in and jumped into Cleopatra's embrace.

Supriti stumbled backward as she watched her catch the other woman. Cleopatra kissed her full on the lips and the woman slipped her tongue inside of Cleopatra's mouth. They kissed as if they were alone and not in the middle of Times Square. Hordes of people maneuvered past them in the after-work rush. The woman put her hands to Cleopatra's face, taking in more of her, and Cleopatra palmed the woman's ass and pulled her hard into her body. Supriti knew Cleopatra was married, and hadn't cared until now. But something about seeing her with her wife messed with her head. She decided she didn't like Jacqueline, based solely on her title and the position she held in Cleopatra's life. She wanted to pull her off of Cleopatra, but managed to control herself by stuffing one hand in her coat pocket and pretending to check her cell phone with the other.

Supriti had momentarily thought Cleopatra's smile was directed at her, but it was for her wife. Now all she could do was stare. They acted as if they had been apart for months instead of an eight-hour workday. Supriti could finally examine her wife up close, since she had managed to avoid looking at their wedding photo in Cleopatra's office. To her dismay, Jacqueline was beautiful, and though she was bundled up, looked to be as fit as Cleopatra. She was taller than Supriti even without the Giuseppe Zanotti boots she had on. Supriti studied her black suede shearling coat—Burberry, she assumed—and black leather Tom Ford shoulder bag. She was definitely well taken care of. It was rare that Supriti came across a woman that she considered true competition, let alone a woman she considered more attractive than she was.

The woman could barely take her brown eyes off of Cleopatra, and for that Supriti could not blame her.

Supriti couldn't pull her own eyes away from the mass of diamonds weighing down Jacqueline's ring finger. How many karats is that, anyway? she wondered. Everything about the woman was immaculate—her clothes and her skin, which was flawless even without makeup, and not a strand of her long, wavy black hair was out of place. She looked on top of the world. How could anyone married to Cleopatra not be happy?

When the newlyweds managed to pull away from each other, Cleopatra realized that Supriti was standing in front of them. "We meet again." Cleopatra smiled at Supriti as she held her wife's hand.

"Yes, we do. Is this your bitch?" Supriti asked in a deep Indian accent.

"Wait … what?" Jacqueline barked at her.

Cleopatra held out her right arm and pulled Jacqueline into an embrace when she felt her lunge toward Supriti, patting her on the hips to help calm her down.

"Excuse me? This is my wife, Jacqueline," Cleopatra corrected Supriti.

Jacqueline simmered down a bit and decided she would let her wife handle whoever this woman was.

"We just met, Ms. Khan, but don't ever address my wife like that again, or your tenure here will be over before it even starts. Do you understand?"

"I'm so sorry, I didn't mean … I just thought that's what you all called each other," Supriti lied. Her mother was biracial and she herself had only dated black women, so she knew that 'bitch' wasn't a word to throw around without repercussions. She'd tried to get a rise out of Jacqueline, to see what type of woman she was dealing with. But instead she got it from Cleopatra. While it was Cleopatra's intention to set her straight, her aggressiveness only turned Supriti on.

"I don't care how sorry you are, or what you did or didn't

mean. Don't let it happen again. If you forget her name, feel free to address her as Mrs. Giovanni. Clear?"

"Very clear. Again, I apologize."

Cleopatra brushed it off. She stepped aside and allowed Jacqueline full access to Supriti now, but put her hand at the small of her wife's back, and massaged her with her fingertips.

"Jacqueline, this is Supriti Khan."

Supriti extended her hand and Jacqueline snuffed her, managing to eek out a maniacal laugh at Supriti's nerve. She tugged on Cleopatra's coat.

"You ready to go home, baby? My mom is keeping the kids for the weekend."

"Mm-hmm." Cleopatra kissed her and Jacqueline slid her tongue into her mouth again.

Supriti looked away. She cleared her throat loudly in an attempt to interrupt them.

Jacqueline pulled away from Cleopatra and smiled at Supriti. "Regarding your earlier statement, you were actually correct."

"I'm sorry. I don't understand."

"I'm about to be her bitch in…" Jacqueline looked at her diamond-encrusted watch. "About half an hour, depending on traffic." She winked at Supriti. "I'll be her bitch all night long, into tomorrow morning, afternoon, and night. Then again on Sunday morning, afternoon, and night. However she wants it. I'm that, bitch."

"Where do you get your hair from?" Supriti smiled, raising a hand to touch Jacqueline's hair. "It looks so soft and shiny."

Jacqueline matrixed her body back and Cleopatra smacked Supriti's hand away as she stepped in front of Jacqueline, blocking her path to Supriti yet again.

"No this bitch didn't … I woke up like this. I got it from my mama, you thirsty-ass piece of—" Jacqueline yelled at her.

"Ok. I'm getting tired of holding her back," Cleopatra said to Supriti.

Supriti glared at Jacqueline, and Jacqueline met her stare. The disdain was mutual. Jacqueline motioned that she was cold and ready to go home. Supriti thought it was interesting that the $4,000 coat she was cloaked in wasn't a sufficient barrier against the winter chill.

"See you around." Cleopatra grabbed Jacqueline's hand and kissed it as they turned and walked down Broadway.

"Count on it." Supriti watched them walk away. Jacqueline looked back and caught her observing them, and a sinister smile spread across her lips as she walked off with a prize Supriti obviously wanted to win.

Cleopatra lit up when she looked at her wife. Supriti could see her love for Jacqueline in her eyes, and how they couldn't keep their hands off each other, but still didn't care. Cleopatra should have been hugging and kissing *her* in the street. Supriti was the one who should have been wrapped in that incredible coat, with that ridiculous wedding ring on her finger. A powerful and dominant woman like Cleopatra needed a formidable woman by her side. And Jacqueline wasn't it. Supriti had convinced herself of that much during their brief face-to-face.

Now all she had to do was make Cleopatra realize that she had the wrong bitch on her team. And she was willing to do just about anything to prove it.

"Who the hell was that?" Jacqueline asked as they stopped at the intersection. She pulled on Cleopatra's coat to keep her from crossing the street.

"Mandisa's architect." Cleopatra buttoned the top button on her black leather pea coat and tightened her gray scarf around her mouth.

"Mandisa? I should have known. So *Coming to America* is recruiting team members now? Is *Bollywood* the newest member of the We Want Cleopatra Club?"

"Wait." Cleopatra held her stomach. "You just called her Bollywood? And Mandisa Coming to America? That's so wrong." She keeled over, laughing.

"First of all, you know no one believes Mandisa is really from Africa. And Bollywood called me out of my name, so I called her out of hers. I hate her." Jacqueline nodded her head, agreeing with her own statement. "Yeah. I hate her."

"I gathered that from the way you lunged at her." Cleopatra glanced at the stoplights again. She was ready to get to the other side of Broadway and grab a cab. She wanted to get out of the cold and go home.

Jacqueline pulled her back. "I don't trust her. She's sneaky. She's all in love with you after a week?"

"That's how long it took you to fall in love with me." Cleopatra kissed her wife's cheek, trying to lighten the moment.

"I was in love with you before we ever met. We aren't talking about me. We're talking about Ms. Is That Your Bitch. Baby..." Jacqueline shook her head. "She wants you."

"Come here." Cleopatra embraced her, kissing her softly on the lips. "What's going on with you?"

"Women come on to you all the time. But she bothers me."

"I only have eyes for you, and you know that."

Jacqueline grabbed her hand and looked up at her, speaking slowly as if Cleopatra was hard of hearing. "Stay away from her."

"So you don't trust me?"

"I don't trust her."

"It's not like you to get so riled up over one chick giving me attention."

"So you admit she came on to you, even though she knows you're married?"

"You are my world. I would never do anything to jeopardize our relationship. I love you." She kissed Jacqueline gently on the lips.

"And I love you. Look at me." Jacqueline grabbed her hand and pulled her back to face her. "Stay away from her." She held Cleopatra's face in her hands.

"I don't care about her. All I can think about is doing you with those boots on." She pushed Jacqueline up against a street sign and licked her lips. "I want those boots wrapped around my neck."

Jacqueline folded her arms across her chest in defiance.

Cleopatra stepped back from her. "Seriously? Why do I have to prove to you that I'm not going to do anything to jeopardize our marriage? I'm committed to you. As long as we're together, I'll never go to her or any other woman."

"I'm sorry, baby." Jacqueline looked at her wife. "You don't have to prove anything to me."

"How about you focus on me right now? You came to get me at work and you had this look in your eyes like you wanted to go home and break some furniture."

Jacqueline smiled. "But I got distracted."

"Yeah, you did. So what were you thinking about when you put those on?" Cleopatra pointed to her 'fuck me' boots.

Jacqueline's tongue peeked out the corner of her mouth, and she arched her back. "I was thinking about your reaction. I know you can't control yourself."

"You know what I like. And you always give it to me."

"That's because you make me happy. I love you more every day. And you know what? The fact that we've been together a while and my feelings just grow stronger is crazy. You still give me butterflies. Your kisses still make me dizzy. Every time we kiss, I want to make love to you. Just like the first time."

"I love you more every day too, baby." Cleopatra kissed her.

"Don't start anything on this street," Jacqueline teased as she pushed her away.

"Then can we go home?"

"Yes, baby. I have something special planned just for you, too." Jacqueline raised her hand to hail a cab. "Just one last thing, so we're clear, and I'm done," she continued. "You already know the lengths I went to just to be with you. So I don't put anything past any woman."

A cab screeched to a halt in front of them and she flashed a smile. "So like I said before, baby—I love you, but I don't trust her. Stay away from her."

FOUR

....

SHE WANTS HER TOO

Supriti went home to her Soho loft alone after leaving Cleopatra and Jacqueline, consumed with thoughts of her new obsession.

Why does she have to be married? Why does her wife have to be perfect? She needed to find out if Cleopatra was happy. If her wife gave her everything she needed. If she satisfied her. She wasn't necessarily one to break up relationships, but when she decided she wanted something, nothing stood in her way. She had stood up to her own father—a heartless and cruel excuse of a man—so Jacqueline would be nothing for her to eliminate.

She thought back to her fourteenth year, when she'd first defied her father's wishes. He wanted her to leave California and return to India, to enter an arranged marriage.

Supriti hadn't even said "I'm a lesbian." She dared not while she lived in his house, but she couldn't remain quiet, knowing what he'd planned for her future.

"I'm not marrying that man," she declared to her father. "Ever. I'm going to college. I'm going to be an architect."

"Men are architects," he laughed. "I won't pay for school. So how the hell are you going to go? Look at your mother. She has her PhD but what does she do every day? Makes my tea, cooks my meals. Washes my underwear and cleans my house. What is that PhD good for? Washing my underwear? You can go to high school until I say you're finished. Then you'll marry."

A full academic scholarship to UC Berkeley later and Supriti had answered the question. Who was going to pay for college? The state of California.

Supriti remembered vividly the last time she saw her father. It was going on five years now. She'd been giving a speech at her college graduation. She surveyed the crowd for her mother's face, and spotted her—a beautiful, distinguished woman of Indian and African American heritage. Her black hair was pulled back into a flawless bun, and she looked nearly two decades younger than she was, and more like a big sister. Supriti was stunned when she saw her father sitting next to her, looking more like her mother's father than husband, his receding gray hairline showcasing his prominent forehead, his broad smile showing every cigarette-stained tooth in his mouth. As if he had anything to do with her accomplishments.

After the ceremony, her mother found Supriti in the crowd. She grabbed and held Supriti, who was visibly upset. "Shut up and let him talk," her mother whispered in her ear. "Wait for your graduation present. Trust your mother."

She released Supriti from her embrace and they both faked a smile. Supriti was quiet as her father went on about how proud he was of her to a group of her classmates's parents.

Various thoughts ran through her mind as they celebrated at what had been her favorite Indian restaurant as a child—the same one that she had outgrown long ago, and that as an adult she had come to despise, his taking her back there was further proof that her father had no idea who she was anymore, she wasn't a little girl, she was a woman now. The silence was deafening as they ate dinner. Supriti huffed and sucked her teeth just to hear something besides the clanking of forks on their plates. She replied sarcastically to her father whenever he tried to start a conversation, and her mother kicked her hard under the table.

Supriti swore she mouthed "Shut the fuck up." She had never heard her mother curse in her entire life, so that was what she did. Shut the fuck up.

After dessert, her father requested Supriti's attention as he spoke across the table in the secluded corner booth. "I have something for you. As you know, my mother was a very successful businesswoman back home in Delhi, and died wealthy. She wanted to ensure that her only granddaughter reaped the benefits of her hard work. But let me say this first." His face grimaced into a frown. "She was successful in business, but not at home. I never understood her need to work and be independent. I just wanted her to be a mother like every other woman in my family. All the neighborhood boys were greeted by their mothers when they came home after school. But not me and my brothers. The time and energy she should have put into our home life went to her job instead. She overshadowed my father and made more money than him. That shattered him, and eventually our entire family."

"Is this a fable? What does this have to do with anything?" Supriti asked, annoyed. She snatched her leg back in anticipation of her mother kicking her again, but her mother didn't move.

"I promised myself as a boy that my wife was not going to work, and that if I had a daughter, neither would she. It's the woman's job to take care of the home."

"I don't understand what this has to do with anything," Supriti said confused.

He pulled a manila envelope from the inside of his suit jacket. "Happy graduation, pretty."

"Pretty?" He must be dying. He hadn't called her pretty since she was ten years old.

"Thank you." She took the envelope and laid it on the table.

Her mother coughed. "Open it." She kicked Supriti swiftly under the table again. Harder this time.

Supriti tore open the envelope and pulled out a cashier's check. She did a double take and brought the check closer to her face to examine all of the zeroes, and then examined the name on the check—hers. Her mother burst into intermittent fits of giggles. Supriti sat the check back down on the table.

"You're dying aren't you?" Supriti raised her eyebrows.

"No, this is your trust fund money set up by your grand-mother."

Supriti folded the check up neatly and placed it securely inside of her bra. "Let me get something straight." She rubbed her forehead with the tips of her thumb and index finger. "Grandmother left me all of this money and I'm just hearing about it now? I'm assuming since you gave it to me today, it was contingent on my graduating from college?"

Her father reluctantly nodded his head.

"Son of a bitch." Supriti smirked. "So why would you try to marry me off at fourteen?"

She interrupted him before he could fix his lips to tell a lie.

"Wait. If I got married young, before graduation, I would have forfeited the money." She stared hard at him. "Isn't that right?" she yelled, attracting the attention of the other restaurant patrons.

"Calm down, Supriti." Her mother touched her hand softly.

"No, Mother. It's too late for all of that." She turned her attention back to her father. "What would have happened to all of this money if I'd gotten married? Hmm?"

Her father was silent for a moment. He looked to be struggling to find the right words. Then he confessed. "I would have gotten the money."

"Supriti," her mother interjected. "Sweetheart. None of this matters now. He's trying to right a wrong. It's yours. It's all yours."

Her father's head hung low; he couldn't look either his wife or daughter in the eye.

"So that little prologue, that little speech about wanting your wife and daughter to stay at home because I guess you didn't get enough hugs as a child, was all bull. You expect me to believe that's why you tried to marry me off so young? You never spoke about marriage to me until after grandmother died. That's when you found out about the money. You wanted me to get married so you could have it all to yourself, because I guess you don't already have enough money. You need more." She pointed to the check tucked safe and snug inside of her bra, then agreed with her mother.

"You're right, Mother, nothing matters anymore. Nothing." She leaned back in her chair and unfurled a slew of insults that nearly got them kicked out of the restaurant. She cursed her father for forcing her mother to abandon her career as a college professor to hand wash his shit-stained underwear. Then she blasted him for accusing her mother of cheating with a black man and threatening to divorce her when Supriti was born looking less than full-blood Indian. She ridiculed him for calling her and her mother the N-word whenever the mood struck him, after Supriti's mother had learned that she was adopted and her biological father—and Supriti's grandfather—was actually African American.

"You put your hands on my mother. Yes, Mother, I know." She looked at her and tears welled up in her mother's eyes. "You will forever have to look over your shoulder, old man. What makes you feel so safe when you walk down the street or start your car?"

"And let's not forget that trying-to-marry-me-off bullshit. I've got news for you: I'm gay. Always been gay, always will be." She sat back, folded her arms, and waited for his reaction.

Her mother tried to feign ignorance of her daughter's announcement. But she was in admiration of her. If nothing else, she raised a strong woman, and she was proud.

Her father heard nothing but "I'm gay." So he went on a rant of his own inside of the packed restaurant. She was a disgrace. He cursed the day she was born. Declared her dead, spit in her face, and in the same breath forbade her mother to speak with her ever again, or he would kill both of them.

Supriti wiped the spit from her eyes, rose from the table, kissed her sobbing mother goodbye, and walked out of the restaurant, a check for $4 million comfortably secured between her breasts. That was nearly five years ago. And it marked the last time she had seen or spoken to either one of her parents.

"Whoa," Supriti said suddenly, emerging from her day-dream and looking at her watch. "Where did the time go?" It was almost seven o'clock. She came back to reality as she gathered her thoughts and regained her composure.

Instead of fantasizing about Cleopatra all night, she called Mandisa over for a late dinner. The former college roommates had remained close through the years. In college, Supriti suffered from the pretty girl curse, and couldn't hold on to friends for very long. She only had rivalries with other women; everything was a competition, or the women would somehow morph into Supriti, dressing and acting like her. Or they would develop feelings and want more than friendship. In either case, it always ended badly, and she stopped trying to make friends altogether. Supriti had lived a lonely existence, constantly thinking everyone wanted something from her. And they often did.

She had several short-term relationships, but never found a woman she felt was on her level, or deserving of her. She began to think that she would need to settle. Luckily, she could distract herself with her career. Then Mandisa, the only person she'd ever called a faithful friend, convinced her to move to New York. She'd only been in the city for a few months now, and had no problem getting attention. She had been out on many first dates, though no one had made it to a second. But now she had met her match—the woman she wanted. Cleopatra.

....

FIVE

ROMANTICAL

"Ooh baby, get it," Jacqueline moaned as she scratched the rug with her nails and held her breath. The pain shot through her breast and she pointed to her nipple and arched her back, lifting up off of the floor. Cleopatra took her nipple into her mouth, sucking the hot caramel clean off, leaving no trace of the sticky dessert topping. Jacqueline pointed to the ladle.

"Mmm... Baby, do it again."

Jacqueline struggled to focus her eyes in the candlelight; the tiny flames that illuminated their chocolate master bedroom coupled with the glow of the fireplace was one big dizzying blur, only intensified when Cleopatra laid her body down on top of hers. Cleopatra pressed the massive bulge held captive in her underwear into Jacqueline's bare pussy. She licked and kissed at her neck, alternating with playful and harsh bites. Then she kissed her lips as Jacqueline wrapped her legs around her waist, drawing her in closer. Cleopatra's soft lips sucked hungrily on hers as she pulled them into her mouth. When Jacqueline's tongue found hers, Cleopatra's thickness rubbed her clit just right through her underwear. Jacqueline gasped for air as Cleopatra backed away. Cleopatra smiled as she looked down at the wet spot Jacqueline left on her briefs, visible even in the dim lighting.

"That's your fault, Daddy. You shouldn't be so damn sexy." Jacqueline licked her lips. Cleopatra traced the wetness with her thumb, creating a delicate thread of her wife's cum when she pulled her hand away and sucking it into her mouth.

"That's so sweet." She winked at Jacqueline.

"I have a lot more of that. You want it?"

"You know I do." Cleopatra leaned over and picked up the large bowl of caramel, hovering it just above Jacqueline's stomach and stirring it slowly with the ladle. Jacqueline studied the rips in Cleopatra's stomach as she worked the spoon, fantasizing about how her muscles contracted whenever she was inside of her. The muscles in her arms, her back, her ass, and thighs— all a well-oiled machine that sent her body into fits of lunacy every single time they made love. Jacqueline's eyes were always drawn to Cleopatra's Adonis belt—the deep V in her stomach, leading down into her briefs. For some reason, her underwear tonight struggled more than usual to hold her strap, causing a massive tent, and the head of her cock peeked out of her waistband, further torturing Jacqueline.

Her cock was even bigger, as if its size tonight was in direct correlation to her excitement. But Cleopatra had always worked her strap like she was born with it. Had she figured out how to make it grow, too? Jacqueline wasn't sure if it was the Ciroc or her wife that was driving her to hallucinate—or both—and she didn't care. Her anticipation rose as Cleopatra loaded the large spoon with the hot caramel and drizzled it over her stomach and thighs. She gasped when the sauce hit her skin and then cooled slowly. Cleopatra licked the caramel off of her, alternating between using her tongue and a cold chunk of pineapple to scoop it from her body. Jacqueline pulled her to her mouth and kissed her hard, tasting the sweetness and stickiness still on her lips, the remaining caramel temporarily gluing their bodies together. Then she trailed her hands up and down the length of Cleopatra's shaft through her briefs, pressing her fingertips on the wet cotton and enjoying its coolness. In an instant, she felt another rush of wetness between her thighs.

Cleopatra rose up from the floor and sat on the edge of the bed. Jacqueline bit her lip as she watched her wife spring the strap from her briefs; she was erect and ready. Jacqueline crawled across the floor, over to Cleopatra, and positioned herself between her legs. She bit at her thighs and licked her way up to Cleopatra's dick.

"I'm all yours. Do you know that?" Jacqueline looked up at her. Cleopatra nodded. "My heart, my mind, and my body all belong to you. My pussy belongs to you. You never have to ask, just take it."

Jacqueline pushed Cleopatra's hand away from her strap and stroked her cock with both of hers. Her eyes widened when Cleopatra said, "How about you just take that. All of it."

Her pussy swelled at her wife's request, and she took the head of Cleopatra's cock in between her lips. Cleopatra brushed the hair from her face and their eyes met. Jacqueline groaned and slid her fist down the shaft, followed close behind by her mouth. She took her deep to the back of her throat and slid her fingers inside of her own pussy, fucking herself as Cleopatra arched into her mouth.

The sensation of her dick on her lips, the motion with

which Cleopatra pushed her hips up in the air to fuck her mouth, and her own fingers inside of her pussy, made Jacqueline want to explode. She struggled not to lose total control as Cleopatra's slick thickness had its way with her mouth. She loved the effect sucking the strap had on Cleopatra. The visual of sliding her dick in and out of Jacqueline's mouth alone could make Cleopatra come. To see Jacqueline down there sucking her and loving it, and not the obligatory kiss or lick, was a total mind fuck for her. Jacqueline sucked the life out of her cock and lived for her reaction. If Cleopatra wanted her down on her knees, that's exactly what she got.

Jacqueline pulled Cleopatra from her mouth and circled her cock with her tongue. "I want you baby. I need to come." She grabbed Cleopatra's hand and crawled up on the bed.

"Feel how wet I am." She pulled Cleopatra on top of her.

Cleopatra ran her hand across Jacqueline's clit.

"See what you do to me?" Jacqueline squirmed underneath her wife.

"And that's my fault?" Cleopatra rubbed her slick fingers together.

"Every time you touch me, or kiss me, every time I think about you."

"So what are you going to do about it?" Cleopatra kissed her way down Jacqueline's body, feeling the heat radiating from between her thighs.

"Nothing I can do but take it." Jacqueline's body tensed up in anticipation of her woman's hot mouth on her clit. Cleopatra rose up on her elbows and stuck her tongue out at her. She grabbed Jacqueline by the hips to keep her steady, and tilted her closer, right where she wanted her. Jacqueline buckled and gasped at Cleopatra's strength, but Cleopatra gripped her thighs tight and kept her steady. She was in complete control of her body.

Cleopatra dove inside of Jacqueline's wetness and pushed the full length of her tongue into her pussy. Jacqueline sucked in a mouthful of air and held her breath. Cleopatra licked her in one long, agonizing drag from the bottom to the top of her. And she didn't relent. Jacqueline slammed her hand down on the bed as Cleopatra's tongue lapped at her clit. She bucked her body and arched her back while Cleopatra teased her and worked her tongue painfully slow. Jacqueline clawed at the sheets and moved her hips, thrashing up and down on Cleopatra's tongue. Cleopatra made love to her with her mouth, drinking her, sipping, inhaling, and swallowing her flow of cream.

Jacqueline couldn't hear Cleopatra, but her noises and moans vibrated on her pussy. She dug her fingers into Cleopatra's locs as their sexy sounds filled the room. Cleopatra's tongue was relentless as she flicked it back and forth while her fingers slid inside of Jacqueline, prepping her for what was to come next. Jacqueline bucked her hips and arched her back, meeting Cleopatra's hand, then taking three fingers into her hungry pussy. But she wanted it deeper. She rolled her hips and pushed against Cleopatra's hand and mouth. Cleopatra lapped up Jacqueline's wet pussy as her fingers continued to invade her.

"Right there, don't stop baby," Jacqueline cried.

Cleopatra alternated between sucking hungrily on her clit and slipping her fingers and tongue deep into Jacqueline's pussy. Jacqueline almost choked when Cleopatra mushed her entire face into her slippery pussy. She locked her arms around Jacqueline's thighs, restricting her ability to fight back. Jacqueline squeezed her thighs tight around Cleopatra's head, trying to trap her there as an orgasm flooded her body, but Cleopatra freed herself from Jacqueline's locked thighs. She kept pleasuring Jacqueline until she heard her cry out in climax again a few moments later.

"Beautiful," Cleopatra whispered against her thigh, watching as her wife shook.

"Shit." Jacqueline's body jerked as Cleopatra teased her clit again with the tip of her tongue. "You are going to pay for that." She exhaled as she looked down at Cleopatra licking her lips and wiping her cum-soaked face. Then, before she knew it, and before she could say "Don't touch it," Cleopatra was on her, sliding into her sensitive and tight pussy.

"Make me pay, baby," she whispered in Jacqueline's ear.

Jacqueline dug her nails into Cleopatra's back and matched her thrusts while biting at her neck.

"Mmm," she moaned. Cleopatra moved her ass just the way she liked it. She fucked her slow and steady at first, and under control. Jacqueline gasped for air. "I know what you want."

"That fat ass," Cleopatra said softly.

She slid out of Jacqueline and repositioned herself behind her as Jacqueline rolled over onto her hands and knees. Cleopatra caressed her body, teasing her between her thighs, and Jacqueline looked over her shoulder, bracing herself and biting her lip. Cleopatra rubbed her cock between her thighs, torturing her. When Cleopatra took hold of her hips, Jacqueline moaned, arched her back, and threw her ass up in the air. Cleopatra spread her open with her hands as Jacqueline's anticipation rose.

"Stop fucking with me, Daddy," Jacqueline demanded.

That's what Cleopatra was waiting for—for her woman to get mad. She steadied her hips and eased into Jacqueline's pussy slowly from behind. In that position, Cleopatra stroked Jacqueline deep. Her wetness slicked her dick as she pulled out and pushed back into her—so wet that Cleopatra could hear it, and loved every intoxicating slippery stroke of it as she marveled at how Jacqueline took all of her dick. Cleopatra's intensity built, and she didn't want to make love anymore. Then her wife said the magic words.

"Fuck me."

That was Cleopatra's queue to stop being gentle; to give it to her, to slam into her pussy and make her woman scream her name. She grabbed Jacqueline's legs and rolled her over on her back without slipping out of her. Now, with her maddening thrusts, Jacqueline lost everything to her, coming so intensely that she trembled uncontrollably underneath Cleopatra, who pumped her hard, pressing her entire thickness into Jacqueline as her body convulsed. Cleopatra lifted Jacqueline up by her ass, pulling her in closer so she could go even deeper. Jacqueline's legs fell over her shoulders while Cleopatra pounded into her, cock to balls. Jacqueline dug her nails into Cleopatra's thighs, unable to control the sensations taking over her body.

"It's yours." Jacqueline repeated her name when she grabbed Cleopatra's face and looked into her eyes. Their eyes locked on each other's as Cleopatra slowed her thrusts down to a torturing pace. Jacqueline rocked her body with hers, catching her strokes and opening up for her wife. She dragged her nails deep across Cleopatra's back, where she had left her mark every time they made love. She pulled Cleopatra closer and closer into her as her body shook.

"I want you to come again for me, baby," Cleopatra whispered in her ear.

Jacqueline was lightheaded and already losing control. But she'd give Cleopatra what she asked for, and wrapped her thighs around Cleopatra's waist to draw her in deeper. She squeezed her pussy around Cleopatra's cock as her body shuddered, their bodies still slick with sweat and caramel as Cleopatra pumped hard inside of her. Her pussy pulsed uncontrollably around her dick, Cleopatra hitting her spot with each stroke until she came. This time Cleopatra joined her, kissing her, taking in her breath as the orgasm took over their bodies.

Jacqueline locked Cleopatra in and forbid her to move.

"You ok?" Cleopatra kissed her wife's forehead.

Jacqueline didn't answer. She wouldn't look at Cleopatra. Then she shook her head no. She struggled to hold back her tears because she knew if she started she wouldn't be able to stop. Cleopatra rolled over on her back and held her wife in her arms. She kissed her cheek and tasted the salt of her tears as they began to stream down her face and to her neck.

"I'm ok." Jacqueline wiped her face with the palm of her hand. Cleopatra kissed her softly on the lips, and she burst into tears again.

"Everything is different now," Jacqueline whispered.

"What do you mean, baby?"

"It's different now that I'm your wife. I'm different. I belong to you. I can't say no to you, and I don't want to. Still, after all of this time, all I want to do is just be with you. I love you so much." Jacqueline kissed her. "I'm sorry I got upset earlier. It's just that now, even more than before, if I feel someone is threatening our happiness or our marriage, I black the fuck out. But I know how much you love me; you prove it to me every day. I just don't ever want you to lose that look in your eyes."

"What look?"

"You have these different ways you look at me. When you first see me. When we're about to make love, after we make love, and then other times when it's quiet and we're just looking into each other's eyes and not speaking. No one has ever looked at me the way you look at me, with such love and passion in their eyes. I don't ever want that go away."

"It won't," Cleopatra assured her.

"When you look in my eyes," Jacqueline whispered, "I can tell how much you truly love me, and when you look at me, I know that you're mine."

"That's because I am."

For a moment Jacqueline worried that she'd scared Cleopatra with her intensity. But she hadn't. Instead her wife pulled her close and kissed her. Jacqueline snuggled safely into her wife's warm embrace. They both closed their eyes, and fell asleep in each other's arms.

✿✿✿

Cleopatra awoke a short time later in the middle of the night to Jacqueline slapping her in her chest. "What is it, baby? Baby.

63

Baby, wake up." Cleopatra got control of her wrists and pinned her arms down. Jacqueline was covered in sweat and stared at Cleopatra hard, almost looking through her. "You were dreaming." Cleopatra caressed her face.

Jacqueline pushed Cleopatra off her and sat up in bed. "You cheated on me with Supriti and I divorced you."

"That's never going to happen," Cleopatra laughed and tried to comfort her. "So I don't know why you're looking like you're mad at me. It was just a dream. Look at me. That is never ever going to happen."

"I know, because there is no way I'm ever giving you a divorce. Just so you know. You fuck with me, you stuck with me." She gave Cleopatra a dirty look. "That's not even an option," she warned. "Over Supriti's dead body."

....

SIX

OBSESSION: INVESTIGATION AND DISCOVERY

"I'll tell you everything so we don't have to have this conversation again." Mandisa was annoyed. Supriti had invited her over to her loft under the guise of having dinner and catching up, but she really wanted more information about Cleopatra. Mandisa realized the purpose of the invite when she saw Indian take-out containers on Supriti's dining room table. She was expecting a home-cooked meal, and she wasn't at all pleased.

"Why are you so dressed up?" Supriti asked. "Look at me." Supriti looked down at her old t-shirt and shorts. "And are you going to tell me what the hell happened to your face?" Supriti stared at her.

"I had a severe reaction to some shellfish," Mandisa lied. It had taken the bruises from her fight with Alexis an especially long time to heal. The makeup artist who camouflaged her injuries for the board meeting wasn't available on such short notice, so Mandisa was forced to do her own face. And she'd done a half-ass job. "And not that it's any of your business, nosy, but I have plans later." Mandisa laid a napkin over her lap to ensure she didn't stain her little black dress.

"Hmm ... ok. I would stay in the house till that heals. Looks like you were in a fight and got your ass kicked."

"Like I was saying. Cleopatra broke up with Jacqueline when she found out that Jacqueline was married to a man." Mandisa laid napkins underneath the takeout containers. Supriti's dining room table and chairs were all bright white, and even though Mandisa had a white sofa herself, she was always uncomfortable in Supriti's home, terrified of making a stain that couldn't be removed.

"What? Was she straight? A man? Really?" Supriti opened the container of basmati rice.

"No, just in the closet. She was separated when she started dating Cleopatra. Is there a way to make it a little darker in here?" The dining room resembled a Soho art gallery, with its bare walls and a spotlight over the table. Supriti got up and dimmed the lights to Mandisa's liking.

"Thank you," Mandisa continued. "They got back together after Jacqueline got a divorce. Cleopatra proposed to her and then an ex of Cleopatra's, whose crazy ass is in prison now for trying to kill Jacqueline, told Cleopatra that Jacqueline had kids. She did a background check on her. That's how Cleopatra found out she had children. She hid her kids the whole time." Mandisa shook her head.

Supriti stared at Mandisa. "Who does that? Her wife is a liar?" She took a sip of her mango lassi from the tall white foam tumbler.

"She did what she thought she had to do to get with Cleopatra and keep her. That's how I see it." Mandisa took a bite of a vegetable samosa. "I did things with Cleopatra that I'm not proud of. She was trying to get over Jacqueline when we got together, but she never did. They were meant to be together. That's what you need to understand. She never really touched me, and she could have had all this."

Mandisa leaned back in her chair, momentarily forgetting that the chair had no support. She caught herself, tweaked her back, and cursed all modern architects. "Can you get a regular chair for when I come over that's not a piece of art?" She rolled her eyes. "Anyway, she never opened up to me—not her mind, her heart, or her body, because it didn't belong to me. It belonged to Jacqueline. Still does. Always will. You understand?"

Supriti glazed over Mandisa's words. "I can't believe you never got a chance to ride that." She shook her head and took a hard bite of a pakora. She would have fucked Cleopatra into submission if she ever had the chance. When she got the opportunity—and she was convinced she would—there would be no turning back. No real woman would have been in a relationship with Cleopatra and not put it on her.

But Supriti wasn't surprised. Mandisa had never wanted for anything. So of course she didn't really know how to set her sights on a goal and work to obtain it. She'd never had to try to do anything; everything had been handed to her just for the asking. In college, Mandisa was a bully, but like with most bullies, when their back was up against the wall, it came to light that they were full of shit. Mandisa was all talk and no action. She may have wanted Cleopatra, or so she thought. But Supriti wondered what Mandisa was willing to do to get her. She may have done some things she wasn't proud of during her college days, but this was real life now. You had to get down and dirty to get what you wanted in the real world. Being her closest friend, Supriti knew that type of focus and determination wasn't in Mandisa's blood. But it was in hers.

"Cleopatra is an amazing woman," Mandisa continued. "But you need to let it go. She's taken. You are going to end up in a whole lot of pain and heartbreak. A world of hurt. She loves her wife. The only way something would possibly go down is if her wife didn't want her anymore. And the last I checked, Jacqueline was not blind, stupid, or crazy."

Mandisa was still not seeing that look of recognition from Supriti—one that indicated she understood and would let go of whatever crazy ideas she had in her head.

"I'm sorry, I can't help the attraction I have for her. Forget the sexiness. That's obvious and by itself enough, but she's smart, confident, and accomplished. She's funny and charming. She commands everyone's attention and she doesn't even want it. You do realize how hot that is. Do I even have to mention the power? Everything about her is immaculate, from her body to the diamonds in her watch. Her energy is so warm and overwhelming. Her aura fingered me, and there was nothing I could do about it." She laughed and exhaled hard. "I can't even explain it. You must understand: I want her. I think she's the one for me. The woman that I've been searching for all my life. I've been bullshitting myself all this time. I'm sorry. I know she's your ex, but this pull that I feel toward her, this need to be in her space and in her face, is not going away overnight. I can't just turn it off."

Mandisa scowled at her. "I'm warning you, you better learn to deal with it. Just like everyone else. Involving yourself in Cleopatra's life would cause nothing but trouble. Are you forgetting that we are in the midst of a multi-million dollar real estate deal? All of that power you fawn over in Cleopatra lets her flip the kill switch on the deal if she so desires. Are you willing to risk that? Besides—newsflash—Cleopatra would never betray her wife. And how do you figure Jacqueline would just lay down and watch someone steal her? If she gets wind of your little obsession, all hell will break loose. And honestly, I hate to say this, but I'm not completely over that motherfucker yet. No woman is ever really done with Cleopatra Giovanni. She's everyone's one that got away. I'd hate to have to fire you and find a new friend. So seriously, back off."

Mandisa checked her beeping cell phone. A large grin spread across her face as she read the text message, and a deep moan roared in the back of her throat. She popped up and gathered her coat and scarf. "So, you see my plight?"

"I understand," Supriti reluctantly said.

"Good. Because I have to go. Promise me that we won't have to have this conversation ever again."

"Promise." Supriti nodded.

She was surprised at Mandisa's little outburst over Cleopatra, but that spoke to how strongly she felt. She would lay low for the time being. She'd try and leave Cleopatra alone, but at the first sign of trouble in paradise, she vowed to be all over her. She would worry about the repercussions after she got what she wanted.

❖❖❖

The following Monday, Supriti visited Cleopatra in her office. She stalked her, waiting until Racquel was away from her desk. Racquel didn't like her—she had told her as much on an intense elevator ride—and could pose a problem if Supriti wasn't strategic. She'd tried to get past her on several occasions and failed. Racquel never seemed to even use the bathroom or take lunch. On rare occasions when she was away from her desk, the Cleopatra-obsessed assistant Nikki was at her post, holding it down in her absence. Nikki took pleasure in not letting Supriti pass when she realized she didn't plan on heeding her earlier warnings to stay away from Cleopatra.

When Supriti saw that the coast was finally clear, she knocked on Cleopatra's door and opened it without waiting for a response. No exchange of formal greetings or pleasantries.

She peeked her head inside of Cleopatra's office. "Your wife is beautiful." She'd come prepared with a light cashmere shawl wrapped around her arms to combat the cold air that gushed from Cleopatra's vents in an attempt to shorten visits.

"She is, isn't she?" Cleopatra smiled as she sat behind her desk.

"But she doesn't like me. Does she?" Supriti walked up to Cleopatra's desk and dragged her finger along its beveled glass edge. "I wonder why?" She smiled sarcastically.

"Now, why would she not like you? Maybe you calling her a bitch?"

"That was an innocent cultural mistake." Supriti shrugged her shoulders and inhaled Cleopatra's cologne, then sat down in one of the armchairs in front of her desk.

Cleopatra stood up and walked around her desk to confront Supriti up close. "A mistake coupled with an Indian accent that I haven't heard you speak in before or since?" She pushed all of her weight on the chair arms, trapping Supriti to ensure she understood. "One of your parents is of African descent. Am I correct?"

"My mother is biracial," Supriti admitted.

Cleopatra rolled her eyes. "So feigning ignorance to the weight that the word 'bitch' carries is bull. Listen to me closely. Don't ever call my wife a bitch again. You can go now," she finished, dismissing her.

Supriti swallowed hard. She was a little afraid, but also turned on by how Cleopatra protected her wife. Cleopatra walked away from her and sat back down behind her desk.

"I did apologize to her. And I will apologize to you again. I'm really sorry. Truth is, I don't trust myself with you."

"Neither does my wife. Like I said, you can leave now."

....

SEVEN

DUMB AND DUMBER

"Shawn hasn't been going to work. Her ass is about to get fired." Robin rested her elbows on the cold black granite countertop. "Hello ... I'm talking to you. Damn!" she yelled at Jacqueline.

"Oh, sorry." Jacqueline shook herself back to consciousness. "I still can't believe you went and got your neck tattooed. What are you going through?"

"Shawn likes neck tattoos. She thinks they're sexy."

"Really?" Jacqueline mushed her sister in the face and twisted her head so she could examine the tattoo closer.

"I've heard enough from Mom and Dad already." She pulled away from Jacqueline. "Ma isn't even speaking to me. You have tattoos!"

"I have one. And it's not on my neck. Who the fuck tattoos a hand choking them around their neck? I should punch you in your throat." Jacqueline shook her head. "Who have you been hanging out with? Is this all for Shawn? I don't understand how you got so hood when you didn't grow up in the hood. The half-Mohawk you have going on is cute, though. I like it. It'll grow back eventually, but that tat? Planning on getting a job ever?"

"I don't have to work. So no, I don't plan on getting no damn job," Robin snarled at her.

Robin had dropped in on her big sister unannounced, as she had been doing more and more recently. Each time she came over, her appearance had changed. And her girlfriend Shawn appeared to be the cause of the transformation. If she wasn't wearing clear high heels, she had on Jordan heels or animal print everything, or she'd pull Popeye's Chicken or Cheddar Bay Biscuits that she'd copped from Red Lobster the night before from her purse. On this day, she showed up in some pocketless jeans, a nameplate necklace, and smelling like Chef Boyardee beef ravioli.

They were just sitting down in the kitchen to chat when Robin started complaining about Shawn—her girlfriend, and Cleopatra's best friend.

"Anyway, Shawn is about to be out of a job if she keeps it up. Payroll called the house for her to come and pick up her check because she's called in sick four days in a row. And I didn't even know about it. You believe that shit?"

"Why is she getting paper checks and not direct deposit?" Jacqueline took a sip of wine.

"Her student loans are in collections like crazy, and her bank account got frozen."

"Um … what school? I didn't know she went." Jacqueline raised her left eyebrow.

"She went to a bunch of them. Truck driving, plumbing, welding, massage … she went to every school but beauty school, girl. Anyway, she asked them to give her paper checks, and cashes them at that dirty check cashing place by the house."

"So how is she paying the bills? I know her check doesn't cover them."

"Yes it does. She got wads of money. How you think I stay not working and looking this good?" Robin ran her hand over the shaved side of her head.

Jacqueline shook her head. "Sweetheart, not from working in a mailroom, she doesn't. I bet Cleopatra gave her some money. At least you better hope that's how she's getting it. Are you sure about this relationship with Shawn?" she asked. "Every time you come over, you're unhappy and beefing about something she did or didn't do. She doesn't appear to be the best influence on you. On Cleopatra, either. She's put up with her sheniggagans for decades."

"Did you say sheniggagans?!" Robin laughed. "That's a fucked up thing to say. That's my girl. But we just go through shit. And Cleo is like her blood. Don't judge us, sis. Just because me and my woman are kind of hood."

"What hood are you talking about, Robin? Because you went from Mommy and Daddy's cushy house in New Jersey straight to Shawn's apartment in Inwood. Nothing is popping off in Inwood but gentrification and baby strollers. All I'm saying is, I thought you were trying to build a life with Shawn and she doesn't seem to want anything or have any goals. Speaking of which. What happened to yours?"

"Hmmph." Robin got defensive and didn't answer her sister's question. "Don't let all this shit go to your head." She looked around the gourmet kitchen, swimming in custom cabinetry, granite, and stainless steel. "The house, the money, the clothes, the black card. Your perfect little life, that big-ass diamond ring—" She pointed to Jacqueline's wedding ring. "—Can be taken away from you just as easily as you got it. There are a lot of haters that would love to see this all disappear. Fine-ass wife that loves the shit out of you. Your kids are good. You can have and do whatever you want. When you want. Hmmmph." She sucked her teeth.

"You sound like you're the one hating," Jacqueline said, calling Robin out on her jealous rant. "Is my life a problem for you? Because you don't have to be sitting in the house that I share with my fine-ass wife," she mocked.

Jacqueline had gotten used to her baby sister's jealous moments, but was slowly beginning to tire of them. "There was nothing easy about getting to where I am with Cleopatra, and you know that. And I'm not letting anyone take my wife away from me. I would die for her. I would kill for her, too. But this isn't about me." Jacqueline rolled her eyes. "So what do you think is going on with Shawn?" She took another sip of Chardonnay.

Robin smirked as she jumped down from the stool. "Uh, what do you think? She's fucking cheating on me. Not everyone is super faithful like your wife." She stood in front of the refrigerator to check her reflection and hair in the stainless steel door.

"I work hard to keep my woman's attention," Jacqueline sneered. "And to make sure she brings that ass home every night."

"OMG! You saying I don't?" Robin yanked open the refrigerator door, pulled a bowl of fresh-cut pineapple and mango out, along with a bottled water, and placed them on the counter.

"Trick. I can see your thong. My wife is in this house. Pull your pants up," Jacqueline scolded.

Robin rolled her eyes and pulled her shirt down and her jeans up high, then went to search the cabinets by the sink for a glass. "Why can I never find what I'm looking for?" she asked.

"I'm not saying you don't work hard to keep her. Drink out of the bottle," Jacqueline said. "You don't live here. You don't need to know where anything is."

Annoyed, Robin sat back down at the island across from her big sister.

"Listen." Jacqueline bit into a piece of mango. "You don't work, you're not in school, you don't cook, don't clean, don't do laundry. You aren't chipping in on the rent or utilities. You use crazy toilet paper. You just started going down on her like..." Jacqueline looked up at the wall clock. "Um, like five minutes ago. I mean, what do you do? Ma didn't raise us that way, and you know it. So what happened to you?" Robin looked pissed. "Before you get mad, hear me out."

"I ain't no damn housewife." Robin threw a chunk of pineapple into her mouth and cringed at its sweetness. "Hmmph. This is good. This is what Shawn needs to be eating—some damn fruit. Every time I see her big ass she got a grape soda in her hand, or a bag of BBQ pork rinds or Funyuns and Munchos. Who the fuck still eats Funyuns and Munchos?"

"Cooking and making sure the house is clean is not being a housewife." Jacqueline spotted Cleopatra, Maya, and Amir's Timberlands thrown in the corner. Cleopatra's pair looked like they had given birth to two pairs of baby Timberlands. She stood from her stool and lined them up neatly by the door to the terrace. "It's taking care of your woman. Cleopatra and Shawn are alike in a lot of ways. Women come on to them all the time, so you have to keep your game up. Trust me, I know. There's this bitch drooling over Cleopatra right now that knows she's married and doesn't care. She wants an oral transaction with my woman. But that snake is mine."

Robin sat up straight, at full attention. "Are you going to handle that?"

Jacqueline smirked. "Eventually I'm going to have to. Anyway, Cleopatra only wants to be with one woman. I can't say that about Shawn. Her idea of settling down was two women, not one."

"We don't spend no time together, she don't take me nowhere. We don't even fuck. I'm about to fuck somebody else, for real." Robin took a gulp of water from the bottle and did a double take. "Is this that $11 water? That shit is good. What was I saying? She's never where she's supposed to be or where she says she is. She can't seem to find her way to work anymore. And she's always hanging out with Cleo. I don't see how you put up with it."

Jacqueline questioned her. "Since when? We've been all over each other since the honeymoon. They've probably hung out once in the last few weeks," Jacqueline admitted as she refilled her glass of wine. "If she told you she's been hanging out with Cleopatra, she's lying."

Robin looked at Jacqueline suspiciously.

"I'm serious. Baby!" Jacqueline yelled. "She's upstairs with the kids." She buzzed Cleopatra on the intercom and asked her to come down to the kitchen.

"You think she knows something?" Robin asked.

"I have no idea."

"I think the question is, will she tell us if she does," Robin said.

"I know how to make her talk." Jacqueline winked.

Cleopatra came down into the kitchen a short time later and kissed Jacqueline. "You rang, sweetheart? Hey, Ms. Robin." Cleopatra kissed her sister-in-law on the cheek. "How are you?" She moved to stand behind Jacqueline, rubbing her shoulders.

"That's going to depend on you. So what's going on with your dude?" Robin tapped her tri-colored manicured nails against the glass water bottle.

"Who?" Cleopatra pulled a banana off the top of the refrigerator and began to peel it.

"Shawnette," Robin said in an accusatory tone.

Cleopatra knew she was in trouble when Robin referred to Shawn by her government name. "Um…" She bit the banana and took note of the glares both sisters were shooting at her. "I have no idea what you're talking about. You live with her." Cleopatra sat down on the stool next to Jacqueline and slipped her arms around her wife's waist, not wanting any part of the conversation.

"Robin thinks she's cheating," Jacqueline admitted.

"Thanks, sis," Robin said, annoyed.

"Well, you do." Jacqueline shrugged.

Cleopatra's shoulders dropped and she exhaled hard. She figured it wasn't the response Robin was looking for, but she asked anyway. "Why do you think that?"

Robin smirked at her. "I've caught her in lies a bunch of times. And you've been her Ali Baba more than once."

"I'm sorry, her what?" Cleopatra crossed her eyes and cupped her hand to her ear. She looked at Jacqueline, who had lowered her head in shame and rocked back and forth in mourning over the brain cells that her sister appeared to have lost since she'd started dating Shawn.

"See what happens when you don't read?" Cleopatra whispered to Jacqueline. "Never leave her alone with the twins." She turned back toward Robin and pointed to her own chest. "Me? I'm her alibi?" She finished the banana and threw the peel into the stainless steel garbage can.

Jacqueline nodded. "You, baby."

"Some nights she don't bring that ass home at all." Robin said.

"At all? Damn," Cleopatra said. "Sorry, I haven't seen Shawn in weeks. I don't even see her at work anymore."

"That's because that motherfucker don't go to work," Robin blurted out.

Cleopatra leaned back and side eyed Robin as if to say don't misplace your aggression. "And we haven't talked lately. Jacqueline knows that."

"So she's definitely lying to me?" Robin stared at Cleopatra. "Is there another woman?"

"I don't know." Cleopatra shrugged, and could tell that Robin didn't like her answer at all. "I know that's not what you want to hear. Honestly, I don't know."

"Would you tell me if you knew?" Robin prodded.

Cleopatra looked at Jacqueline. "Ugh … probably not. It's not my business." Cleopatra cringed. "Sorry, just being honest.

I don't know what she's doing. Everyone knows Shawn does stupid shit. If she has an all-out relationship with someone else, you would know about it already. She's messy. She's probably just sleeping with random chicks outside of your relationship. But I doubt it's serious."

Both sisters looked at Cleopatra with their mouths hanging open.

"What? That's real. Robin, you know that. She's a cheater. If you want to know for sure, next time she leaves the house, check to make sure she doesn't have her strap with her."

"Duh. I've done that. I've checked the drawers and it's still there."

"Uh-huh. You mean the one that she uses on you is still there?" Cleopatra smirked. She now had Robin and Jacqueline's undivided attention. "Check her backpack before she leaves the house."

"Duh. I've done that before, too. I check her bag before she goes to the gym."

"Of course you do, because you know that ass hasn't seen any part of a gym in a minute, right? Right. Why are you with her, again? Anyway, she's probably wearing it, because she can't do the mailbox trick since you live together and you have a key now."

"What? The mailbox trick?" Jacqueline asked. "No. Really? In the mailbox?"

"She can't be wearing it—I would see it," Robin said, annoyed. "Everyone would see it."

"Not if she puts it on loose, lets it hang down low between her legs, and has on baggy jeans or sweat pants. And then there's always tucking it into your sock and strapping the harness around your calf."

Jacqueline waved her hands in surrender. "Ok stop, baby. I don't want to hear anymore."

Cleopatra laughed. "I just made all of that up. Why would I tell you how to bust my girl? Damn. And I had you both, too. You were all in," she chuckled.

Robin rolled her eyes, annoyed.

"Anyway, good luck," Cleopatra said. She got up from the black leather stool and began to walk out of the kitchen.

But Robin approached her, cutting her off and invading her personal space, backing her up into the counter. "Look, I need you to find out what's going on."

Cleopatra laughed. "Did you just flex on me, Thug Life? Did you grow some balls when you shaved your head and got your neck tatted up? Jac, get your sister off of me, please." Cleopatra raised her hands in the air so she wouldn't be tempted to push Robin.

"Robin, come on. Sit down." Jacqueline pulled her away from Cleopatra and made her sit back down on the other side of the island.

"Thank you," Cleopatra said. She looked at Robin. "You want me to grill my best friend and then report back to you?"

"That's exactly what I want you to do."

"No. Why don't you just step to her yourself, like you just did to me?"

"Because she won't talk to me, she's never home, and she doesn't answer my calls or texts."

"Well, that's too bad. Good luck with that, though." Cleopatra attempted to walk away again, wanting no part of the sideshow that was Robin and Shawn's relationship.

Jacqueline got up from her stool and pulled Cleopatra to the side. "Baby. Did you give Shawn money?"

"Yeah." Cleopatra nodded. "And I'm paying her rent right now."

Jacqueline rolled her eyes. "Can you just talk to her for me? Get her to talk to Robin. Ask her to stop running from her. Please, baby?" She breathed into Cleopatra's ear. "If you say yes, she'll leave and we can go and do what we do."

"No. I don't get involved in Shawn's relationships. I only bail her out of jail. That's it. End of conversation." Cleopatra walked back upstairs.

Jacqueline turned to Robin. "I'll see what I can do."

"Well I'm out of here." Robin grabbed her coat and prepared to leave. "Tell Cleo I'm counting on her."

EIGHT

....

BACK IN THE DAY WHEN I WAS
YOUNG I'M NOT A KID ANYMORE

"Ok. I'll track Shawn down and talk to her." Cleopatra surrendered to her wife's request to find out what was going on with her former partner in grime. But she had no intention of telling Robin or Jacqueline what Shawn was really up to. Robin might be her sister-in-law now, but Shawn and Cleopatra had history. She would choose Shawn over Robin every time. And even though she knew Shawn had probably gotten herself into something stupid, as usual, this time felt different. She didn't have a good feeling, and she didn't foresee laughing this one off.

Shawn and Cleopatra had been best friends for over twenty years. They were family. But the more settled down Cleopatra became, the more tired she grew of Shawn's antics and lifestyle. They were both approaching thirty now, and things they'd done at nineteen were no longer cute, and nowhere near smart. Cleopatra had become a grown-ass woman while Shawn was not only stuck reenacting her reckless teen years, but happy right where she stood.

Thinking back on their history now, Cleopatra realized that from day one, she'd ridden hard for Shawn, no matter what. She was Shawn's 'ride or die.' They even had their own saying: Friends help move couches, best friends help move bodies.

They first crossed paths at eight years old in their East New York neighborhood section of Brooklyn. Shawnette grew up with her parents and four sisters. They were a close-knit Trinidadian family heavily grounded in the Catholic Church. Her parents worked hard and gave their spoiled daughters everything they asked for, deserving or not. They lived comfortably in a multifamily home that they owned, were a two-car family, and sent their daughters to all-girl Catholic schools to ensure that they raised respectful, proper, and smart young ladies. Shawn eventually convinced her parents to send her to the neighborhood public school, instead. She liked being surrounded by all girls, but hated the Catholic school rules and uniforms. Although her parents were initially wary of sending her into the public school environment, they finally agreed.

Just a few blocks away Cleopatra, her parents, and brother lived on the top floor of a five-story walk-up in a two-bedroom apartment. Cleopatra shared a bedroom with her brother, who was fourteen years her senior and lived at home well into his late twenties. Cleopatra herself was a good kid—got good grades, cooked, cleaned, did what was asked of her, and stayed out of trouble.

Shawn didn't really know any kids in the neighborhood, as her parents kept their daughters sheltered and all of their free time was spent at church. So switching schools long after the school year began only filled Shawn with anxiety. But she immediately recognized Cleopatra, who she'd watched playing out in front of her apartment building, from the backseat of her parents' Oldsmobile on the way to church. Cleopatra stuck out because she was big and tall, and never wore dresses—only overalls or jeans. She also wore her long hair in cornrows down her back. She had baby hair and long sideburns—not the kind Shawn's sisters cultivated with Vaseline, rat tail combs, and toothbrushes, but real baby hair that laid down on its own. And she carried an Archie and Veronica lunchbox, and had covered Archie's face with a Polaroid of hers.

On Shawn's first day of school, she wandered around the playground alone, then spotted Cleopatra rolling on the concrete with two little girls. And it was at this playground, covered with spray-painted gang tags, broken bottles, crack vials, and discarded fast food wrappers on a random day in third grade, where the lifelong friends first met.

Cleopatra had on red Oshkosh overalls and a red knit hat. The girls were in what had formerly been very pretty but not age-or playground-appropriate pink dresses. They were now covered with dirt, ketchup, and mustard stains.

Shawn pulled the girls off Cleopatra and shouted at them to leave her alone. The girls scattered off to opposite ends of the playground.

Cleopatra jumped to her feet and said, "What are you doing? Those are my girlfriends."

It was then that Shawn realized for the first time that she wasn't the only girl who had a thing for other little girls. The two little beauties, one Puerto Rican and the other Haitian, ran back over to Cleopatra, both kissing her on opposite cheeks before running away to play on the other end of the playground again. Shawn admired that, and from that moment on wanted to be just like Cleopatra.

"I thought they were beating you up."

"You thought those girls were beating me up? Really? Look at me." Cleopatra held her arms out. "Look how big I am." In kindergarten, Cleopatra easily passed for a third grader. Now, at eight, she could pass for a twelve-year-old. "I'm fine. When it comes to girls, I don't need any help. Thanks." She walked away, dusting off her overalls and adjusting her knit cap, pulling it down over her ears.

Shawn ran after her. "So you like those girls? And they like you?" She tried to understand.

"Yeah. You saw them lay two big fat ones on me. You got a problem?" Cleopatra huffed and folded her arms across her chest.

"No. No." Shawn shook her head. "Does your mommy know? I mean does she…"

Cleopatra was annoyed now. "For my last birthday she said I could have any cartoon character on my cake. I chose Popeye." She posed with her little biceps curled. "He was like this on my cake. Yeah, she knows." Then she rolled her eyes and looked Shawn up and down. "Are you comfortable in that? Because you don't look like it."

She was referring to Shawn's red velvet dress with the white bow on the chest and black patent leather Mary Janes.

"You look like a boy in a dress." Cleopatra cocked her head to the side, studying Shawn harder and taking her all in now. "You look like how I would feel in a dress. Do you feel like throwing up? I would throw up, if I were you."

Shawn collapsed to the ground and started to cry. She rolled back and forth, her dress now a canvas similar to that of Cleopatra's two little girlfriends.

Cleopatra freaked out. "I'm sorry. What did I say?"

"I hate it." Shawn stood up, her face covered with tears and snot. "I feel like a boy in this dress. I just didn't know that I looked like one." She wiped her face on her arm, and a line of snot spanned from the crook of her elbow.

"Eww." Cleopatra swiped at it and rubbed it on Shawn's ruffled sleeves—the first of many messes she would clean up for Shawn. "Follow me."

She took Shawn into an empty classroom and began rifling through her teacher's desk.

Shawn walked around the vacant classroom, crammed with forty neon orange chairs shoved snuggly under forty old, fossilized wood tables. She ran her fingers over a blue ink pen carving in one of the desks: Peace in the Middle East. Streamers in every primary color hung from the ceiling with no particular purpose or pattern, with various loop sizes.

"Is that you?" She pointed to the bulletin board titled Thriving Third Graders.

Cleopatra looked up momentarily. "Yup," she said, and continued rummaging through her teacher's drawers.

"How did you get on the bulletin board?"

"It's not hard. Pay attention. Do your classwork, your homework. Be quiet and polite. Stay out of trouble. Ah ha." She grabbed a pair of scissors and charged toward Shawn. "Hold out your arms." She cut the ruffles off of Shawn's sleeves and two Almond Joy candy bars fell out.

"Um … why are you hiding candy bars in your sleeves?" Cleopatra giggled.

"Because I ran out of room in my lunchbox." Shawn hung her head.

"You don't have to do that. Tomorrow I'll just hold them for you in mine." Cleopatra took a staple gun and stapled the dress between Shawn's legs so it looked like she was wearing a shorts set. Then she ran into the girl's bathroom. Shawn scooted quickly behind her with her legs confined by the newly stapled dress.

"See, you look like Wonder Woman now. Kinda." Cleopatra squinted. "Well, if you do this." She scrunched up her face and closed her eyes.

Shawn shook her head as she looked at herself in the mirror. "Um … no, I look more like a buff Superman."

Cleopatra looked at Shawn in the mirror again, and shrugged. "Ok … Superman it is."

"Yeah, Superman." Shawn posed with her hands at her waist. "Wait, what happens when I have to go to pee?"

"Easy. I'll just wait for you and staple you back up again." Cleopatra smirked. "What's your name?"

"Shawnette."

"Nice to meet you Shawn. I'm Cleo."

And so it began: a friendship and Shawn's fascination with Cleopatra. A fascination and appreciation that helped them form a bond that would be constantly tested, but grow from that day forward.

✿✿✿

Unlike Shawn, Cleopatra didn't have the picture-perfect

family. Her mother was a hardworking woman and a loving parent, but she had given up hope on Cleopatra's brother, David, who was lazy and unmotivated. Cleopatra didn't care; she idealized him. He was tall, handsome, and attracted the most beautiful women.

And he never held a job, but always had money, the newest porno magazines, and the flashiest jewelry. The finest clothes hung up beside Cleopatra's in the small bedroom closet that they shared. He let Cleopatra wear his suits and shoes to school after her growth spurt, and when she fit comfortably into his size 10s. She was the only girl who wore a double-breasted silk suit and alligator shoes to eighth-grade graduation. And she wore it well.

Her brother would have ten girlfriends at any given time, and Cleopatra marveled at how he juggled them, sometimes with her help. She would learn much from her brother about women, but mostly how not to treat them. She saw women make fools of themselves over her brother; not unlike the shenanigans women would later pull in the name of getting her affections. By her early teens, there wasn't much Cleopatra hadn't seen. She would run into the jaded black and Latina zombies her brother created well after he was only a distant memory.

But Cleopatra was altogether different. She was her mother's pride and joy; her mother saw a bright future for Cleopatra and held her to a different standard. Cleopatra grew up demanding that same type of love and devotion in her intimate relationships.

Cleopatra had once been the apple of her father's eye, too.

She helped him around the apartment with home improvements and repairs. And she packed such hearty lunches for him that his fellow construction workers often tried to trade with him. He took Cleopatra everywhere—to the liquor store, the racetrack, and to play the lottery. She was his good luck charm, picking the winning numbers and horses with ease. He took her to Popeye's and White Castle and watched her polish off a ten-pack with admiration, or down a spicy three-piece chicken, not like an eight-year-old girl, but like a grown man.

Then one day, everything went to hell and their relationship would never recover. Cleopatra's uncle, her father's big brother, died suddenly, and it was like the life in her father died right along with him. Her father just stopped going to work, never to go again, and went from a weekend drunk to a daily drunk, stealing money from her piggy bank to buy corn chips and Miller High Life. That was when Cleopatra began to hate the man. She was no longer daddy's little girl; whiskey was his girl now, and rumors were that Ms. Berry down the street was his bitch.

Her already strained relationship with her father was irrevocably broken when ten-year-old Cleopatra was awakened by another argument between her parents. But her father's tone was more volatile than usual. He had never hit her mother before, but he'd turned into a man Cleopatra no longer trusted. She ran into the kitchen, grabbed a butcher knife, and stood in the doorway, waiting.

Her father caught a glimpse of her and said, "What the fuck do you want, Cleopatra?"

"If you touch her, I'll kill you," Cleopatra responded coolly.

Her mother's lips curled up into a smile. He didn't stand a

chance between the two of them. Cleopatra's mother carried a .45 in her purse and pulled it out whenever necessary. After that night, he slept with one eye open, and never had a peaceful night's sleep again until he left the family for good.

There was an uneventful span of nearly four years, then, and in that time Cleopatra spoke less than ten words to her father. She was fourteen now, and her mother's debilitating stroke was the final straw—his cue, his out to leave, never look back, and not feel any kind of way about it. The last thing he said to Cleopatra as he left with his lone suitcase, in his house slippers and with a bottle of Remy Martin in a soiled brown paper bag, was: "Sometimes things just don't work out."

Cleopatra saw him a few days later. He had taken up with Ms. Berry down the block, just like the rumors said. But he acted like he didn't know Cleopatra. Didn't acknowledge and didn't speak to her as he walked down the street with his mistress and her three kids, one of whom was in Cleopatra's eighth-grade class. Another was a little girl of two or three years old that looked a lot like Cleopatra at the same age.

Shortly after her father left, her brother disappeared. Left like a thief in the night, and never said goodbye to Cleopatra or her mother. Cleopatra told her mother she didn't think he was dead but didn't think he was ever coming back either. Her mother was heartbroken and didn't speak a word for days.

She never did hear from her brother again, but many years later a woman claiming to be his wife appeared at her door with two children, looking for him. She said he had a habit of disappearing for weeks, and sometimes months at a time, and she thought she would look Cleopatra up, on the off chance that he was with her.

"That relationship died long ago," Cleopatra told the woman, who looked her age—much too young to be dragging her kids all over, looking for their no-good daddy. She slipped a few hundred dollars into the girl's hand. "Feed your kids instead of looking for that motherfucker. They look hungry."

The two most important men in Cleopatra's life had left her. Was that what men did? They left? But it took her to a conclusion: If her father and brother could pretend she didn't exist, she would do the same. It would have been easy for her to begin hating everyone at that point, but she never did; just those that called themselves her family. From then on, she convinced herself that she didn't need family and didn't need love. She would take care of herself and her mother. There were times in her life when that thought process appeared to work for her, and times when it didn't. But Cleopatra never complained. She never spoke a harsh word against her father or brother in her mother's presence. She kept her emotions in check and did what needed to be done. She supported herself and her mother by using their benefits sparingly. There were times she didn't eat, but made sure her mother ate well. She held down after-school and weekend jobs at supermarkets and fast food joints, sneaking meals when she could.

Cleopatra continued to see her father in the neighborhood, with that same woman and her children and the little girl that looked remarkably like her. When she moved to the freshman dorms at Columbia University, he was still on the block. When she finally moved her mother out of Brooklyn to the cushy Upper East Side, he was still on the block.

She would go on to live without her father. Without his love, supervision, or support, and she would be just fine. She decided as a teenager that she would never forgive him, and she was well with that. At that early age she vowed to live her life doing right by those she loved, and to live with no regrets. Life had to, and would, go on. Cleopatra became super-focused on revenge against those who had wronged her and her mother. Those who had either left, disrespected, or underestimated their resolve. Not a violent revenge, but the sweetest form: success and prosperity.

Cleopatra knew education was the only way to a better life for her and her mom. She was dedicated to her schoolwork, and at times studied with a flashlight when their electricity had been cut off. Or at the library or the twenty-four-hour White Castle on Pennsylvania Avenue, right off of the ho stroll. The same one she'd frequented with her father many years before.

But eventually, Child Protective Services found out that both Cleopatra's father and brother were no longer in the home. Refusing to believe that a smart fourteen-year-old and her wheelchair-bound, stroke-surviving mother could take care of themselves, Social Services broke up what was left of Cleopatra's family. Her mother was shipped to a nursing home in the Bronx, and Cleopatra to a group home in Queens. Cleopatra ran away almost immediately, preferring to live on the streets after realizing that with all the fighting, stealing, and sexual abuse in the group home, the streets were actually safer.

She bounced around the homes of various girlfriends for a while, until the girls's parents realized that Cleopatra was more than just a boyish friend. Then she slept in school bathrooms and locker rooms. And restrooms of expensive hotels all over the city.

Through it all, even after Cleopatra's mother fell ill and her father and brother left, Shawn's parents refused to offer any type of help. Once, after Cleopatra had been living on the streets during a harsh winter, Shawn snuck her into her room so she could get a peaceful night's sleep and a hot meal. But Shawn's mother found Cleopatra and kicked her out of the house. She even took the plate of food right out of Cleopatra's hand.

Shawn's parents had always hated Cleopatra. But they constantly compared Shawn to her, hoping to draw a wedge between the two. They were dumbfounded at how a kid in Shawn's position, with so many privileges and resources, was so unaccomplished when a kid like Cleopatra—who they had labeled a sexual deviant—excelled at everything she did.

They'd always blamed Cleopatra for their daughter's rough, boyish appearance and mannerisms. So back when Shawn came out to them at age twelve, her parents kicked her out and sent her to live with Cleopatra.

"Since you want to be just like her, go on and fucking live with her!" Shawn's mother screamed.

Shawn stayed with Cleopatra and her family for nearly six months—so long that Cleopatra's mother threatened to put Shawn on her taxes if her parents didn't take her back in. Shawn's parent's agreed only after she promised to "become" straight and stay away from Cleopatra and girls.

Of course Shawn had no intention of doing either. Cleopatra was the only person who knew, accepted, and loved the real her unconditionally. Cleopatra would go on to prove that many times over in the following years, though Shawn's parents hypocritically berated and belittled Cleopatra and her sexuality to Shawn at every possible opportunity, often right in

Cleopatra's face. Cleopatra'd had enough of their verbal abuse, so when she finally pointed out that every evil thing Shawn's mother said about her must also be true of Shawn, Shawn's mother threw a pan of hot fish grease at her. Shawn's mother only escaped prosecution because Cleopatra wasn't injured and wouldn't press charges.

Those were some of the roughest years of Cleopatra's young life. But instead of destroying her, those years made her. Eventually life would turn around, when a fifteen-year-old and homeless Cleopatra walked into a woman's shelter in lower Manhattan and met Teresa Benjamin, the director, a thirty-something, petite woman with warm chocolate skin and widely spaced eyes. The dreadlocked former attorney-turned women's advocate knew Cleopatra was special when she asked where her belongings were and Cleopatra answered, "In a storage locker by Port Authority. I don't need things. I just need my books."

"Well go get your things anyway, and by the time you come back I'll have your bed ready," Teresa said.

Cleopatra refused to give Teresa any information, fearing she would turn her back over to the city. But Teresa took her in anyway, and advised her not to start any shit.

"You're tall and lanky." Teresa looked up at Cleopatra. "That doesn't mean I can't knock your ass out," she warned her.

Teresa gave her room and board, and in exchange Cleopatra tutored the other children, helped the women study for their GEDs, and taught other skills the women could use to get jobs. She did well at the shelter, and they became her family. They knew Cleopatra to be a loving, kind, and sympathetic kid. She eventually opened up about why she was living on the streets. Teresa became her temporary guardian and later helped reunite her with her mother, after her mother made incredible strides in her rehabilitation. Although she was still wheelchair bound, she was practically self-sufficient now. Eventually, Cleopatra and her mother moved into a first-floor-accessible one bedroom back in their old neighborhood in East New York, and once again around the corner from Shawn.

Times were tough just as before, and money continued to be tight. But all that mattered was that her and her mother were back together. Cleopatra would be forever indebted to Teresa.

But just when Cleopatra wanted to collapse from exhaustion from taking care of the house, school, and working two part-time jobs, a chance meeting changed her life forever.

....

NINE

SLEEPING WITH THE STARS

Sixteen-year-old Cleopatra and Shawn were in the West Village on a Saturday night—a hot summer evening, and a rare outing. Cleopatra had gone reluctantly only after her mother convinced her to have some fun with her friends in the city. They were hanging out on the Pier, along with hundreds of other gay teens, most of them black and Latino. They had all marched down Christopher Street and formed their own impromptu queer parade, snaking toward the waterfront, as was the norm on weekend nights. They were packed in groups of ten and twenty, and the air was electric with pride as boys locked hands with other boys and girls kissed each other out in the open, sliding their hands down into their panties freely, without a care as to who was watching. The Pier was where Cleopatra and Shawn could be themselves, not being able to express their sexuality as freely as they wanted to in the neighborhood where they lived. At the Pier, they laid out on benches, danced to music, and prowled around for cute females.

It was on this night that Cleopatra met Olivia, an attractive former runway model with deep-set almond eyes and full lips.

Cleopatra was already tall and muscular, her locs just past her shoulders, she had on baggy jeans and Timberland boots. But her baby face gave her away every time.

The chocolate woman, who was a bit taller than Cleopatra in her stilettos, laughed in Cleopatra's face. She flipped her long, flowing weave out of her eyes as the wind off the water jostled her hair across her cheek. Olivia was trolling the pier, looking for at-risk teens in need of a particular method of mentoring.

"How old are you, sweetheart?" She perused Cleopatra's body. The body had definitely outrun the face, she thought.

"Age ain't nothing but a number." Young Cleopatra charmed the woman, but she didn't get into Olivia's pants as she had originally planned. Instead, Olivia became her mentor of sorts, her advocate, her champion, and even her benefactor. She helped with her mother's bills, and rent money, and enough pocket money so that Cleopatra didn't have to work part-time jobs anymore.

Olivia groomed Cleopatra into a renaissance woman. She exposed her to different cultures, languages, the fine arts and cuisine, and the ins and outs of business. She challenged Cleopatra to become well read, and read books outside of high school. She taught her how to handle her money, how and where to spend it, and how and where to save it. Cleopatra was gifted academically and athletically, but Olivia taught her etiquette and how to handle herself in any given situation. Cleopatra was already courteous, generous, and thoughtful, but Olivia would teach her to act like a true gentlewoman.

Cleopatra was unsure of what Olivia did for a living and never asked, but her level of wealth was confirmed when she gave Cleopatra the key to one of her vacant penthouse apartments. Unbeknownst to Cleopatra, Olivia had big plans for her.

Olivia brought Cleopatra into her circle of female friends. Cleopatra had her suspicions about the introductions to the women, but she wasn't overly concerned; she was overwhelmed by them, each more beautiful than the last. And every introduction Olivia made ended in a hook up, though Cleopatra never forgot the first night she realized what was really going on. It was the night of her seventeenth birthday.

"You do know who this is, don't you?" Olivia smiled as she put her arm around Cleopatra and introduced her to a new woman.

"I do." Cleopatra licked her lips as her eyes danced up and down the woman's body.

The woman was spread out across Olivia's leather Chesterfield sofa, drinking champagne, her black stiletto heels thrown underneath the antique marble-top coffee table. She got up slowly, her body constrained by her tight black dress, and slithered toward them.

"Nice to meet you, Cleopatra." She took Cleopatra's hands in hers and caressed them. "Olivia says that I'm one of your favorite singers."

"My favorite," Cleopatra corrected her as she looked down at the woman's cleavage and bit her lip. She was even sexier than in her videos, Cleopatra thought.

"I'm your one and only? I love that." The woman looked up at Cleopatra. "So, when Olivia told me about you, I really wanted to meet you. And then she told me you have a little crush on me." She pinched her fingers together.

"There's nothing little about what I have." Cleopatra smiled as she flirted back with the woman. She was mesmerized; the woman was petite, and she figured she could pick her up and throw her over her shoulder with one arm.

"I like her," the woman said to Olivia, who had walked across the room and was watching them from the chaise in the corner. She whispered in Cleopatra's ear, "She's told me about you," and slipped her hand into Cleopatra's locs to run her fingertips through her scalp. Cleopatra's body shivered. When the woman spoke it was breathless, as if she was mid-orgasm, and it drove Cleopatra wild.

"What's going on?" Cleopatra asked Olivia.

She didn't know what the international superstar was doing at Olivia's penthouse. Why did she know or even care who Cleopatra was? And why could she not keep her hands off her? The woman picked up the glass of champagne she'd been sipping on and chuckled a bit. Cleopatra looked back at Olivia, who continued studying them. The woman traced her finger across Cleopatra's bottom lip, and Cleopatra stuck out her tongue and pulled the woman's finger into her mouth to suck it.

"Mmmmm ... that must be the snake," the woman moaned as her eyes rolled back. "I can only imagine what else you can do with that."

Cleopatra pulled the woman's finger from her mouth and kissed it before giving her back her hand. She was a junior in high school, but looked to be in her early twenties and was getting into clubs now with fake IDs. She had her hands full following in her absent brothers footsteps, juggling multiple girlfriends her own age, but what was this endless parade of grown and sexy women that Olivia was serving her?

The woman turned her back to Cleopatra and grinded her ass into her. Cleopatra grabbed her and held her by her waist.

"Mmmm…" The woman turned around. "Olivia said you were strong." She pulled a pin out of her updo and let her curly black hair fall down to her shoulders.

"Beautiful," Cleopatra whispered.

"Olivia also said you're an amazing lover."

Cleopatra didn't know what else to say. "Um ... thank you, Olivia." Olivia smiled, confirming that she had indeed praised her skills. She had taught Cleopatra a lot in the bedroom, but Cleopatra was already experienced and detail-oriented. Now she was an even better lover.

"Why don't we go upstairs now so we can celebrate your birthday?" The woman grabbed her hand and Cleopatra looked back at Olivia, who nodded her head in approval.

The next morning, Cleopatra woke up in the bed with the singer, their arms and legs intertwined, the woman clinging to her and not wanting to let her go.

She whispered in Cleopatra's ear, "I wish you could come on tour with me. When can I see you again?"

Olivia walked into the bedroom right as Cleopatra said, "Whenever you want."

Olivia interrupted. "Call me if you want to see Cleopatra again, and we'll set something up." She yanked the duvet off of them, exposing their naked bodies, and pulled the curtains open, letting the sunshine in on their faces.

"We discussed overnight, if you recall." The woman snuggled her head under Cleopatra's chin.

Olivia checked her watch. "Yeah and it's 6AM."

The star looked at Cleopatra and clutched her arm tight. "I don't care about my allotted time."

"Cleopatra has another engagement," Olivia said.

Cleopatra looked at her, confused, while Olivia handed the woman her crumpled up dress. "Contact me to set up another date with her."

"Is it someone else?" the singer asked Cleopatra. "I don't want you with anyone else. When can I fly you out for a visit?"

"Um." Cleopatra looked at Olivia, who was visibly upset now. Olivia reiterated again that she would be in touch. The star didn't take too kindly to being kicked out of the house, as she wanted to stay in bed with Cleopatra. But Olivia hurried her along and slammed the door in the woman's face, right as she yelled at the top of her lungs, "Call me, Cleopatra!"

After the woman left, Olivia found Cleopatra in the bathroom and handed her a thick manila envelope.

"What's this?" Cleopatra asked as she dried her naked body, fresh out of the shower.

"That's payment for a job well done. I didn't think she was going to leave," Olivia laughed.

"What just happened?" Cleopatra wrapped the towel around her waist. She opened the envelope and flicked through the stack of bills.

"You just fucked her and got paid for it. Do you have a problem with that?"

Cleopatra flicked the bills through her hand again. "There must be a few thousand here."

"You spent the whole night with her. That's a lot of work."

"No the hell it wasn't, that wasn't work. I think I'm in love. She told me she loved me last night, like every time she came."

Cleopatra smiled. "I didn't even know she was gay. Why does she have to pay for it?"

"No one knows she's gay, and no one will find out, you got that? You can't tell anyone, not even Shawn. No one. She's an icon. America's sweetheart. No one can find out she's gay. Cleopatra. Look at me. "

Cleopatra looked at her. "Ok. No one. I got it."

Olivia leaned against the bathroom vanity. "So let me ask you again. Do you have a problem getting paid to do this?"

"Not if they all look and fuck like her. Oh my God, look at my back and shoulders." She twisted her body so Olivia could see. "My skin is raw, it's burning. She was a beast."

"I know. I heard."

Cleopatra smiled and caught herself. "So ... this is what you do? You're basically a pimp?"

Olivia laughed. "No, sweetheart. I run an escort service—the largest and most exclusive in the city."

"What's the difference?" Cleopatra put on a fresh pair of underwear from her emergency stash.

Olivia pointed to the large stack of bills. "That's the difference. And by the way, don't ever call me a pimp again. Can't stand the word. What I do and what we will do as a team is on another level. So if you want to do this and you're committed, we can make a lot of money together. Set you up for life."

"Me? My mother?"

"You, your mom. College and grad school, if you want. You're a smart kid and you'll get scholarships, but they don't cover everything, and when you turn eighteen they'll cut off the little benefit checks. You can have everything you want if we do this right. Last time I'm going to ask you: Do you have a problem with this?"

"Only problem I have is we didn't start this sooner. What do I have to do?"

"Keep your mouth shut. I'm going to be connecting you with some wealthy, powerful, and well-known women. Some are married, some aren't. Some are in the closet and some aren't. And you can start with not fucking them so good. I don't want them all falling in love." Olivia caught herself. "On second thought, never mind. Let them fall in love." She laughed. "Now hurry up, finish getting dressed, and get your ass to school."

....

TEN

DON'T CALL IT A COMEBACK /NO BUSINESS LIKE HO BUSINESS

Cleopatra kept her promise to Jacqueline and Robin to try and meet up with Shawn. She left multiple voicemails for her, but before Shawn called her back, she got a phone call from an old friend.

"As fine as ever." Olivia kissed Cleopatra on the cheek. "I always did love you in a suit." She ran her hand down the length of Cleopatra's back, caressing the gray Italian wool between her fingers. Olivia had summoned her to one of her favorite restaurants on Manhattan's East Side, and Cleopatra had come directly from work.

"Look at you." Cleopatra beamed. "Flawless." Olivia was gorgeous and ageless. Back when she was a teenager, Cleopatra had thought Olivia was in her thirties or forties, but she hadn't aged a day, and Cleopatra really had no clue how old she was now. Today, she wore her short brown natural hair slicked back, accentuating her long neck and large almond eyes. Never one to be caught without a fur when the temp was under 50 degrees, today she wore a tight black cashmere sweater dress with a low-cut mink collar.

"Thank you for meeting me on such short notice." She sucked her bottom lip into her mouth as she ran her hand over the white tablecloth, smoothing it out to the corner.

"Of course. ASAP. Just like old times." Cleopatra sat down across from her at the intimate corner table overlooking the East River.

"Have you had lunch? Are you hungry?" Olivia inquired as a short redheaded waiter brought her food to the table and delicately placed the dish in front of her.

"Basil poached frog, cured beets with chive oil, Swiss chard with cloumage ravioli, and white and green asparagus."

"Thank you, dear," Olivia said to the waiter. She motioned for him to direct his attention to Cleopatra. "Order whatever you like."

Cleopatra scrunched her face. "Did you say poached frog?" she asked the waiter.

"Yes, Ms. Giovanni." He nodded and smiled.

"How do you know my name?"

"Customer service," Olivia interrupted. "You get what you pay for." She smiled.

"I'll just have a glass of water with lemon," Cleopatra said to the waiter as she examined the frog on Olivia's plate. She imagined it had probably been alive and hopping around no less than ten minutes before, and that killed whatever hunger she may have had. "Thank you. I can't stay long," she said. "I have to get back to the office." She looked down at her watch.

"So, it's been a long time." Olivia sat back and studied Cleopatra as she carved into her frog.

"My mother's memorial service," Cleopatra said. "Thank

you again for everything. I wouldn't have been able to get myself together and handle the arrangements without your help."

"No thank you necessary. You're like family. Speaking of family, how is married life? It looks to be treating you extremely well." She winked at Cleopatra.

"She's treating me extremely well. It's been wonderful." Cleopatra smiled at the waiter when he returned to the table with her water. "Thank you."

"You've come a long way from the young stud I met all those years ago on the Pier. I owe you. You made me a lot of money. Are you sure you don't want some of this? The frog is magnificent."

Cleopatra immediately shook her head no. "You set me up for life, just like you promised. And it's still paying off to this day." She smiled.

"You're talking about Alexis, among others?"

"Non-disclosure agreements, remember?"

"There is a piece of work," Olivia chuckled. "All that money and she still can't have you. Do you see her often?"

"Not really. She tends to show up when I'm in some sort of trouble. Just in time to save the day."

"That's because she loves you, always will. That woman is dangerous, but you know that already, don't you?"

"I do." Cleopatra nodded as she took a sip of water.

The waiter brought Olivia a decanter of cognac and she smiled. "Thank you, sweetheart." She picked up the cognac and refilled her own glass. "I forgot. How did you actually meet Alexis, anyway?"

Cleopatra smiled. "I was, um … with a client in the ladies' room of this restaurant."

Olivia laughed. "One of your favorite spots."

"This client liked to do it in public. Alexis heard us and saw us leave the stall. Long story short, I dropped my cell phone, Alexis found it, kept it, and answered it every time it rang. I eventually called my cell and Alexis invited me to her penthouse to pick it up. The rest is history."

"It was definitely historical. She was so obsessed with you that she paid to have you on call twenty-four hours a day, just so you couldn't have any other clients. And didn't she try to leave her husband for you? And leave all that money behind."

"Crazy, right? It was always business for me, nothing more. But that was a long, long time ago. The Pier has even changed. The city cleaned it up; they show Disney movies there in the summer, now. That shit is disturbing." Cleopatra shook her head, remembering the seedy things she used to do on the Pier. "First Times Square, now the Pier. Can nothing stay grimy and sacred in this city?"

"Doesn't seem like it." Olivia laughed as she sucked an asparagus into her mouth.

"You sounded stressed on the phone. I can't recall the last time I heard that in your voice," Cleopatra said, though she feared being pulled back into something she wanted no part of.

"I'm sure there's one thing about you that hasn't changed." Olivia dabbed her mouth with the white cloth napkin. "How you take care of your family. I called you as a last resort, because of Shawn. I'm sure you know by now." Cleopatra raised her eyebrows, confused. "She's costing me a lot of money and has a lot of clients in a frenzy, because not only does she have their contact information, but now she's hitting them up for business and money. Some have even taken her up on her discounted offers. But most of them don't like it, and I hate it. You can imagine how this makes me look. This is a breach."

Cleopatra waved her hand and shook her head to get Olivia to stop talking. "Are you telling me Shawn is back in business?"

"You didn't know?" Olivia sucked a sliced beet into her mouth.

"Hell no, that's crazy. For how long?"

"That's how I feel. A few weeks, maybe longer. You of all people know the most important part of this business is privacy; ranks right up there with amazing sex. These women are paying to get fucked silly, and for no one to ever find out about it. So it's a problem that she has their contact info and is trying to freelance. She's been dodging my calls, but I have someone watching her apartment, and she hasn't been home in days. You're my last hope, or I should say her last hope." Olivia took a gulp of cognac, held her left hand up in the air, and snapped her fingers twice.

Cleopatra looked around, confused. She didn't know what that signal was for, but she'd heard that tone of voice and seen that vacant look in Olivia's eyes before. She was fortunate to have never been the object of her unhappiness.

"What do you want me to do?" she asked.

"Simple. Get her to stop."

"I think I know what this is about. She wants to pay me back; she got into some trouble and I bailed her out of a few situations."

"That's admirable of her. But not my concern."

The waiter scurried over to the table. "Your double shot of Jose Cuervo 250 Aniversario, Ms. Devereaux."

Cleopatra smirked. How did he know that Olivia snapping her fingers twice meant to bring her tequila? *Now that is customer service*, she thought. She looked down at her watch: 12:15. "Hitting the liquor a bit hard and early, are we?" She smiled, but Olivia didn't participate in her humor.

"Would you like a shot?"

"No, thank you." Just then Cleopatra realized what the waiter said. "Isn't that like $300 a shot?"

"Something like that." Olivia threw back the double shot without flinching or shedding a tear. "You sure you don't want?" She pointed to the now-arid 2-ounce glass.

"I'd rather have the $300. Or is that $600?" Cleopatra joked. Again, her humor was lost on Olivia, who was all business now. "Ok. What if you just let Shawn work until she pays off what she owes me, and then she'll stop?"

"How much does she owe you?"

"A little over $100,000."

"Now that's funny. You know how long it will take her to make $100,000? And on her own? I didn't come to negotiate with you, Cleopatra. Just offering you a warning as a courtesy. It would be a shame for you to find out what happened to her after the fact."

"What are you going to do?"

"If she continues, I'll hurt her. You're probably the only one who can convince her to stop. She either quits altogether or comes back and works for me—her choice. I'm not even asking that she pay me the money she's costing me by taking some of my clientele. I've already talked at length to her voicemail, and I'm not dealing with her anymore. If you can't get her to stop, I will. She can fuck for me or not at all. It's on you now."

"You've known us since we were kids. Don't do this."

"And I've never liked her. I only dealt with her because of my feelings for you. She was always insubordinate; she wanted it all, but she was lazy and unwilling to work for it. I always cut her slack, since day one. She has seven days."

Cleopatra cringed. She'd heard of the seven days of warnings before, but hadn't seen or heard much from those to whom the warnings had been issued, after the fact. They usually gave in long before the seven days of daily punishment were up.

"You said you owe me," she pleaded.

"That's why I'm here telling you that your friend is about to get fucked. How would you feel if I had her ass whipped and said nothing to you? You would be furious, right? Right." Olivia answered her own question as Cleopatra nodded.

"Look, I'll give you forty-eight hours to find her and talk some sense into her. If she's still working independently after that, she'll be in a world of hurt." Olivia picked up a frog leg and slurped it into her mouth. "Then, every day for seven days, I'll have at least one part of her body fucked up, and on the seventh day I'll break her jaw personally. The last time I broke someone's jaw, I broke a nail. And that really upset me."

Cleopatra had been in many precarious situations before, and rarely feared anything—even Olivia—but in that moment she wanted to pee a little. She wanted to plead for Olivia to spare her friend, but knew that Olivia had already been incredibly patient with Shawn, just because of her. She had seen women and men fucked up for much less than what Shawn was doing, with less warning. Nobody messed with Olivia's money and got away with it.

"So that's it, huh?" Cleopatra asked.

Olivia nodded, her mouth full of beets.

"I'll talk to Shawn and see what I can do. I promise you that," Cleopatra said. "But it's all on Shawn. After I speak with her, this right here is between you and her."

Olivia smiled. "You should be tired of cleaning up her messes; you've cleaned them up for as long as I can remember. You need to think about dropping that dead-ass weight." She dabbed the corners of her mouth with her white cloth napkin.

"You're right. I'm in a different phase of my life. I'm settled. I'm happy. I don't need this."

"In fact," Olivia paused. "I can beat Shawn's ass for seven days straight and she still won't acquiesce to my conditions. She's that much of a fool. So I need a little insurance policy to ensure that she does." Olivia took a sip of her cognac. "Handle Shawn or innocent people will get hurt." She stared at Cleopatra.

Cleopatra looked around, twisting her eyebrows in confusion. "Wait. Are you fucking threatening me?"

"I would never hurt you. You know that. I love you too much. But I don't love your wife or your kids." Olivia smiled, her teeth stained with beet juice. "Handle Shawn."

Cleopatra couldn't believe that after all she had been through in her life, and all she had overcome to create her own happy family, it was being threatened. And because of Shawn.

She sat quiet for a moment, then leaned into the table and spoke, her voice just above a whisper. "Listen. Olivia." She reached across the table, took Olivia's glass of cognac out of her hand, and gulped it down. "You are not going to hurt my family. You want to know why? Because then you would leave me with absolutely nothing to lose. And then I would kill you. So this is what's going to happen instead."

Olivia cleared her throat and attempted to speak.

"Shut it up. Put one of those nasty-ass frog legs in your mouth and listen. I'll talk to Shawn because I promised I would. Then I'm walking away from both of you motherfuckers. As of right now, you and I are done."

ELEVEN

....

KEEPING ENEMIES CLOSER

"How are you going to go back in the business and not tell me? What's wrong with you? And why are we meeting in the park? It's dark and freezing out here." Cleopatra kicked a small pile of snow and threw the hood of her black North Face jacket over her head.

"I'm sorry, man." Shawn slipped the fur-trimmed hood of her vintage white Triple Fat Goose down coat over her short Caesar hair cut as the wind whistled through the trees.

Cleopatra had finally caught up with Shawn a day after meeting with Olivia, and it was Friday evening by the time they met on Parkside Avenue, just outside of Prospect Park in Brooklyn. She needed to knock some sense into Shawn; she had until the next day at noon, then the seven days of ass whippings went in to effect.

Cleopatra looked at her friend and twisted her head sideways to get a better view of her face as they walked into the park. Who was this person? An even better question: Why was she there wasting time with her? She had been asking herself that for some time now, but had failed to distance herself from Shawn. Shawn had been her family for as long as she could remember, and she just dealt with Shawn and her choices because that's what you did with family. Cleopatra had her share of incidents in the past, but she didn't seek them out or revel in the nonsense. She had long outgrown the bullshit, but was just now realizing it. Shawn's fiascos weren't funny anymore. The childhood friends had grown apart. Their lifestyles and goals were different now. Cleopatra had matured while Shawn appeared to retreat even further from adulthood. The energy and patience that it took to deal with Shawn's ridiculous situations were wearing on Cleopatra. And now her family was being threatened. That was it for her. She was done.

"Olivia is going to put a hurting on you, and your girl thinks you're cheating. But forget all of that. Olivia threatened Jacqueline and the kids. Your business is in my house, and I will not have that."

"I tried to keep you out of it." Shawn walked over and sat on a wooden bench just inside the entrance to the park.

Cleopatra pulled her hood tighter over her head and sat down next to her. "I'm in it now. After we discussed you not going back into the business and how you didn't have to worry about paying me back, you go back and do this shit anyway?"

Shawn hung her head like a scolded child.

"So you're going to be a freelance ho with broken fingers, broken legs, and your tongue in a jar?" Cleopatra asked.

Shawn took a package out of her backpack and handed it to Cleopatra. The smell of McDonald's wafted up in to the night air and Cleopatra shook her head as she grabbed the brown paper bag. She took her black leather gloves off in order to unwrap it.

"What's this? Are you crazy?" She stood up from the bench.

"How are you going to hand me a brick of cash in the park? This isn't New Jack City." She threw the money back at Shawn and yelled, "I told you I don't want the money. You're crazy for doing this behind Olivia's back, and especially when you have a woman at home."

"You did that shit back in the day."

"My girl back then knew I was an escort and she was cool with it. Robin has no idea. You plan on telling her?" Cleopatra twisted her lips because she already knew the answer.

"No. And she won't find out unless you tell her," Shawn said. "Here, take it. It's like 10 Gs." She unzipped Cleopatra's backpack, shoved the money down into the bottom, and closed it back up. "I owe you a lot more. But I got you. I promise."

"Whatever, man. Robin asked me to talk to you. Don't you think you at least owe her some type of an explanation?"

"And tell her what?" Shawn twisted her eyebrows.

"Something? I don't know, make up some shit. I thought you were actually trying to have a real relationship with her. You can't keep avoiding her—you live together." Cleopatra sat back down on the bench.

"I know that. I know everything about this shit is wrong. I shouldn't be fucking with Olivia's clientele. And I did this behind your back when you told me not to. I hate that I have to do this at all. And do this to Robin. She has her issues, and man, she's got a filthy-ass mouth on her, but deep down she's a good girl. I think I'm ruining her."

Shawn leaned back on the park bench and exhaled hard into the brisk night air. "But it's the only way I can pay you back.

It's my only option. That's more important to me than any-thing right now. Nothing else matters. I don't want that debt hanging over my head. I can't move on with my life until I've wiped the slate clean with you. I'm tired of owing you, man. I'm tired. I have to do this."

Cleopatra shook her head. "I understand you want to pay me back. But not like this. And it's not a rush, at all. You don't pay the rest of your bills on time, if at all."

"I know that. But you've bailed me out of jail more times than I can count, gotten me lawyers—and good ones. I haven't forgotten all that. You do realize that I've never paid you back for anything? Like, ever in my life. I had to do something. You're my family, you pay family back."

"You got it mixed up. Family can't ruin your credit or re-possess your truck."

"How did you know it got repossessed?" Shawn asked.

"I saw you get off the B41 bus before you went into that McDonald's." Cleopatra shook her head. She was beginning to lose her patience. She badly wanted to just get up and walk away and be done with Shawn, but there was no convincing Olivia to change her mind. It was all on Shawn. And even after everything, she couldn't just turn her back on her friend, know-ing the beating she had coming in a few hours and the potential harm that could come to her family if Shawn refused Olivia's conditions.

Cleopatra's only option was to convince Shawn to contact Olivia and come to some type of agreement.

"Look. I talked to Olivia. She's going to hurt you and I don't want anything to happen to you. And I won't allow my family to be pulled into your bullshit. This is your shit, Shawn. You have to stop stealing Olivia's client's altogether, or just go and work for her. It's simple—she's giving you a choice. She's putting the seven days on you. And you know what that means. You have to contact her by noon tomorrow to straighten this out."

"I ain't stopping, and I'm sure as hell not working for her again. She's not going to do anything."

"You're a dumb shit!" Cleopatra yelled. "What do you mean she's not going to do anything? We've seen what she can do! Did you even hear me? She threatened my family! And she is going to put hands on you. There's nothing I can do to stop her. Do you not understand that?"

Shawn stood up, angry, and stood over Cleopatra. "I'm not asking you to do anything. I'm not asking you for shit. I didn't ask for your help with this."

Cleopatra looked up at Shawn. "What's wrong with you? Why are you getting upset with me?"

"You think you're better than me?" Shawn pounded her chest.

"What did you just say to me?" Cleopatra stood up and looked her in the eyes. She thought Shawn must be high.

"You heard what I said."

Cleopatra stepped back and stared at Shawn. "Seriously, what is wrong with you?" She assumed that Shawn had smoked some cheap strain of weed, because it usually made her hallucinate and become belligerent.

"You think you're better than me!" Shawn pounded her chest again.

"No, *you* think I'm better than you!" Cleopatra yelled back, realizing that Shawn was serious. "You really want to do this?"

she asked. "You want to take it there?"

"Come on with it then," Shawn egged her on. "You got something you want to say to me? You got something on your mind?"

"You had more opportunities than I ever had, Shawn. It's not my fault you didn't take advantage of them. You don't know anything about struggling to survive."

"How you figure?" Shawn smirked.

"What do you know about paying for two chicken wings with a bag full of nickels? Or walking around the city at night with a razor in your mouth because some bitch might try to jump you or some dude might try to rape the lesbian out of you because you're gay and living on the street?"

Shawn couldn't hide the shock on her face. Cleopatra looked at her and thought about what an ungrateful piece of shit she was. She'd done nothing but be there for Shawn from day one—no questions asked, no judgment, just fucking there every time she needed her. And this was the thanks she got.

"Nothing to say, Shawn? You are fucking lazy. If you wanted what I had, you could have done something about it. You're used to everyone doing for you and giving you shit. But the moment you have to be held accountable and maybe follow a fucking rule or two, you turn into a quivering little bitch." Cleopatra's emotions were bubbling up inside her, and she didn't have the energy to contain them.

"Fuck you. I never asked you for shit."

"You simple motherfucker. That's all you do is ask me for shit. Are you high? Seriously. Because like two minutes ago, right here on this bench, you talked about all the attorney's fees I've paid and all the times I saved your black ass. Isn't that why we're here in the first place? Because for some reason you're set on paying me back for the first time in your life? Get your story straight. How many calls have I gotten at three in the morning, asking me to come get your ass out of jail and bring my checkbook? That was me, every time. You never called your mama, your four sisters, or any of the bitches you were fucking. It was me, every single time."

Cleopatra clapped her hands together. "Who's been paying your rent for the last few months? Who gave you first and last month's security and the broker's fee to get the apartment in the first place? That was probably my money that paid for that stank-ass McDonald's in your bag. Who paid for your daddy's funeral when you all found out he left his money to his other wife and kids in Trinidad? That was me. I paid for the funeral of a man who hated my fucking guts. You need to stop smoking that cheap shit—your memory is fucked up."

Cleopatra was tempted to just walk away, but stopped herself. "I'm only going to say this one more time. She's going to hurt you if you don't do what she wants. You know she will. We've seen it happen to other people. She doesn't care anymore that you're my family. Please, I'm asking you. And I've never asked you for shit. I need you to just work something out with Olivia. Because there's nothing I can do."

"How many times do I have to say I'm not fucking asking you to do anything?"

"How did you get so damaged? What happened to you?"

"I've heard what you had to say. Now will you shut the fuck up?"

"See how you do without me." Cleopatra threw up the

peace sign and turned to walk away. She would figure something else out. She thought briefly of contacting Alexis, but Alexis and Olivia were two women that you didn't want on the opposite side of anything. And if Alexis knew of Olivia's threats, she and Olivia would probably succeed in destroying each other.

She would go back to Olivia and make some type of deal with her on her own, she decided. She'd beat the brakes off of Shawn herself, if it came down to that. The way she felt at that moment, she could beat the shit out of Shawn right there in the park and not feel the slightest tinge of regret.

"Fuck you!" Shawn yelled after her. "You know, from that first day on the playground in third grade I told myself that I wanted to be just like you. And every single day since then. I hated you, but at the same time I wanted to be you. You've always gotten the baddest bitches, the most intelligent and classy bitches, with the most money. You were smart, could master anything you set your mind to. Cleopatra snaps her fingers and can have whatever or whoever the fuck she wants. And there I am, more a fan than a friend. I'm needy, irresponsible, up for a good time and a few laughs, I'm a fuck up and a taker. That's what I do, I take."

Cleopatra turned back around and saw a disdain in Shawn's eyes that she had never seen before. "I should have never forgiven you after you fucked my girlfriend. My life would be so much better without you in it."

Cleopatra walked up close to Shawn and stared at her in confusion. "That was well over ten years ago. I didn't know that was your girl, and you know that. And you forget everybody fucked Niecy, and I do mean everybody—that was everyone's three-hole whore. We used to call her 'dic tac,' you know like tic tac? Because if it looked like a dick she swallowed it. She fucked a deacon in your church, she fucked your cousin Teddy."

"What?" Shawn asked.

"Ugly-ass Teddy. I know that's your family, but that motherfucker can bite an apple through a picket fence. Oh, and she fucked Leanza. That's right, your sister. Didn't know your own sister was gay, did you? Anybody that fucking homophobic is gay. After I turned her down, she got some from your girl. Your sister may pretend like she has a problem with me for your mother's sake, but she's one of my biggest fans."

"My mama doesn't hate you, at least not anymore."

"That's because I've been keeping her lights on for how long, now? She still hates me, but she's not dumb enough to hate me to my face." Cleopatra was furious now, and years of pent-up anger and resentment began to spill out of her. "I know you don't want to bring up old shit, because I'm done cleaning up your messes and taking the rap for you. From the time you stole money from your parents and told them I took it and they called the cops on me to the time you put your weed in my backpack and the principal caught me with it."

"Whatever, man." Shawn rolled her eyes at Cleopatra.

"Yeah … it's whatever. Don't call me the next time you fuck up, and you will. That's what you do best." Cleopatra reached into her backpack, grabbed the wad of bills, and threw the money on the ground. "Take that back. Most freelance hos haven't bothered to sign up for Obamacare yet. You'll be out of a job soon, and you're gonna need that for your hospital bills. In the meantime, pick a struggle." She turned to walk away.

"Don't worry about your perfect wife and kids, Cleopatra Giovanni," Shawn said. "You're the big family man, now. Right? Protecting them is your job. If you can't do that, maybe they should be taken away from you."

Cleopatra stopped in her tracks for a moment. She laughed out loud and then exhaled hard, turned around, hauled off, and struck Shawn in the jaw with a right hook. Shawn dropped to the ground on top of a fresh pile of snow. Cleopatra stood over her and kicked her in the ribs.

"Look at me and listen."

Shawn rolled around in the snow, holding her face. Blood trickled from her mouth onto her white coat as she struggled to focus her eyes on Cleopatra.

"Olivia threatens my wife, who has nothing to do with this, and two little children who have nothing to do with anything, and you don't give a shit? You better pray to whoever you pray to that nothing happens. Let my wife get a hangnail or one of my kids even stub their toe or get a runny nose. If Olivia does anything and you let it happen, I'm going to kill everybody."

Cleopatra walked away from Shawn, back toward the entrance to the park.

"Fuck you, Cleo. Your daddy left, your brother left, and your mother died mad young, just to get away from you. Now I'm out!" Shawn sat up in the snow.

Cleopatra stopped, but didn't look back or respond. She just stood there. She exhaled deeply, a strange calm coming across her. She didn't feel hate, disgust, or animosity. She felt nothing. There was nothing left. She was relieved—almost at peace. She took another deep breath and a slight smile spread across her lips.

You hateful, petulant child. You can't fire me, because I quit.

···

TWELVE

WE GON ~~PARTY~~ ACT STUPID LIKE IT'S YO BIRTHDAY

"Open it." Jacqueline struggled to contain her excitement, her foot playing with Cleopatra's leg under the table. "Happy birthday, baby, I love you so much."

"Another one?" Cleopatra smiled as she sipped her glass of seltzer water. Jacqueline had showered her with birthday presents all day. "You're spoiling me, baby. Will whatever's in this pouch help me get you out of that red dress any quicker?"

"Be good, baby. Don't make this harder than it has to be. I already want to come across this table at you." Jacqueline winked at her.

Cleopatra blew Jacqueline a kiss and looked around the large, candlelit dining room. They were by the fireplace in a secluded corner in one of the city's most exclusive establishments overlooking Central Park. For her birthday evening, all Cleopatra wanted was to have a romantic dinner and make love to her wife. The wandering of her stare up and down Jacqueline's body affected Jacqueline just as strongly as it had the first time they'd laid eyes on each other. The lust was there, and the sexual tension between them was as thick as Jacqueline's thighs.

"Sorry, I can't help but picture that dress on the floor. You look beautiful tonight." Cleopatra winked at her.

"Look who I'm stepping out with," Jacqueline said. "When I saw the black velvet tuxedo jacket and the bow tie I knew you weren't playing. I had to match my woman's birthday sexy. Ok. Now back to your present. Selfishly, this is kind of for me too." She smiled, excited as she watched Cleopatra dump the contents of the small black satin bag on to the table.

Its metal contents chimed against the centerpiece, a towering arrangement of lilies.

"What's this?" Cleopatra asked. She picked up the silver and pink gadget, which looked to be a remote control of some sort, and a small skeleton key. She took the key and rubbed the cold silver between her fingers, then put the remote up to the candlelight.

The waiter approached the table and sat down the first course of their dinner. "White bean flan with black winter truffles. Enjoy."

"Thank you." Cleopatra smiled and wondered where the rest of the portion was.

"Baby, it's nine courses, remember? You aren't going to have a bunch of food falling off your plate."

Cleopatra laid her arm across the table and extended her hand to Jacqueline. "Back to what you were saying."

"I have a small vibrator inside me." Jacqueline smiled as she put her hand in Cleopatra's and interlocked their fingers. "It's strapped around my thighs and secured with a lock. That's the key." She leaned back in her chair, grabbed her fork, and dug into her flan. "The only way I can pull it out—" She licked her lips and shifted in her seat. "—Is to unlock it with that key."

A smile spread across Cleopatra's face. "It's all the way in there?" She pointed under the table with her fork.

"Mm-hmm…" Jacqueline closed her eyes and nodded.

"And this?" She picked up the remote.

Jacqueline smiled. "You already know what that is, baby."

The waiter came, removed their dishes, and laid down their next course. "Ladies, here we have sweet corn sorbet with poached huckleberries. Enjoy."

Cleopatra moaned when she tasted the sorbet, then read the number on the side of the remote control. "That's good. Wait, 1 to 15? Damn. What does 15 feel like?"

"I don't know. I was hoping you could help me with that." Jacqueline laid her spoon down on the table and held the table tight with both hands. "Start slow, baby, be gentle with—"

Cleopatra pushed the power button and turned the dial to 1. Jacqueline closed her eyes and leaned back in the chair.

"Really? Number 1 made you stop talking?" Cleopatra laughed. "You are going to regret giving this to me."

She turned it up to 5 and Jacqueline slammed her hand down on the table, causing the silverware to clash together. She tried to grab for the remote but Cleopatra quickly snatched it away.

"No, this is mine. I'm going to wear your pussy out at this table, then I'm going to take you home and wear your pussy out again." She laughed as she downed the last spoonful of her sorbet.

She pushed the dial up to 10 as Jacqueline took a sip of wine and Jacqueline almost spilled it on herself. Cleopatra keeled over with laughter. "I don't believe you didn't test this before you gave it to me." Cleopatra kissed the remote. "Happy birthday to me."

Suddenly the waiter came again with the next course. "Charred eggplant with Armenian cucumbers and artichokes. Enjoy, ladies."

"Thank you." Jacqueline smiled at him. "You want to maybe turn that off now?" She exhaled hard.

"I've been trying to work my way up. Can I just see what 15 does? Please?" Cleopatra pleaded with her. "Remember, it's my birthday."

"Go ahead." Jacqueline covered her face with one hand as she stuck her fork in to the eggplant. Cleopatra pressed the remote until the LED read 15.

"Whew…" Jacqueline's head flew back. "Oh my fuck. Off … off." She waved her hands, surrendering, and Cleopatra turned off the vibrator and looked around at the other patrons looking at them. "I'm going to get you." Jacqueline bit her lip.

Cleopatra was in awe. "Ok. Ok. So you really can't take it out without this?" Cleopatra held up the little silver key as she took a bite of cucumber.

"Mm-hmm." Jacqueline slowly regained her composure and picked at the food on her plate.

"I should swallow it," Cleopatra joked.

"I got something you can swallow. You want to get the food to go?"

"Baby? For real? It's my birthday. I have on velvet, and you're wearing the hell out of that red dress. Didn't you make these reservations like four months ago? I know you can't just pop up in here unless you have old money. And like they have take out containers." Cleopatra smirked.

"I know, baby, but I need you. You don't have this fire-cracker inside you."

"Your fault." Cleopatra winked. "You just have to sit in that puddle you're creating over there."

"Can we go to the bathroom?" Jacqueline pleaded.

"Nope. You have to wait until we get home." Cleopatra smiled.

"Uh…" Jacqueline threw her head back. "You remember what happened the last time you made me wait too long? I broke your dick."

"Hmm … that was so hot. But I'll make it worth the wait, baby."

"You always do." She stuck her tongue out at Cleopatra. "So what do you think of this place? Is it what you thought it would be?" She rubbed her wife's hand.

Two waiters approached the table and took their dishes. "We hope we have been building up your appetite. Now we present fillet of Atlantic black bass with chanterelle mush-rooms, sweet carrots, and puffed wild rice."

"Thank you." Cleopatra smiled at the tall, brown-haired, blue-eyed Frenchman. She looked around the vast dining room, decorated in muted grays and browns with its hyper-attentive and informative wait staff. "This place is a bit much. Not our style, huh? I could eat some mac and cheese about now."

"I know, baby. But it's what you asked for. It's ok to do something different. You were curious, and this is supposed to be the best restaurant in the city."

"It's definitely special." She rubbed her wife's hand and

looked around at the rest of the patrons, who looked nothing like them. Everyone else was looking right back at them. The waiters had on tuxedos and spoke in thick French accents. "Think we can stop and get me some rice and beans and plantains on the way home?" She took a bite of the bass.

"If that's what you want."

"Wait a minute. That fish is good." Cleopatra bobbed her head. "Eat, baby," she said to Jacqueline, who reached down into her purse to check her phone to make sure their new nanny hadn't called. Instead, she found a dozen missed calls. "Uh oh. Robin."

"Baby. Don't." Cleopatra went to grab her phone.

Jacqueline snatched her phone away. "Let me just listen to her voicemail. There must be something wrong."

Cleopatra rubbed her hand as she watched her wife frown. "What now?" Cleopatra bowed her head toward her plate and put a forkful of fish into her mouth.

"She had a fight with Shawn and in the middle of it Shawn got a call from another woman and left to be with her." She put the phone back up to her ear.

"What are you doing?" Cleopatra asked. "Your food is getting cold."

"I'm calling her. She sounded really broken up, baby."

Cleopatra knew it was the end of her romantic evening when she heard Jacqueline tell Robin it was ok to come and join them at the restaurant.

"Wait. Are you serious? You told ratchet Robin to come here? Here?" She pressed her index finger down on the table. "Inside?" Cleopatra twisted her eyebrows. "The *maître d'* has tails on his tuxedo, he's wearing white gloves, and she's coming in here? The newly crowned ghetto queen? Ms. Hood? You need to go get your coat and meet her outside."

"I'm not waiting on the street for her in this dress and these heels in the snow and ice. It's like 20 degrees outside. Besides, she knows it's your birthday and how long I've been planning this. She knows better than to try and ruin it. She'll be in and out. It will be fine."

Cleopatra smirked at her in disbelief.

Jacqueline tried to plead her case. "She's my baby sister. I have to look out for her. I know she's nouveau ghetto right now, but my sweet little sister is still in there somewhere. I think she does love Shawn as much as she's capable of loving someone. I just want to be there for her. She was there for me when you and I were going through it. She needs me right now. Eat, baby." She pointed to Cleopatra's plate.

They enjoyed two more courses—sea scallops with olives, peppers, and pine nuts, and corn ravioli with peaches and radishes—before Robin arrived. She announced herself by making a commotion at the front of the restaurant. Both Cleopatra and Jacqueline heard her at the same time. They looked up and their eyes locked as they both mouthed "No."

Cleopatra hopped up from her chair and went to the front, where she found Robin.

But Robin didn't notice Cleopatra; she was too busy arguing with the *maître d'* about not being properly dressed to enter the dining room. She had unfortunately checked her winter coat, which covered a majority of the nonsense that lay underneath. So now she stood in confrontation with the *maître d'* in an orange floral headscarf, a wife beater, black baggy jogging pants, and black Uggs with salt stains, on top of the exposed fist tattoo on her neck. Cleopatra looked at her, spun around, and acted like she didn't know her.

"Where is she?" Jacqueline asked when Cleopatra returned to the table.

"She has on a wife beater." Cleopatra rolled her eyes. "And it's dirty. You need talk to her."

Annoyed, Jacqueline left the table in a huff and approached the front of the restaurant. The first thing she saw was Robin's orange headscarf-covered head rolling back and forth and her index finger extended as she pointed at the *maître d'*. For a split second Jacqueline wanted to do just as Cleopatra had done—return to the table unnoticed—but there was no one left at the table to come and save Robin from herself.

"Excuse me," Jacqueline interrupted the confrontation. "Please accept my apologies for the interruption and her poor manners." She grabbed Robin's hand and squeezed it so hard that Robin's knees buckled. "I know she's not properly dressed and our reservation is only for two, but is it possible that she could sit at our table just for a bit?" Jacqueline flashed a smile.

"Sorry, *mademoiselle*, but it's against policy. She cannot enter the dining room in such attire. There are no exceptions." The tall, tanned Frenchman was apologetic as he rubbed his white-gloved hands together.

Jacqueline realized that she would have to take a simpler approach. "I know for a fact that as the *maître d'* you run the show here, and part of that is making the customer happy." She winked at the man and flipped her hair over her shoulder. "I can't imagine that this has never happened before. You must have a spare suit jacket somewhere that she can borrow?

Would you be a sweetheart and check?" She stuck out her chest and ran her hand down between her breasts. "Please." She cocked her head to the side and quivered her lips.

The man's eyes followed Jacqueline's hands to her breasts and he appeared to lose his words momentarily. "Excuse me one moment," he finally said. He disappeared and left Jacqueline and Robin standing there.

"Let go of my hand." Robin snatched it away and massaged it in an attempt to regain the circulation in her fingers. Jacqueline snatched the headscarf from Robin's head and tied it around her neck, covering her tattoo. Then she ran her fingers through Robin's hair to make her a bit more presentable.

A moment later, the *maître d'* returned with a spare tuxedo jacket from the waiter's locker room. "This should fit her," he said. "Please follow me."

Robin slid the jacket on over her stained wife beater, buttoned it, and followed the *maître d'* and Jacqueline back to their table.

Cleopatra looked up and saw both of the sisters as they appeared with the *maître d'*, who carried an extra chair for Robin. She shook her head, annoyed that they were accompanied by a very-much-unwanted guest: Robin, looking like a seven-year-old in her daddy's church blazer.

"They aren't too happy with us right now. He was trying so hard to be nice."

"How did she get back here?" Cleopatra asked. "You flipped your hair, touched your boobs, and did the lip quiver didn't you?"

Jacqueline laughed and nodded. "Yes."

"Let's make this quick, you got ten minutes," Cleopatra said to Robin.

"Have some sympathy, Cleo. Damn," Robin scolded her. She and Shawn were on the verge of breaking up, and Robin was annoyed by Cleopatra's insensitivity.

"Why?" Cleopatra took a sip of her water. "You don't have any sympathy for my birthday."

"So, what's going on?" Jacqueline asked. "Your voicemail said Shawn got a call from some woman and packed up some clothes and just left."

Their waiter stopped over and offered a menu to Robin, but as Robin fixed her lips to say thank you, Cleopatra interrupted.

"That won't be necessary. She's not staying, but thank you."

Robin scowled at her and Cleopatra smiled and pointed to the pitcher. "You can have some water."

Robin just looked at her sister to come to her defense.

"You chipping in?" Jacqueline asked. "That's what I thought. I can't help you." And she shook her head no.

Moments later, the waiter returned with the next course. "Black winter truffles with charcoal-grilled filet mignon."

Robin licked her lips as the sizzling steak was delivered to the table and Cleopatra began to carve into her meat. Both Cleopatra and Jacqueline groaned when they stuck the buttery steak into their mouths, further infuriating Robin.

"Anyway." Robin cleared her throat, trying to get their attention away from their food. "That motherfucker finally came home, so I confronted her."

"Keep your voice down," Jacqueline said. "Inside voice." She patted Robin's hand.

"All right. Damn," Robin said. "She walked in the door and I was like, what's good?" She started talking with her hands as she told the story.

"Keep your hands down, too," Cleopatra reminded her. "We don't need air traffic control in here." She popped a piece of steak into her mouth.

Robin rolled her eyes and sucked her teeth at Cleopatra. "So. I'm like you don't bring your ass home, you don't go to work. What do you do all day? We don't fuck, we don't spend no time, we don't do nothing. We just don't. What's good? What are we doing? Why am I even here?" Robin's voice began to rise again, and Jacqueline put her fingers to her own mouth to remind Robin to bring it down a notch.

"Then you know what that fluffy motherfucker had the nerve to say to me? She said she didn't owe me no explanation. We ain't fucking married. I don't work, cook, clean, don't do laundry, pay for shit, and don't do shit. And I'm lucky to have somewhere to stay."

Cleopatra and Jacqueline both nodded their head in unison, in agreement. "Mm-hmm. I already told you that," Jacqueline said.

"Yeah. Not helping right now, sis. So right then I go in on her. I'm like you messing with another bitch. I'm like, ain't you? Ain't you? She goes I ain't gotta tell you shit. I ain't gotta tell you nothing. But since you all in your feelings, I ain't fucking with no other bitch. I'm fucking with other bitches."

Cleopatra sat her fork down across her plate and exhaled hard. "I'm sorry. But I can't with the I ain't. Every once in a while, who cares. But it's like an onslaught. 'I ain't got no, I ain't with no other.' Damn. You do understand that my reading level has plummeted sitting here listening to you?"

"Fuck you, Cleo." Robin sucked her teeth.

"No thanks, I'm fucking your sister." Cleopatra winked at her.

"Fuck you, Robin." Jacqueline grabbed Robin's wrist and twisted it.

"Ouch," Robin gasped.

"Listen to me. Don't talk to my wife like that. This is her birthday that you're intruding on. Don't think that just because we're in this bougie-ass restaurant, I won't drag you across these tables. Don't ever come for her like that. That's my daddy, show some respect."

Cleopatra got turned on when Jacqueline went for her own sister's head in her defense, and blew a kiss across the table.

Robin, meanwhile, sat silent for a moment and watched both of them. "I'm sorry, Cleo. I'm just upset right now, and didn't mean to take it out on you."

"Apology accepted." Cleopatra began to eat again.

Robin continued her story. "So I'm asking her about this other bitch and she says I ain't fucking with no other bitch. I'm fucking other bitches. Then her cell phone rings. She goes and locks herself in the bathroom. Comes out, throws some clothes in a bag. And get this, Cleopatra." Cleopatra looked up, stunned that Robin was addressing her directly. "She put her dick in her bag. Now ask me how I know that? Ask me how I know that shit."

Cleopatra cringed. "Um how do you know that?"

"She let me see her put that motherfucker in her bag. She did it in front of me. She didn't care. I'm screaming at the top of my lungs that if she fucking left the house with that dick to fuck another bitch, we were over. And you know what the bitch did? Ask me what the bitch did," she said to Jacqueline.

"What did the bitch do?" Jacqueline asked.

"She left."

"Shit" slipped from Cleopatra's lips.

"I know, right?" Robin agreed with Cleopatra.

But Cleopatra wasn't addressing Robin; she thought she'd spotted someone who looked a lot like Shawn on the other side of the restaurant.

She popped another piece of meat in her mouth, pretending she was listening to their conversation, and started praying to herself. *Please don't let them turned around, don't turn around, don't turn around.* Robin and Jacqueline were still talking about Shawn, and Cleopatra's prayers had totally drowned them out. She had to get up and do something. She had to get up and leave her steak.

"Excuse me, baby." She wiped her mouth. "I'm going to the bathroom. Don't touch my filet mignon, Robin." And with that, she made a detour toward the bathroom, turned before she reached it, and headed to Shawn's table.

There was the largest lobster Cleopatra had ever seen on Shawn's plate and she wondered how she'd missed that on the menu. Shawn had on a dark brown suit that was much too tight and Cleopatra envisioned the button on her white shirt popping. She caught herself squinting for fear it would take her eye out.

Shawn got an attitude with Cleopatra when she saw her standing at her table. "What the fuck do you want?"

"Fuck you. Robin is on the other side of the restaurant." Shawn's dinner companion looked to be a client, which meant she hadn't stopped poaching Olivia's clientele, and the inevitable beat down was looming. She figured it was only a matter of time before Olivia found Shawn and put the paws on her.

"Fuck!" Shawn covered her mouth, the tightness of her slacks lifting her inseam up just enough to showcase her white tube socks.

Cleopatra couldn't resist. "The white socks, though?"

She turned her eyes to the woman on the other side of the table. Shawn's date was an older black woman. She screamed old wealth—the exact kind that could show up at that particular restaurant unannounced and count on them to scramble to get her a table. The kind that never spent it on her appearance but was quick to drop $1,000 on dinner. And who knew how much else to stay in the closet, and pay for what she did in the dark with other women. The woman had on a navy blue pants suit, and wore a bang with a prominent crease from the pink foam rollers she probably still slept in.

"Hope you're enjoying your evening," Cleopatra said. The woman's face was twisted in confusion; she was not happy. When Cleopatra turned to leave the table, she ran right into Jacqueline. "Shit."

Jacqueline moved Cleopatra out of the way. "Shawn, are you serious right now? Who is this?" Jacqueline pointed to the woman, who now looked like a deer caught in headlights.

Cleopatra backed away, wanting nothing to do with it. She grabbed Jacqueline's hand. "Baby. Don't."

"What the hell is she doing?"

"Robin doesn't need to see this," Cleopatra whispered to Jacqueline.

"What the fuck?" Robin yelled from the other side of the dining room.

The entire restaurant had stopped now, and everyone

zoomed in on the loud and only black people in the whole establishment.

"Damn." Cleopatra shook her head. She thought briefly about standing between Robin and Shawn, but changed her mind. Instead, she grabbed Jacqueline's hand and backed away from the table. "Let's stay out of this."

"Baby, you are in the middle of it. You knew she was here."

"I was trying to get her to leave because I knew—"

The manager, a fat, bald man in a tuxedo, swooped in and asked if there was a problem. Cleopatra tried to assure him everything was under control. But then Robin ran over and pushed through all of them to get to Shawn's table, where she took a bottle of champagne and poured it on Shawn's head.

Cleopatra covered her face with her hands. "I knew it would get physical."

Robin then tried to turn the table over and dump the food in their laps. She goaded Shawn to get up. Shawn's older woman grabbed her purse, quickly scooted out of the booth on the opposite side of Robin and ran out of the dining room.

"You better run, you old, wide bitch!" Robin yelled after her.

Several waiters, the *maître d'*, and the manager had all swarmed around them now. They corralled Robin, Cleopatra, Jacqueline, and Shawn like a group of wayward sheep that needed to find their way out of their establishment, and as soon as possible.

"I'm sorry. But we have to ask you all to leave. Please," the *maître d'* informed them.

Cleopatra and Jacqueline nodded in agreement. They didn't have the energy to put up a fight. It was time to go. The *maître d'* and the manager escorted them toward the front, but on the way by their table Cleopatra grabbed the rest of her steak and wrapped it in a napkin, then swiped a basket of bread off of another nearby table on their way out of the dining room.

The manager retrieved their coats from coat check and stripped Robin of her tuxedo jacket. He, along with two waif-thin waiters, escorted Cleopatra, Jacqueline, Robin, and Shawn downstairs in the elevator.

"I've never been thrown out of such a distinguished establishment, and with such care. Do you think they'll hail us a taxi as well?" Cleopatra joked to Jacqueline.

Jacqueline whispered in her ear. "We missed a couple of courses but at least we didn't pay, baby."

"Didn't you have to give them a credit card to hold the reservation?" Jacqueline nodded. "Then we paid, baby."

Cleopatra slapped two pieces of warm bread around her steak and made her own to-go sandwich. Robin looked at her like she wanted a bite.

"You have got to be kidding right?" Cleopatra said. She took a bite of the sandwich as they walked out onto 59th Street and Columbus Circle.

"Talk to your girl, baby." Jacqueline side eyed Shawn, who stood a few feet away from them, typing frantically on her cell phone.

"What are you talking about? We aren't cool and you know that."

"You were cool enough to warn her."

"I didn't want an altercation in the restaurant. Especially not this restaurant. We were the only people of color in there, baby. We're not even in the kitchen in that place. Not even washing dishes. And your salty-Ugg, dirty-wife-beater-wearing That Ho Over There sister had to come in and set the race back two hundred years."

"Did you just call my sister a THOT?"

"I did. Would you like to debate that?"

"No, I just wanted to be clear. I'm still not sure on the exact definition."

"Me either. But calling her that in this exact moment makes me feel better. I'm in that type of mood right now. Anyway, I just wanted to finish dinner alone with my wife. Damn, I'm hungry."

"I'm going to try and calm Robin down so we can get out of here," Jacqueline said.

"Hurry, baby. It's cold out here." Cleopatra bit into her sandwich again as she watched Jacqueline walk over to her sister.

"Look, Robin. What you did in there, making that scene, was unacceptable." Jacqueline flipped up the collar on her black cashmere coat and rubbed her cold hands together. "You take that out on the street or back home and handle your business. You ruined my wife's birthday dinner."

Robin paced back and forth, wanting to run up on Shawn. "Well, we're on the street now. Let me at her." Her red bubble jacket was open, her wife beater exposed and her wool scarf in her hand. Her anger appeared to have rendered her immune to the winter elements.

Jacqueline pushed her sister back. "No. You aren't going any where until you calm the hell down. Someone is bound to get hurt the way you're acting."

Cleopatra stood a few feet from Jacqueline and her sister.

She had lost track of Shawn, and wondered if she'd snuck down to the subway and gone home. She wouldn't blame her if she had, because that's exactly what she wanted to do. She reached inside her pocket and her hand suddenly grazed the vibrator remote. During all the commotion, she'd completely forgotten about it. Now she couldn't resist.

She turned it on and punched it up to 5.

She studied Jacqueline and saw her body twitch. Jacqueline glared at her as she tried to keep her composure. She may have been mad, but she was also going to be horny if Cleopatra had anything to do with it. She was impressed initially as she watched Jacqueline control her reaction to the sensation. But then Jacqueline waved her hand across her neck, telling Cleopatra to cut it out, and she turned it down to 1. It didn't take long for Jacqueline to realize that it was still on. Jacqueline came over to her.

"Give it to me." She held her hand out.

"That's not happening. You know why? Because it's cold as hell out here and because I don't care about their bullshit. All I care about right now is you, me, and that vibrator." Cleopatra turned it back to 5.

"Fine. Where the hell is Shawn?" Jacqueline asked. She still saw Robin close by, but Shawn was nowhere in sight.

"I don't know." Cleopatra shrugged her shoulders.

Jacqueline waddled back over to her sister. Cleopatra watched as she masterfully maneuvered her Louboutins in the ice and snow. She imagined Jacqueline clenching her pussy to control the increasing vibrations. Jacqueline's fists were balled up when she looked at Cleopatra.

"Listen. I'm not going to be out here all night with you,"

Jacqueline told Robin. "My wife and I have grown-folks business to tend to. Just go back uptown, pack some shit, and go home to Mom and Dad. We'll figure out what to do later, because this is not a good look. Just leave; it's not worth it and she's not worth it. I think you know that now."

Cleopatra was watching the two sisters when Shawn reappeared out of the blue, with three hot dogs that she must have bought from a nearby cart.

They stood silent for a while, shooting each other hateful looks that lifelong enemies wouldn't be able to duplicate.

"Enjoy those franks, you should get some popcorn too. Because in less than a week your jaw is going to be wired shut," Cleopatra said confidently.

"You seem pretty sure of yourself."

"Olivia showed me the menu of what she has in store for you. Actually I probably shouldn't stand this close to you. Her goons should be looking for you, now." Cleopatra looked down at her watch.

"You sound awful confident in the safety of your family, too." Shawn said with her mouth full of beef hot dog. "If I don't give in after the seven days, they'll be next."

"About that." Cleopatra smiled. "You were actually right for once. I met with Olivia again. She's not going to do anything to hurt my wife and kids. It was all a trick ... or should I say a test. She knew that you wouldn't come through for me. But she felt the need to show me. Because I would never have believed it. I would have said Shawn rides just as hard for me as I ride for her. But wait, you're not ride or die. You don't ride for me. You're not even in the car, you're not even on a bike alongside of the car. Hell, your ass is still in the house on the couch. Olivia watched you and me for years and felt the need to open my eyes. It took her pulling this little stunt for me to realize how close I had been keeping my enemies. Good luck. You're going to need it." Cleopatra winked at her.

In the meantime, just several feet away, Jacqueline had managed to calm Robin down and convinced her to go home, pack a bag, and go to their parents' house. She made Robin promise not to pick a fight with Shawn, but to get her belongings and just go.

"Looks like Shawn is back and waiting for you. Don't start any thing, remember. Just get your shit and go home to Jersey," Jacqueline said. She took a $100 bill out of her purse and slipped it into Robin's pocket, then walked back over to Cleopatra, ignoring Shawn. She grabbed Cleopatra's hand and kissed her.

"Take me home and fuck me."

✿✿✿

"Ciao, Bella." César, the twins' nanny, gave Cleopatra a full report on their activities for the last few hours. Jacqueline checked on them and found Amir and Maya both sound asleep. The tall, gay Italian man with generous gray eyes teased Cleopatra as they watched Jacqueline come down the stairs and pace back and forth.

"She's ready to celebrate your birthday, eh?" He elbowed Cleopatra as he put on his coat and walked toward the front door. "We took pictures and videos while we played, they're all on the camera in the children's room. I didn't want you to miss any special moments."

"We've been gone three hours," Cleopatra laughed. "Thank you." She patted him on the back. "You're so thorough. Nuts, but thorough."

César had barely walked down the front steps when Jacqueline slammed Cleopatra up against the front door. She turned the child monitor up on high and threw it somewhere in the living room, then ripped open Cleopatra's velvet tuxedo jacket and threw it down to the floor.

"I'll get you a new one," she said as it lay on the floor mat and soaked up the melting snow.

"Damn," Cleopatra gasped as Jacqueline grabbed her by the neck.

Jacqueline looked down as two buttons from Cleopatra's French cuff shirt bounced onto the hardwood floor and rolled into opposite corners. "I'll buy you a new shirt, too," she said as she yanked Cleopatra's shirt from her body and took her face into her hands and her mouth into hers, thrusting her tongue inside as if she couldn't get enough of Cleopatra's lips.

"Give me the damn key." Jacqueline extended her hand and snapped her fingers.

"What key?" Cleopatra asked. "Oh, hell no." She shook her head and ran into the living room.

"Give it to me now." Jacqueline chased after her, but stopped momentarily to take her wife all in, running around the living room in a black sports bra, black dress slacks, and boots. She watched the rips in Cleopatra's stomach contract as she panted. "When I get that key, I'm going to do the hell out of you," Jacqueline said. She cornered Cleopatra and dug her hands down into her pants pockets, frantically searching for the vibrator remote and the key, and Cleopatra let her.

"You better hope I don't turn this bitch up to 15 again." Cleopatra flicked on the remote, which she held in her hand, high overhead and out of Jacqueline's reach.

"Shit." Jacqueline keeled over and then sprang up erect to pull the red silk dress off her body. Now bare-breasted, with only the securely fastened red thong on, Jacqueline plopped down on the brown Moroccan leather couch.

"Come here." She motioned for Cleopatra to join her. There had been many an episode on that couch, which Jacqueline had once judged to be brown, soft, and strong … just like Cleopatra.

Jacqueline moaned in anticipation of making love to her wife. "This is not the time to play with me."

Cleopatra stood over her. "When would be the time?" She turned the vibrator up to 15 again, and Jacqueline flipped over on her stomach and buried her face in the couch cushions. She arched her ass up in the air and threw her head back to look up at their reflection in the mirror over the black marble fireplace. She purred when she saw Cleopatra standing behind her.

"Damn, it's like that?" Cleopatra palmed Jacqueline's ass. She tugged on her red G-string and slid her hands between Jacqueline's thighs. Her fingers met the heat from Jacqueline's pussy, and Jacqueline growled at her touch and flipped over onto her back. She grabbed Cleopatra by her bow tie, pulled it loose, and wrapped it around her fist. Then she drew Cleopatra hard to her lips.

"Turn … that … shit … off … right … now. I'm not playing with you."

"All right." Cleopatra turned the vibrator down but not off.

"I said off, baby." Jacqueline pulled Cleopatra down on top of her, their bodies slamming together.

"You are so sexy right now." Cleopatra kissed her and slid the shiny skeleton key down between her wife's breasts.

Jacqueline whispered, "No foreplay." Cleopatra slithered down between her wife's thighs, found the little padlock, and unlocked it. "Slow, baby," Jacqueline pleaded with her.

Cleopatra grabbed the wet rocket and eased it out of Jacqueline as her body shuddered. Jacqueline pulled Cleopatra by her locs.

"Let me taste you. I want you. Let me…" Jacqueline begged. She was serious about wanting her mouth elsewhere on Cleopatra's body, and though Cleopatra was the dominant one, Jacqueline wanted to please her first tonight.

But Cleopatra didn't give in so easily. She kissed Jacqueline and slid her tongue into her mouth. She laid Jacqueline back down on the sofa and kissed her way from her lips down to her neck, before she sucked her nipple in to her mouth.

"Suck it." Jacqueline pushed her breasts together so Cleopatra could lick them in one fell swoop. "Bite it. You're going to make me come if you don't stop baby." She threw her head back as Cleopatra pulled on her nipples with her teeth.

Suddenly Jacqueline sprang up. "No. I said … I wanted you."

Cleopatra sat back and held her hands up with a slight smile on her lips.

A tinge of nervousness shot through Jacqueline as her strong and beautiful stud surrendered her dominance. She pushed Cleopatra down on the sofa and straddled her, kissed her as she cradled her face, controlling their intensity, and kissed from Cleopatra's lips back down to her throat, pressing her mouth to her neck.

Cleopatra nodded her head in satisfaction and a deep growl spilled from her lips. She lifted her hands to Jacqueline's head, moving the hair back from her face. Jacqueline moved away a bit, just enough to pull off Cleopatra's sports bra and expose her wife's breasts. She teased Cleopatra's nipples, then kissed the muscles in her stomach. She slid down Cleopatra's body and unzipped Cleopatra's pants to slip her hand inside and stroke her.

Cleopatra's moans ignited Jacqueline's desire. She tugged Cleopatra's pants and boxer briefs down her legs and onto the floor.

Cleopatra kept her gaze on Jacqueline's face, watching her eyes as Jacqueline's hands traveled up her calf muscles to her knees and then up to her thighs. She stopped at Cleopatra's pussy, then dove down and licked her in one swipe of her tongue, but neglecting her clit.

"Damn. I'd never do that to you," Cleopatra moaned.

It would have been easy for Jacqueline to concede to her wife's complaint, but she wasn't willing to give her what she wanted just yet.

"You tease me like this all the time." Jacqueline's lips spread into a smile on Cleopatra's pussy. Jacqueline had been practicing her authority and she liked it. She drove her tongue in again, this time taking Cleopatra's clit into her mouth and sucking her gently, her eyes never leaving Cleopatra's. She licked across her clit once more, savoring the sweet taste and giving Cleopatra the full warmth of her mouth. Cleopatra let out a moan when

Jacqueline pulled her lips away, and Jacqueline teased her, fondling her clit with her thumb while she slipped two fingers inside of her.

Cleopatra was dizzy as she watched Jacqueline pull her soaked fingers from her pussy and slip them back inside. Then Jacqueline sucked her hand into her mouth and twirled her tongue around her fingers, sucking Cleopatra's juices clean off.

"You taste so good, baby." Jacqueline closed her eyes and pushed her tongue back into Cleopatra's pussy. Cleopatra's stomach muscles tensed as Jacqueline's moans vibrated on her clit. Her clit grew bigger between Jacqueline's lips.

Jacqueline hadn't thought about whether or not she intended to suck her wife to orgasm yet, but suddenly she needed Cleopatra to come. She pushed her face into Cleopatra's pussy and sucked and licked on her hungrily. Cleopatra gasped, gripping Jacqueline's hair between her fingers, pulling till it hurt.

Soon, Cleopatra took control of Jacqueline, holding her head steady over her pussy as she fucked her tongue, and Jacqueline let her. But only because the moans that came with Cleopatra's thrusts made Jacqueline's pussy throb. So much so that she had to fight the urge to flip over on her back and beg Cleopatra to fuck her. Cleopatra's body trembled with her impending climax, and her moans grew louder as she rocked against Jacqueline's tongue. Jacqueline's name escaped her lips as she grasped her head, holding onto her. Jacqueline pulled Cleopatra's hands away to free herself from her grip and raised her head up, pulling her mouth from her pussy.

Jacqueline moaned. "You are so sexy when you're getting your pussy eaten," she teased as she licked her lips.

She climbed up Cleopatra's body and spread her legs, straddling her waist. Cleopatra could feel the wetness from Jacqueline's pussy run down onto hers, and her eyes widened with desire as she smiled. She took Jacqueline's naked ass into her hands and Jacqueline leaned down to take her lips into hers. Cleopatra's kiss was hungry and devouring, and she worked her tongue inside of Jacqueline's mouth.

"What do you want?" Cleopatra asked.

They had been testing their boundaries and it challenged Cleopatra to let Jacqueline control their lovemaking. But she did it because she loved her wife, and it really turned Jacqueline on. That was a big step for both of them and, though a huge part of Jacqueline wanted to let Cleopatra take her in whatever way she wanted, she was committed to trading places, at least for the moment.

But she hadn't yet answered Cleopatra's question. What did she want?

"Play with my nipples. Suck on them again, hard," Jacqueline said.

Cleopatra pinched her nipples between her index fingers and thumbs, and Jacqueline's nipples hardened immediately, her breasts excited and alert as Cleopatra caressed them in her big, soft hands. Jacqueline bent over to kiss her. As she took Cleopatra's mouth between her lips, Cleopatra took the opportunity to slide her hand between Jacqueline's thighs and swipe her fingers across Jacqueline's wet clit.

"Bad girl," Jacqueline gasped, admonishing her.

Cleopatra winked before she took her nipple back into her mouth. As she sucked, Jacqueline's resolve to stay in control began to waver again. She screamed when Cleopatra took intermittent bites of her nipples and breasts, teasing her.

"Still in control?" Cleopatra twirled her tongue lightly around her nipples. Jacqueline's whole body shuddered.

"You want my fingers inside of you, don't you?" Cleopatra had switched it up on her. She had turned Jacqueline's body to Jell-O.

Jacqueline finally gave in to her wife. But she wouldn't give in completely, as she wanted to retain some semblance of control.

"Eat my pussy, now," she said softly as she lay back on the couch.

Cleopatra smiled—her eyes even lit up—but she didn't make a move to fulfill her wife's command. Instead, she kissed and bit at her wife's neck, evoking uncontrollable moans that grew progressively louder until Cleopatra stopped.

Then she whispered in Jacqueline's ear, "You aren't ready. You don't really want it, just yet."

"What? I do want it. Give me the snake, now," Jacqueline sneered.

Cleopatra smiled again. She knew at that moment that she had Jacqueline right where she wanted her. In one nimble move, she dove between Jacqueline's legs and had her thighs locked in her arms and wrapped around her ears.

"I love it when you get mad," Cleopatra laughed.

THIRTEEN

....

PUNKS JUMP UP TO GET BEAT DOWN

"You are not walking out on me again." Robin took off her coat and blocked the apartment door, Shawn's only escape route. She'd dragged Shawn home in order to confront her in private, and not just pack up and leave like Jacqueline advised her to do. They were silent the entire subway ride uptown to Shawn's quiet Inwood neighborhood. But once they got inside, Robin was ready to have it out once and for all.

After they keyed into the apartment, Shawn turned on the living room light. They paused momentarily as they always did before taking off their coats, so the mice and roaches that needed to scatter could do so in an orderly fashion. Neither of them took care of the place, and Shawn just slept there occasionally. The furniture was sparse; Shawn had made no real attempt to furnish it. The futon was positioned in front of a nineteen-inch tube TV perched upon a still-unopened U-Haul box from her move over a year earlier. She had been sleeping on that same futon for years, until Cleopatra gifted her a real bedroom set. There was not one picture on the wall, which always annoyed Robin … but not enough to purchase one and hang it up.

"Cleopatra wouldn't tell me what happened between you two the other day. But she was pissed."

Shawn walked up to her. "I know what you need to get you acting right." She puckered her lips to kiss her.

"Get off of me. Don't touch me." Robin pushed her away, beating her in her chest. "I don't know where your mouth has been."

"I'm sorry I've been neglecting you. Come here." Shawn reached her arms out and called her like a timid puppy.

Robin slapped her arms away. "Neglecting me would be one thing. But you've never been committed to me. I've told you a million times what I want, what I need, and you aren't living up to my standards."

"Since when did you get standards?" Shawn burst into laughter as she took off her brown suit jacket. "What the hell are you talking about?" She sat down on the lopsided black metal futon and her tight brown slacks rose up, revealing her white tube socks.

The white socks, though? Robin thought to herself. "I told you I needed time and attention." Robin began counting on her fingers. "I need to be taken out on dates and treated like a fucking lady. Surprise me with presents. Bring your ass home so you can fuck me every night. Look at me like you love me and shit."

Shawn laughed again, only making Robin madder. She laid her head down on the futon and held her stomach, laughing, but quickly removed her face from the cushion. The futon was soiled with everything imaginable. Cleopatra had long refused to even sit on it; she knew enough of what had happened on the futon to know better. Everything had been on that futon cover but hot water and laundry detergent.

"What's so damn funny?" Robin glared at her.

"You're describing Cleo." Shawn got up from the futon and the metal squeaked aggressively with relief. "That is not how I get down. You see what she does for Jac and decide that's what you want late in the game. You're not working, but you got a place to stay don't you? You're not up in your mama's house. You're not hungry. You sure don't look hungry." Shawn grazed her hand along Robin's ass.

Robin smacked her hand hard. "I told you not to fucking touch me."

Shawn sat back down, leaned over, and turned on the TV with her thumb.

"I give you money to have in your pocket so you can get your hair and nails done. I pay your cell phone bill." She reached over and opened a bag of cheese curls that lay on a pile of dirty clothes, then started popping them into her mouth three at a time.

"So what, you pay my little cell bill. Cleopatra gave Jacqueline her own black card," Robin said under her breath as she walked into the kitchen to get a glass of water. The smell of onions and garlic from the Tex Mex joint downstairs married with the mildewed laundry marinating in the corner overpowered her nose. The kitchen was as bare as the living room, with just the appliances the apartment came with and a microwave that Cleopatra bought after she visited Shawn and had to heat up her Chinese food in the oven.

"What did you just mumble under your breath?" Shawn

asked when she came out of the kitchen. She sucked the caked-on powdered cheese off her fingers.

Robin cleared her throat. "I said so what you pay my cell phone bill. Cleo gave my sister her own black card."

"Man, fuck Cleo!" Shawn yelled.

Robin mumbled something under her breath again.

"What did you say to me?" Shawn scowled at her.

Robin smirked at her. "I said I would if I could."

At that, Shawn ran up on Robin and shoved her hard. Robin's head snapped back and hit the wall, and she screamed and grabbed her head, then pushed Shawn off of her. Shawn looked as if she wanted to hit her but Robin ran to the other side of the living room before she had a chance.

"Don't you ever fucking touch me again. Are you crazy? Don't come near me."

"She doesn't want you!" Shawn yelled. Her fists were balled up and her arms were shaking. "And for your information, same way I'm not Cleopatra, you sure as hell aren't Jacqueline, so don't get that shit twisted. It's never going to happen."

"Fuck you. This is not about Cleopatra."

"You're the one that keeps bringing that motherfucker up. I know what she does for Jacqueline. She fell in love with her, wifed her, that's what you do."

"What is that shit supposed to mean? Huh?" Robin goaded, walking over and getting up in her face again. "So you don't love me? Is that what you're trying to say? Who was that woman tonight?" She rubbed the back of her head, expecting to feel a knot form at any moment.

"A friend."

"Bullshit. You're just like Cleopatra. Studs don't have

femme friends—they're just women you haven't fucked yet that want to fuck you, or women you fucked who haven't gone away because they want to fuck some more. And that romantic restaurant? Where you get all that money? Cause I saw your check. Why can't you just admit you're a dog?"

"Out of everyone, you are the only one that I have a full-blown relationship with." Shawn realized that she needed to say something to calm Robin down. At least until Robin packed her things and left, and she had a chance to change the locks. Unfortunately, she wasn't that quick on her feet, and only made things worse the more she spoke. "Our relationship … it's just different with you." She knew she'd messed up as soon as the words came out of her mouth, but there was no way to take them back.

"Out of everyone? Our relationship is different from your other relationships?" Robin stood with her hand on her hip. "Hmm … look at me Shawnette. Fucking more than one? Really? Cause you said that shit before."

Shawn exhaled; she needed to come clean, all the lies and leading a double life had worn her down. She didn't have the mental or physical stamina to keep up the high-stakes game she was playing. Plus the clock was ticking, and Olivia's men could be kicking down her door at any moment. She didn't know what she was doing, didn't have a plan, and anxiety was building up inside of her. If she got everything off her chest, maybe Robin would get mad and leave, and they could both just get on with their lives. She had thought for a while that she was ready to slow down a little bit, and Cleo and Jac's wedding had given her a glimpse into the possibility of a different life, but she knew deep down that she wasn't about *that* life. She didn't want to be tied down or have someone expecting anything of her. She didn't want to come home, provide, or most of all stay faithful.

"I'm not cheating. It's not like I care about them. I'm just fucking them," she admitted.

Robin backed up. The wind was knocked out of her. "And that makes it better? That makes it ok?"

"It makes it different. I don't love them, I love you." But Shawn's definition of love was tolerance. She only tolerated Robin, her presence in her apartment, and her demands on her time and attention as she longed to live the single life again. She tolerated Robin like one who could barely stomach their day job and did just enough not to get fired. But one could only keep up that charade for so long.

"You don't love me." Robin shook her head. "You don't know what love is. I knew you couldn't be with just one woman. Why can't you be like Cleopatra?"

Robin said that knowing it would piss Shawn off. She knew that Shawn had her insecurities and at times could be insanely jealous of her own best friend.

"You think Cleo is so perfect? Why don't you pack up all of your shit, bounce up out of my house, and go after her?"

"I've thought about it, believe me." Robin ran her nails through the shaved side of her half-hawk and sucked her teeth loud. Shawn clinched her fist again and Robin could see her chest heave. She moved clear across the room, not sure what Shawn would do. She had never hit her before but Shawn was good for shoving her hard. They were both verbally and mentally abusive toward each other, but it had never come to blows.

Why she didn't leave the first time Shawn shoved her into a wall she couldn't explain. In her own way she did love Shawn, and she knew that deep down Shawn loved her … at least Shawn's warped version of what she thought love was. Shawn was the wounded lifelong underdog, a consistent screw up, the constant misunderstood disappointment.

Robin knew she'd promised Jacqueline that she would pack her bags and go, but she didn't want to give up on Shawn just yet. Especially now, after her best friend of over twenty years had said she wanted nothing to do with her.

"Cleo isn't perfect—she's just as much of a ho as I am. Who do you think got me into this business?" The words spilled out of Shawn's mouth so quickly that she couldn't stop herself, and, truth be told, she didn't want to stop. She was in the mood to air dirty laundry now. She was tired of everyone thinking that Cleopatra was so perfect. She wasn't; she had her secrets too.

"What the hell are you talking about?"

Shawn told Robin every last detail of Cleopatra's past, from her first meeting with Olivia up to the present. She explained how Cleopatra got her money, the mysterious sugar mama who gave her a house in Greenwich Village, and how even though she hadn't been in the business in years, it was still bankrolling her lifestyle. How Jacqueline didn't even know.

"You're a prostitute?" Robin stood back and eyed Shawn up and down.

"I'm an escort. It's different. I've been one off and on since I was about seventeen."

"Do you or do you not fuck women for money?" Shawn

didn't respond, only shrugged her shoulders. "That's a prostitute. I'm done with you." Robin went into the bedroom and
packed up everything she could fit in her old duffle bag and
suitcase.

Shawn unceremoniously sat down back down on the futon
and turned the television to ESPN Classic to watch an old
Knicks game, almost satisfied that it had been that easy to get
Robin to leave. This only infuriated Robin even more.

"I'm done with you, for real this time." Robin took the
house key off her key chain and threw it at Shawn. When the
key hit her in the chest, she grabbed it and sat it down next to
her on the futon. Her lack of emotion killed Robin. But never
one to be outdone, she would dig deeper until it hurt.

"You know I don't owe you shit. I'm not married to you,
you are not my wife or my family like Jacqueline is to Cleopatra." Robin stood what she thought a safe distance away
from her.

Shawn cut her eyes away from the game momentarily. "You
know Jacqueline would forgive Cleo."

"Yeah well, she's not a ho for dough anymore. You are, and
I keep trying to tell you, you are not Cleopatra." Shawn sprung
up and caught Robin tight by her wrist. "Let go. That hurts."
Robin squirmed and tried to yank her arm out of Shawn's grip.

"I'm tired of your smart-ass mouth," Shawn said. "How
many times do you think you're going to get away with talking
to me like that, and nothing happens to you?"

Robin twisted her body and freed herself from Shawn's
grasp. She stood eye-to-eye with Shawn for a moment and tried
to think of something else to say, but no words would come.

Shawn turned around and sat back down in front of the television while Robin put on her coat and went to the door where her bags sat. She put her hand on the knob and as she turned the cold brass in her hand, hesitated for some reason.

"Before you go," Shawn called out, "you might want some advice. You'll never be your sister. So stop trying. It's never going to happen."

"What?" Robin turned back around and put her hand on her hip.

"You'll never be Jacqueline. Your sister is a bad bitch. And well, you … you are just her sister."

"That's real funny." Robin readied herself to move her bags out into the hallway. Always needing the last word, though, she gave one last dig. "I never said anything because hey, I didn't want to hurt your feelings, but now I do." Robin caressed her own stomach. "Let's just say a big belly that comes out three times as far as her breasts is not sexy on a stud, especially when you got big-ass titties already." She twisted her lips.

Shawn slumped her shoulders in and looked down at her chest and stomach.

"Yeah, bitch, bigger than mine and I'm good. Real good. Lay off the beer, the pork, high-fructose corn syrup, the grape soda, all that. When you strap up we want to feel dick, not belly. You get winded after two strokes. Why you think I always want to be on top?" Robin clapped her hands. "That makes me wonder who you're actually getting paid to fuck. Oh yeah, old bitches like the one you were with tonight. Makes sense now. But why don't you use some of the money you're making in the escort business—" She did the quote sign with her fingers. "—And hire a personal fucking trainer. Thanks."

Robin turned her back to open the door. As she turned her head to mouth "Fuck you," Shawn's smartphone whizzed past her head, grazing her nose, hit the door, and shattered into pieces.

"Are you fucking crazy?" Robin yelled.

Shawn leapt across the room with her hands stretched out, ready to take hold of Robin's neck. She shoved Robin hard up against the door, slamming it shut as she tried to press her fingers into Robin's throat. But Robin punched Shawn in the stomach and escaped to the other side of the room. Shawn dead bolted the door and hooked the chain.

"I'm tired of your bullshit. I'm tired of your voice. I'm tired of you breathing." Shawn corned Robin and caught her, grabbing her by the forearm and flinging her across the room like a rag doll. Robin got up and ran frantically into the kitchen to get something to protect herself. She was convinced that someone was going to get hurt before this night was over, and it wasn't going to be her.

Shawn followed her into the kitchen. She pushed her hard up against the counter and wrapped her hands around Robin's throat, choking her hard again.

This bitch is really trying to kill me. Robin struggled and reached back on the counter, grabbing the first thing she felt: a tall, dusty bottle of decorative red peppers sitting in extra virgin olive oil left behind by the previous tenants. She swung it as hard as she could, bashing it across Shawn's head. The bottle shattered.

Robin freaked out when Shawn fell to the black and white checkered floor and lay there, motionless. It seemed like forever, but only a couple of minutes passed before Robin finally got up the nerve to nudge Shawn with her foot. Shawn rolled around the floor, holding her head and groaning in pain. Simultaneously relieved she hadn't killed her, but still angry, Robin kicked her as hard as she could, square in her exposed belly button.

Then she walked to the door, grabbed the handle on her rolling suitcase, threw her gym bag over her shoulder, and strolled out of the apartment.

She heard a commotion as she waited for the elevator, and saw Shawn stumble out into the hallway looking for her. Robin dropped all of her belongings and ran down the side staircase. She burst out the door onto the sidewalk of the busy block, into the frosty night air, with Shawn right on her tail.

"You think you're just gonna bash me over the head and get away with it? You probably gave me a concussion!" Shawn yelled as she wiped the olive oil and blood from her face. "I don't care who you are, you're going to pay for this." She swung on Robin.

Robin moved, but the blow grazed her arm. She screamed and doubled over as she held her bicep.

At that, a teenage boy in a blue bubble jacket yelled to the man inside the newsstand kiosk on the corner. "Yo, that dude is beating on that girl."

"Hey, man," an older Dominican man dressed in a post office uniform said, "you can't hit on a woman like that. What the hell is wrong with you?"

"Mind your business, old man." Shawn turned to him. "She hit me with a fucking bottle." The man backed off when he realized that Shawn was a female and not a man, as she appeared to be from farther away.

An older Jamaican woman screamed at Shawn in her thick accent. "She look like a bad man, and she put her hands on her just like a bad man."

Suddenly Robin's body straightened as she recovered and swung upward with her clenched fist. She struck Shawn hard in the jaw.

Shawn keeled over, holding her face in her hand. But she shook it off, stood up, and staggered toward Robin. "Oh, you want it, don't you?"

Robin backed up and the gathering crowd backed up behind her.

"Give the little one some room!" a man in the crowd yelled.

"The big one will kill her!" a female onlooker shouted.

"I'm just going to slap the shit out of her a few times. Remind her who I am!" Shawn yelled.

And at that moment, a large snowball thrown from someone in the crowd pelted Shawn on the cheek. The onlookers howled with laughter.

Robin leapt forward and hit Shawn with a short hook to her chin, snapping her head back, and dug her fist square into her belly. Shawn let all the air out of her lungs and Robin danced around her, waiting to strike again.

"Somebody stop this shit!" a woman hollered.

"The big one is getting her ass kicked. Leave it," the Jamaican woman said.

Shawn was tired and swung a slow punch at Robin, who ducked and dug both fists into Shawn's fluffy stomach again. Shawn doubled over in pain and Robin punched her in the face with a left and then a right, square into the cuts she already had from the bottle of olive oil. Blood spewed from Shawn's face.

She grabbed at Robin, but Robin stepped back, ready to deliver more punches. Shawn fell to her knees.

Then an onlooker threw something else at Shawn. It whizzed past her head, just missing her. Robin scurried to pick it up, looked at it quickly, and suppressed the urge to throw up. With Shawn charging toward her, Robin extended her arm and mushed it into Shawn's face. The crowded roared in laughter and disgust as Shawn struggled to pull the glue trap off of her forehead, the body of a dead mouse dangling lifelessly from it.

"Don't ever touch me again." Robin stood in front of her. "And don't let me see your ass on the street."

She pushed Shawn down to the ground as she still fought to pull the glue trap from her head without pulling the skin and eyebrows from her face, and without pressing the body of the mangled mouse against her cheek.

"Just so you know," Robin yelled as she made her way through the crowd, "all pretty girls should know how to fight. My sister, you know that bad bitch, taught me that."

FOURTEEN

....

THE SECRET

"Baby, get the door before they wake up the kids." Jacqueline pushed Cleopatra out of the bed in the middle of making love. They had moved from the sofa up to the sex room—the off-limits adults-only playroom across the hall from their master bedroom. Cleopatra was taking full advantage of what that silver bullet had started at her birthday dinner hours before. But now someone was banging on the front door and ringing the doorbell.

"It might be Robin," Jacqueline said.

Cleopatra put on a pair of black basketball shorts and a Brooklyn Nets t-shirt and ran down the stairs. She saw Robin through the stained glass, standing on the other side of the door.

Jacqueline had just finished apologizing for allowing Robin and Shawn's business to interfere in their relationship, and now this.

"What now?" Cleopatra yelled, but didn't open the door. She was having second thoughts about ruining the last few hours of her birthday.

"Open up, Cleopatra," Robin cried from the other side of

the door. Cleopatra relented and let her in. She wore the same oversized jogging pants and salty Uggs she'd had on at the restaurant earlier in the evening, and came in and hugged Cleopatra. She sobbed on her shoulder as Cleopatra held her up.

"Where is my sister?" Robin threw her bags in the corner of the foyer.

"Oh no," Cleopatra said when she saw Robin's luggage. "Jac!" she yelled.

Jacqueline came down the stairs in nothing but her short black silk robe and bare feet. "You woke the kids up, Robin. What's going on?" She tied her robe tight around her waist.

"I'll get them back to sleep, baby." Cleopatra ran up the stairs.

"What happened? Whose blood is that?" Jacqueline took Robin into the living room and sat her down on the couch as she looked at her t-shirt.

"It's Shawn's. I fucked her up. We broke up," Robin cried as she covered the blood splatter with her scarf. "She was cheating on me with a bunch of women."

"A bunch? How much is a bunch?"

"Does it matter? That's not even the point. She's a prostitute." Robin wiped her tears with the palm of her hand. "An escort, is what she called it. She gets paid to have sex with women."

"What?" Jacqueline was confused. "You're joking, right?" She laughed out loud and covered her mouth when she caught herself. "Shawn?"

"I would never joke where I come out looking this fucking stupid." Robin rolled her eyes.

Cleopatra came down the stairs, stopped, and stood in the

archway of the living room.

Robin looked at Cleopatra as she wiped more tears from her face and raised her voice. "And she's an escort too." She pointed to Cleopatra as if she was identifying the defendant in a courtroom.

It had all come to a head. Robin was jealous of Jacqueline, who had met Cleopatra and fallen in love so easily. And no matter what they went through, that love had never dimmed. They had a beautiful relationship, and Cleopatra treated Jacqueline like a queen. Meanwhile, Robin had wasted too much of her life tangled up with Shawn, a loser that wanted nothing but to put her hands on her. Robin longed for a love like the one that Cleopatra and Jacqueline shared; they epitomized love conquering all.

But not this time, if she had anything to do with it. If she couldn't have a love like that, then no one should.

Cleopatra froze as the two sisters looked at her.

"What do you know about that, Cleopatra? Why don't you tell your wife what you used to do for money? How you got this house and all that dough," Robin said proudly. Nothing felt more satisfying than shattering her sister's perfect little utopia. She thought she had it all, but Robin knew she could knock her down off her high horse. She would sit back now and watch it all fall to pieces ... and enjoy every moment of it.

"What are you talking about?" Jacqueline looked at Robin suspiciously.

Cleopatra stared at Robin, disgusted. "Wow. You really do hate your sister, don't you?"

She glared at Robin and exhaled deeply, but Robin moved before Cleopatra was able to say anything.

She hopped up from the couch and approached Cleopatra. "Cleopatra used to be a ho, too. I'm sorry, a pro. A ho for pay. She's the one that got Shawn into it. She fucked wealthy, closeted women for money for years. And they're still paying her to keep quiet. One of her sugar mamas gave her the deed to this house. That's how your life of luxury is being financed."

Jacqueline looked at Robin like she was crazy. "What the hell? I don't believe you. Baby?" She walked over to Cleopatra.

"It's true." Cleopatra glared at Robin, who stood next to them with her arms folded, proud of herself. "Silly little girl. You really are a vile, jealous piece of—"

Jacqueline grabbed Cleopatra by the bottom of her t-shirt and pulled her to the corner of the foyer. "Explain this to me. She's really telling the truth?"

"Yes." Cleopatra nodded.

"You had sex for money?"

"I supplied companionship and I got paid for it. It was just a job that I had a very long time ago."

"Companionship? What does that mean? It got sexual?"

"Sometimes. Most of the time … just about every time."

"Wait. So you gave me shit for how long over lying about being married and having kids. You know what you put me through for keeping that from you?"

"We are not going to compare lies. I didn't tell you about a job! A job that I quit years before I ever laid eyes on you. You didn't tell me about three actual human beings."

"Why did you keep this from me?" Jacqueline's eyes began to water.

Cleopatra could see the pain in her face, but didn't relent. "Did you tell me about every job you ever had?"

174

"Yeah, I have actually." Jacqueline raised her voice. "That's how you got this house? Exactly how long ago was this?"

"I quit like six or seven years ago. Four years before we even met."

"Please." Jacqueline caressed Cleopatra's face. "Make me understand why you never told me about this. We said no more lies after what I put you through."

"What is there to understand?" Robin interrupted. "She and her best friend are hookers."

"Shut the fuck up, Robin!" Jacqueline yelled. "Cleopatra and I were just fine until you and Shawn came up in our house with your bullshit."

"Hookers don't make what I made Robin," Cleopatra jabbed back at her.

"You were a high-priced hooker."

"Say something else Robin, I'm warning you." Jacqueline glared at her sister.

"High-priced hookers don't make what I made either!" Cleopatra yelled. "Not everyone was blessed to have a father that gave a shit and mother in good health. I was doing what I needed to do to support myself and my mother. What do you know about that? You haven't had a job since you were trying to sell fucking Girl Scout cookies outside of a massage parlor. Oh and FYI, happy endings aren't supposed to be free. Why don't you go to school, learn a trade, and stop leeching off of everybody and shut the hell up? I don't owe anyone an explanation or an apology for what I did."

Cleopatra looked at Jacqueline. "It was my body."

"And now it's my body too." Jacqueline shook her head. "So that's how you did it? Undergrad and grad school with no student loans, no debt. Took care of your mother. This house. My wedding ring. The ceremony. The trust funds for your god-children. Everything. Baby, why didn't you just tell me the truth?"

"Why would she tell you? She's no better than Shawn."

At that, Cleopatra got up in Robin's face. "I've had it with your big-ass mouth. When Shawn was busy blowing me up, did she tell you about the case she caught for fucking an underage girl and videotaping it?" A look of horror crossed Robin's face, who was speechless.

Jacqueline wasn't. "What the hell did you say?" She grabbed Cleopatra's arm.

"I didn't think so." Cleopatra ignored Jacqueline and focused on Robin. "Did she tell you she almost went to prison because of that shit, but the attorney that I paid over $50K kept her ass out?"

"You kept that shit from me too?" Jacqueline yelled at Cleopatra. "Are you serious? That's my sister."

"She begged me not to tell you. She promised she was going to change her ways," Cleopatra said.

"And you believed her and kept it from your wife?" Jacqueline was even more furious now.

"You weren't my wife at the time," Cleopatra sneered at Jacqueline. "I'll talk to you in a minute. I'm not done with her." She turned her attention back to Robin and cornered her.

"Did Shawn tell you how she had to pay all the money she made from selling her ass back in the day to that girl's parents in a civil suit? Hmm?" Cleopatra widened her stance and pressed her right palm against the wall, blocking Robin from escaping. "Now that girl Shawn fucked for free. She was cheating on your ass just for the hell of it that time. I'll tell her to send you the videos, she still has them. She had the nerve to say I pulled her in? She begged me to bring her in." Cleopatra got angrier as she beat herself on the chest.

"Baby. Calm down." Jacqueline pulled Cleopatra away from Robin.

"No. She's in my house, I can talk to her however I want to. As a matter of fact..." Cleopatra ran into the living room and found her and Jacqueline's clothes still puddled in front of the couch from when they returned home from her birthday dinner. She pulled her wallet from her pants pocket, walked back to the foyer, and took Robin's bags, opened the front door, and threw them down the steps and into the snow.

"Get out." She took a handful of bills from her wallet and tossed them in Robin's face. "Get a room somewhere, because you are not staying here."

"You think you can just throw money at me and I do what you want? I'm not you or your bestie," Robin said as she picked up the $100 bills anyway.

"How are you going to throw my sister out?" Jacqueline yelled.

"Do you want to go with her?" Cleopatra shouted. Jacqueline didn't move. "I didn't think so."

"You act like you're proud of what you did," Jacqueline said.

"I'm out of here." Robin picked up the rest of the cash. "Your perfect life isn't so hot, now. And your perfect wife ain't so perfect now, is she?" she asked Jacqueline.

"Get out of my house." Jacqueline shoved Robin out the

front door. She turned around and looked at Cleopatra, but didn't speak. She just stared at her.

"I don't have any delusions about what I did in my past," Cleopatra admitted to Jacqueline. "But it's done, it's over. That was who I needed to be at that moment. You do the best you know how at the time. I was a kid when I started. But I was able to make sure my mother lived comfortably for the rest of her life, and I was able to secure my future at the same time. I make no apologies for that."

"How can you act like this is not a big deal?" Jacqueline asked.

"Because it's not. You knew I could feed you in more ways than one. You never really cared where the money came from. Did you? I make a whole lot of money from my career but our lives are beyond that. Did you think I was a drug dealer? Would that have been better? You love this life. There is nothing you and the kids can't have, and you know that."

"I don't care about the money. You know that. The first time I saw you I thought you were a damn bike messenger, and I wanted you then. And I knew you had been with a lot of women. I know what you went through and that you would have done anything to take care of your mother. I don't fault you for that. It's that you kept it from me. You felt you couldn't tell me and I'm your wife now. You still didn't trust me enough. Even after we got married."

Cleopatra got defensive at that. "You lied to me about being married and I took you back, then you lied about having kids and I forgave you both times." She threw two fingers in the air. "Twice."

"So why the hell are you bringing it up now?" Jacqueline

yelled at her.

The kids scooted down the stairs. They ran to Cleopatra and she scooped them both up in her arms.

"What are you two doing down here?"

"We still couldn't sleep," Amir whined.

"Will you tell us a story?" Maya asked.

"Sure, I'll tell you one right now." She looked at Jacqueline. "You're going to have to have this argument by yourself. I'm not doing this." She climbed the stairs with both children hanging off her, took them to their room, and tucked them into their beds. She told them a bedtime story as Jacqueline watched from the door, reading to them until they were sound asleep. Then she kissed them both gently on their foreheads, and turned out their lamps.

Jacqueline followed close behind, kissing the kids goodnight as they slept peacefully ... just as they always did when Cleopatra read to them. Cleopatra waited in the doorway and grabbed Jacqueline's hand as she passed by.

"I need some time," Jacqueline whispered to her. Her eyes were red from crying.

"What does that mean?"

"I'm going to take the kids to Jersey tomorrow and stay with my parents for a while. I'm so mad at you that I can't even ... I don't know what to say to you." She pulled her hand away.

"How long is a while?"

"I don't know."

"And you think being apart will solve what you're feeling right now?"

"I don't know that, either." She couldn't look at Cleopatra.

"What do you know, exactly?" Cleopatra was getting impatient with the whole situation. "As big as this house is, you don't want to be in it with me?" She waited for Jacqueline to answer her. "Never mind. You don't have to leave. I don't want the kids displaced. I'll go. I don't stay where I'm not wanted anyway." She tried to move past Jacqueline in the doorway, but Jacqueline grabbed her hand to keep her from leaving.

Cleopatra looked at Jacqueline for a moment as her eyes began to water. "You do realize that you're mad at me because of who I am, right? I take care of the people that I love no matter what. I would do it again in a heartbeat if I had to, no regrets."

"You're not understanding me. And I can't even think about your not telling me about Shawn and some teenage girl right now. I'm not mad at who you are. I'm mad that you didn't tell me who you are. Why didn't you just tell me? Why couldn't you open up to me?"

"I don't have a reason that would satisfy you. It was my past and I chose to leave it there. Everyone has a past and you have nothing to do with that." Cleopatra shrugged her shoulders. She went into their bedroom, where she threw on some jeans and a sweater and packed a large duffle bag with a few changes of work clothes.

Jacqueline was silent, she just watched Cleopatra pack and did nothing to stop her from leaving. She followed Cleopatra downstairs to the front door as she prepared to walk out.

Cleopatra put on her coat as they stood face-to-face, looking into each other's eyes. She kissed Jacqueline and Jacqueline kissed her back and held tightly onto her coat.

"I love you," she said as Cleopatra opened the front door.

"You know how to reach me if you or the kids need anything," Cleopatra responded.

"Did you hear me? I said I love you." Jacqueline raised her voice.

"I heard you." Cleopatra turned around. "Love is facing you right now but you're letting it walk out the door. Like I said. You know how to reach me."

FIFTEEN

....

IF SHE WON'T, I WILL

"And where are you going?" Supriti perched her hands on her hips. Cleopatra was stepping out of a cab in front of the Soho Grand Hotel, a short ride from home, when she ran into her.

"Hey." Cleopatra forced herself to smile. *Great.* She threw her hood over her head as the wind howled down West Broadway. She had managed not to run into Supriti at work since she threw her out of her office, so running into her on the street was particularly annoying.

"Are you going to answer my question?" Supriti twisted her lips and examined the big brown Louis Vuitton duffle bag on Cleopatra's shoulder. "You must be meeting your wife here or something."

"Something like that," Cleopatra lied as she looked through the glass doors of the hotel, wishing a doorman would come out and save her. But it was so cold she couldn't blame them for standing inside.

"You want some company while you wait for her?"

"Um ... no." Cleopatra noticed that Supriti was glammed up—she had her red lipstick on, her hair blew freely in the wind, and the short open coat she had on covered an even shorter sapphire dress. "You look like you're about to go out anyway, don't let me keep you." She walked closer to the hotel entrance.

"I have a blind date. Mandisa set me up with some chick. You sure you don't want me to wait with you?"

Cleopatra looked at her watch. "That won't be necessary. You have a date now?" She smiled. "The later the dinner the bigger the winner, huh? Don't worry about me. Enjoy your evening." She walked away again.

"Are you ok?" Supriti grabbed Cleopatra's bicep, forcing her to stop.

"Yeah. I'm good," Cleopatra mumbled, not really wanting to look in Supriti's pretty, dark brown eyes.

"You're lying. No you're not. I can see it in your eyes, in your body language." Supriti moved in front of Cleopatra in order to see her face. "What is it?"

"I'll be fine, trust me. You really look beautiful." Cleopatra smiled as she took all of Supriti in. "I'm sure your date is waiting for you."

"Thank you." Supriti blushed, flattered that she noticed her.

"But you need a real winter coat," Cleopatra chastised her. "You know that, right? No one told you that when you moved from Cali? You have on a rain trench and it's not even buttoned."

"I know. I'll get a winter coat this weekend, I promise." Supriti smiled, loving that she cared.

"Good," Cleopatra said. "You should go on ahead now. I'm fine, really."

"I don't want to leave you when you're feeling like this."

"And how am I feeling? Hmm?" Cleopatra was annoyed that Supriti, a virtual stranger, was so in tune to her energy. She'd held in her emotions so far, not even showing Jacqueline how much pain she was in. But keeping her feelings in check was starting to get to her, and in this moment she wasn't sure what she wanted to do more—curl up in a ball and cry her eyes out, scream at the top of her lungs for her wife, or punch a hole in the wall.

"It's not good. You're sad," Supriti said. "You're obviously upset, and checking into a hotel without your wife."

"I'm going to go." Cleopatra turned and walked away.

Supriti grabbed Cleopatra's arm again. "Ok. I'm sorry, I don't mean to push. I'm just worried about you. Am I allowed to be worried?"

"That's sweet, but there's no need. I'm a big girl."

"I know you're a big girl and can take care of yourself. But you don't have to. How about you humor me? Take my cell number, call me if you want to talk."

Cleopatra pulled her phone from her pocket. When Supriti saw they had the same model, she pulled up her contact info and bumped phones with Cleopatra, exchanging all of their contact information instantly.

"Thank you," Supriti said.

Cleopatra walked off and finally made it inside the hotel lobby. She exhaled, believing she was safe from Supriti. But Supriti had followed her inside.

Cleopatra turned around and huffed at her. "What?"

"Nothing." Supriti looked in her eyes. "Just wanted to say good night. I'll talk to you later. Ok?"

"Don't call and wake me up."

"I have a feeling you'll be up." Supriti smiled.

"You feel better now?" Cleopatra asked.

"A little bit." She smiled. "I'm going to call you and see how you're doing later. But if you need me before then, you call me. I'm going to keep checking my phone."

"Rude," Cleopatra teased her. "I'm glad I'm not going out on a date with you. I would have a real problem with you constantly looking at your phone. You do know that's a first date 'fail,' right?"

"If I were going out with you I would much rather look at you than my phone, so that wouldn't be an issue."

Supriti winked, making Cleopatra smile. She waved goodbye to Supriti as a porter approached her and escorted her to the reservation desk. Cleopatra checked in to the only room they had available, a queen. She hadn't slept in a queen bed in years; her long body didn't fit and her legs hung off the end, but it would have to do for now. When she got there, the hotel room was about the size of her freshman dorm room, but much nicer. Thanks to its flat screen TV and a mini bar full of junk food, she had everything she needed for a short stay. She hoped she wouldn't be there long but she wasn't too confident in leaving any time soon.

Her cell phone didn't make a noise for a couple of hours, until Olivia texted her.

{*Olivia: FYI, 7 days began tonight. First up, Shawnette's ribs with a side of face.*}

Cleopatra ignored Olivia. The last person she was thinking about was Shawn and her big-ass mouth.

Jacqueline wasn't picking up her calls or even responding to her text messages, and eventually Cleopatra got the picture: Jacqueline meant what she said about not having anything to say to her. All she could do was give her time and space to cool off and sort out her feelings. So she showered, settled in, and relaxed, and before she knew it Supriti was ringing her phone.

"What are you doing?"

"Watching television. How was your date? No night booty cap? Wait." Cleopatra looked at the time. "Is it over already?"

"Definitely. No way could I be with someone else as heavy as you were on my mind. She was nice, but not you. She was very understanding."

"What does that mean?"

"I explained why I was late and I basically only showed up to cancel the date in person."

"And why was that?"

"I was worried about you and she was in my way of making sure you were ok."

Cleopatra shook her head. "In your way? You're nuts."

"About you? Absolutely." Supriti laughed. "So do you want some company?"

"Um … what are you talking about?" Cleopatra sat up in bed and looked around her hotel room.

"You heard me. Do you want some company? Can I come up to your room?"

"What do you mean come up? Where are you?" Cleopatra jumped out of the bed.

"I'm at the bar downstairs. I said I would check on you later, and that's what I'm doing. I'm a woman of my word."

"I thought you meant call and check on me."

"I did initially, but I'm old fashioned. I like to do certain things in person. And I don't live all that far from here. So what's it going to be? Am I coming up?"

"I'm on my way down." Cleopatra didn't want Supriti anywhere near her room. She threw on some jeans and a black t-shirt, put her keycard and cell phone in her pocket, and took the elevator down fifteen floors to the lobby.

Supriti's eyes bulged out of her head when she saw Cleopatra, who was sexy even in the simplest clothes. And then her eyes went right to her left hand. "Where's your wedding band?"

Cleopatra looked at her hand. "Oh. I forgot to put it on after I showered. Sometimes I forget. Jacqueline hates that." She looked at her naked finger as she rested her hand on the gold marble-topped bar.

"Oh. I thought you took it off for me." Supriti smiled.

"You really do flatter yourself," Cleopatra said. Now that Supriti wasn't covered by her coat, Cleopatra took note of how stunning she looked in that low cut blue dress. But she knew giving Supriti the slightest compliment would be blown way out of proportion. So she kept her thoughts to herself.

Suddenly there was a commotion at the entrance to the bar, and Cleopatra saw some of the front desk staff and some of who looked to be kitchen staff in their white chef jackets huddled in a group. They started clapping and chanting, "Cleopatra, Cleopatra Happy Birthday!" and then broke out in a chorus of Happy Birthday, accompanied by the other patrons in the bar. They presented Cleopatra with a three-layer chocolate cake. Cleopatra blew out the candles.

"How did they know it was my birthday?" Maybe they saw

it on her driver's license at check-in, she thought.

"Your birthday is in the contact information you beamed to my phone." Supriti smiled. "Why didn't you tell me?" She pinched Cleopatra's arm.

"Because it's almost over. And I figured you wouldn't leave if you knew. It's not a big deal." Cleopatra shrugged as she looked at her watch.

"Well it is a big deal and you have fifteen minutes left. You're right—I wouldn't have left. How about that?" She stood up off of the nail-headed bar stool and laid a fat kiss on Cleopatra's cheek, though she wanted her lips. She used her thumb to wipe the lipstick from her face.

"Thank you." Cleopatra blushed. "This was all very sweet. I appreciate it."

"You're very welcome."

Cleopatra picked up the knife to cut into the cake. "How did you get a cake so quickly, and with my name on it?"

"I have ways of getting things when I want them badly."

"Are we still talking about the cake?"

"I'm not," Supriti said with a serious look on her face. "Don't cut it yet." She reached down into her purse and pulled out a long, flat box wrapped with a red bow.

"Seriously?" Cleopatra laughed. "Wait, you did all this in a couple of hours on top of kicking ole girl to the curb? Where did you get this?" Cleopatra shook the box.

"Open it," Supriti laughed.

Cleopatra was slow to unwrap the gift as her wife had just uttered those same words earlier in the evening. "Open it." For one of her many birthday gifts … and now they weren't even under the same roof. It hurt her that her cell phone hadn't rung or beeped with a text from her wife, saying something. Saying anything. She and Jacqueline didn't play games, so instead of her thinking that Jacqueline was being stubborn or trying to punish her, Cleopatra had started to feel like Jacqueline just didn't care.

"Hey." Supriti rested her hand on her shoulder. "You ok?"

"Yeah. I'm good," Cleopatra assured her. She opened the box and pulled a scarf from it. "What? Is this Burberry?" She examined the charcoal-checked, crinkled cashmere scarf with its fringed ends. "Um ... did you get this from Canal Street? Is this a Furberry?" she laughed.

"No!" Supriti exclaimed. "It's not from Canal, baby." Supriti realized what she called her and lost her train of thought momentarily. "Um ... that's real Burberry, I promise you that." She rubbed it on Cleopatra's cheek and down to her neck. Her tongue peeked out the corner of her mouth as she caressed it against Cleopatra's skin.

"You're right." Cleopatra smiled and took the scarf from her. "And how did you get a Burberry scarf at this time of night?"

"This hotel has a hell of a concierge." She smiled.

"Wow." Cleopatra was impressed. "Thank you very much. You went through a lot of trouble for all of this. I really appreciate it."

"I know you do. And you're very welcome." Supriti smiled at her and rubbed her back. "Now, you can cut your cake." She clapped her hands, excited.

"I love chocolate," Cleopatra said as she removed the lone candle and pushed the chef knife into the cake.

"I was hoping you would say that." Supriti broke off a piece of cake with her fingers and pushed it into Cleopatra's mouth.

As their eyes met, Supriti whispered, "Happy birthday ... baby."

Cleopatra and Supriti sat and talked at the bar into the early hours of the next morning, eating cake and drinking Bailey's Irish Cream.

"How long have you two been together?" the female bartender finally interrupted them.

"Excuse me?" Cleopatra asked, perplexed.

Supriti immediately saw her opportunity. She touched Cleopatra's hand. "Not long, but it feels like we've known each other forever." She winked at Cleopatra.

"You make a beautiful couple," the bartender said. "I can tell how much in love you are."

"No. No." Cleopatra waved her hands. "We're just friends. I'm married, and not to her." She attempted to clear up the bartender's confusion.

"Oh." She smiled and put two champagne cocktails in front of them. "Well, to friends then. On the house," she said, and walked away.

"You're so bad. You were going to let her think we're a couple."

"Hey, she's a romantic. She obviously saw something going on over here. Who am I to burst her bubble?" Supriti took a sip of the cocktail. "Mmmm ... that's good. Would it be the worst thing in the world? Look." She pointed to the mirrored wall in front of them, behind the rows and rows of liquor bottles. When Cleopatra looked up at their reflection, Supriti laid her head on her shoulder. "Beautiful couple, just like she said."

Cleopatra rolled her eyes and thought better of responding.

In another lifetime she could be with Supriti, who was beautiful, intelligent, and ambitious. She had a bitchy and at times aggressive side to her that Cleopatra was attracted to. But this wasn't another lifetime, and she was married and dangerously in love with her wife.

She probably shouldn't have been sitting at that bar with Supriti. But she didn't want to be alone. Supriti was an incurable flirt, but nothing Cleopatra hadn't dealt with before. Cleopatra needed a distraction, and that's all Supriti was. She hoped Supriti knew that she didn't have a chance in hell of finding herself between her sheets. She was just taking Cleopatra's mind off of what lay ahead for her and Jacqueline.

What was going to happen now, she wondered? They could recover from just about anything, she tried to reassure herself. Jacqueline just needed time. Jacqueline compared this to her keeping her marriage and children a secret. It wasn't even close in Cleopatra's mind, though she realized that she probably should have trusted her wife enough to tell her about her past. But right now, Cleopatra was weak and hurting. She missed Jacqueline and had acted out a bit because, right or wrong, she felt entitled to.

"Ms. Giovanni?" A woman Cleopatra recognized from check-in a few hours before approached her. "A king opened up, and we've switched your reservation. Here is your key card. You can move to the new room at any time."

Cleopatra's eyes lit up. "Thank you very much. This is so much better."

Supriti studied Cleopatra. "What do you need a king-size bed for?"

"I'm used to sleeping in one." Cleopatra slipped the card

into her back pocket. "I need a lot of room."

Supriti licked her lips. "Yeah. You are long." She smiled.

Cleopatra enjoyed Supriti's company immensely that night. They parted ways around 6am, when she put Supriti in a cab home. She was happy for the distraction and Supriti just wanted to be with her no matter what the circumstances. They didn't talk about Jacqueline or her marriage. Cleopatra didn't offer any details on why she was out of the house, and Supriti didn't press her on it.

She didn't care why Cleopatra wasn't with her wife; she was just glad she wasn't.

Supriti was convinced that their running into each other that night was destiny. Because, as she saw it, she and Cleopatra would eventually be together. If Cleopatra's wife allowed her out of her bed, sooner or later Cleopatra would find her way in to Supriti's.

SIXTEEN

....

MENTAL AND DEFECT

"What the hell do you want?" Cleopatra asked when she saw Robin standing outside her hotel room. It was a couple days later, and Cleopatra and Jacqueline still hadn't spoken, only traded brief text messages and emails, resolving nothing in the process. That evening, Cleopatra had worked out in the hotel gym. When she returned to her room, she saw someone standing outside her door.

"I know you're really angry with me. My sister told me where you were. I just came to talk to you, that's all," Robin lied.

"Jacqueline did not tell you what hotel I was staying in." Jacqueline wasn't one hundred percent trusting of Robin around Cleopatra. Robin coming on to her at their first meeting had never left the back of Jacqueline's mind; although she forgave her sister, she sure as hell never forgot.

"Ok, I saw your text message to her," Robin admitted.

"And how did you see my text messages? Never mind." Cleopatra pushed the key card into her door and went into her room without inviting Robin in. She spoke to her from the doorway while making Robin continue to stand out in the hall.

"Make this quick." Cleopatra wiped the sweat from her face with a hotel towel. She couldn't imagine what Robin had to say to her.

"I can wait inside if you want to go and jump in the shower right quick." Robin stared at how her sweaty black muscle shirt and basketball shorts stuck to her body.

"Why are you here? I haven't talked to Shawn and don't plan on it, so I can't help you." Cleopatra leaned on the door, ready to slam it.

"I don't want to talk about Shawn. We're over."

"How is Jac?"

"Furious with me for taking so much pleasure in blowing up your spot and hurting her." Robin hung her head.

"You took a sickening pleasure in it. It was all over your face. But I meant how she is where I'm concerned?"

"She's not exactly confiding her innermost feelings to me right now. I don't want to talk about her, either."

"So why are you here?" Cleopatra jiggled the doorknob in her hand making an audible noise so Robin would know her time was up.

Robin was silent for a moment, then undid the belt on her trench coat and let it fall open and off her shoulders, revealing a little black dress. She stuck her foot in the door. "I was hoping maybe we could talk for a while."

"Ha. Get the fuck out of here." Cleopatra kicked her foot from of the doorway. She couldn't believe Robin was dumb enough to pull this stunt again. She should have known—when you saw the trench coat, you automatically knew what it was.

Robin started to speak.

"Shut the hell up," Cleopatra interrupted. "Are you really

this broken? What is wrong with you? You tried to purposely hurt your sister. You took pleasure in it. You're trying to break up her marriage. Now you show up like this? You just want whatever your sister has. You need to grow up and get over that shit. Shawn is fucked up and she hurt you, but this right here—" She pointed to Robin's dress. "—Is only making it worse."

"Do you know how hard it is being her sister?" Robin shook her head. "I mean, she is good to me. But Jac has always been the beautiful sister—flawless, smart, cute perfect children, Ivy Leaguer, scholarships, valedictorian, prom queen, cheerleader, dancer, blah, blah, blah. You have any idea how it is growing up in her shadow? It's like my sister is fucking Beyoncé or something," Robin ranted.

"I'm sorry, but you are no Solange," Cleopatra smirked. "My heart isn't bleeding for you. You have an amazing sister that loves you despite the fact that you keep fucking up. And you have probably the most loving parents I've ever seen. I'm sure they welcomed you back home with open arms, didn't they?" Robin nodded. "You look real stupid. All this energy you're expending being mad at your sister's life you could be putting toward getting a life yourself."

✿✿✿

A few minutes later, Cleopatra was about to hop in to the shower. But once again she was interrupted. There was a loud banging on the door to her suite. She assumed it was Robin again, not knowing when to give up.

"You can't take no for an answer can you?" Cleopatra swung the door open.

Shawn stood in the door. She grabbed Cleopatra by the collar of her robe and shoved her hard. Cleopatra almost fell over the small armchair next to the flat screen TV. Shawn ran up on her again, grabbing her robe.

"Get off me." Cleopatra pushed her, and Shawn fell back into the door, slamming it shut, but then ran up on her again.

"I just saw Robin get on the elevator. What was she doing here? Did you fuck her?" She pushed Cleopatra again.

Cleopatra took a deep breath to calm herself down as she tightened the white hotel robe around her waist. "You have one more time to put your hands on me," she warned Shawn. "If I fucked her, she would have been limping out of here, not walking."

Shawn swung on her. Cleopatra ducked and punched Shawn square in the jaw, knocking her to the floor.

"Are you serious?" Cleopatra shook her right hand as the pain from connecting with Shawn's jaw shot through her fingers. Her hand hadn't totally recovered from the last time she'd had to punch her. "You're mad over that? She's not even your girl, remember? She was here trying to fuck, again! You want to do this?" Cleopatra stood over Shawn, who was holding her jaw, curled up on the floor.

Then Cleopatra looked closer at Shawn's bruised and swollen face. She had a bandage across her cheek. "Your face is fucked up. And why are your fucking eyebrows missing? Never mind, I don't even care. Why are you here?"

Shawn held her jaw as blood trickled out the corner of her mouth. She was scared when she looked up at Cleopatra. She would never get used to seeing the amount of anger she now saw in her former best friend's eyes whenever she looked at her. "You weren't answering your cell so I called the house and Jacqueline said you were here. I came to check on you."

"For what? We aren't friends." Cleopatra studied the bandage again. She knew she was responsible for some of the damage on Shawn's face, and Olivia'd had her face pummeled as well, but why Shawn was missing most of her eyebrows was a mystery.

"I came to apologize." Shawn sat up on the floor and rested her head on the side of the armchair and her back against the wall. "I want my best friend back. I'm sorry, man. For our fight, for all the fucked up things I said, for telling Robin about your past. You know Jac will take you back."

Shawn seemed sincere, but it was much too late for Cleopatra. She knew people often had regrets and managed to channel up mounds of sincerity when they were on the brink of hitting rock bottom.

She sat down on the edge of the bed. "You couldn't wait to bust me. But at the same time, you neglected to come clean on your own activities. Don't worry, I filled Robin in." She glared at Shawn. "You want to be my friend again? That's funny."

Shawn pulled herself to her feet and sat down in the chair across from Cleopatra, but Cleopatra'd had enough by now.

"What do you need? Giovanni Savings and Loan is out of business."

"That hurt, Cleo." Shawn shook her head and held her stomach. Her breathing was shallow and Cleopatra noticed.

"So Olivia tells me you've met with her team." Cleopatra folded her arms across her body. "Tapped out on the first day.

That didn't last long."

"I guess she told you I'm back working for her, now. Well, as soon as everything heals." Shawn straightened out her clothes as she stood up and walked toward the door.

"You know, it's fascinating how important the ribs are when you want to breathe, isn't it?" Cleopatra smiled.

"We've been through too much to end up like this." Shawn held her side as she winced in pain. "We're still family. I know you're going to be mad at me for a while. I know I deserve that shit. I'll be around when you need me." Her head hung low as she stepped outside into the hallway.

"That's where you're mistaken," Cleopatra corrected her. "I don't need you."

....

SEVENTEEN

NOT A GOOD LOOK

"Jacqueline wasn't sleeping. She was cranky and struggling not to take missing Cleopatra out on the twins. Maya had asked one too many times when Cleopatra was coming home and Jacqueline snapped at her, causing her to burst into tears. Amir had then consoled his mother.

"We just miss Mama Cleo, that's all. She is coming back, right?"

Jacqueline tossed and turned in their bed each night without being wrapped in her wife's embrace. Cleopatra literally put her to sleep after they made love. Without that, and without the warmth of her wife's body, she was left staring at the ceiling or watching TV all night. The final straw was when Supriti crossed her mind; her wife wasn't home and she knew that hungry shark must have been circling. It was time to go get her woman and bring her back home where she belonged.

"You just missed her. You should have called," Racquel said to Jacqueline. Racquel herself was packing up for the day. "She just went down on the elevator as you came off. What's going on with you two? What's your problem?" Racquel was ready to get into it with Jacqueline, especially with Cleopatra nowhere around to shield her.

"Some other time, Racquel, I'm going to try and catch her. Thanks." Jacqueline escaped to the elevator, hit the button for the bottom floor, and ran to security in the lobby. They directed her to the door Cleopatra had just gone out of. Jacqueline flew out of the revolving door and saw Cleopatra on the sidewalk. But she was with some chick, standing in the taxi line. Jacqueline ran over and grabbed Cleopatra's arm, yanking her away from the woman. Cleopatra balled up her fist and was ready swing when she realized it was Jacqueline.

"What the hell?" Cleopatra exclaimed.

"Who is this?" Jacqueline immediately assumed that Cleopatra had reverted back to her old bachelor habits. She wouldn't risk assuming that married Cleopatra was any different.

"This is Mrs. Randall from the New England office. VP of Mergers and Acquisitions for the Boston area. This is my wife, Jacqueline."

The studious woman extended her hand. She had deep-set brown eyes under thin eyebrows, and straight, shoulder-length chocolate-colored hair worn in a simple style. She was short and wide-hipped. Her pale skin clashed harshly with her wardrobe—a simple navy wool coat with a purple scarf thrown casually around her neck, as the mild NYC winter had nothing on the Boston temperatures she was used to.

"Pleased to meet you. I've heard so much about you." She smiled warmly at Jacqueline as she shook her hand. "So this is the mother of those beautiful children. I'm a newlywed myself—six months now." The woman beamed, and Jacqueline felt smaller with each word she uttered.

She only conjured up a "Pleased to meet you."

"Excuse us for a moment," Cleopatra said to her colleague. She escorted Jacqueline by her arm, weaving through the after-work rush hour crowd and out of ear shot of the woman. "How could you embarrass me like that?" Cleopatra scolded her. "I have a business meeting. That is a colleague, nothing more."

"So all of a sudden you have business meetings in the evening with women I don't know, and you never had them before?"

"You're right, because my wife and my family came first; after 5PM wasn't an option and I was unyielding on that. Now it is an option. If you will excuse me, she wants to get back to Boston and home to her husband by a decent time."

"Cleopatra." Jacqueline ran behind her and grabbed the back of her coat. She hugged Cleopatra tight. "Baby, I'm sorry. You know how I get when we're apart. You know I can't function being away from you, and I get crazy. I get jealous and insecure. I'm sorry."

"This is what you wanted."

"I know that's what I said. Come see the kids after dinner? They miss you."

"If it's not too late."

Cleopatra walked off with her colleague and jumped into a taxi. She enjoyed a productive business dinner with her Boston counterpart and saw that she made her 8PM Amtrak Acela train departing from Penn Station with plenty of time to spare, then kept her word to Jacqueline and went to visit the kids in time to help with their bath. She was heavy on the bubbles, as always, and they made a huge mess of the floor, splashing and throwing water at each other and Cleopatra. Then she told them a story and tucked them in, kissing them goodbye instead of goodnight.

She had her garment bag with her and packed more work clothes. She was ready to leave all the while, not speaking or making much eye contact with Jacqueline. She put on her coat and prepared herself to go back to her hotel, but Jacqueline stopped her as she opened the front door.

"I was under the impression you were coming home when I saw your bag," Jacqueline said.

"I don't recall being asked to come home to stay. You asked me to come and see the kids. Are you asking?" But Jacqueline hesitated too long for Cleopatra. "I'll see you later." She walked out and slammed the door behind her.

Jacqueline ran to the door and opened it. She called out to her, "Baby, please come back!" Cleopatra stopped at the bottom of the steps and looked back at her. "Don't leave, not like this. Don't you miss me?" Jacqueline pleaded. "Come."

She extended her hand out to Cleopatra, who hesitated, but finally jogged up the steps and came back into the house. She laid her bag down in the foyer. Jacqueline pulled her coat off and dropped it on top of her bag, then led her over to the couch in the living room.

"Sit and talk to me."

Cleopatra sat on the couch, feeling like a guest in her own home.

"How are you?" Jacqueline asked.

Cleopatra scowled. "How do you think I am?"

"You haven't hugged or kissed me. You're so cold. You just come to see the kids, get some clothes, and leave. That's it?"

"The kids didn't want time away from me. You did. You came by my job to tell me the kids missed me and asked me to come home and see them. I did that. Now what?"

Cleopatra was upset. She missed Jacqueline, but the longing had turned into anger and more hurt when Jacqueline had refused to take her calls over the course of the last few days, and she hadn't done herself any favors when she showed up at Cleopatra's job accusing her of wrongdoing with a colleague.

"I want to come home." Again Jacqueline was silent and didn't answer Cleopatra as quickly as she should have, so Cleopatra stood up. "Good night, Jacqueline."

Cleopatra had no desire to argue, and left the house. She'd had enough with just about everyone in her life, and her tolerance was now nonexistent.

Jacqueline, on the other hand, saw a change in her wife, and it scared her. Cleopatra's face didn't light up when she saw her … in fact, she barely looked at her. She didn't stop everything she was doing and wrap her tight in her arms and kiss her.

That look in her eyes that she promised would never go away was fading.

EIGHTEEN

....

SERIOUSLY, IF SHE WON'T I WILL

Cleopatra worked late for the next few days. She was in the office after hours on a Friday and not in a hurry to go to her hotel suite and spend the weekend alone. Nothing had changed between her and Jacqueline; they were growing more distant. Jacqueline hadn't called her and she hadn't called Jacqueline, outside of talking to the twins and giving them their bedtime stories via Skype. It wasn't getting better, and Cleopatra didn't know what to do or how to fix her marriage.

She was in her office with the door closed when Racquel knocked and proceeded to walk right in.

"Thank you again for the tickets." She smiled.

"Of course." Cleopatra looked up from her computer screen. "Happy Valentine's Day. I hope you enjoy the show tomorrow night."

"Oh we will. Motown on Broadway, orchestra seats. We're going to be right up there with Diana Ross." She did her best lead Supreme imitation.

"You know this is a just musical? Diana won't actually be there."

"I am Diana," Racquel corrected her.

"Your Ms. Ross fetish is so disturbing," Cleopatra laughed as she leaned back in her chair.

"Have you changed your mind about coming home with me for dinner tonight and spending some time with your godchildren?" Racquel danced in front of Cleopatra's desk. "Stop in the name of love…" she sang, out of tune.

Cleopatra laughed. "Not tonight, but soon, I promise."

"I'll make your favorites. Rice and beans and sweet plantains."

"As tempting as that is, I can't. But you can always bring me the leftovers on Monday." Cleopatra batted her eyes as if to say "Pretty please."

"Just as well. I'm gonna fill those children's bellies, rub some whiskey on their gums, and get them to bed early so I can put on my I Want Muscles wig and give my man some loving." She did a slow grind.

"Ooh, I just threw up in my mouth." Cleopatra gagged. "What is an I Want Muscles wig?"

"I put on my Diana hair and we put on the song and reenact the Muscles video."

"Wait there was a video?! Let me find it on YouTube." Cleopatra turned to her monitor and keyed it in. She covered her mouth as she watched. "Wait … Kelile ain't got no muscles. Ya'll do this? Oh my God."

"Hmmph. Kelile got a muscle all right."

"Eww." Cleopatra gagged again and waved her hands in surrender. "Just stop."

"Don't be mad 'cause I keep my marriage hot," Racquel laughed.

"Don't come back up in here with any more godchildren

for me. Three is enough!"

"Don't worry about that. How about you go home?"

"I don't feel like it." Cleopatra played with her cell phone.

"I don't mean your hotel room. I mean your house where your family is."

"You know I can't do that."

"No, I don't know that. I thought you would have been back home already. That's your house, you pay the bills."

"We just need some time. That's all."

"Do you know if she got her Valentine's gift?"

"Yup. The jewelry store called me to confirm delivery."

"And she didn't call to say anything? Text? Like thank you for the damn diamond necklace? Maybe you should have canceled the order like you were thinking." Racquel folded her arms and huffed.

"No call. No text today. I haven't heard from her."

"I'm giving her through the weekend before I get involved. And she don't want none of this."

"No she doesn't," Cleopatra laughed at her. "Have a good weekend, kiss the babies for me."

"You know I will." Racquel waved goodbye, went to her desk, and packed up her belongings.

Supriti had been lurking in the shadows, careful until the coast was clear and Racquel was gone. When she got up the nerve, she walked to the doorway of Cleopatra's office and knocked lightly on the open door.

"I finally have you all to myself, huh?" She'd managed to run into Cleopatra just about every day that week, but was never fortunate enough to get her alone. She would make up for that tonight.

Cleopatra turned her attention from her monitor. "Hey."

"I saw your light on. What are you still doing here?"

"Just hanging." Cleopatra shrugged. "Look at you." She eyed Supriti's shape in the tight scarlet pencil skirt and matching silk blouse.

Supriti smiled. "I would think you would have been rushing home to your beautiful wife."

"You would think that, wouldn't you?"

"Wait. Are you not back at home yet?" Supriti walked around Cleopatra's desk, forcing her to face her. But she quickly changed the subject. "Do you ever get hungry?" she asked. "What do you do in those instances? Have dinner with me."

"I can't do that. It's Valentine's Day. It's not appropriate. It would be wrong."

"Oh and our talking for hours at your hotel bar was appropriate?" Supriti smiled. "Our going out to dinner is no more wrong than your not wanting or not being able to go home. Which is it?" Cleopatra didn't answer. "Come on, an innocent dinner out in public, and you can pick the most crowded and open restaurant you can think of. I'll feel better knowing you weren't alone and had a good dinner, at least. No one wants to be alone on Valentine's Day. Do you?"

✿✿✿

"This is convenient," Supriti said.

"How so?" Cleopatra asked as they emerged from the subway. She had picked a Thai fusion restaurant not far from her hotel.

"It's close to my loft and even closer to your hotel." Supriti stuck her tongue out at her.

"You're out of your mind, you know that?" Cleopatra asked as she held the door open for her. "Mere coincidence. I love this place. The food is addictive."

The restaurant was packed, with it being Valentine's Day, but the wait staff recognized Cleopatra, as she had been eating there almost every day for the last week and was a notoriously big tipper. They scrambled to get a table ready for her. And fought over who would wait on them.

"Hold on a sec. I need to call my wife." Cleopatra excused herself from Supriti momentarily in order to call Jacqueline. She was hopeful that she would answer the phone and tell her to come home, but her call went to voicemail again. Cleopatra tried to fight the overwhelming disappointment in her wife's actions ... or lack of action. No Happy Valentine's Day call or text. No thank you for the present. Nothing. She hung up her phone, deep in thought about how their first Valentine's Day as a married couple found them not even speaking to each other.

While they stood and waited for their table, Supriti's eyes roamed over Cleopatra, liking the way her toned body filled out her navy blue suit underneath her camel hair coat. She wore the Burberry scarf Supriti had given her for her birthday, loosely wrapped around her neck. It brushed her cheek when she turned her head and it warmed Supriti's heart to see Cleopatra wearing a present from her. It was only a morsel of what she could give Cleopatra if she would only let her. It was a $900 scarf, but in her eyes it was much too small—scraps compared to how she would spoil her if she were hers. Cleopatra deserved so much more.

Supriti struggled to pull her gaze from Cleopatra, who was in a conversation with the restaurant owner. She tried to ignore the visions of kissing Cleopatra in her head. She wondered what the repercussions would be if she ever worked up the courage to kiss her.

There were many attributes to appreciate about Cleopatra, but at the moment Supriti decided to focus on her eyes. That would be safer, she thought. She was wrong. She stood there staring at her without speaking, and felt exposed and naked, though not how she wanted to be naked in front of her.

Just lead me to your hotel room and take it, she thought. Why are we wasting time bullshitting? "Damn."

"What's wrong?" Cleopatra turned her attention to her.

"Hmm ... oh, nothing. I just remembered something," Supriti lied.

"Everything ok?"

"Yeah," she lied. "No," she whispered as she inhaled Cleopatra's cologne and thought of all the things she would do to her. The throbbing between her thighs grew more intense and she stood with her legs tightly crossed. Right when she thought she would pass out, the hostess approached them and announced that their table was ready. Supriti was annoyed at how the petite Thai woman gazed at Cleopatra. She was evidently charmed by her, and joking about how she hadn't seen Cleopatra in forever, when Cleopatra told Supriti that she'd been there for dinner just the evening before, and nearly every night that week. She led them through the dimly lit restaurant to an intimate table in the corner, always polite. There, Cleopatra pulled out Supriti's chair for her.

"You are such a gentleman," she teased. "Thank you." She smiled, feeling like the most beautiful woman in the world.

The hostess handed them their menus and recited the specials, but before she excused herself she asked Cleopatra what she thought of her red Valentine's Day dress as she dragged her hand from the bottom of her thigh to the top of her hip.

Before Cleopatra could respond, Supriti said, "It's miraculous that as tiny as you are, you still managed to find a dress two sizes too small. What does she think?" Supriti pointed to Cleopatra, who was stunned at Supriti's candor. "Probably what I'm thinking—how much? And do you charge by the hour, or the act?"

Both Cleopatra and the hostess's mouths dropped open.

"Seriously? I'm so sorry." Cleopatra apologized to the woman. "Do not put anything in my food. Please. Hers, I'd understand, but not mine." She winked at the woman as she ambled away, stunned, then turned her attention back to Supriti.

"Wow, out of pocket. You are in rare form tonight."

"I didn't like how she was coming for you."

"But it's ok for you to do it?"

"Basically." Supriti opened up her menu.

Cleopatra opened her menu. "You forget that I'm married. And not to you. Women come on to me all the time. That's my wife's business, not yours. I know how to handle myself."

There was never a dull moment with Supriti, and once again Cleopatra welcomed the distraction, but Supriti could be exhausting at times.

Cleopatra looked around the crowded restaurant packed

full of lovers, each couple seeming more enamored with their partners than the next. The garden-style dining room featured low, wooden ceilings with billowing Thai-silk, and flickering vanilla candles floating on a central pool, as trance-like instrumentals were softly piped in.

After studying the menu and learning the Valentine Day specials, Cleopatra ordered Tempura shrimp with grilled eggplant and palm sugar-tamarind sauce, and Supriti selected the Thai organic chicken roulade with maitake mushrooms and sesame-soy sauce. They chatted casually until their food arrived. Then, in the middle of dinner, Cleopatra finally opened up, feeling somewhat safe. She would never tell another woman specifics on what went on between her and her wife, but she admitted to Supriti that she'd kept something from her past a secret. And that she and Jacqueline had been living apart for nearly a week.

"Not that I believe everything I hear, but I heard she kept a few things from you, too. Well, three things, to be exact. I would think she'd understand, or at least have no grounds to be upset with you about withholding something from your past." Supriti took a sip of Chardonnay. "But I guess I would be upset too, at first. You do understand where she's coming from?"

"Yeah, I do." Cleopatra lowered her head. "But you said you would be mad at first, and it's been a week." She stuffed her mouth full of eggplant.

"That's true. Like for an hour I would be mad. And!" Supriti held up her index finger. "I would not have let your fine ass leave the house. That's just madness. Sorry." She shrugged her shoulders as she cut up her chicken. "I would just have to be mad as hell lying underneath you, naked."

Cleopatra nearly spit out her Thai iced tea because she laughed so hard. "That's pretty funny." She covered her mouth with her red napkin. "You make me laugh. I needed that."

"I'm so serious." Supriti winked at her. "Anyway, give her some time. I'm sure she'll get over this. From what I saw, it looks like she really loves you."

"Thanks. I need to hear that right about now."

"Can I ask you a question?" Supriti was ready to turn the conversation to her favorite subject. She reached her fork across the table and stole a shrimp from Cleopatra's plate.

"Really?" Cleopatra's mouth dropped open. "A shrimp?"

"I'm sorry." Supriti apologized, chewing. "Here, you can have anything over here that you want. Anything." She leaned back in her chair so Cleopatra had full view of her body.

Cleopatra shook her head and smirked. "I want my shrimp back. What was your question?"

"Oh yeah. I wanted to know. What do you think of me?" She gazed into Cleopatra's eyes, awaiting her answer. She had wanted to ask that question for the longest time.

"Honestly?" Cleopatra raised her eyebrows as she swirled a shrimp around in the sweet tamarind sauce.

"Of course, honestly. Give it to me, I can take it." She licked her lips. She had stopped eating and folded her arms, giving Cleopatra her complete attention.

"It's not like we've known each other all that long." Cleopatra popped another shrimp into her mouth.

"I know your type. You're kind of quiet. You listen twice as much as you speak because you're making observations. So ... yeah, go ahead."

Cleopatra swallowed and wiped her mouth with her napkin. "You strike me as someone who likes to be in control. You hate it when you're not." She took a sip of her Thai iced tea before focusing her eyes back on Supriti. "You're very intense, which limits your ability to have meaningful friendships with women. Your need to be the center of attention and the most desired woman in the room doesn't win you fans, either. You like to live life to the fullest, so you often live in the moment when you should plan more for your future. Architects are artists, so you need unconditional love and deep spiritual and physical connections to be happy ... or so you think. You want a soul mate who sees you for what you actually are."

Supriti sat and stared at her, not sure how to respond. She wanted to be mad. But mad at what? That Cleopatra could see through her? She was shocked at how Cleopatra analyzed her so thoroughly.

"I don't mind relinquishing control if the other person knows what they're doing," Supriti said, annoyed. "And what am I, really?" She swallowed hard as she awaited her response.

Cleopatra was unfazed by her defensiveness. "Someone who needs to appreciate herself for her mind and spirit and not just her sensuality." She pointed to Supriti's exposed cleavage with her fork as she continued to eat her dinner.

"What if that is especially difficult because that's all that people seem to value in me?" Supriti leaned back in her chair and proceeded to rock back and forth as she clutched her wine glass in both hands, sipping it as if it were hot tea.

"Then you should probably eliminate those people from your life. Do you want me to continue, or do you want to keep getting agitated because I'm not telling you what you want to hear?"

Supriti was taken aback. She wasn't used to a woman just talking to her any type of way, but she liked it. "Go ahead."

The hostess interrupted them, then, speaking only to Cleopatra. "Would you like dessert?" she asked as she motioned for a server to come and clear off their table.

"Yes. We would." Cleopatra decided to order for both her and Supriti to avoid another awkward confrontation with the hostess. "We'll both have mango and sticky rice. Thank you, sweetheart," she said as the hostess walked away.

"Sweetheart?" Supriti scowled at her. "Don't encourage that wench."

"Seek help, Supriti. Let's see, where was I?" Cleopatra continued as she smoothed out the red tablecloth in front of her. "Oh. You need to learn to be alone and be okay with it. If you're single you hate it; if you're with someone you hate that, because you're waiting for something to pop off so you can end it before they hurt you. Sound familiar?"

Supriti was silent as she reflected back on her daddy and abandonment issues.

"Hey." Cleopatra waved her hand in front of her face. "I'm sorry, I didn't mean to offend you."

"You didn't. I didn't know you were paying attention. You know a lot about me. I'm not sure how I feel about that."

"I hope I haven't made you too uncomfortable."

"You haven't, only because it's you. My soul feels naked, but I trust you with it." Supriti squirmed in her chair. Cleopatra wasn't helping Supriti want her any less.

"I'm glad you aren't mad at me."

"I don't think I could ever be mad at you. You know, no

one wants to be alone."

"I know. I don't want to be alone any more than the next person, but I find myself there again. I have a wife and two kids and yet I'm living alone in a hotel room."

"You're not alone, or at least you don't have to be." Supriti caressed her hand.

"Thanks. I've been through much worse. Being alone won't kill me." She slid her hand away from Supriti's.

Their server arrived with their mango and sticky rice and a side order of whipped cream.

"I don't recall you asking for that on the side?"

"I didn't. She remembers I like a lot of extra whip." Cleopatra dropped a dollop on top of her sticky rice.

The hostess was officially an enemy now. Supriti leaned over and looked toward the front of the restaurant, where the woman was staring right back at her. She stopped herself just as she was about to put a forkful of sticky rice in her mouth.

"I actually think I'm full." Supriti sat her fork down on the plate and pushed it away. The woman laughed uncontrollably and walked back into the kitchen.

"Does your wife have any idea how much this is hurting you? What it means for you to be out of the house?"

"It's not about me. It's about her being kept in the dark." Cleopatra cut into her rice with the side of her fork.

"I don't care. You just got married and you're already separated."

"We aren't separated," Cleopatra snapped at her.

"What would you call it, then? You aren't living in the same place," Supriti snapped back, not letting up.

"It's not forever."

"But it feels like forever to you right now. Doesn't it?"

"It does. She's behind my every thought. I miss my wife." Cleopatra had suddenly lost her appetite, and pushed her plate toward the middle of the table to touch Supriti's.

Supriti saw the pain in her eyes and hoped that one day Cleopatra would feel that deeply for her. "If she's smart, she'll come to her senses quickly. She can only shut a woman like you out for so long."

"What does that mean?"

"It means if she's not willing to be your woman, she needs to step aside and make room for someone who is."

Cleopatra laughed. "She's more than willing to be my woman. We're just going through something right now. You really aren't out to make friends, are you?" She leaned back and folded her arms across her chest.

"I call them as I see them."

Cleopatra smirked. "And you think I would give up on my marriage that quickly?"

"No I don't, but it takes two people to make a marriage work."

"Point taken. Enough about me. I'm curious how you negotiate your sexuality with your culture. The Indian women I've dated were hiding in several closets. It wasn't fun."

Supriti smiled. "You've dated an Indian before?" Her lips curled. "More than one?"

"Yeah." Cleopatra smiled. "I have a thing ... never mind." She gazed off into space.

"Mmmm that is so sexy and good to know." Supriti couldn't contain her excitement. "So tell me about them." She leaned across the table full, of curiosity.

"Ayesha was my first real girlfriend. Her father owned a bodega in my neighborhood. She always gave me free stuff—whatever I wanted. Candy, chips, soda, and honey buns. One day I asked her why, and she said if I wanted I could pay her with kisses." Cleopatra smiled. "So that's how we started messing around. I was ten or eleven. She was fourteen or fifteen. Her father found out about us and sent her back to India to live with her grandmother. So that was the end of that."

"So you never saw her again?" Supriti asked.

"She actually found me a couple of weeks ago on Facebook. She's married to this old rich fat dude and has like six kids. Anyway there were many others, but back to what I asked you."

Supriti smiled wide as she squirmed in her seat. "Um ... what was your question? Oh. How is it being a lesbian and Indian? Actually it's not so hard. My father had already disowned me for other reasons long before I even came out. I'm not really that connected to the Indian community, since I'm so new to the city, but I was no better back in Cali. I pick and choose the parts of my Indian and African American heritage that I participate in. But I speak Hindi. I practice Hinduism, Ayurveda, and yoga. I can cook the food. I love Bollywood movies and I know the Kama Sutra like it's my social security number. So I don't think it's been that hard for me. From outward appearances most people assume I'm just African American. Sometimes...what do they say nowadays? It's not bi-racial. Ethnically ambiguous? Yeah. So it's not really like ooh look at that Hindu lesbian."

Cleopatra smiled. "Thank you," she said to the waiter as he removed their dessert dishes from the table. "You don't sound like that bad of an Indian to me. You're being a little hard on yourself. So who are you dating? And why aren't you with them tonight?"

"I'm single at the moment."

"By choice, I'm sure."

"I need to make myself available for someone that I've had my eye on for several weeks." She winked.

Cleopatra looked around. How did she find herself in such a precarious position?

"Um ... Supriti, I love my wife more than I could ever put into words. You need to understand that we could never be more than just friends. And I do mean never."

"Something you need to know about me is that once I set my sights on something I want, I get it. Every single time."

Cleopatra was missing her wife and kids, and not interested in beating Supriti off her. "That's admirable, but I'm not a job, a pair of shoes, or the bridal bouquet at a wedding reception. I'm a woman, a married woman. Is that going to be a problem for you?"

"It's not a problem for me if it's not for you."

Cleopatra smiled. "You know I have to laugh. You are really trying to wear me down. You have incredible stamina."

"You haven't seen even a glimpse of how long and hard I can go."

Cleopatra nearly choked on her water. She wiped her mouth and made a mental note not to drink when Supriti was speaking. "You are so inappropriate that it's hilarious."

"I'm not laughing."

"Like I said, I plan on moving back home, where I will be back into my own bed, going long and hard on my wife."

"If you're trying to make me jealous, its working and I hate it."

"I'm trying to make you visualize me with Jacqueline so you can knock the thoughts of me and you out of your head."

"Understood." Supriti leaned back in her chair.

"You don't like rejection do you?"

"What type of question is that? Who does?"

"So why do you keep putting yourself in a position to be turned down?"

"I'm willing to put myself in any position you want me in."

"Thank you," Cleopatra said to the server as he brought her a peppermint tea with a side of vanilla soymilk.

"Wait. When did you order that?"

"I didn't have to." Cleopatra turned around and made eye contact with the hostess and mouthed the words "Thank you" as she waved.

"Really? I've had it with her. How does she know I didn't want any tea?"

"Do you?" Cleopatra poured the soymilk into her cup.

"No. But how does she know that? Ugh. She's going to make me come back up in here."

"Please don't do that," Cleopatra laughed.

"Does your wife please you?"

"You are so out of order right now." Cleopatra looked up from her tea.

"You come across as very erotic to me. You're a very sexual person aren't you?" Cleopatra didn't answer. "Being out of the house probably has your body all in knots, doesn't it? You're probably a freak," Supriti said. "The quiet ones usually turn into animals when the lights go out."

Cleopatra was thankful that Supriti hadn't made extensive contact with her exes outside of the receptionist Nikki, who she was certain had tried to scare her off. "I'm not about to discuss my sex life with you."

"Well I guess you don't really have one right now, sleeping in a hotel and all. How is that working for you? Ok. I'm sorry. I'm sorry, really. I will behave. But just in case I haven't been clear. If you at any point need my body, you just let me know."

Cleopatra shook her head. "You are exhausting." She remembered a time when she would have taken Supriti into the restaurant bathroom and fucked her in the stall just to shut her up. She hadn't been faced with such persistent temptation since she and Jacqueline had gotten married, but she hadn't allowed herself to be in such a dangerous position. She'd been home with Jacqueline, burning a hole in their marital bed every night.

Now she was constantly facing temptation from a beautiful and aggressive woman who Cleopatra knew was nothing but trouble. But Supriti was giving her the attention that her wife wasn't. Cleopatra flipped her cellphone over. No missed calls or text messages, as usual.

"So, I'm sorry. What do you think of me again?" Supriti pressed her.

"Short version?" Cleopatra asked. "I think you are beautiful, intelligent, and sweet."

"And how do you feel about me?" Supriti smiled.

"Interesting question. I'm human, so yeah I'm drawn to you for some reason. Probably because you remind me of my first girlfriend. And you know, that little Indian woman fetish thing."

Supriti beamed. "My first girlfriend was black, too."

"Like chocolate, huh?"

"Love it." Supriti winked. "So you know all about my culture and the traditions? Did your Indian girlfriends teach you?"

"They taught me a lot of things." Cleopatra smiled hard but didn't elaborate.

"You're so sexy. Do you know that?" Supriti leaned forward across the table. "There is no reason for you to be alone tonight." She slid her hand under the table, onto Cleopatra's knee.

"Don't do that." Cleopatra pushed her hand off of her leg. She wished Supriti would stop talking about sex. It was wreaking havoc on her emotions, and each time it just reminded her that she couldn't make love to her wife. "I love my family. If I wasn't married it would be different, but I am, and you and I are just not going to happen. You know studs and femmes can actually be friends."

"Can they really?" Supriti raised her hands in surrender. "I'm sorry. Your smile makes me melt."

"Apology accepted."

Cleopatra's cell phone vibrated on the table and a smile crossed her lips when she saw that it was Jacqueline. She'd been expecting her call much earlier, as she'd been reading the kids bedtime stories every night before they went to sleep. It had been the only bright spot in her day over the last week.

"Excuse me. I need to take this," she apologized to Supriti. "Hi."

"I stopped by your hotel but you weren't there." Jacqueline hesitated, waiting for Cleopatra to volunteer where she was at 9PM on Valentine's Day, but she didn't. "I packed up your things and checked you out. Please come home, baby."

"Really?"

"Hurry, I'm waiting for you. I've missed you so much."

Cleopatra smiled. "I've missed you too."

Supriti felt a knife puncture her heart as she pretended not to listen.

"You need me to bring anything?"

"You have everything I need," Jacqueline whispered into the phone. "I love you."

"I love you too, baby. I'm on my way." She hung up and looked at Supriti. "So I guess you couldn't help but hear."

"Congratulations. I told you she wouldn't let you stay out of the house too long. No sane woman would."

"I'm going to put you in a cab and then head home." Cleopatra motioned to their server for the check.

"You don't have to do that. I can walk—I'm not even a fifteen-minute walk from here."

"Absolutely not. It's dark. It's late. And it had already started to snow when we first arrived. Plus, I always make sure a lady gets on her way safely. You're taking a cab, end of discussion," Cleopatra informed her.

"If you insist," Supriti relented.

Spending the evening with Cleopatra had not quelled Supriti's desire for her. And Supriti was only making things worse, because it was a no-win situation. Everything and everyone had told her to leave Cleopatra alone, but she was going after this woman who was married, desperately in love with her wife, telling her 'no' every step of the way, and whose wife would probably inflict great bodily harm on her. She decided she'd try again to contain her emotions for Cleopatra; as long as her wife was making her happy, Supriti would do her best to leave her alone. Yes, she wanted her, and that wasn't just going to change overnight. But for now, she would try and harness her desire.

As they exited the restaurant, dozens of cabs snaked down Sixth Avenue. One of them pulled up the second Cleopatra extended her arm.

"Thank you for tonight." Cleopatra opened the door for her. "I really needed a friend. Thank you for being there."

Supriti looked inside the cab but turned away, not ready to leave just yet. "You're very welcome. At this point I'm ready to be whatever you need me to be, Cleopatra. Even though you're going home to your wife, I'm glad to see that beautiful smile back on your face and that light back in your eyes. I really do want you to be happy."

"And I want you to find someone that makes you happy. Someone deserving of you."

"I'm starting the meter, we can do this all night," the cab driver barked at Supriti.

"Congratulations," she shot back at the driver.

Supriti looked back into Cleopatra's eyes. Her breathing slowed, and so did her heart. She reached up on her tiptoes, placed her arms around Cleopatra's neck, and brought her mouth to hers. Her heart pounded hard in her chest the moment their lips touched and shook every nerve in her body until she feared losing control. The kiss was instantaneous, and so was the moistening of her panties. It sparked a blaze between her legs until she felt like she was on fire. At that moment she wasn't aware of anything but needing to stick her tongue into Cleopatra's mouth. She wanted to caress her, feel her tongue stroking hers; but the rush of sensations between her thighs overpowered her.

Cleopatra pushed her away and wiped her lips with her sleeve.

Supriti smiled and laughed, proving that she wasn't sorry. "I don't have to find someone deserving of me." She licked her lips. "I've already found her. Goodnight." She ducked into the taxi.

"Goodnight." Cleopatra closed the cab door and waved goodbye as the cab pulled off. She touched her lips, making sure she didn't have any lipstick on her mouth.

So much for controlling herself, Supriti thought. Maybe she would start tomorrow, or the day after. She watched Cleopatra in the cab's rear view mirror and traced her lips with her tongue, still tasting her there. She hadn't counted on not being in control when she kissed her, but if that kiss had lasted any longer, she would have lost it completely.

Forget about leaving her alone, she would make sure to put herself in the position to lose control with Cleopatra as soon and as often as possible, wife or no wife.

NINETEEN

....

AFTERMATH

Jacqueline stood in the doorway when Cleopatra arrived. "Baby, I'm sorry." She jumped into Cleopatra's arms. "I've missed you so much. You have no idea."

"I've missed you." Cleopatra pulled off her coat and walked into the living room, where she plopped down on the couch.

"Where are the kids?" Are they sleeping?"

"Nope. At their grandparent's house, remember?"

"Oh yeah. Valentine's weekend and you wanted me all to yourself."

"I sure do."

Jacqueline held both of Cleopatra's hands in hers and kissed her fingers. She moved in closer.

"The other night I got scared," Jacqueline admitted. "Scared of losing you. I've felt so disconnected from you; you've been so cold, and I knew it was because you were hurting. I don't ever want to feel like that again."

"I had to turn off my feelings. I shouldn't have to do that with you." Cleopatra spotted the diamond pendant between her wife's breasts. Jacqueline pinched the pendant between her fingers, brought it to her lips, and kissed it.

"I love it, baby. Thank you. It's so beautiful. Happy Valentine's Day." She kissed Cleopatra softly on the lips. "Come on." She pulled Cleopatra upstairs toward the bedroom. "Are you tired?"

"I haven't slept well in days. You know I can't sleep without it," Cleopatra whispered in her ear as they entered their bedroom. "You tired?"

"I haven't slept either." Jacqueline came out of her clothes and undid the belt on Cleopatra's pants. "You ruined me. I can't function without you. I don't ever want to be without you again."

Cleopatra scooped her up and carried her over to the bed and laid her down. "You won't, baby."

They didn't make love; they just fell asleep in each other's arms. The best sleep they had in a week.

✿✿✿

A few hours later, when she woke up in the middle of the night and found her wife watching her sleep, Cleopatra asked, "So do you want me to tell you everything? If we get this out of the way, it won't creep back into our marriage."

Jacqueline rolled over onto her side. "I do have questions. How did it work, exactly?"

Cleopatra turned on her bedside lamp and looked into her wife's eyes.

"Weren't you breaking the law?" Jacqueline took Cleopatra's hand, reassuring her wife that she could confide in her.

"Eh. Legally there were some age of consent issues for a

bit. But as far as the business aspect, it's a fine line. I was contracted to supply companionship. I was never paid for sex. And how did it work? Well, where a man usually wants to just do the act and be done, women for the most part want the girlfriend experience. Dinner, a show, conversation, and then the physical. My job was to make them feel good before I ever touched them."

"Tell me about the woman that gave you this house."

"She checks in periodically, when she thinks I'm in trouble. She's overprotective and just likes to make sure I'm good."

"What's her name? I want to meet her."

Cleopatra buried her face in her pillow and laughed. "Ah, that's never going to happen, baby. Those women paid for discretion and privacy. And you don't need to know her name."

"So this woman has, or had, feelings for you? You didn't love her?"

"Never. Understand, I went to Ivy League institutions. Scholarships helped, but this is still New York City and I had my mother's medical bills, her rent, my rent, utilities and food. It was just a job—a really good-paying job, but still, just a job. Besides, a lot of women have loved me that I didn't love back."

Jacqueline burst into laughter. "That's the most conceited shit I've ever heard."

"It's true!" Cleopatra laughed.

"That makes it even funnier," Jacqueline laughed. "But this woman took care of you back then, and she still is in a way. What does she get out of it?"

"We haven't had sex since I quit the business, if that's what you're asking."

"When was that last time she popped up?"

Cleopatra thought back to how Alexis had made quick work of her crazy ex, Kenya, framing her for a slew of offenses that caused her to be sent off to prison, and away from Cleopatra and Jacqueline. "She knows how much I love you and she respects it," she assured Jacqueline. "We wouldn't be together if she didn't. She's that powerful. She has systems and the means to make things go her way if she so desires. She truly only wants my happiness. Nothing more."

"So I have nothing to worry about?"

"Absolutely nothing." Cleopatra smiled. "Can I ask you something?" She sat up in bed and pulled Jacqueline to her. "Has this changed how you feel about me?"

Jacqueline kissed Cleopatra softly on the lips. "There is nothing you can't tell me. The day we got married I promised to take care of your heart, but you have to give me a chance to do that, baby." She took Cleopatra into her arms and held her tight. "Nothing will ever change how much I love you. Nothing."

✿✿✿

"Baby, your phone is beeping."

Jacqueline had come out of the shower first, slathered herself with coconut oil, and wrapped a towel tight around her body. Cleopatra's cell phone was chirping, signaling what Jacqueline thought was her text message alert. She looked at the time—2:28 am—but shook it off. Cleopatra's smartphone with her various apps always beeped for one reason or another.

But then the phone rang. Now Jacqueline was pissed.

"Pick it up!" Cleopatra yelled from the shower. The phone stopped ringing by the time Jacqueline crawled across the king size bed to Cleopatra's nightstand. She picked it up and started to go through it, but decided against it.

"Who was it?" Cleopatra called from the bathroom.

"I don't know, they hung up."

"Check, baby. It's late; maybe it's an emergency."

Jacqueline picked up the phone again. It beeped once more in her hand and two unread text messages popped up.

{*S: I'm home safe*}

{*S: Thank you for tonight, Cleopatra. I needed you just as much as you needed me*}

"Who the fuck is S?" Jacqueline yelled.

Then the phone beeped yet again in Jacqueline's hand. A multimedia message popped up with a subject titled, "Because you went home to your wife." Jacqueline opened it and saw a picture of a vibrator laying on a woman's stomach. It glistened in the moonlight and looked to be covered in cum.

Jacqueline stormed into the bathroom and opened the glass door to the marble walk-in shower, then threw the phone at Cleopatra. "What the fuck is this?"

"What?" Cleopatra caught the cell phone as it grazed her nipple. "Oww. Really?" She glared at Jacqueline. "What are you … my phone's not waterproof…" Cleopatra turned her back to the showerheads and read the text messages. "That's Supriti." She said dismissively as she tried to hand the wet phone back to Jacqueline.

"Look at the picture!" Jacqueline demanded.

Cleopatra looked at the phone again. "What the … ew! Is that cum?" She tossed it at Jacqueline.

"Wait!" Jacqueline yelled as she caught the phone. "You were with that bitch tonight? That bitch? Tonight?" And she accosted Cleopatra in the shower, getting part of her already-dried body wet again. Then she went back to Cleopatra's text messages and deleted the picture.

"We had dinner after work." Cleopatra shrugged her shoulders. "That's where I was when you called. I left to come home." She took her bottle of shower gel and lathered up her body some more. As soon as she turned toward Jacqueline full frontal, Jacqueline lost her train of thought.

"Mmmm." Jacqueline walked away and turned her back on her. "What the hell does, 'I needed you as much as you needed me' mean?"

"She was there when I needed a friend tonight. I was missing my wife."

"And I'm sure she loved that shit." Jacqueline threw her hands up in the air.

"She is not the issue," Cleopatra said. "This being separated shit—I can't do that again. I didn't commit my life to you to live apart. You don't run or push me away if we're fighting. I can't deal with that, it hurt. Sleeping in a hotel for a week? Not making love to my wife? Not hot."

Jacqueline turned back around to look at Cleopatra. "I never wanted you to leave. I was hurt and I was angry at Robin. It all happened so fast. It just got way out of control. I didn't think you would really leave, and then you got mad." She moved to stand in the doorway of the shower. "I'm sorry, baby, as soon as you hit the steps I missed you. I cried myself to sleep that night, thinking you didn't love me anymore."

"I will never stop loving you." Cleopatra kissed her softly, her lips still moist from the water and steam of the shower. "I don't want to argue. I missed you, and I was hurting. She offered to take me to dinner and I didn't want to be alone. Simple as that."

"I could strangle you right now, you know that?" Jacqueline grabbed a handful of locs and pulled Cleopatra away from the showerheads, then drew her face down to hers. "If you're lonely and you miss your wife, come home. I don't care if we're fighting or not. Don't spend time with some woman that you know for a fact wants you."

Cleopatra opened her mouth to speak and tell her about the kiss, but Jacqueline covered her lips and shushed her.

"Don't talk. I don't want to know. I'm not about to fight with you and send you back out on the street. That's what she wants—you away from me again," Jacqueline said.

Then she dropped her towel to the floor and slid back into the shower to join Cleopatra.

"You seem to have forgotten that you're all mine and I'm all yours." Jacqueline kissed her. "I'm about to remind you again and again.

TWENTY

....

GIMME A BREAK

"Let me get this straight. You're taking the subway with four kids all under the age of five?"

"Yup," Cleopatra said, proud of the day she had planned with Maya, Amir, and Racquel's twins at the Children's Museum.

"They're going to love that, baby." Jacqueline hesitated. "So wait. I'm going to be at the spa all day by myself? Too bad Robin, my number one stalker, hater fan, can't come. She lost," she laughed.

As a make-up present, Cleopatra gifted Jacqueline with some time off from the kids and arranged a special day for her at one of the city's most exclusive spas: a facial, manicure, pedicure, massage, steam bath, a little champagne, relaxation, and a chauffeured Escalade. The works, and whatever else Jacqueline's heart desired.

Cleopatra and the kids saw Jacqueline off to her day of beauty and readied themselves to leave right after her. The kids had their own special routine before they left the house with Cleopatra. First, everyone peed, then they had body checks, where Cleopatra checked for sticky fingers, boogers, and lint in their hair. Cleopatra, having just cut Amir's hair the night before, was impressed that he had kept his little wave cap on all night, but had to now coax him to take it off.

"No. You're not wearing that outside, boy. You are not about that life," Cleopatra warned him as she snatched it off of his head.

Cleopatra started counting the numerous barrettes that Jacqueline had snapped on to Maya's four jumbo ponytails.

"Mommy knows that you're going to be running around today, right?" Cleopatra asked her.

"Yes," Maya nodded. "She said it doesn't mean I can't be cute while I'm doing it." Cleopatra laughed. "Don't laugh, Mama, look." Maya started to jog in place and the barrettes started to smack her in the face.

"Ok. Stop. Stop." Cleopatra chuckled and started to re-move some of the barrettes. She put them in her pocket, cer-tain that she would be rebraiding Maya's hair at some point before the day was over.

Then they had an impromptu fashion show, as they never left the house without looking their absolute best, no matter what the occasion. On this day it went particularly quickly, as they all wore the same thing: black hoodies, black jeans, black Air Jordans, and their gray North Face jackets.

Then Cleopatra had the mandatory 'don't' talk with them. Maya and Amir were always well behaved, but gentle reminders never hurt anyone.

She sat them down on the living room couch and paced back and forth in front of them. "We're going to have a great time today," she said, excited. "But it's important that you do exactly what I tell you to do, just like always. So don't ask for anything, don't touch anything or anyone you aren't supposed to touch, don't look at anything or anyone that doesn't need looking at, don't talk unless you are spoken to or unless it's important, or you have to do #1 or #2. If you understand, nod your head yes."

They both nodded their heads yes and smiled.

"Good. Now what do I always tell you?"

Amir raised his hand. "Don't try you because you will whip us in front of white people."

"My man." Cleopatra high-fived him. "One last thing. It's freezing outside." She pulled a container of Vaseline from her backpack, looked in the living room mirror over the mantel, and started to slather her face with it and rub it in.

"I want some." Maya tugged on Cleopatra's pants leg.

She bent down and covered Maya's face with the petroleum jelly, and Maya helped her rub it in.

"You're next, Amir," Cleopatra said.

Amir stuck his face out, but as soon as Cleopatra plopped a glob of the Vaseline on his forehead, he started to whine.

"Just take it, Amir," Cleopatra laughed.

"Man up, boy," Maya chastised her brother.

"Hmmph. I'm not a man yet," Amir fussed.

"My mama did this to me," Cleopatra said. "And now I get to do it to you." She smiled. "You'll thank me when we get outside."

"I'm getting hot, Mama," Maya said.

"That's right, baby, that's when you know you're ready to go."

By the time they walked to the end of the block, Cleopatra

239

was already checking in with Amir. "How's that Vaseline working for you? Not cold, are you?"

Amir lifted up his little arm and formed a thumbs up sign with his Scooby Doo mitten.

Cleopatra beamed. "That's my boy."

They hopped on the uptown D train to Racquel's apartment on East 180th and Grand Concourse in the Bronx. After they arrived, they visited for a while with Racquel, her husband, their twins Amare and Ayana, and Cleopatra's youngest godchild, Gabriela. Then Cleopatra and both sets of twins jumped back on the subway and headed to the museum in Manhattan.

Cleopatra had arranged a private tour. The kids were all excited and giddy, and even Cleopatra was filled with anticipation … until she saw who their tour guide was.

"Cleopatra." The woman jumped into her arms. "Oh my God."

Cleopatra didn't embrace the woman. Instead, she waited for it to stop. *Can I not go anywhere without running into an ex?* The girl topped the long list of Cleopatra's past mistakes. She'd failed to realize the position she'd put herself in when she stripped naked for Cleopatra in the first hour of their first date. She had destined herself to the jump-off hall of fame, never to emerge as anything more.

"I just found out this morning that I was going to have you today."

Shit, shit. "How you doing, Bri … Brianna?" The girl's name escaped Cleopatra until she spotted her nametag.

The kids looked at the woman with eager anticipation, waiting to hear about their day. But she just stood there, staring intently at Cleopatra.

"Ok, so you want to address the kids? They're excited." Cleopatra pointed to them standing behind her. "This is Amir, Maya, Amare, and Ayana."

"Oh, hi kids." The attractive, petite woman turned so quickly that her long box braids smacked Cleopatra across her cheek. She appeared to be stunned that there were children actually standing there. "I'm Brianna, but you can call me Bri. Should we get started?"

Cleopatra nodded. "That would be nice."

The children screamed and jumped up and down, and Cleopatra let them lose control, as they had been holding in their excitement all morning long.

"Just one second," Brianna told the children. "So how have you been?" She turned her attention back to Cleopatra. "You look amazing." The woman raised her hand to brush Cleopatra's arm.

"Excuse me, Mama." Maya swooped in between the woman and Cleopatra. "May I say something?"

"Yes, baby girl." Cleopatra looked down at Maya. "Go ahead."

"Stop flirting with my Mama Cleo, please." Maya looked up at Brianna. "She's married to my mommy. See?" She pointed to Cleopatra's hand. Cleopatra held up her wedding band, wiggled her finger, and smiled.

The woman was equally stunned that Cleopatra was married and that this little girl told her to step off.

"Oh. I had no idea." She straightened her posture. "Shall we get started? For real this time."

Maya grabbed Cleopatra's hand as they listened to the day's agenda. Cleopatra intended to tire the children out, but she would be exhausted right along with them before the day was done. They built robots and made ice cream with liquid nitrogen. They launched boats down a winding stream. Learned which objects floated in water and which ones sank and experimented with sand to create rivers and lakes. By the end of the day, regardless of whatever protective gear they had on, they were all moist and sticky.

When they stopped for lunch, Brianna figured it was her chance to catch up with Cleopatra.

"So when and why did you get married?"

"I'm a newlywed." Cleopatra took a bite of her veggie burger and wiped her mouth. "I got married because I'm in love with my woman. What type of question is that?" Cleopatra rolled her eyes.

"So are those all your kids?" Brianna took a hard bite of her hot dog.

"No, just the two that are dressed exactly like me." Brianna looked down the table and noticed that Amir, Maya, and Cleopatra all had on black. "The other two, Amare and Ayana, are my godkids."

"You know I still think about you often."

Maya slid down the table, motioning Amir, Ayana, and Amare to move down with her. She laid her head on Cleopatra's arm. And began to mean mug the woman. "Excuse me, Mama."

"Yes, baby," Cleopatra answered.

"You know how you tell me things one time because you don't like to say it over and over?" She side eyed the woman.

"Be respectful, baby."

"Yes, Mama."

Cleopatra wanted to burst into laughter. Instead, she held it in. Jacqueline had blamed Cleopatra for Maya's fresh mouth. She was quick and sarcastic for a four- going on five-year-old. She was never disrespectful, but was definitely going to be a handful when she got older.

"She's got a point, Brianna," Cleopatra said. "Show some respect, especially while I'm with my children. How about we finish the day on a positive note? No hard feelings. Can we do that?" Cleopatra wiped her hands with a wet nap and proceeded to rebraid one of Maya's pony tails, which had exploded from its barrette.

"Yeah. We can." Brianna smiled as she watched Cleopatra take care of Maya. "And I'm sorry, Maya." She winked at her.

"Thank you." Maya turned her attention back to her pile of French fries.

That evening, Jacqueline arrived home feeling and looking brand new. She found Cleopatra facedown, asleep on the sofa in the living room.

"Hey, baby. How was your day?" She kissed Cleopatra. "Ewww. Why are you wet?" she screeched.

"Hey, sweetheart." Cleopatra sat up on the couch and exhaled. "Let's see, we built a replica of the Empire State Building with garbage. Oh, sorry, recycled materials." Cleopatra did air quotes. "We rode bikes, danced, ran, bounced, and jumped on everything constantly. And there was water. A lot of it. We crawled up a giant tongue and waded through fake guts in plastic suits." Cleopatra exhaled.

"I've had water sprayed on my head, did I say water? There was water. We got covered with a green, snotty-looking goo that looked like baby diarrhea. I think I'm losing my hearing because of all the screaming. And someone's kid threw up on my new Jordans. So yeah … you're going to be working this off for a while." Cleopatra flopped back down on the sofa.

"You look exhausted." Jacqueline laid down next to her.

"I just put the kids to bed. I hosed them down on the terrace with Mr. Bubble and dishwashing liquid." Cleopatra smirked.

"You're kidding, right?"

"Uh, no. They loved it. They even washed my locs for me. We made it a game. They're upstairs, knocked out."

Jacqueline laughed. "I'm going to kiss them goodnight. Be right back, baby."

Cleopatra fell back to sleep. A few minutes later, she awoke to Jacqueline's lips on hers.

"Thank you for today." Jacqueline smiled at her. "Not just for my day, but for the babies. They were up when I went in. They said today was the second best day of their lives. They said our wedding day was the best."

"Mine too." Cleopatra smiled, fighting not to doze off again. "I love you. I'd do anything for you and the kids," she whispered.

"You're so tired. Let me get you upstairs." Jacqueline sat her up.

Cleopatra opened her eyes again and caressed Jacqueline's face. "You look beautiful."

"I feel amazing. I had a facial, a mani/pedi, and a brown sugar body massage, then I sat in the sauna for a while. And I got a Brazilian." Jacqueline licked her lips. "I want you, baby. But you're so tired. I tell you what." She stood up and took Cleopatra by the hand and began leading her upstairs to their bedroom. "How about you let me do all the work? All I've been thinking about is how good you are to me. And how I was going to repay you when I got home tonight." When they arrived at their room, she laid Cleopatra down on the bed and undressed her.

Jacqueline tore off her own clothes, but by the time she slipped into bed, Cleopatra had fallen asleep. Jacqueline didn't wake her, just watched her wife sleep peacefully, knowing how exhausted she was.

"I love you so much, baby," she whispered. "I wish I could put into words just how much. I wish I could make you understand." She laid down behind Cleopatra and wrapped her arms around her.

"I love you more than life itself. You're my everything."

TWENTY ONE

···

ABANDONMENT ISSUES

"Where am I going to find a woman who can handle me like you can?" Supriti asked Cleopatra. "Someone who can pinpoint my personality like you did? That analyzes me to such an extent without judgment?" Supriti hovered around the office thermostat, tempted to turn on the heat.

"Who says I would know how to handle you?" Cleopatra asked as she took off her suit jacket and sat down behind her desk. "Don't touch my thermostat."

"I say you know how to handle me." Supriti came and bent over Cleopatra's desk, giving her all the cleavage her sleeveless black dress had to offer and longing for her undivided attention. "Can you look at me for a minute, please?"

Cleopatra turned her head from her monitor.

"Thank you. What I'm saying is you know who I am and yet you like me anyway."

Cleopatra's lips parted slightly and at that moment Supriti remembered the kiss. Just reminiscing on it sent vibrations through her body. Cleopatra's eyes fell to her mouth and to her breasts, and Supriti was certain that she was thinking of it too.

"Wrong and wrong." Cleopatra opened up her email. "You

can really never know who anyone is. You can live with them forever and still not know. And I like you, I don't *like* you."

Supriti was standing so close to Cleopatra that she could smell her—the mysterious, masculine musk of her, the scent no one could ever place or replicate because her pheromones were downright primal. It opened Supriti up, awoke the animal in her.

"I need a good woman." Supriti swallowed hard.

Cleopatra's cologne lulled her into a daydream. She thought briefly back to her first girlfriend. Most people had difficulty letting go of their first loves, and Supriti had been no different. Her first serious relationship started and ended messy, as is often the case with young love. Even though it was Supriti who was the heartbreaker that first love had long been the woman that Supriti thought got away. She had yet to meet anyone that surpassed her, who moved her emotionally, spiritually, intellectually, and physically, until she met Cleopatra. Cleopatra tugged at her heart, and she did it effortlessly.

"Everyone needs a good woman." Cleopatra interrupted Supriti's daydream. "I think you would be quite a handful. You're going to keep someone very busy once you decide to give them your heart. I hope they don't have a career, because they need to work you like a full-time job."

"What does that mean?" Supriti folded her arms across her chest.

"I'm just saying. And it's nothing wrong with it. You require a lot. You get bored easily, don't you? You get tired of people quickly. When was the last time you had a relationship that lasted more than three months?"

Supriti thought about it, but came up with nothing.

"Uh-huh, that's what I figured."

"So what do you do when you've found that person and they're married?" Supriti asked.

"You suppress the hell out of it and keep them as a friend until your true love comes along," Cleopatra said without hesitation.

"No, I don't like that idea. Cleopatra ... look at me. Um, never mind." She turned to leave her office. "No, I need to say this." She stopped and turned around. "I've wanted to say this for a long time. You're such a good woman. I'm falling in love with you, and I don't know what to do about it."

Cleopatra was silent for a moment, staring at Supriti. "I'm sorry." She shook her head. "You know nothing will or could ever happen between you and me. I've said that before. My love is blind and I don't see anyone but Jacqueline."

"I know. That's why I think it might be best if we stay away from each other. That I stay away from you. What do you think?" Supriti asked, hoping Cleopatra wouldn't agree to part ways.

Cleopatra was motionless. "What I want doesn't really matter. But I understand."

"Don't say that, it matters to me."

"If our friendship is only causing you pain, then you should do what you need to do."

"Our friendship isn't causing me pain, the fact that I want you as more than a friend and can't have that is killing me. I don't see any other option, because I can't just turn my feelings and my desire off. I've tried. You will say something funny or brilliant or do something incredibly sweet and I can't stop falling."

"I can be corny, stupid, and mean if that works better for you." Cleopatra tried to lighten the mood, because Supriti was taking herself and her status in her life way too seriously.

"This is not what I want, but I think it's best," Supriti said.

"Well, going to miss you, friend," Cleopatra said flippantly.

"I'm going to miss you too." Supriti hesitated and looked down at the floor. "We shouldn't call or text. I need to do this kind of cold turkey."

"I'll respect your wishes." Cleopatra side eyed Supriti, waiting for her to burst into laughter, but she didn't. "What about around here? Since you have an office here now for the project, do you want me not to speak if I see you?"

"Don't go to that extreme. That would break my heart." Supriti sighed. "Deep down, I know you don't want to be away from me any more than I want to be away from you. I really don't want to leave you alone. I don't want you to feel like I'm abandoning you."

"Don't worry about it." Cleopatra forced a smile and wondered if Supriti was really serious or auditioning for a part in a remake of *Gone with the Wind*.

"I can't help but feel that way. You're black and white, there's no gray area with you. I know when it comes down to it, whether you admit it or not, you're going to feel like I'm leaving you. Like I'm just walking away from you."

"Umm … no. I'll be fine. Do what you need to do," Cleopatra tried to convince her. *She's really serious. Yo, she's nuts.*

Supriti exhaled hard. "Don't do that to me. Don't just dismiss this. What's happening with my emotions, what's going on inside of me when I'm with you or even just thinking about you, is not good for anyone. I just can't do this with you any-more. You love your wife, I get that, and she loves you. I feel like I'm banging my head against a wall. I know I can't win, I know I can't have you. And what's crazy is I know I can't even have a little piece of you, because if I could that would be enough for me and I wouldn't be doing this."

"You're right. I do love my wife and she loves me. You are banging your head against a brick wall, you could never come close to winning or having me. This is for the best." Cleopatra took a more serious and forceful tone with Supriti now. "Take care of yourself." She dismissed her and turned her back to look out her window.

Supriti ran up to Cleopatra and hugged her hard, then turned back toward the door.

Cleopatra glanced over her shoulder and watched her high tail it out of her office without looking back. She felt a tinge of sadness at the loss of her new friend, but was used to people she cared about leaving. She'd developed a tough skin and in-stantaneous rebound skills … which were applicable to every-one but her wife.

She dug her hand into her pants pocket, where she found a note that Jacqueline must have slipped to her that morning.

To My Wife,

There is no doubt in my mind that we were meant to love each other. I appreciate all that you do and the beautiful ways that you express your love. You make me happy, you make me laugh and you bring me joy and peace. Most importantly, you make me feel safe and loved. I cherish each morning that I wake up next to you and each night that I fall asleep in your arms. Thank you for loving me, putting up with me, being patient with me, and thank you for making me feel like the most beautiful woman in the world every time you look at me. I want forever with you.

I love you,

Jac

A smile spread across Cleopatra's lips. She grabbed her backpack and coat, left the office, and went home to her wife early.

She missed Supriti for all of sixty seconds. They only saw each other sporadically at work after that, and shared short, generic greetings, usually followed by Supriti abruptly excusing herself and running off. She continued to pull away from Cleopatra, but they would soon be thrown together in close proximity, testing Supriti's willpower once again.

TWENTY TWO

....

LET'S GET READY TO RUMBLE

"Hey." Supriti tapped her on the shoulder.

"Shit," Cleopatra said. "What are you doing here?" Midtown Properties was having the annual executive retreat at a secluded resort off the coast of Maine. Cleopatra would be away from Jacqueline for three days and two nights, so Supriti was the last person she wanted to see.

Cleopatra had spent most of that first day participating in team-building exercises with colleagues she didn't like or didn't trust. She had called Jacqueline after lunch and Jacqueline could tell in her voice that her wife missed her. But she didn't give away that she was sitting in a private car, on her way to surprise Cleopatra at the resort.

Meanwhile Cleopatra would be left to fend Supriti off all by herself.

"I came with Mandisa." Supriti smiled, excited. "I've never been to New England before. Look I'm dressed properly." She modeled her bright red ski jacket for Cleopatra. "It really is beautiful up here." Her eyes glazed over Cleopatra's body and she beamed. "It's so good to see you. You look well." She ran her fingers along Cleopatra's white cashmere cardigan.

"Thanks. Enjoy your stay." Cleopatra turned and walked away.

Supriti grabbed her arm. "Don't walk away from me like that."

"What's the problem? I was cordial, now I'm leaving."

"That's what I don't want you to do anymore. You have an amazing ass but I would rather look in your eyes than always watch you walk away from me. I miss your eyes."

"Hey, Cleopatra." Mandisa swooped in and saved the day. Supriti was annoyed by the interruption; she always wanted Cleopatra to herself, now Mandisa was just in her way. Never mind that if it weren't for Mandisa she wouldn't be at the retreat in the first place, or even know that Cleopatra existed. Friends or not, deep down, Supriti wished that Mandisa would just disappear.

"Great idea bringing her, Disa," Cleopatra whispered in her ear.

"What do you mean?" Cleopatra's sarcasm was lost on Mandisa, since she had no idea of the time they had spent together or the moves that Supriti had been making on Cleopatra every chance she got.

Cleopatra spoke softly in Mandisa's ear. "You need to do something about your girl. There's nothing wrong with a little harmless flirting, but she means harm. Talk some sense into her before things go horribly wrong and she gets herself in real trouble."

Cleopatra cleared her throat and spoke so Supriti could hear her. "I was just about to head to the next session. Check you later, ladies." She threw her hand up and waved goodbye.

Mandisa yelled. "Save me a seat at dinner, Cleopatra." Her

nostrils flared as she veered at Supriti. "We need to talk."

☼☼☼

At dinner, Mandisa didn't show up, but Supriti did.

"Disa came down with a nasty bout of diarrhea." Supriti smiled. "It was horrible. Seems she got her teas mixed up and had two cups of Smooth Move instead of her usual chamomile. She's still riding it out." She laughed.

"Damn. Two cups?" Cleopatra cringed and held her stomach.

Cleopatra and Supriti sat together and had dinner. The whole time Cleopatra debated whether she should tell Jacqueline that Supriti was there, though Supriti was on her best behavior—probably only because they were sitting in a group of ten. Cleopatra was certain that the large group setting had foiled Supriti's plans for an intimate dinner with her, since she assumed that she was responsible for Mandisa's bout with the violent diarrhea. So Supriti switching Mandisa's usual tea for a laxative tea was a wasted effort. Dinners at job retreats were never intimate affairs, and Cleopatra was thankful for the protection her coworkers afforded her. But fighting off Supriti's subtle advances and discreet innuendos could still be exhausting.

After dessert, she got a text from Jacqueline to go back to her room so they could video chat. Cleopatra said her goodnights to everyone and made her way to her room. When she approached the door to her suite, Supriti bolted off the elevator behind her and called her name.

"Wait, Cleopatra."

Cleopatra stopped and looked down the narrow, dimly lit hallway. "What?" She grabbed the doorknob to her suite.

"What else? You and me?" Supriti walked up to her and slid her hand around Cleopatra's neck. Cleopatra quickly pulled it away. "Let me come inside. Your wife never has to know. She doesn't know I'm here, does she?"

"I haven't talked to her since you popped up, but of course I plan on telling her. I'm not keeping this from her." Cleopatra leaned back on her door. "Good night. My wife is expecting my call."

"Don't you want me?"

"Not even a little bit. I love my wife."

"You don't mean that. And I didn't ask if you loved your wife. One thing has nothing to do with the other."

"Good night." Cleopatra was convinced that Supriti was actually nuts because she refused to hear her. Her aggressiveness wasn't attractive; it just reeked of desperation. The only person who could pull off that level of aggression was Jacqueline. And that was because she was her wife, and could get away with it. Cleopatra pushed the door open to her room.

"Let me come in for a night cap," Supriti pleaded with her.

Suddenly the door to Cleopatra's suite flung all the way open. Jacqueline stood in the doorway in a black lace teddy and stilettos.

"Damn." Cleopatra's mouth fell open. "It must be hard to be that fine." She smiled.

Jacqueline pushed past her and mushed Supriti in the face, shoving her back up against the wall in the hallway.

"Her bitch is here. You can leave." Jacqueline pointed down

the hall to the elevator.

Supriti froze, with both of her palms pressed firmly against the wall, stunned that Jacqueline had magically appeared. She was frightened of Jacqueline, and couldn't hide it.

Cleopatra didn't think someone so bold to openly chase someone else's wife would back down so easily.

Jacqueline took Cleopatra by the hand and motioned to her. "Get down on your knees."

Cleopatra wasn't sure what she was about to do, but she kneeled before her wife. Jacqueline lifted her leg and flung it over Cleopatra's shoulder, who caught her thigh in mid-air.

Supriti saw the large tattoo on Jacqueline's inner thigh with Cleopatra's name on it. Then she saw Cleopatra kiss the tattoo, stand up, and kiss her wife.

"I've been thinking about you all day, Daddy," Jacqueline said to Cleopatra. "You got something for me?"

"You know I do." Cleopatra kissed her and went inside the room.

Jacqueline crossed her arms and stared at Supriti. "Don't you have somewhere else to be? Or do you plan on listening at the door? You know what? You'll probably be able to hear us from there, because it's so good. And I can get loud. You should whip out that pink vibrator of yours when you listen to us. But put it on the lowest setting. We can go for hours, because my wife likes to take her time."

Supriti gasped.

"Yeah. I saw the picture. Cleopatra never mentioned it to you? That's because she's too nice. We laughed, hard. How you manage to maintain such a high level of thirst consistently escapes me. I mean it's commendable. It's real and I respect it.

You're not half-ass in your quest to quench that thirst. Like I always say, go hard or go home. So I'm gonna go in the room now with my wife and go hard and uh … you go home."

Supriti walked off down the hall.

"Before you go." Jacqueline snapped her fingers. "How many times does my wife have to tell you she doesn't want you? I heard it with my own ears. Look, I understand. If she wasn't mine I would be chasing after her too. She's actually everything: sexy, smart, sweet, and intelligent. And you know what else? She's married, and she's loyal. So I don't know why you keep putting yourself in danger."

"Danger?"

"Don't get confused because I'm not hollering or cursing or rolling my neck and popping my tongue or clucking like a bird when I talk to you. I'm not a basic bitch, I'm a grown-ass woman." She walked up to Supriti and touched her nose with her own. "So when I say danger, I'm asking what price you're willing to pay. How far are you willing to go for her? This can get dirty, it can get real physical if you want to take it there. Keep it up."

Supriti turned to walk down the hall without answering.

"You'll never have her." Jacqueline said.

Supriti stopped and looked at her as she waited for the elevator.

"Never." Jacqueline smirked as she opened the door and joined Cleopatra.

TWENTY THREE

....

CASE OF THE EX

"Does anyone know that man?" César pointed across the playground to the eerie stranger. It was the beginning of April, spring was in the air on an unseasonably warm day, and César had taken Maya and Amir to the park not too far from the house. He watched the children play on the jungle gym as he sat and chatted with the other nannies. It was a sight to see, the 6'4" gay Italian man gossiping among the petite Latina and Caribbean nannies.

All of the other nannies shook their head "no" at his question, though. They had all seen the strange man before, but they didn't know him and he didn't have a child.

"I don't like it." César watched the man lurk around the perimeter of the playground, looking intently at the children. On this day, César was convinced that the man had zeroed in on Maya and Amir.

Just as César crept across the park to approach the man, the mysterious stranger ran off. But the next day he returned and César confronted him directly. He was immediately hostile, and that raised César's suspicions. The other nannies flagged down a police officer, who removed the man from the park and warned him not to return.

But he returned again anyway, and appeared to take pictures with his camera phone. César, convinced that he'd taken pictures of Amir and Maya, approached the man. They exchanged words again, and César demanded to see his cell phone. Backed into a corner, the man swung on César and missed. César—an otherwise gentle soul—pummeled the man right there in the middle of the park in front of Maya and Amir and all the neighborhood children. The other nannies gathered the kids to shield them from the fight and called 911.

The man was no match for César, who beat and detained him until the police arrived. César immediately called Jacqueline, who had just returned home from the three-day retreat a few days before, and was finally unpacking her and Cleopatra's suitcases and doing laundry.

By the time Jacqueline got to the playground, the ambulance had already taken the strange man away. She panicked until she had her arms wrapped around both Amir and Maya and saw that they were fine.

But the story César told her didn't calm her nerves. Some man taking pictures of the kids. "Who was it?"

César tried to describe him to Jacqueline as an EMT tended to his bruised and cut-up knuckles. He showed her a grainy video that he had taken. The man was a tall, skinny, scraggly black man with a receding hair line, wearing old clothes.

César leaned over and whispered in Jacqueline's ear. "I said nothing to the police, but at one point when I was beating him, he said he was their father."

A short time later, after she left work, Cleopatra emerged from the subway and turned her corner only to see someone standing outside their house.

"What the hell?" Her cell phone went off, alerting her to a seven missed calls from Jacqueline, and it didn't take long before she realized it was Shawn pacing back and forth on the sidewalk.

"I know you were out of town last week, but I haven't heard from you in a while. You haven't responded to my texts or anything. So I figured I would catch you on your way home. I came to ask what's up."

Cleopatra ignored her and didn't speak a word, just walked past her and proceeded up the steps to her front door. She stopped, then, and walked back down the steps and looked Shawn in the face.

"What the hell is that?" She pointed to the scar on Shawn's left cheek where the bandage had been, then noticed she was eating a bag of Funyuns. "Who the hell still eats Funyuns?"

"It's not what you think. It wasn't Olivia. Robin did it." Shawn patted her face lightly where the stitches had just been taken out a few days earlier. "She kind of cracked a bottle over my head the night we broke up." She cringed in anticipation of Cleopatra's reaction.

"What?" Cleopatra leaned in to get a closer look at the wound.

"I'm going to a plastic surgeon, so you won't even be able to tell I had it." Shawn smiled, seemingly proud of herself.

"Robin is a lot of things, but I didn't know she was violent. Why the hell would she bust you over the head with a bottle?"

Shawn looked at Cleopatra, knowing she would be even more disappointed in her, and stuttered a bit. "I, um…" She exhaled hard and shrugged her shoulders. "I choked her."

Cleopatra had a blank look on her face. She thought for a moment, unable to hide her disgust. "Since when do you put your hands on a woman? Are you crazy? What the hell is wrong with you? You're lucky." She shook her head, realizing Shawn had no excuse for her behavior. "I would have stabbed your ass in the stomach with that broken bottle after I cracked it over your head and left you to bleed out." She turned and walked back up the steps.

Shawn followed her up to the front door. "At least hear my side."

"You have no side. That's abuse, plain and simple."

"It's not like I hit her," Shawn said.

"Pushing and shoving, choking, that's abuse. This isn't your first time is it?" Shawn didn't answer her. "It's a good thing she left your ass, kept her from having to kill you, and I wouldn't have blamed her. Your ass is too big to even be fighting some men. You need help."

Shawn nodded her head. "I'll think about it."

"Whatever you do, you better hope Robin doesn't tell her sister that you put your hands on her. Jacqueline's the one who taught Robin how to fight. She'll fuck you up."

"Why you think I'm out here walking back and forth? I didn't want to take a chance."

"Shh … You hear that?" Cleopatra stopped and listened at the front door. "Yelling." She rushed to put her key in the door and walked in on Jacqueline in the foyer, standing with a man she didn't recognize immediately and César.

The man had wide black eyes. His thick, wavy, soot-black hair was worn in a style that reminded her of guys who still wore Dax and doused their hair with S-Curl before stepping out on a Saturday night. But his hairline was retreating from his forehead and he was sweating profusely.

He was tall, but much thinner than the muscular build that Cleopatra remembered from years before. His skin was dark and his face was bruised and swollen, like he had just taken a beating. He had a crooked nose and small feet for his height. He was unshaven and his stonewashed jeans were wrinkled as if they had dried in a ball.

His name was Alonzo.

This is probably how I would look too, if Jacqueline divorced me, Cleopatra thought to herself.

"Hey, César." Cleopatra noticed his bandaged hand and how he paced about, and pointed to Jacqueline's ex-husband. "What's he doing here?"

"Baby." Jacqueline pulled Cleopatra to the side and hugged her hard. She could tell that Jacqueline had been crying; her face was wet with tears and she shook as Cleopatra held her.

"What is it?"

"He's trying to take the kids." She held tightly on to Cleopatra. "He's suing for full custody."

"No." Cleopatra shook her head. "That's never going to happen."

"Never gonna happen." Shawn folded her arms across her chest and leaned on the arched doorway to the living room.

"Never," César agreed.

"I'm going to go upstairs and check on the kids. They were taking their nap; I want to make sure we didn't wake them up."

Cleopatra wiped a tear from Jacqueline's face with her thumb and watched her go up the stairs. César followed close behind her. Then she and Shawn surrounded the man and stared him down.

"Stonewashed jeans? Who wears stonewashed jeans still? And how wrinkled do they have to be to actually look wrinkled?" Shawn laughed at her own joke.

Alonzo laughed nervously. "I know you're going to try and hire the best attorney that money can buy," he said to Cleopatra. He ran his hand across the mahogany side table in the foyer, and looked into the living room. "Look. I'm in a piece of shit hotel by the airport. I have enough money to last me about three more days here." He pulled on the hair at the nape of his neck.

That's when Cleopatra saw the burn marks on his fingers.

"I'm not trying to take this to court, that's not what this is about," he whispered. "Just write me a check now and this can all go away." He laughed. "You can just give me all of that attorney money and however much it would take to support them until they're about eighteen and ready to go off to college. And then I'll need whatever their college tuition would be." He rubbed his palms together. "You keep the kids. I'll leave like I was never here. Jacqueline doesn't have to know a thing. She'll get emotional and it'll get messy. Let's leave her out of it." He winked at Cleopatra.

Cleopatra was in shock, but she burst into laughter, then sniffed the air and stepped closer to Alonzo. When she sniffed him again, she smelled the pungent scent of ammonia. "This motherfucker is high. Or he's just coming down. What are you on, meth?"

Shawn grunted and pushed him up against the wall, catching him off guard.

"Stop. What are you doing?" Cleopatra pulled Shawn away

from him.

"She's trying to kill me!" Alonzo yelled at the top of his lungs.

Just then Jacqueline and César rushed down the stairs.

"What are you doing? Putting your hands on people is how you solve every problem? Get the fuck out of here," Cleopatra yelled as César grabbed Shawn by the scruff of her neck like a cat and pushed her toward the front door. "I don't even know why you're here!" Cleopatra screamed at her.

"He can't just run up in here and think he can have his way."

"Get out!" Jacqueline yelled, terrified.

Cleopatra slammed the door in Shawn's face. Alonzo looked at Cleopatra and Jacqueline, and burst into laughter.

"You sic your mannish friend on me and your man nanny already beat the shit out of me." His face twitched as he talked and he wiped the sweat from his forehead with the sleeve of his black bubble jacket. "My attorney will love this."

"You'll never get custody. You have never been a father to them. How are you just going to show up over four years later and try to claim them?"

Alonzo paused and his eyes trailed off to the right, his pupils dilated. "You lied about being a lesbian."

"Motherfucker, you were the only one that knew I was gay. Remember?" Jacqueline said.

"You can't prove that." He smirked. "We had sex once, you got pregnant, I tried to be a man and marry you, and I got nothing in return. Well, that's about to change. You think a judge is actually going to believe you? And your millionaire escort wife here?" he said.

How in the hell would he know about me being an escort? Cleopatra wondered.

"No judge will ever let you keep my kids," he said to Jacqueline. "I mean, how many women have you been with anyway?" he asked Cleopatra.

"This is not about Cleopatra."

"It will be by the time I'm done with her. You gave up the kids for her before, you can do it again."

"They were nine months old when you left. They don't even know you." Jacqueline scowled at him. "And you think you're just going to swoop in and take them? All of a sudden you're interested in them? Why is that? You may be their biological father, but Cleopatra has been their daddy. She takes care of them, provides them with a roof over their head, clothes on their backs, and food in their bellies." She grabbed Cleopatra's hand.

"I'm remarried now, to a straight, God-fearing woman. She's in church every day of the week. And we look good on paper. Judges like that."

Cleopatra laughed out loud. "Sorry." She cleared her throat, reminiscing about the many sweaty weekends she'd spent with those God-fearing five-nighters.

The corners of Alonzo's mouth turned up slightly as he turned and flicked through the *O Magazine* on the side table in the foyer. "I could get used to this."

"You need to leave." Cleopatra opened the door, letting the cold air rush into the house, and stared at him. As he stepped out onto the steps, he turned and spoke to her in a whisper so neither Jacqueline or César could hear.

"Fancy house, fancy job. Think you can have everything? My wife, my kids? Actually, you can have them. But all that money? I'm gonna need most of that. Someone has to pay. Might as well be you."

Cleopatra stared at him without speaking for so long that it made him uncomfortable. He got jumpy and couldn't control his facial tics. He cleared his throat and nervously straightened out his jacket, then handed her a slip of paper. "Here's how you can reach me. You have forty-eight hours. Pay up and everyone wins. Or you'll hear from my attorney, and you don't want that. Given how ridiculous your world is, the courts will rule in my favor, no doubt about it." He turned to leave.

"I know your type," Cleopatra said. "You'll never get a dime from me."

He turned around and was greeted by her sinister smile, one eyebrow towering over the other.

"You know why?" Cleopatra continued. "Because you're the ridiculous one. You think you're going to come back and scare my wife, and blackmail me into financing your dusty-ass life and your little drug binges. Jacqueline told me you weren't shit. Look, I'll give you whatever's in my pockets." Alonzo smiled as he looked down at Cleopatra's hands in anticipation.

She dug into her coat pocket, pulled out her clenched fist, and jerked her arm like she was going to punch him. He flinched and tripped over his own feet, then fell down the steps.

✿✿✿

"How the hell are we going to prove that he just wants money?" Jacqueline was furious when Cleopatra told her later that night about her exchange with Alonzo. Cleopatra only waited because she'd briefly considered paying him off to go away, and then thought better of it.

"I don't know. But he asked me straight out to write him a check," Cleopatra said. "I think we know how he's living. He admitted to staying in some hot sheets hotel by the airport and he was clearly high on something."

"That's crazy. I never knew him to do anything but smoke weed. But even if he is broke, and I'm sure he is because people don't change, that's not proof of anything. We need proof that he asked for money to drop the case."

"It's a motive for him coming out of nowhere. It makes sense. He just doesn't want you to know he wants money."

"I believe you, baby, but there's no evidence. The only thing we know for sure is that he can't be trusted. What if it's some kind of trap? What if we gave him something and then he turned around and accused us of bribery to make this case go away?"

"That's a good point. I hadn't thought about that," Cleopatra admitted.

"I don't know. Maybe he is having regrets and actually does want to be with the kids."

"Really?" Cleopatra looked at her sideways. "I know you don't have a lot of experience dealing with hustles, but this is a big one."

"I'm not taking any chances with my children." Jacqueline said. "We're getting an attorney."

TWENTY FOUR

....

IF IT PLEASES THE COURT

"I need to know how far you two are willing to go to ensure you're awarded custody of the kids. You're paying me a lot of money, so with that comes a certain level of creativity."

Vanessa Cohen, who didn't sleep much, looked like she didn't eat much either, and liked people even less than she liked food. Vanessa, who as Vanessa Goldberg lost her husband to a younger and more attractive woman and later on her three children and her home in a bitter divorce and custody battle. Her ex-husband's money and connections were no match for the naïve and unskilled high school graduate. She swore from that day forward to fight for those who had no voice, and after college and law school, and a few high-profile court battles, she became exactly what she despised: a high-priced Upper East Side attorney that would do anything to win.

Jacqueline and Cleopatra had met with Vanessa once before, but only briefly, to discuss the custody case. That first meeting was an uneventful one; they gave basic information and she agreed to take them on as clients. She called and asked to meet with them on short notice once she reviewed the paperwork from Alonzo's attorney. Not liking her tone and the urgency in her voice, both Jacqueline and Cleopatra dropped everything when she summoned them to her office to have what she called a "no bullshit" conversation.

The unseasonably warm weather had continued—62 degrees in April—and Cleopatra wondered why Vanessa was dressed like a cat burglar, in a black wool turtleneck and black slacks. The attorney looked at Cleopatra and Jacqueline without speaking. Her nose and mouth were often scrunched together as if something stunk; otherwise she would have been a fairly attractive woman. Cleopatra wondered if her choice of profession had soured her face and strengthened her chin.

"Alonzo refuses to settle this in mediation." Vanessa's shoulders dropped. "He wants to go before a judge. But I'm not surprised. He has a solid case." She drummed her fingers on the top of her mahogany desk. "Look at it from his lawyer's perspective. You have Jacqueline, a switch hitter, bisexual."

"I'm not bi. I'm a lesbian." Jacqueline raised her eyebrows as she turned and looked at Cleopatra.

"Ok." The woman was startled at Jacqueline's correction. "The facts." She stuck her pen into her curly, ash gray hair. "Jacqueline conceived twins with him, married him, shipped the children off to her parents in New Jersey, left him to be a lesbian, pursued Cleopatra while keeping her marriage and children a secret from her, and then divorced him."

Cleopatra shook her head and sunk lower in to her chair. "Damn, just sounds bad." Jacqueline scowled at Cleopatra. "What?" she shrugged her shoulders.

"Do you mind if I smoke?" Vanessa asked them.

"Yes, I do," both Jacqueline and Cleopatra said in unison.

"No problem." She got up and poured herself a glass of scotch from a mini bar disguised as a file cabinet behind her desk.

Cleopatra looked at her watch: 12:11PM. "Cigarettes and scotch. That breath must be kicking."

"I heard you," Vanessa snapped at her.

Jacqueline slapped Cleopatra's arm.

"There seems to be a few things that you neglected to tell me during our first meeting, ladies." Vanessa began. "We need to straighten everything out right now. You want me to convince a judge that you're serious about being a family? That the kids are where they're supposed to be? You need to explain this to me, be honest with me. I need to know everything if we're going to prove to the court that the kids are in a stable, nurturing, and loving home."

"They are," Jacqueline defended herself. She leaned over to Cleopatra and whispered, "I thought you said she was the best."

"She is." Cleopatra nodded. "I didn't say she wasn't a bitch."

Only a few days had passed since Alonzo came back into their lives, destroying the peaceful home they had worked so hard to build. Now they sat in the office of one of NYC's sharpest family law attorneys. She wasn't friendly, compassionate, warm, or a hopeless romantic. What she was, was a winner and a shark. Cleopatra wasn't sure what she was alluding to when she asked how far they were willing to go. But from the moment they sat down, it didn't feel right to her. She wasn't a fan of her cigar bar-like office housed in the basement of a brownstone, with no windows. Her body craved sunlight, and she even entertained purchasing a seasonal depression lamp and having it sent to the office anonymously.

"This is what it comes down to," Vanessa continued. "He's suing you on the grounds that you're an unfit mother. And to support that claim, he has listed a slew of offenses against you, your lifestyle, and Cleopatra and her associates." She took a gulp of scotch. "I was reading through these allegations earlier … I mean, really? You can't write this stuff." She started to laugh but caught herself when she saw that neither Cleopatra nor Jacqueline shared in her amusement.

Cleopatra sank back in her chair. She knew that even though there was a good reason behind all the claims, it looked terrible on paper, and she wasn't confident that they would be able to overcome them even with Vanessa leading the charge.

"Cleopatra is a bad influence and no role model," she continued. "Her associates? An ex-lover Kenya Rampersad is in prison now for plotting a contract killing against you, Jacqueline. Your nanny César Santo pummeled Alonzo in front of a playground full of kids, including yours. Her friend Shawnette Donovan is just downright dangerous. She jumped him in your home. Seriously? You're lucky he didn't call the police."

"She didn't hurt him," Cleopatra attempted to explain. Jacqueline covered her face, mortified that she tried to defend Shawn's behavior.

"She shouldn't be anywhere near the children. I think you both realize that now. See that she stays far away from them. Did you know there are videos online of her fighting in the street?"

"What? Really?" Cleopatra was stunned. Olivia's goons

didn't do public beat downs, but who else could she be fighting? Probably Robin. She made a mental note to check World Star Hip Hop for the video.

"She was fighting some girl that was much smaller than her," Vanessa continued. "But she got her ass kicked. The glue trap killed me." She shook with laughter, then cleared her throat. "Cleopatra, consider that friendship a wrap."

"Not a problem, we don't hang anymore." Cleopatra dragged her thumb across her neck as if to cut her own throat. "Glue trap?"

"Cleopatra, there's also an unsubstantiated claim that you were involved in the escort business several years ago."

"How the hell did...? Excuse me." Cleopatra caught herself. "Now how would he know anything about that?" She sneered at Jacqueline. *I wouldn't grant us custody, either,* she thought to herself. Then she regained her composure. "There's no proof of that."

The woman looked at Cleopatra and exhaled. "You know what? If you say there's no proof, I believe you." She rubbed her temples. "But if there isn't proof of that, there is proof that you were incredibly promiscuous."

"I'll give you that," Cleopatra agreed. "I was also single at the time."

"What about Shawn's activities?"

"Uh, there is a way to prove all that," Cleopatra acknowledged.

"I know. I have her record right here." She patted a thick manila folder. "Shoplifting, receiving stolen property, endangering a child, public intoxication, resisting arrest, writing bad checks, sex with a minor, producing child porn, possession of child porn, a civil suit involving a statutory rape case that she settled out of court for an undisclosed amount of money, and she has the lowest credit score I've ever seen." Jacqueline scowled at Cleopatra. "She's taken out at least ten restraining orders on ex-girlfriends and an ex burned her apartment building down. I mean, what are you two doing to these women?" She laughed.

"Can we focus here?" Jacqueline interrupted.

"And several arrests for unlawful possession of marijuana," Vanessa continued. "How is she still walking the streets?"

Jacqueline looked at Cleopatra. "Who are you hanging out with?"

The attorney and Jacqueline waited for Cleopatra to answer.

"We don't hang anymore."

"But you've been friends some twenty years," Vanessa reminded her.

"How many times do I have to say we don't hang anymore? Ok I didn't know about like two or three … five of those. Or the marijuana possession. She doesn't usually keep weed long enough to get caught with it, so that's a surprise."

"Enough about Shawn. I have to ask you, are all of the other accusations listed here true?"

They looked at each other and at the same time said, "Well."

"You first," Cleopatra conceded to Jacqueline.

"He knew I was gay when we had sex that one and only time, because we were best friends before. So that's a lie. He thought he could change me. He got mad because he couldn't."

"He claims that you cheated on him with Cleopatra when you were still married."

"Legally, we were still married. But we had separated long

before I ever met Cleopatra. He dated women throughout our entire marriage. If I cheated on him and he gave a damn, why didn't he claim that shit in the divorce proceedings?"

Cleopatra looked at Jacqueline, shocked that she cursed at the attorney.

"He claims he wanted out of the marriage as quickly as possible because you had already moved on with your life and he was anxious to move on with his." She flipped through the papers. "And the kids?"

"My parents took the kids because I was in grad school and working part time, and couldn't afford daycare. I couldn't do it all by myself. He never did his part, even back then. It became too much and I left school to go to work full time so I could support us. But even after I got a full-time job I still couldn't afford daycare for two kids with all our other expenses. So they stayed with my parents in Jersey the majority of the time. You do know it's expensive to live in New York City, right?"

Vanessa let Jacqueline's sarcasm role off her back. "Did you lie to Cleopatra about your marital status and that you had two children?"

Cleopatra nodded her head. "Yup."

"And there is truth to the allegations, Cleopatra, that you have a reputation for having a lot of women. And you slept with some of them for money?"

Cleopatra twisted her lips. "You asked me that before. He won't be able to prove it. Next question."

Jacqueline looked at Cleopatra, annoyed. "What?" Cleopatra asked nonchalantly, but she knew she was going to have to put a stop to any further investigation as far as previous associates. That was not an option.

And as they sat there listening to Vanessa, both Cleopatra and Jacqueline, without uttering a word to the other, decided that Alonzo's sudden appearance out of the blue and his wealth of information on them had big-mouthed Robin written all over it. And again, without words or eye contact, they both planned to deal with Robin in due time.

Cleopatra thought that she might have to get Olivia and Alexis involved … and if she did, Robin would be in a world of trouble. Jacqueline would be the least of her worries. Her big sister could rough her up, but Alexis and Olivia would wreck her. First Robin had told Jacqueline about her past as an escort, now she'd seemingly brought Jacqueline's ex-husband back into the mix, undoubtedly for a payday. She had caused nothing but trouble in their marriage, and would have to be taught a lesson sooner rather than later.

Jacqueline reached over and squeezed Cleopatra's hand. "Isn't what's best for the children always taken into consideration? Would they really take them from me?" she asked Vanessa.

"There are many factors. It's always in the best interest of the children. And it has to be pretty bad for them to take the kids away from the mother. The court looks at who has been the principal caregiver all along, their parenting skills, and so on. But you never know…" She shrugged her shoulders.

Cleopatra was annoyed that Vanessa wasn't more positive.

"Honestly, this doesn't look great. He looks like a victim. Jacqueline, whether you were honest with him or not about your sexuality, you got pregnant, married him, and then told him you wanted to be with women."

"He left the kids before they were even walking and barely talking, and hasn't seen them or given me a dime to support them since. They never said 'daddy,' they said 'mommy.' They don't know him. They don't ask about him. He was never a father. How does that look good?" Jacqueline was getting upset now. "He had his boys over to the house smoking weed around my babies, and had random women over when he was supposed to be watching the babies, while I was at work or at school. I'd come home to hungry, crying babies that had been in soiled diapers all day long. How does that look stable?"

"He never gave you a dime because you didn't sue for support, that's interesting," Vanessa said.

"Sue for what? He wasn't working. Anyway, if he could pick up and never see his kids again I didn't want a dime from him—didn't want any contact with him at all. He didn't even want visitation then, much less custody when the marriage ended."

Vanessa leaned back in her chair. "You have any dirt on him? Anything we can use?"

"Besides him being a deadbeat, runaway father? No," Jacqueline said. "I hadn't seen him in over four years until last week."

"I think he's on meth. He was definitely high when we saw him. And he's just here for money," Cleopatra interjected. "He told me he didn't want the kids. Said I could have them. Said I was going to have to pay, and asked me to write him a check."

Vanessa was stunned. "He said that? And you're just telling me this now? Do you have it on tape or video?"

"Who do I look like? James Bond?" Cleopatra shrugged her

shoulders.

Vanessa looked like she wanted to respond with a smart quip of her own, but caught herself and instead took another gulp of scotch. "Ok, so there's no proof that he actually said that? We would need him on tape, otherwise it won't matter. We can't use hearsay to get this case dismissed."

"He complained about my having money. He was looking around our home like he was shopping and taking inventory."

"Being broke doesn't mean he just wants money rather than his kids. And remember, we don't know that he's not setting us up," Jacqueline said.

"I know that, but he actually said he didn't want the kids, Jacqueline. He wasn't lying about that." Cleopatra was annoyed. "He said I could have them. Damn, what else does he need to say?"

"He needs to say a lot more and we need some type of proof that he said it," Vanessa intervened. "Look, I know you're frustrated, Cleopatra, and it makes a lot of sense now, him coming out of the blue all of a sudden when he'd shown absolutely no interest before. What did he say specifically about the money?"

"He said that he was going to need my money. Most of it, he said. He wanted however much it would cost to support them to eighteen, and put them through college, and then he'd disappear like he was never here. I plan on hiring a private investigator. They'll get into his background and even his financials."

"None of this will make a difference," Jacqueline said, frustrated at the entire conversation. "He didn't come out and say give me money or I'm taking the kids. And he's not going to."

Cleopatra rolled her eyes. "He actually kind of did."

"Cleopatra, have your investigator dig deep. It can't hurt. I'll request that he be tested for all illegal substances as well. If he's an addict this case is a wrap, so cross your fingers for that. Because there has to be something to combat what you two and your associates have going on here in these files. And make sure they look into his new wife's background too; no one is as squeaky clean as he's claiming. Since she's the kids' step-mother, any blemishes on her record can only help your case."

"Are we done with this subject?" Jacqueline asked Cleo-patra. "Can we discuss how we're going to win this so we can move on with our lives? What's your strategy?" she asked Vanessa.

"You should know that if the court finds neither of you or Alonzo is a suitable parent, which in this instance is entirely possible, they can order the kids into foster care. In that case, your best strategy would be to try to get them placed with their grandparents. Your parents Jacqueline, not his."

"Of course mine. His aren't even in the picture anymore."

"Yes they are. They're listed as next of kin as well."

Jacqueline was furious. "They haven't spoken to me or seen the kids in years! Not since I came out. They wanted nothing to do with us and told me as much."

"Are you seriously doing this right now? That's not what she meant by strategy, anyway," Cleopatra snapped.

"Cleopatra, I have to think one hundred steps ahead of eve-ryone. Every possible scenario and outcome. You have to trust me."

There was a knock on the door and Vanessa's young, blonde assistant entered.

"I'm sorry to interrupt, but it's about the Giovannis' case.

You asked me to let you know as soon as a judge was assigned."

Vanessa pulled her to the side, where they began whispering in the corner of her office. Then Vanessa let a "shit," slip from her lips. She grabbed the back of her neck as if to dull a sharp pain. Her assistant left the office, closing the door quietly behind her. Vanessa sat back down and looked at Cleopatra and Jacqueline for what seemed like forever before she spoke.

"Your judge has been assigned." She exhaled. "Honestly, he's a homophobe. He will rule against you before he even sees you. Just because he can."

Jacqueline leaned forward, with her head in her hands. "Then what are we supposed to do?"

"Listen carefully to what I'm about to say. Cleopatra, just listen before you get upset."

Cleopatra's ears perked up and she was now prepared to do just that—get upset.

"There's something that I've done in the past with this judge, and it's worked. I've won every time. That's why I'll ask again: How far are you willing to go?"

"Would you just say it?" Cleopatra asked, annoyed.

"The last lesbian couple that went before this judge broke up. That's it. That simple." Vanessa leaned back in her chair. "They got a divorce and lived in separate residences until it pleased they court."

Cleopatra stared hard at her, confused.

"Hear me out, Cleopatra." She held her hand up to keep her from interrupting. "The birth mother declared that she would resume a heterosexual lifestyle and agreed to court-ordered counseling."

"You're serious?" Cleopatra burst out laughing. Jacqueline laughed too, but her smile soon turned to a frown.

"And the judge awarded her full custody," Vanessa continued.

"You're out of your mind, that's crazy," Cleopatra dismissed her.

"Did they get back together?" Jacqueline cut Cleopatra off. "Did they get remarried?"

"Yeah. Of course," Vanessa said. "They only did it to win the case. They were very much in love." She hesitated for a bit. "But they broke up again a few months later."

"So wait, you're basically saying that this judge would rather have the kids in a straight one-parent home than in a gay two-parent home?" Cleopatra asked.

Vanessa nodded. "That's what it comes down to."

"Why the hell are you even telling us this?"

"I wanted you to know your options. That's what you're paying me for. You want to keep the children? This is how we play the game. This is how we win it."

"I'm not playing games and I'm not paying you to break us up. Do your damn job."

"Cleopatra. When I've played by the rules with this judge, I've lost. You know what that means? It means the kids were taken. Then the marriages suffered and eventually ended in divorce anyway."

"So you won against him? Every time you've used this strategy?" Jacqueline interrupted.

"Five times now. Every time I've tried this tactic. Every time the couple got a divorce."

"Did the other four couples get back together?" Jacqueline

asked.

Vanessa hesitated. "No, they pretty much stayed divorced. A few of them remarried other people, though, and they still co-parent. I sincerely doubted you would agree to this tactic. But I did want to tell you about the option."

Jacqueline was quiet, and Cleopatra was shocked silent.

"So this is how it would work, if you were to go this route," Vanessa continued. "I'll advise the court of your intentions to divorce. You'll file separation papers first." She turned to Jacqueline. "This shows that you're serious, and then as we get closer to the court date, Jacqueline, you'll file divorce papers. You'd need to live separately starting almost immediately. That's the first thing this judge will investigate. Cleopatra, you can come and pick the kids up for visits, but no extended time or overnight stays with Jacqueline. If they think you're still living as a married couple, and not just co-parenting, this won't work."

"Seriously? Ok. Thanks. You can stop talking now," Cleopatra interrupted. "Now I hope you have a better strategy than that because your check hasn't cleared yet."

Jacqueline was surprised by how angry Cleopatra was getting, but Cleopatra was so beside herself that she didn't notice Jacqueline's lack of participation in her tirade.

"This is crazy. This is New York City, the gay and lesbian capital of the planet. Can't we just petition for another judge and site prejudice?"

"I'd advise against that. It would start a whole new wave of trouble that we don't want, thanks to the influence this veteran judge yields. His prejudice aside, Cleopatra, you and your associates have a shady past and present, and it's hurting Jacqueline's case tremendously. It's frankly better if you aren't a factor."

"Not a factor? This not a factor just wrote you a fat check."

In the midst of her tantrum, she looked over at Jacqueline, who was deep in thought.

"You have nothing to say? Nothing at all?" Jacqueline bit her lip and looked down at the floor. "You aren't actually considering this, are you?"

Jacqueline tried to speak, but nothing came out.

Cleopatra's eyes filled with tears, but quickly dried as the sorrow was replaced with rage. "Wow." She stood up so abruptly that the chair tipped over behind her. "Well, there it is." She grabbed her messenger bag and flung it over her shoulder. "Ok, so it's obvious I'm not needed here—I'm only in the way. I'm going to go, you just needed my money right? You two can figure this shit out yourselves. Looks like you already have."

"Please don't leave," Vanessa pleaded with her.

"Oh and it gets better—the attorney asks me to stay and my own wife doesn't say shit. Thanks for pretending to care, Vanessa. That didn't go unnoticed." She walked out of the office and slammed the door behind her.

Cleopatra went straight home and started packing. She was loading up her suitcases when Jacqueline got home. She did nothing to stop her; only sat and watched. Cleopatra packed suitcases, rather than a duffle bag like before, and took her luggage downstairs to the front door, where she readied to leave. Neither of them said a word as Jacqueline followed close behind her.

"You know what?" Cleopatra said. "I'm not leaving until

you tell me you don't want me and don't want to be married to me anymore. Look me in my eyes and tell me you want a divorce."

Jacqueline looked Cleopatra square in her eyes. "You know I can't do that. You know that's not what I want. When I married you, it was forever. But your past and friends aren't going to help my case."

"My past? You lied to me about being married and even having children in the first place, and he knows that. That's not necessarily helping either," Cleopatra fired back. "Speaking of which, any idea how he knows all our dirty laundry? Hmmm? You need to check your sister before I run up on her myself."

"Don't touch my sister. That bitch is mine," Jacqueline warned her. "Forget about her right now. I want to fix this. I just want us to be happy again. But I can't lose my children. I won't lose my children."

"You're not going to, baby. It's going to be all right. I promise."

"How can you promise me that? How do you know it's going to be all right? You can't make it go away. You can't fucking fix everything, Cleopatra. Look at me. This isn't what I want." She grabbed Cleopatra by her arm.

"Are you telling me to stay?"

Jacqueline was silent. Cleopatra shook her head, turned around, and started to zip up her garment bag. "Do you want me to move out?" she asked with her back turned, not being able to look Jacqueline in the face.

"No, I don't want you to move out. I don't want you to leave me and the kids, not again."

Cleopatra exhaled a huge sigh of relief.

"But I don't know what else to do. I've made my own mistakes, but your past isn't helping. I've made a decision. We can't—"

Maya and Amir came down the stairs. They'd been napping in their room when Cleopatra arrived home and relieved César.

"Where are you going?" Maya asked when she saw Cleopatra's bags. She tugged on her pants leg.

"I have to go away for a little while."

"Is it work?"

"No. It's not business baby." She picked Maya up and rubbed the sleep out of the corner of her eyes with her thumb.

"Then what? You promised you would never leave again," Maya wailed, immediately going from 0 to 10 as only Maya could do. Cleopatra hugged her tight. "I know, and I'm sorry, sweetie."

Maya clung tight to her neck, nearly choking her. "I want to go with Cleo!" Maya screamed.

Tears streamed down Cleopatra's face as she looked down at Amir, who was looking up at her, wanting her to pick him up too. She extended her arm and scooped him up, now embracing them both.

"You guys are getting heavy." She smiled at them. "I won't be able to do this much longer. I'll come and see you both as soon as I can. Ok? Please take them. I can't," Cleopatra said to Jacqueline.

Amir cried, "No, I want to go with Cleo too."

"Why do you keep leaving us?" Maya asked.

Jacqueline pulled the kids off of Cleopatra and sent them into the living room.

"This right here is why I never dated women with children.

It's not fair to them. They don't understand or deserve any of this."

"We're not dating, you're my wife," Jacqueline said, angry. "We're a family."

"Really? Whatever." Cleopatra sucked her teeth. "What happened to not letting anything or anyone come between us?"

"These are my babies. I put you above them before; I just can't do that again. I can't."

"What happened to you putting off grad school because you wanted our first year of marriage to be perfect? Your exact words were 'I want to be able to focus on my family right now,' and you asked if I would allow you to take care of me for a while!" Cleopatra raged. "What happened to you saying you would never give me a divorce?"

"I know. And I meant all of that." She paused. "But this won't be forever."

Cleopatra was shocked. It appeared that Jacqueline had decided that she was really going to go through with Vanessa's plan. A tear rolled down her cheek.

Jacqueline rarely saw Cleopatra cry and it broke her heart. Tears poured down her own face.

But Cleopatra felt nothing for Jacqueline's tears in that moment.

"So you're going to stop making me a priority after I marry you because you think you got me?" Cleopatra asked her with a smirk on her face as she moved her bags outside to the steps. "That's a big mistake, and so was my falling in love with someone who isn't brave enough to love me back."

Jacqueline ran to the door and grabbed Cleopatra's arm, yanking her back to face her.

"Don't you ever say some shit like that to me again! All I've done since the moment we met is love you. All I've done is be brave in the face of losing everything and everyone I've ever known to love you. Don't ever say anything like that to me again." She pushed Cleopatra outside the door onto the steps. "You know I have no choice!"

"You have a choice." Cleopatra sat one of her suitcases down on the steps. "You could trust and believe in your wife when I tell you I'm going to handle it. When I said to sit your pretty ass down and watch and learn. That was your choice."

"I can't leave it up to chance. I can't risk it."

"Have it your way. I won't do anything, then. I'm not involved in this. I won't hire a private investigator, even though it's obvious that your ex is shady as hell. And I'll just continue paying the bitch that so easily convinced you to divorce me."

"This is not about you!" Jacqueline screamed.

"It's *only* about me. I'm the one you're divorcing. Kicked out of my house, just waiting to be kicked out of my family. Everyone always leaves me. Everyone I love leaves me. My father, my brother, my mother, Shawn. I'm so tired of it. I'm leaving this time."

"That's not fair to your mother and you know that."

"She gave up, Jacqueline. She was sick and didn't want to be here anymore. She wanted to die more than she wanted to stay and be here with me." Tears gushed from Cleopatra's eyes.

Jacqueline was at a loss for words. She had never heard Cleopatra admit her true feelings about her mother's death, and she'd never seen her so inconsolable. She was almost irrational.

"I'm a good person, Jacqueline, I'm an even better wife. I don't expect or ask a lot from people because all they do is let me down. But I do expect a lot from my wife. I wanted you to say I'm not giving my woman up because it was too hard to get here. This is what the fuck is wrong with marriage. It's not a game. Divorce is not a game. You were the first person besides my mother that loved me for who I was, unconditionally. You loved me, you're all I have, and yet you're willing to throw me away. I want you to stick up for me. I want someone for once in my fucking life to think about me and not abandon me. That's what I want."

Cleopatra wiped her face with her sleeve. "I hope you're not so delusional to think that when you divorce me I'm going to stay in a relationship with you, much less remarry you when it's convenient for your life."

PART TOO

FOOLISHNESS

TWENTY FIVE

....

HERE WE GO AGAIN

"Hey there handsome stranger." Teresa hugged Cleopatra tightly as she let her in the back door of the woman's shelter. "What are you doing here at this time of night?"

"I was in the neighborhood." Cleopatra was lucky to catch Teresa before she left for the evening. She'd slept on the old leather couch in her office many nights before when things in her life had gotten out of control.

"Uh-huh. You just happened to be on 11th Avenue? With Louis Vuitton luggage?" Teresa teased.

Cleopatra had stormed out of the house without a plan. All she knew was she didn't want to be alone. So she went to her safe haven. The shelter had changed significantly since she lived there as a teenager, primarily due to her charitable donations. Even though Teresa relented and let Cleopatra make over her office years before, she wouldn't let Cleopatra touch that leather couch. There was now more masking tape holding it together than actual leather.

The small office was otherwise immaculate; and it always smelled of fresh brewed coffee. It was late and the building was eerily quiet. She assumed most of the women and children were in their rooms for the night. Thelonious Monk's *Round Midnight* was whispering from Teresa's speakers when Cleopatra walked in.

"How's your lady doing?" Cleopatra played with Teresa's locs in an attempt to change the subject. Cleopatra was the only one besides Teresa's partner that she let touch her long, silver-gray locs, which had grown down past her knees. Teresa was the reason Cleopatra locked her hair as a teenager.

"My lady is good." Teresa smiled. "She's waiting for me at home. You know, we're getting married. I figured she's not going anywhere now, and we might as well do it."

"Get out of here. After twenty years? You're finally going to do it? That's so romantic of you," Cleopatra teased her. "I told you any woman that takes care of you like you're sick twenty-four/seven when you're not sick—put a ring on it."

Teresa and her partner had always been Cleopatra's role models of black lesbian love when it worked well. It was a love that she had aspired to, even when she ran through women like crazy as a teenager and in her early twenties.

"Your woman can get out on these streets and still get it, and she loves your Birkenstock, lumberjack-with-the-hat-to-match ass anyway," Cleopatra joked. "Tell her I said congratulations. I'll be waiting for my invitation in the mail." She plopped down on the couch. "Are your beds full for the night? I was thinking about staying."

"You know all the beds are full, but you can sleep on the couch as always. It still has your ass groove in it."

"I don't know why you won't let me buy you another couch." She rubbed her hand across the gray masking tape that had curled over and was sticking to her jeans.

"You've bought enough around here; your money is put to better use on other things. Besides, it reminds me where we came from. It's sentimental. But why would you want to sleep on that couch anyway, with that beautiful townhouse of yours and that beautiful wife up in it?"

"Domestic difficulties."

"I see." Teresa shook her head, remembering that the last time Cleopatra popped up unannounced, she'd been out of the house, too. "You didn't want to go to a hotel like you did last time?"

"Don't really want to be alone tonight. You need help with any thing?"

"I think we're pretty much set."

"All right." Cleopatra got up and looked at the bulletin board behind Teresa's desk. Teresa sensed a sadness in her that she hadn't seen in a while.

"How are the kids?"

"They're ok." Cleopatra smiled when she saw the picture that Amir and Maya had drawn for Teresa thumbtacked to the bulletin board. "I'll try and bring them around soon. They love it here."

"You know you'll never be alone here. You're always wel-come. No matter what."

"I know. But it's still good to hear, anyway," Cleopatra said. She smiled as she fingered the yoga class flyer in the activities section of the bulletin board. "Since when do we have yoga classes? That's great."

"Oh yeah." Teresa beamed. "We have a volunteer. She just appeared one day, and she's amazing. She gives so much of her time and love to the women. They're really getting into it. She's even teaching us meditation. You know we need that around here."

"I know you do," Cleopatra laughed.

"I want you to meet her. She's such a sweetheart. I know you love Indian women, and she's stunning."

"I'm good on the Hindu princesses." Cleopatra held her hand up. "Thanks."

"Well if you still want to help out, there's a class going on right now. It should be wrapping up soon. You can help her clean up afterward. I'm going upstairs to the wife. Lock up for me. Come upstairs if you need anything." She kissed Cleopatra, handed her a spare set of keys, and headed out.

"No problem. I got you." Cleopatra walked down the hall to the community room and peeked through the glass pane in the door. The dark, candlelit room was filled with about twenty women, all laid out on their yoga mats. They were in savasana pose, flat out on their backs and covered with blankets.

Cleopatra studied the instructor from behind. *Nice body*, she thought, eying the woman's curves in her yoga shorts and sports bra. She struggled to avert her eyes from the yoga teacher's ass as she walked around the room, guiding the women through a deep meditation. Cleopatra had never seen the usually rowdy group of women and girls so peaceful; this woman was a miracle worker. The instructor went to the front of the room and then banged on a set of Indian singing bowls to bring the women back to full awareness. She put her hands together in Namaste and the women rose and crowded around her, hugging her goodnight before leaving. When Cleopatra entered the room they ran over to greet her, not having seen her as much since she got married.

"Hey, handsome," a soft voice spoke behind.

Cleopatra turned around and saw Supriti. She hadn't recognized her with her hair in a ponytail, practically no clothes on, no makeup, and no Louboutins. She smiled wide when their eyes met and Cleopatra returned her enthusiasm.

"What are you doing here?" Cleopatra asked as Supriti embraced her. She caressed Cleopatra's back with both hands. "So you're the stunning Indian that Teresa was talking about?"

"She's sweet. I was wondering when I would run into you. I was touched by what you told me about this place, so one day I came to see what I could do, and here we are."

"You're kind of incredible for doing this."

"Not really. I understand now what you meant by them giving you way more than you could ever give them. And they love you here. Everyone. I've heard some of the sweetest stories about you. It's so good to see you."

"Good to see you, too. I'm here to help you straighten up, so tell me what you need."

"I'll get the mats, but it would be great if you could grab the blankets and fold them up for me. Please."

"Ok." Cleopatra smiled. "So how have you been?"

"You mean without you in my life?" She slipped a pair of jeans and a t-shirt on over her yoga clothes.

Cleopatra frowned. "That's not what I meant."

"I'm just playing with you." Supriti poked Cleopatra in the stomach. "I've been ok. This place helps tremendously. I hope you don't mind sharing it with me."

"I don't mind at—"

Supriti interrupted Cleopatra. "I have missed the shit out of you." She grabbed Cleopatra and embraced her tight. "Not seeing you is one thing, but not talking at all is crazy," she whispered in her ear, resting her head on Cleopatra's shoulder. "I'm sorry. I had to get that out." She pushed herself away from Cleopatra.

"I thought that's what you wanted."

"It was never what I wanted. It was what I needed to happen so I could try and shut off my feelings for you."

"Did it work?"

"Right now, standing this close to you, I can honestly say … no, it didn't work. And seeing you at that resort in Maine with your wife didn't help."

"I don't know what to say. I'm sorry you're still going through it."

"Don't be." She shrugged her shoulders. "So how are you? What are you doing here at this time of night?"

Cleopatra put her head down a bit.

"What's up with you?" Supriti prodded for more information.

"I came to spend the night. I'll probably stay on T's couch in her office."

"Are you shitting me right now? Why would you have to spend the night here?" She threw her hands up in the air. "Why am I staying away from you when your wife doesn't treat you right? When are you going to have enough of her hurting you?"

"What?"

"You heard me. I'm talking about everything she's put you through. What is it now?"

Cleopatra shook her head. "You don't know the whole story. But I don't want to talk about it. I decided to come here instead of a hotel so I could get a little love."

"And you run into me. Isn't that something?" Supriti smiled. "You asked me to back off and I did. But you're not happy and I have a real problem with that. Come on." She grabbed her hand. "You're coming home with me. I'll take care of you."

"Uh, hell no." Cleopatra snatched her hand back and stopped in her tracks.

"I'm not taking 'no' for an answer."

"That's why I'm not going home with you," Cleopatra laughed.

"There are no beds tonight and you aren't sleeping on that sofa. It's covered in masking tape."

"I know that. Who do you think put all that tape on there in the first place? I've slept on that sofa since I was fifteen years old."

"Yeah and it's time to come up in the world, Cleopatra. I have plenty of room in my bed." She smiled. "I'm kidding. You can stay in my guestroom. I'll be as good as you want me to be. If not better."

TWENTY SIX

....

BETWEEN THE SHEETS

"I love your place." Cleopatra roamed around Supriti's loft. "No TV, huh?"

"No, I don't watch TV."

"That's because you don't have one." Cleopatra smiled.

From the moment Cleopatra set foot in her loft, Supriti wanted to strip naked so Cleopatra could have her way with her, use her body as her personal playground, her own life-sized candy land. But she tried to control herself.

"Are those Taliesin Barrel Chairs?" Cleopatra gasped as she spotted the Frank Lloyd Wright-designed signature chairs. "Oh reproductions, but still, they're perfect," she said as she examined them more closely, still refraining from touching them.

"How do you know about those chairs? Go ahead, you can sit."

"Wright used to be my favorite architect, until I fell in love with Japanese architecture. I wanted to be an architect when I was a kid." Cleopatra sat down and stroked the cherry wood with both hands.

"Damn. I thought it was impossible, but you just got even sexier." Supriti licked her lips. "So what happened?"

"Why am I not an architect? I wanted to make money and be happy."

"Look how I'm living." Supriti shrugged her shoulders and spun around.

"You're renting in Soho when you could own in Brooklyn. And you're paying that rent with family money." She winked at her. "Are you happy?"

"Point taken. Come," Supriti laughed as she grabbed Cleopatra's hand. "So what's your favorite Indian dish?" Supriti escorted Cleopatra to the kitchen, where she poured her a glass of Chardonnay. "Wait. I remember you telling me. Chicken tikka masala coming right up." She winked at Cleopatra.

"You remember that, huh?" Cleopatra asked as she looked through the massive arched windows at the city lights.

"I remember everything about you."

Supriti cooked as Cleopatra downed the bottle of wine. She watched Cleopatra's tongue snake over her lips, licking away the last evidence that the wine had ever been in her mouth. She'd almost forgotten that she wasn't supposed to dive across the kitchen counter, tackle Cleopatra, and rip all her clothes off. When she kissed Cleopatra on Valentine's Day, she'd decided that her lips tasted of milk chocolate, and it was hard to push that memory and the feelings that memory conjured up aside.

Cleopatra, on the other hand, hadn't been this at ease in a while. "I haven't had a good night's sleep in a week, so I probably shouldn't be drinking. Don't be frightened if I fall off this stool." Cleopatra snapped Supriti out of her daydream as she joked. "Just put a blanket over me, I'll be fine."

Supriti had officially taken Shawn's place as confidante, Cleopatra thought; she was there for her when she needed someone, even if Supriti's intentions were far from pure. Despite the distraction of her and the alcohol, though, Cleopatra missed her wife. Supriti would talk to her but Cleopatra would drift off into some random thought about Jacqueline or the kids. She kept checking her cell phone, but not a peep—no calls, no texts, no emails from her wife, nothing.

"No matter where I am, I always say goodnight to the kids and tell them a story." Cleopatra rarely read traditional bedtime stories from books; she made her tales up off the top of her head, or—when Jacqueline wasn't looking—told the twins inappropriate jokes that made them laugh so hard they tired themselves out and immediately fell asleep. The old school 'black man, white man, Chinese man' jokes were their personal favorites. It hurt her to not only be away from her wife, but from her kids as well.

Supriti snatched Cleopatra's cell phone away from her. "No phones at the dinner table," she admonished.

When they started the meal, Cleopatra found it to be better than any food she'd had in the best Indian restaurants in the city. And it officially finished her off. With a stomach full of alcohol and food, she became exhausted and incoherent.

After dinner they sat on the couch and Supriti moved in close to Cleopatra, their thighs touching.

"It looks like you're ready to get into bed." Supriti caressed Cleopatra's thigh and ran her hand down to her knee. She slithered off the couch and kneeled down to the floor between Cleopatra's legs, massaging both of her thighs down to her calves.

She slipped off Cleopatra's black leather boots as she looked up at her, thinking that she could learn to love this vantage point. She licked her lips as she imagined Cleopatra pulling her up off the floor to straddle her. She would ride the hell out of her, she thought.

"Yeah, I'm ready. Where's your guest room?" Cleopatra stood up, unsteady on her feet, interrupting Supriti's fantasy.

"Put your weight on me." Supriti rose up, wrapped Cleopatra's arm around her neck, and walked her back toward her bedroom rather than the non-existent guestroom.

She laid Cleopatra across her king size canopy bed and quickly turned over the two 8x10 pictures of Cleopatra she had prominently displayed on her nightstand before she had a chance to see them.

"Baby. What if we were both single? I mean, when we met," Supriti said. "What do you think would have happened?"

Cleopatra giggled. "You'd be my woman by now."

Supriti's heart raced. Cleopatra snuggled into the white duvet and down pillows. She looked up at Supriti, who was standing over her. "You like me, don't you?" She smiled at her like a sleepy four-year-old.

Supriti said, "No Cleopatra."

"Why don't you like me?"

"Because I love you." She positioned Cleopatra in the middle of the bed, wrapping the bedding around her.

"Why don't you get in the bed with me?" Cleopatra whispered.

Supriti's heart dropped in her stomach. But she knew it wasn't Cleopatra talking; the alcohol and exhaustion played a part. She was damn near delirious. "You've had way too much to drink and the lack of sleep is just hitting you now. When I get in the bed with you, we're going to make love, and I want you to be 100 percent aware of what you're doing."

Cleopatra whispered "ok," and fell asleep. Supriti sat and watched her for a while. She fantasized about slipping into the bed naked and Cleopatra waking up sober and taking her. She even stood up at the end of the bed and stripped naked, all the while hoping that Cleopatra would wake up and see her. But she didn't move.

Supriti decided to take a bath, thinking it would calm the pressure she felt between her legs. She sank down into the deep spa tub full of lavender milk bath and focused on the dozens of lit tea lights, trying to clear her mind of the 6-foot chocolate distraction that lay passed out just a few paces away. She took a sip of merlot and watched as the milky bath water swallowed her body. The creaminess of the milk and the serenity of the lavender did nothing to extinguish her desire for the mound of trouble currently tangled in her sheets. Supriti had been soaking for what seemed like forever, intermittently closing her eyes, making a wish that Cleopatra would appear before her and join her in the spa tub built for two, but to her dismay she continued to soak in her own juices and the now-lukewarm water. She babysat her glass of wine obsessively, taking tiny sips as if it was a much stronger dark liquor that her body was rejecting.

But nothing was working. Her mind was set on Cleopatra, her desire fixated on having what lay on the other side of her bathroom door.

She moaned as she watched the thick milk cover her breasts. She hadn't been prepared to have Cleopatra in her home that night, or to have the opportunity that she convinced herself lay in her bed. She wasn't ready to cook her a meal and attempt to seduce her on such short notice, but that was where she found herself. She had laid Cleopatra right where she wanted her, right where she needed her. Her bed. Now what?

Cleopatra could have stayed and slept on Teresa's couch at the shelter or checked into any hotel in the city, but she'd chosen to come home with her. Supriti had initially thought she was helping Cleopatra, but Cleopatra was doing more for her. Her mere presence simultaneously calmed and excited her. She made her relax, made her laugh and smile. Made her feel beautiful, even though she refused to touch her. She brought out the best and the worst in her. How? She really had no idea, and had tired of trying to figure it out. She'd just accepted it as reality. She only knew that all these weeks later, after being separated from Cleopatra and keeping her distance, she still hadn't been able to forget the way her lips felt.

She puckered her mouth to blow a carved path in the water then reached up and tweaked her own nipples. She tried to ignore the fact that she wanted her nipples between Cleopatra's fingertips, and not her own. Supriti's hands were small and lean as they slid down into the milk, gliding across her body. Cleopatra's hands were massive and strong, yet soft, and would feel intoxicatingly smooth inside of her.

"Mmmm," she moaned as she closed her eyes and slipped her fingers into her pussy. But there was only one person's fingers she wanted. One mouth, one tongue. Cleopatra's. What would it feel like to have Cleopatra's tongue there? she wondered. What about her fingers or her strap? She moaned, feeling flushed and hot as she squirmed in the water. Her nipples were hard, and she wanted Cleopatra to touch them. It wasn't long before she was thrashing against her own hand, imagining Cleopatra's mouth sucking her nipples as she tugged on them, and lost in the fantasy of Cleopatra kneeling between her legs, licking her breasts or stroking her cock into her pussy.

Supriti splashed the creamy water all about the floor, wondering how she had gone so long without making love. She fingered herself faster, slipping in two fingers, and working hard to get yet another finger into her pussy. Would Cleopatra stretch her open wide like this? Would she fuck her hard and fast, and long stroke her? Or would she do it slow and sexy? She pictured Cleopatra pounding into her as an orgasm slammed into her body so hard that not a sound came out when she attempted to scream her name.

Supriti slipped into a white silk robe after her bath and, instead of removing herself from temptation and leaving Cleopatra alone, stood over her and watched her sleep again.

Cleopatra in her bed was the sexiest thing she had ever seen. Her chocolate skin against her white sheets, her long black locs scattered all about the pillow. Her full lips were parted slightly—just enough that Supriti could hear her breathe. She grabbed her hair and twirled a loc around her fingers, praying that Cleopatra would wake up wanting her. She was fixated on riding her.

"Baby? Baby?" Supriti whispered, but Cleopatra didn't move. Supriti stood before her and let her robe fall to the floor. She slipped into the bed naked, next to Cleopatra.

To her surprise and disappointment, Cleopatra didn't stir or wake up at all. Supriti undid her white button-down shirt slowly, taking care with each button, and held the sterling silver

half-heart pendant that hung from Cleopatra's neck in her
hand, but refrained from ripping it from her chest, as she imagined her wife wore the other half. She was distracted by the
black wife beater that clung to Cleopatra's body. She lifted up
her beater to take a peek at her stomach and saw the muscular
V that disappeared inside her Calvin Klein briefs. She wanted
to lick her from her stomach down into her underwear, but
settled on light kisses around her belly button.

She had already gone too far, but couldn't stop herself.

She undid her belt buckle and unbuttoned her jeans. Cleopatra tossed in her sleep and kicked the pants off her legs, and
Supriti got nervous, thinking she was awake. But she wasn't.
She sat back and took her all in, the city lights shining through
her bedroom windows illuminating Cleopatra's body.

"Damn." She moved her hand up inside of Cleopatra's wife
beater, running her fingers over her six-pack. Right as she was
about to mount Cleopatra, the doorbell rang.

"Who the hell?!" Supriti hopped off of the bed and grabbed
her robe off the floor. She ran to the front door before they
had a chance to ring the bell again and wake Cleopatra, and in
the process tripped over one of Cleopatra's boots. She yelped
out in pain as she approached the door slowly and looked out
of the peephole.

Mandisa stood on the other side of the door. "I know you're
in there—I just heard you. Open up." She banged on the door
hard. "I was in the neighborhood. Thought you'd want to have
a late dinner." Supriti opened the door, but was nervous and
anxious. She finally had Cleopatra in her bed, and now Mandisa
was in her way—as usual.

"Ooh you got company?" Mandisa covered her mouth as

she watched Supriti tighten the robe around her waist. "Who is it? What's her name?"

"Nobody you know."

"What's going on with you?" Disa looked around the apartment. She sniffed the air and smelled a familiar cologne; saw a bunch of luggage and a pair of men's boots by the couch.

"Unless you're straight all of a sudden, we have a problem. I don't know any woman but Cleopatra who wears Varvatos boots and has that much Louis Vuitton luggage, and I would know her cologne anywhere," Mandisa exploded. "There is no way she's here. No fucking way." She stormed toward Supriti's bedroom.

"You need to leave, Disa. Come on, let's go." Supriti grabbed her arm and pushed her toward the door. "You gotta go."

Mandisa shoved her back, hard. "Get your hands off me. I don't believe she did this. Did you drug her, or what? There's no way. She may be here, but she's not fucking you, there's no way. I can't believe you would do this to me."

"You forced me to choose between the two of you, Mandisa. I'll choose Cleopatra every time. If I had to choose between having her as a lover for one night or you as a friend forever, I'd still choose her." Supriti unknotted her robe and let it fall open to flash her naked body. "Like I said, it's time for you to go. I need to get back to my woman."

"You have lost your mind. If you think I won't go right now and tell her wife, you're dumber than I thought."

Supriti pushed Mandisa across her threshold. "Get out."

Mandisa slapped Supriti hard across her left cheek. "I told you to keep your hands off me."

Supriti was shocked as she held her face, which stung from the force of the hit. But she shouldn't have been surprised. Mandisa was a sore loser when she didn't get what or who she wanted.

"I'm leaving." Mandisa straightened her coat and threw her purse over her shoulder. "I'll let Jacqueline have you first.

TWENTY SEVEN

....

SNITCH

"What is your problem?" Jacqueline had much attitude when she opened the door and found Mandisa standing there. "You know, it's late and my kids are sleeping." She stepped back from the door as the chilly night air whipped under her pink robe, which was labeled "Hers."

Mandisa knew that telling Jacqueline where Cleopatra was resting her head would cause trouble in her marriage and send Jacqueline on a rampage for Supriti's neck. But Mandisa had played nice for too long, and decided she was going to get just as aggressive as everyone else. She was well aware that she was being low, but she was adamant about removing these two women from her ex's life. She was considering making it her new side project. If she couldn't have Cleopatra, neither would they.

"I know we aren't friends but—" Mandisa began.

"You're right. We aren't friends." Jacqueline crossed her arms. "You're my wife's ex, who watches our every move from her living room window. When are you going to get over her?"

Jacqueline was not in the mood for whatever Mandisa

309

wanted. She was still hurting from Cleopatra walking out earlier. She was furious that Cleopatra wasn't answering her
phone, and Mandisa had rung her doorbell at the wrong time.

"Like I was saying. You should know where your wife is."

"I know where she is."

"If you did, you wouldn't be so calm right now."

"Where is she?" Jacqueline put her hand on her hip.

"In Supriti's bed." Mandisa smiled.

"What?" Jacqueline's eyes nearly left her head.

"Mm-hmm." Mandisa nodded.

"You saw her in her bed?"

"No, but I smelled her cologne and saw her Vuitton bags
scattered all over the apartment. And Supriti was naked underneath her robe. Which she was more than happy to show me.
She said she needed to get back to her woman."

"I don't believe you." Jacqueline grabbed Mandisa's arm
and pulled her inside the house. She called Cleopatra's cell
phone again while Mandisa stood and watched.

✿✿✿

Supriti smiled when she answered Cleopatra's cell phone.
"Cleopatra's line."

"What are you doing with my wife's phone?"

"I picked it up because she's knocked out, and I thought
you would want to know that she'll be in good and capable
hands tonight. Mine."

"Bitch, put my woman on the phone."

"Like I said, she's knocked out. She can't come to the phone right now. It got rough and she's sleeping it off."

"Where are you? I'm coming to get her."

"No you aren't," Supriti laughed into the phone. "How many times do you think you can push her out of her own house and it not backfire on you? I mean, seriously."

"You don't know what goes on between me and my wife."

"I know enough," Supriti said. "I actually gave you the opportunity to really be her woman. Did she tell you I walked away from her? Tried to give you a chance, because I know how much she loves you. But now it doesn't matter. I'm taking her from you. Tell that snitch Mandisa I said hi." And Supriti hung up.

Jacqueline called back frantically, but Supriti wouldn't pick up. Jacqueline thought her head would explode. Less than a minute later both her and Mandisa's cell phones went off, alerting them to a new text message. They both looked at their phones and saw a picture of Cleopatra lying in Supriti's bed.

"What the hell is she doing?" Jacqueline screamed.

"Shit," Mandisa said, angry herself. Supriti was rubbing it in her face now, too.

"How could she go to her so quickly? Just like that?" Jacqueline asked herself.

She called Cleopatra's cell twenty times in succession, but it went straight to voicemail each time. A million different scenarios ran through her head and she tried not to panic, but was failing. She couldn't stop the images of what she thought Cleopatra was doing to Supriti, but she didn't want to believe it. Cleopatra had always been faithful to her, and it was only when they were broken up that Cleopatra had been promiscuous and run the streets with other women. Was that what they were now? Broken up? Why was she there, why didn't she pick up her phone herself? What had Supriti done to get her in her bed?

Jacqueline's train of thought was broken by Mandisa's cell phone going off. Mandisa looked down at the text message.

{*Christopher: Tribeca Grand Hotel, presidential suite in 1 hour. Wear what I like.*}

Mandisa smiled and wondered if she had time to run across the street to her place, shower, and slip into something sexy. "Well, I guess my work here is done." She walked toward the front door, but Jacqueline grabbed her by her arm and spun her around.

"Give me Supriti's address, now."

Jacqueline scared her, and in that moment the situation became real to Mandisa. They were all incredibly passionate women that were being pushed to the brink in the name of love, desire, and jealousy. Mandisa thought about it and decided against telling Jacqueline where Supriti lived. The look in Jacqueline's eyes confirmed that she would put a serious hurting on her.

"No. You're way too upset; it wouldn't be good if you went over there right now."

"You are seriously not going to tell me?"

"I'm seriously not going to tell you."

"All right." Jacqueline massaged her balled-up right hand with her left. "Fine. I'll deal with you another time. That's what I get for not finishing you off sooner," she mumbled to herself.

"Excuse me?" Mandisa turned around.

"Living across the street, pining away for my wife. You're

enjoying this, aren't you? Get out of my house now, before you get what Supriti should be getting."

Jacqueline pushed her out the door and slammed it behind her, then spun around, trying to figure out what to do ... how to find Supriti and Cleopatra. She Googled Supriti after racking her brain to remember her last name, but no address popped up and all of her social media accounts were private. She logged in to Cleopatra's Android account, thinking she could track her through her phone's GPS, but it was turned off. She had tried every idea she could think of, but then remembered that she had sent Supriti's phone number to herself when Cleopatra wasn't looking, just in case she ever needed to relay a message to Supriti personally. Now that time had come. But all her attempts to call were immediately dropped, not even going to voicemail.

A Google search of the cell number only showed her old address in California.

That was it. Jacqueline had exhausted every idea she could think of, and she felt helpless. She was furious and stewed in the house as she thought about strangling the address out of Mandisa. But it seemed insane to call the nanny to watch the kids while she went and beat the shit out of Mandisa just so she could get Supriti's address in order to go and beat the shit out of her.

If the police got involved, she might as well kiss the kids goodbye without a fight. So she sat and waited. And waited.

....

TWENTY EIGHT

SLEEPING WITH THE ENEMY: THE SEDUCTION OR THE FAIL?

This and my heart belong to Jacqueline.

Supriti had slipped, naked, back into bed with the still sound asleep Cleopatra. She was draping her fingers up Cleopatra's thigh when she saw it—the large tattoo on the inside of her thigh, pronouncing who she belonged to.

"Shit." The body art stopped her in her tracks. It was a hell of a deterrent. Supriti hopped out of the bed, frustrated; Jacqueline was continuing to keep her from what she wanted. She knew how much Cleopatra loved her wife, and she hated it. Hated Jacqueline for having what was hers, and hated the tattoo, which was a reminder she didn't need. Supriti had fantasized about this moment for months, and knew just how she wanted the first time she made love to Cleopatra to go. She had laid it out in her head in excruciating detail. She looked back down at the bed and Cleopatra submerged in her sheets. This was her opportunity.

She got back in bed and kissed the muscles on Cleopatra's

stomach, teasing her navel with her tongue.

"Do you need me, baby?" Supriti whispered. "Tell me you need me. I don't give a damn about your wife. I'm the one you really want, I'm the one you need."

"I love the way you touch me," Cleopatra whispered as she grabbed Supriti's head. Supriti smiled and sucked hungrily on Cleopatra's stomach. Cleopatra let out a soft moan. "I love you so much, Jac."

Supriti flipped over on her back, covering her face with her hands. This wasn't her fantasy. In her dreams, Cleopatra was awake and sober, proclaiming her love for her before she turned her out. She really did want Cleopatra to know exactly what and who she was doing when they made love. So she would have to wait. But tonight she would make a compromise.

She took a handful of Cleopatra's locs and draped them across her breasts and stomach. She placed light kisses on Cleopatra's body as she slid her fingers into her own pussy.

"See what you do to me baby?" She took her fingers and dragged them across Cleopatra's stomach, leaving a stream of wetness across her belly. "You got me so wet. You got me playing with my pussy twice in one night." Supriti flicked her clit as she snuggled close to Cleopatra. She slid her other hand underneath the waistband of Cleopatra's CK briefs and caught a glimpse of her pussy.

"Give me the strength." Supriti exhaled and threw her head back as she flicked her own swollen clit until her body exploded.

✿✿✿

Cleopatra woke up a few hours later, after she had slept off the wine. She found Supriti asleep on the couch in the living room.

"I should go." Cleopatra touched her lightly on her shoulder. "It's not right that I spend the night here. I just really needed to sleep off that wine, it knocked me out. But thanks." She stepped into her boots and bent down to tie them.

"Thanks for what?" Supriti stood up over the kneeling Cleopatra.

"For being there when I needed you. I appreciate it." Cleopatra rose up and hugged her.

Supriti melted in her arms. She wrapped her arms around Cleopatra's neck, filled her hands with her locs, and didn't want to let her go. When Cleopatra pulled away, Supriti grabbed her face and tried to bring Cleopatra's lips to hers.

"No. My life is complicated enough."

"I don't plan to do anything else to break up your marriage, but I'm going to be there when it does."

Cleopatra stared at her. She looked down at her cell phone on the coffee table. "Did you turn my phone off?"

"I couldn't find your charger and your battery was dying."

"Thanks."

Supriti held her breath as she watched Cleopatra with her phone. She hoped she'd erased all traces of the picture she shot of her lying in her bed, and Jacqueline's calls and text messages from the night before and that morning.

Cleopatra was saddened when she powered her phone on and saw that she had no missed calls or text messages from her wife. She took a deep breath and grabbed her bags, planning to head into her office early and catch a quick nap before her morning meetings. She'd worry about checking into a hotel later.

But she had an uneasy feeling. Supriti was especially quiet and subdued.

"Did anything inappropriate happen, since I don't remember how I got out of my clothes?" Cleopatra asked as she walked toward the door.

"What would you consider inappropriate?" Supriti smiled. "No. That and your heart belong to Jacqueline." She licked her lips.

"Yes it does." Cleopatra said, knowing for sure now that Supriti had seen her tattoo. Supriti had felt the need to mess with her last night, evidently, so she decided now that she would repay the favor. "So what did you do?" she asked, curious whether Supriti would come clean on her failed encounter.

Supriti loosened the knot on her robe and allowed the silk to slip slightly down and off her shoulders. Her nipples hardened as she walked up to Cleopatra. "What if I said I laid you down on the bed, fully dressed, and covered you with the duvet? And I just stood looking at you, sexual chocolate in my sheets. Just watched you lay in my bed until my pussy thumped. My clit was pounding so hard that it hurt. So I decided to go and soak in the tub. But it didn't help the throbbing, only made it worse."

"So I ended up fucking myself in that milk bath while I imagined that it was you inside of me, and not my hand. I came so hard that when I tried to scream your name not a sound came out. But it still wasn't good enough, so when I emerged from the tub, I stripped you down to your underwear, dropped my robe, and stood before you naked. Then I slipped into bed with the intention of having you. But I saw the tattoo and it stopped me. You called me Jacqueline and that stopped me too. I realized that when you do fuck me—and you will—that I want you to know you're fucking me. So I decided to wait, because our first time is going to be earth shattering and I need you to be 100 percent alert. So I grabbed your locs, draped them across my stomach, and fingered myself until I came for the second time." She cupped her own pussy. "Then I wiped my wet fingers across that sexy-ass stomach of yours."

"That's probably the craziest shit I've ever heard." Cleopatra laughed but immediately straightened up. What was crazy was her spending the night in Supriti's apartment in the first damn place. She knew she wasn't being herself, but she was going through something and about to lose her family—the only family she had. Of course she wasn't making smart decisions by spending time with Supriti, who had already proven that she was certifiably crazy.

But Supriti, regardless of her real intentions, was there for her and wanted her. Cleopatra couldn't say the same about her wife.

"Yeah. That is crazy isn't it?" Supriti smiled. "But I never said that's what happened. I said, 'What if?'"

"You have a beautiful body, but..." Cleopatra licked her lips as she looked at her nakedness, covered by less and less of her robe as Supriti let it slip further down her shoulders.

"Yeah, but you're married, I know," Supriti interrupted. "I don't give a shit about anything. Where we met, how we met, who your exes are or who you're married to now. I have wanted you since the second I laid eyes on you. I want you to know, I will continue to try and seduce you. I'm a woman who gets what she wants." Supriti shook her head, letting her eyes close. "Don't stop me," she whispered as she tugged Cleopatra's locs and ran her fingers through her thick, black dreads, spreading them out across her shoulders. "I can't stop thinking about you, wanting you," she whispered in her ear. "It's all I ever do."

"I know," Cleopatra said smugly.

Supriti nuzzled her nose against her soft earlobe, moving slowly down to Cleopatra's neck. "Please, don't stop me," she begged her again.

"Come here." Cleopatra drew her closer by her robe. Supriti gasped. "Tell me. What does the hair on my pussy look like?" Cleopatra whispered. "Hmm? Tell me." Cleopatra slid her hand inside of Supriti's robe and pulled her in, forcibly pressing her body up against hers.

Supriti panted as the cold metal from Cleopatra's belt buckle pushed against her bare stomach.

"Is it straight ... is it curly? Is there even hair down there at all, what?"

Supriti's body softened with desire, almost to the point where Cleopatra was holding her up.

"I said tell me," Cleopatra demanded, and pushed Supriti off of her, forcing her to regain her composure and stand on her own feet.

"Um ... neither," Supriti whispered as she bit her bottom lip.

Cleopatra moved Supriti up against the wall. She brought her face to hers, forcing Supriti to look into her eyes. Supriti's tongue peaked out the corner of her mouth and she licked her lips as she shyly looked away. Cleopatra closed Supriti's robe and tied the belt tight around her waist.

"Like I was saying, you have a beautiful body, but I don't ever want to see it again. Go ahead. You were saying what my hair down there looks like."

"It's kind of wavy." Supriti smiled timidly.

"Interesting."

"Interesting? Why would you say that?"

"I may not be able to trust your actions or trust what you do, but I can trust you to actually tell me the truth."

"I don't understand."

Cleopatra leaned in as she spoke. Her breath tickled Supriti's ear, making her shiver and giving her goose bumps. "You're sexy when you come."

TWENTY NINE

....

COME CLEAN

"So you aren't home again, huh?" Racquel stuck her head into Cleopatra's office, waking her up.

"How did you know?" Cleopatra sat up on her couch and tossed the blanket off her. She looked at her watch; it was 7:00AM.

"You just told me. And you're here sleeping in wrinkled street clothes." Racquel twisted her lips as she sat on the edge of her coffee table. "Security told me you got here early this morning with a bunch of luggage. What's going on this time?"

Cleopatra filled Racquel in on what had been happening over the last week, with Alonzo, the custody battle, and Jacqueline's willingness to divorce her like it wasn't a big deal.

"He came back and you didn't tell me? Where is he staying? I'll send Kelile and his cousins over there. No need to pay an attorney all that money. Give them each a bottle of Hennessey and they're good to go."

"He's still their father," Cleopatra reminded her.

"That's bull. You're still her wife."

"He'll always be their father. I won't always be her wife."

"That's not going to happen. She's not going to divorce you after everything she did to get you. She's scared now of losing those babies. But she's not going to risk losing you in the process."

"How are you so sure?"

"I threatened her at your wedding. She don't want none of this." She patted the crown of her head with the palm of her hand.

"Yeah. Ok, Racquel. Thank you for caring, but you know with your shady past if you so much as fart on the subway your ass is getting deported right back to Ethiopia."

"This is true." She smiled.

"She hasn't called me or texted me or anything since I left the house yesterday. It's like she really doesn't care." Cleopatra hung her head.

"You know that's not true."

"No, I don't know that. Thanks for trying to make me feel better, though. I'm going to shower and change," Cleopatra said as she rifled through her garment bag. "But if you want to do something for me—" She pulled her black card from her wallet. "—See if you can get me one of the lofts at the Soho Grand."

"For how long?" Racquel reluctantly took the card from her.

"Until I max out the card."

"There's no limit on the black card, you know that."

After a long, panic-filled, and sleepless night, Jacqueline thought better of reaching out to Mandisa for Supriti's address again. She would deal with Mandisa another time. So after César came over to watch the kids, she moved on to Plan B.

She hadn't heard from Cleopatra at all. She hadn't returned any of her text or voicemail messages, so she called Racquel as soon as she thought she was at her desk. "Hi, Racquel. It's Jacqueline. I need a favor."

"What is it?" Racquel was irritated that her phone rang at 7:30AM while she was eating her hard-boiled eggs and Ezekiel Bread, and Jacqueline being on the other end did nothing to simmer her bad attitude.

"Have you seen Cleopatra this morning?"

"She was here sleeping on the couch in her office when I got in half an hour ago. Why?"

"Really?" Jacqueline exhaled. "How did she seem?"

"Groggy until I got some coffee and breakfast into her. She said she drank an entire bottle of Chardonnay last night, and you know she can't handle wine like that. She hasn't been sleeping well, anyway."

"Yeah, wine knocks her out." Jacqueline pieced together the puzzle of what she now knew didn't happen the night before.

"You know I was wondering, since I have you on the phone," Racquel said. "Why would Cleopatra drink that much wine when she knows it pretty much renders her unconscious? Hard liquor she can outdrink any man, but wine? It's like warm milk to her. Any ideas?" she asked in an accusatory tone.

"I don't know," Jacqueline lied. "I need a big favor from you, though."

Racquel only agreed not to tell Cleopatra that Jacqueline

called checking in on her after Jacqueline told her about Supriti's actions of the last evening. How Supriti must have had Cleopatra's cell phone, and probably deleted her texts and phone calls. Racquel confirmed for Jacqueline that Cleopatra hadn't gotten any of her communications, and was so furious that she trolled around the office, searching for Supriti, only to find out that she wasn't coming in that day. But she managed to get her home address from a friend in the human resources department.

Then she called Jacqueline back with Supriti's info.

"You're the best," Jacqueline thanked her.

Jacqueline and Racquel had had their issues in the past, but where Supriti was concerned, they were on the same page.

"Go easy. The last thing Cleopatra needs is your getting arrested. Just be smart—there are plenty of ways to get that bitch."

✺✺✺

"She never touched you" was the first thing Jacqueline said when Supriti opened her door. She pushed her way inside the loft and locked the door behind her. Supriti was stunned and speechless.

At that moment, Supriti spotted the other half-heart pendant dangling between Jacqueline's breasts—the other half of Cleopatra's heart.

"You know how I know she didn't touch you? Two reasons." Jacqueline held up two fingers. "Not even considering that she doesn't drink wine or that she was exhausted, there's something between her legs with my name on it." Jacqueline stood with her legs spread and hiked up her black skirt so Supriti could see her tattoo: *This and my heart belong to Cleopatra.*

"Remember, I showed this to you before, in Maine, when you tried to seduce my wife and failed? And if you saw Cleopatra's tattoo that stopped you in your tracks."

Supriti hung her head and Jacqueline knew she'd seen her name tattooed between Cleopatra's thighs.

"And if she had touched you, you wouldn't be so quiet and timid right now. You would be telling me about the countless ways she fucked you and turned you out. I know, because that's what I would be doing. And just between you and me, after the first time Cleopatra and I made love, I didn't walk right for at least three days. And you're looking mighty swift on your feet right now. So … yeah. Mission not accomplished. My heart and my pussy belong to my wife, and hers belong to me. Nice try. I got a lot going on right now," Jacqueline continued. "So I can't afford to catch a case. I can't burn this loft down, I can't stomp you in the face until you're unrecognizable. I can't cut off your fingertips or pull your teeth out with pliers so they can't identify your body. I can't do any of that right now."

Supriti's body relaxed, and a smirk came across her face as she came to the conclusion that she was free and clear.

"But don't get too comfortable." Jacqueline eyed her in her sweats and oversized t-shirt. "I'm certain that's not what you wore last night."

She slammed Supriti up against the wall and pushed her thumb up into her throat, and her index finger into her temple. "I promise you, mess around with my wife's cell, send pictures, delete my calls and text messages again, and I will make you eat that fucking cell phone. Just because I can't fuck you up at this precise moment doesn't mean you can continue to try me. I don't know if you're stupid or just crazy, or have a death wish, or what. But your luck is going to run out, and I'll be there when it does."

❁❁❁

Jacqueline had been sitting in Cleopatra's office waiting for over an hour and was ready to have it out the moment Cleopatra came in. "Where were you last night?"

"I have a feeling you already know."

Cleopatra was returning from a meeting when Racquel informed her that her wife was in her office and not happy. Racquel just shook her head, knowing Cleopatra was in big trouble.

Cleopatra, to her credit, was honest about going home with Supriti. But Jacqueline took little comfort knowing the detailed truth. She blasted her for putting herself in such a stupid position and for letting Supriti get her phone and delete her calls, texts, and voicemails. She refused to accept Cleopatra's apology and cursed her out like a random chick on the street. Jacqueline pulled up the picture Supriti sent of her laying tangled in her bed and threw her phone at Cleopatra.

"You're my bitch. Not hers!" Jacqueline screamed at her.

Cleopatra tried to remain calm. "I know you don't like her, trust her, or want her anywhere near me. I get that, and I've apologized for being stupid. Please trust me when I tell you I will handle her in regard to her playing on my phone. But the next time you curse at me like that, I'm walking out. You know I hate that. I'm not your child," Cleopatra snarled at her.

"You're right. You're a grown woman. You're my wife."

"Yeah and recently that's only been on paper."

"You belong in my bed."

"That's what you say, but it's awful funny that I woke up in Supriti's bed this morning."

Jacqueline burst into tears. "You know what, Cleopatra? If you really fucking want her, why don't you go and be with her?"

THIRTY

MESSY

"So you're in one piece." Mandisa had gone over to Supriti's loft as soon as she had a free moment. "She must not have been here yet."

"If you're talking about Cleopatra's wife, she's been here and left already. Too bad, you just missed her."

"And yet you appear unscathed." Mandisa looked at Supriti's face. "Or are you hiding bruises under your sweats?" She pushed passed her and sat down on her couch, uninvited.

"You couldn't wait to run and tell her, could you? Nothing happened last night between Cleopatra and me, and her wife knows that."

"So talk. I want to know everything. Cleopatra here in the middle of the night, her things scattered all over the place."

"Like I said, nothing happened." Supriti plopped down on the couch next to Mandisa, since she didn't appear to be leaving anytime soon. "Trust me, if it had I would give you all the juicy details, blow by blow." Supriti pursed her lips at Mandisa.

"Then why did you want me to think it did? Why was she even here?"

"She and her wife haven't been getting along lately. She crashed here for a little while, slept off some wine, then left. Why are you so concerned? Mad that she didn't run across the street and stay with you? Mad that I got further with her than you ever will? Mad that you don't have her scent all up in your sheets? If she wasn't married, she'd be my woman."

Mandisa laughed. "Did she tell you that? Did she say anything even remotely close to that? Or is that your own warped sense of reality?"

"Yes, she did tell me that, now that you mention it. I'm so much better for Cleopatra than Jacqueline whatever her maiden name was." Supriti rolled her eyes.

"Tripp was her maiden name," Mandisa said. "It's Giovanni now."

Supriti smiled. "Not for much longer, if I have my way."

"I told you to leave her alone on more than one occasion, and I told you why. I wasn't over that woman yet. Does that not mean anything to you? I came to you respectfully as a woman and a friend and said leave her alone. I warned you that if you didn't it would be a problem. And now what do we have?" Disa threw her hands up in the air. "A motherfucking problem. There are three things that I don't like. Being lied to. Being disrespected. And being betrayed. Any of them perpetrated against me separately, and you will have me as an enemy. But all together and I won't rest until I've ruined you."

Supriti wasn't moved by Mandisa's threat, so Mandisa stood up and smoothed out her blue dress as she prepared to leave. She threw her large brown leather handbag over her shoulder.

"I don't know what Jacqueline said to you. She obviously let you slide for her own reasons, and that's her business. But she's not the one you need to be worried about at the moment."

"I didn't sleep with her, damn."

"But you wanted to. Didn't you? And you still want to. Right now. At this very moment. You've been trying your hardest to get up underneath her since the moment you laid eyes on her. And you would have if she wanted anything to do with you. We still have to work together—that is, until I find a way to void your contract and fire you. But as of right now, we are no longer friends. Your career as an architect in this city is about to be over. Enjoy it while it lasts. When I'm done with you, you won't be able to build sand castles on Coney Island."

✿✿✿

"Can you come to my office please, we need to talk" was all that Cleopatra said on Supriti's voicemail. She called her immediately after Jacqueline stormed out of her office. She didn't know Supriti hadn't come in to work that morning, but it didn't matter. Once Supriti listened to the voicemail, she changed into a work-appropriate white blouse and black pants suit, hopped into a cab, and was in Cleopatra's office within an hour. But the meeting would not be what she was expecting.

"I wanted to talk to you about last night." Cleopatra closed her office door behind her, after winking at Racquel.

Supriti's body tensed up as she sat in front of Cleopatra's desk. She focused on Cleopatra's wedding band as she watched her unbutton her navy blue suit jacket. Her wedding band really was big and full of diamonds. Supriti had never studied it

333

before. She'd managed to avoid looking at it all this time. But now she couldn't take her eyes off it.

"Last night I let you have your fun. Actually it was probably more fun for me, as you just seemed to be torturing yourself. It was kind of hilarious, so I let it slide. I let you bust your nut, which really was hot, by the way. But make no mistake—you would have never taken me."

Supriti's mouth hung open as she replayed everything she had done and said the night before.

"Jacqueline told me what you did, sending that picture of me in your bed to her and Mandisa. Erasing her texts and voicemails. And that you talked to her. Everything. You had the nerve to pick up *my* phone and talk to *my* wife." Cleopatra got up and stood over Supriti as she sat stiff in the armchair.

Supriti attempted to talk.

"Shut the fuck up." Cleopatra leaned on the edge of her desk and folded her arms across her chest. "I'm not interested in any excuse you can come up with. I have never put my hands on a woman, and I don't condone it at all. But the next time you do anything to cause my wife unhappiness, I will hurt you."

Supriti began to speak again.

"Shut up. I'm not done," Cleopatra interrupted her. "My wife asked me once more to cut off contact with you, and that is for the best. Our friendship has done nothing but cause problems. Until Mandisa figures out how to crush you—her words, not mine—" Cleopatra held up her cell phone to display the text message Mandisa sent her. "—Our interaction will only revolve around work matters, and only during business hours. Racquel and Nikki will see to that."

Supriti blamed Mandisa for everything. If she hadn't run

and blabbed, Cleopatra wouldn't be so furious with her. Why couldn't she just leave her and Cleopatra alone? Mandisa had her shot, and couldn't manage to hold on to Cleopatra. Now it was Supriti's turn. But it would be impossible to make Cleopatra hers with so much outside interference.

"I'm sorry. I wasn't thinking. I'm so sorry," Supriti pleaded. "You make me do things I would never do, things I'm ashamed of. Nothing like that will ever happen again. I promise. I don't want to lose you."

"You never had me. You don't seem to understand that. My friendship was never enough, and that's fine. But to hold on in the hopes that you were going to be with me is nuts. It's not going to happen, like ever. I have amazing control when it comes to my commitment to my wife; my flesh is not that weak. Yeah we're going through something right now, but what my wife and I have is a deep level of intimacy. Yeah we fuck hard, and a lot." Cleopatra smiled. "We make love passionately, and a lot. I know what she needs and not only does she know what I need, she gives it to me. She twists my locs. I paint her toenails. We shave each other. She rubs my back when I'm tired. If I had pimples on my back she would pop them. I don't. But if I did. She would. She takes care of me when I'm sick, she takes care of me when I'm not sick. She thinks I'm smart and sexy. She cooks for me. I cook for her. She puts blueberries and granola bars in my backpack. She knows if I all of a sudden burst into tears it's because I miss my mother, and she doesn't ask questions. She just holds me and lets me cry. Her arms tell me it's going to be all right. And I love her kids as if I gave birth to them. You can't compete with that. And it was downright simple of you to ever try."

Cleopatra stared at Supriti, who couldn't bring herself to look Cleopatra in her eyes.

"And the 8x10s of me on your nightstand?" Cleopatra continued. "Creepy as hell. My wife doesn't even have pictures that big of me on her nightstand. I mean, really? They're damn near life size."

Cleopatra opened her office door and motioned with her hand for Supriti to leave. Racquel was standing in the doorway with her arms folded, waiting to escort her to the elevator. Nikki stood shoulder to shoulder with Racquel.

"Yaas bitch." Nikki snapped her fingers across her face. "I told you from day one, ok?"

Supriti got up and walked toward the door.

"One last thing in case I wasn't crystal," Cleopatra added. "This shit right here, what you did, this is how people get hurt. Fuck with my wife again."

THIRTY ONE

....

POPS

Jacqueline's parents were expecting to see Jacqueline, Cleopatra, the twins, and the rest of their extended family when they stopped by Cleopatra's house early that Sunday evening. But when they arrived, they found instead a surprise anniversary party, with every member of the family but Cleopatra.

It had been a little over a day since Jacqueline and Cleopatra had their fallout over Cleopatra's finding herself in Supriti's sheets, so Jacqueline wasn't surprised when Cleopatra didn't show up to help with the preparations. But when she didn't show up at all, she sent her a 911 text.

{Jacqueline: Where the fuck are you? Get here now!}

Cleopatra smiled as she jogged up the front steps to the house a few moments later. "Hey Moms. What's wrong?" Jacqueline's mother had tears in her eyes as she hugged Cleopatra at the front door and wouldn't let her go. Her mother, a beautiful fifty-something version of Jacqueline, had been waiting for her when she arrived, and Cleopatra could barely get

337

past her and inside the house.

"You two need to stop this nonsense and get back together. Why are you not living in this house? You never leave, Cleopatra. You don't leave," Moms scolded her as she dabbed the corners of her eyes with her handkerchief.

"It's ok. Let me talk to her." Jacqueline's father sent his wife back inside the house to rejoin the party in their honor.

Jacqueline's father, a tall, handsome, gray-haired gentleman, closed the front door behind his wife and pulled Cleopatra back outside onto the steps. "Why didn't you call and tell me what was going on?"

"How is that my place, if your daughter didn't? What would you have said?" Cleopatra leaned up against the stair rail.

"I would have told you what I just told her. What a bad decision this is."

"She's convinced it's going to work. She wants to handle it no matter the sacrifice, no matter what she loses in the process."

"I don't agree with what she's doing, but I understand. I can't imagine how you feel." He sat down on the top step and used his hand to clear a spot for Cleopatra to sit next to him.

"You're right—you can't imagine how I feel right now." Cleopatra wiped her eyes with her hand. She hadn't really discussed what she was going through with anyone—not deeply—because she didn't have anyone to confide in. She had held it all inside, but she was heartbroken.

"We've been married a couple of months and she wants to divorce me already. If she wants it, she can have it. Remember you told me that when you've committed to one another, you just don't leave? Well, you need to tell your daughter that."

Cleopatra noticed the sun going down and figured she could be back to her hotel before dark. She turned and walked down the steps.

"I know you haven't had a father around in a very long time." Pops raised his voice. "And when he was in the picture, that's not necessarily the title you would have given him. You've been like the son I never had. You are my family—my third daughter—and right now you're my second favorite." He winked at her. A dig on Robin. "I expect the same amount of courtesy and respect as if I was the one who helped bring you into this world."

"Yes, sir." Cleopatra walked back up the steps and sat down next to him.

"Thank you. This is not what she wants, you know that. I've never seen her this scared before. I haven't seen her this miserable since you two were broken up the last time."

"Why are you telling me this? She's the one that wants a divorce. There's nothing I can do to stop her."

"Is that why you aren't fighting her?"

"Fight what?" Cleopatra jumped up. He gently grabbed her arm and guided her to sit back down on the step. "She said stay out of it. She would fix it. This is what she wants. This is how she's fixing it."

"This isn't what she wants. You think like me, you think like a man. It's black and white for you. If she divorces you it means she doesn't want you, so you're done. That's all you need to hear and you're out of here. I understand that. Because I know I would be out. There's no way I would stick around and pretend that we weren't divorced when we were."

"And that's what she expects: for me to act like we aren't

339

divorced. But we'd be forced to live separately and sneak around to see each other. And if I'm lucky I might be able to get visits with the kids. All this until the heat dies down. That's not going to happen," Cleopatra said. "So why do you expect me to do something that you wouldn't even do?"

"Because that's my daughter and I want her to be happy. You make her happy. I don't have to worry about her when she's with you, Cleo. She and my grandkids will be devastated if they lose you. She loves the hell out of you, and I know how much you love her. When no one is fighting for the marriage, there's no way in hell it will survive, so it's on you because she's consumed with keeping the kids with her and safe. You have to do it, Cleo. You have to be the one."

Cleopatra rolled her eyes and shook her head no.

"When you were broken up before, both times, she fought like hell to win you back. It's your turn now," Pops said.

"She doesn't want me."

"That's not true, and you know it. At this moment she couldn't want you more. I know how much she's enjoyed being a housewife and taking care of you and the kids. She calls you her wife, her woman, but there are times when she calls you her husband. I've heard her call you her man, the man. Start acting like it."

"Excuse me?"

"Fight for your woman. You're smart, you have money and resources, and you can fix this and still have your family intact. But you can't just do nothing. You have to make the decision. Make the decision that you're going to fight to keep your wife and your family."

"So you're telling me to basically man up?"

"I walked my daughter down the aisle. I gave her to you. I entrusted her heart to you. But that doesn't mean you shouldn't check her when she needs it. There will be times when you know best, and you need to assert your authority and put your foot down."

"Check her? What do you expect me to do?"

"I don't think it will get as far as divorce if you do something now. But if she actually does go through with this, don't leave her. She needs you."

"I would make sure her and the kids were well taken care of. They would never want for anything no matter what, if that's what you're worried about."

"It's not. I said she needs you, not what you can offer her. Just do what you need to do to make sure it doesn't get to divorce. Live up to your name."

"What?"

"I didn't know your mother, but do you think she just picked the name Cleopatra out of a hat? Wise and powerful ruler, clever and well educated." Pops side eyed her. "So yeah, Cleopatra, what I'm saying is man up, woman up, step the hell up."

THIRTY TWO

....

ANNIVERSARY PARTY

"Where the fuck were you?" was the first thing that came out of Jacqueline's mouth when Cleopatra walked into the anniversary party. She grabbed Cleopatra's arm and held it tight.

They stood face to face for the first time since Jacqueline had walked out of her office during the argument over the Supriti slumber party. They hadn't spoken to resolve anything. Jacqueline had only texted about the party preparations, and Cleopatra had gone radio silent on her.

Cleopatra looked down in disbelief. "You're joking right?" She pulled her arm from Jacqueline's embrace. "I fell asleep," she said dismissively.

"I've been texting you all day. You've been sleeping all day? You expect me to believe that? Were you having another sleep over with that bitch?"

Cleopatra looked around the dining room at Jacqueline's family members turning their attention to them. "You really want to take it there? Who are you cursing at? I don't sleep well anymore, so when I do fall asleep I sleep really hard. And for the record, I prefer the hotel bed to Supriti's. The hotel has one-thousand thread count sheets. Supriti's couldn't have been more than eight hundred."

Jacqueline's head was seconds from exploding. Just as "Fuck you Cleopatra" was about to shoot from her lips, Cleopatra said, "Don't take it there if you can't handle it. You want to do this right here, right now, in front of your family? On your parent's anniversary?" Jacqueline was quiet. "We can have everybody in this house up in our business, everybody on this block. What do you want to do?"

Jacqueline exhaled and gritted her teeth. "I'm sorry. I was worried; you were supposed to be here early to help me set up and help with the food. I was just worried. I'm used to knowing where you are and what you're doing. You go to work and to the gym. That's it, then you come home."

"I was home."

"That hotel room is not your home, this is your home, right here, where me and the kids are." Jacqueline caught herself, her heart pounding hard in her chest as she tried to calm herself down. She took a deep breath. She was still furious and hurt, but this wasn't the time or place, in front of her family. "Are you hungry? I'll fix you a plate." She needed to do something with her hands to keep from wrapping them around Cleopatra's neck.

"I'm starving. I can fix my own plate, though. Thank you."

Jacqueline stopped in her tracks, with sadness in her eyes. "I always fix your plate." She shook her head in defiance. "I'm fixing your plate. I'm still your wife." Cleopatra stepped back and held her hands up in surrender.

"Thank you," Jacqueline said as she assembled her wife's food at the massive buffet table she'd set up in the corner.

Jacqueline sat her plate down at the head of a table where other family members were sitting around eating and talking, and poured Cleopatra a glass of lemonade.

Cleopatra pulled out the chair and sat down. Her eyes widened when she saw her plate. "Filet mignon? Thank you." She smiled.

"You're welcome. That's thyme and pepper-rubbed filet mignon with blueberry bourbon barbecue sauce. I only made three. My parents have the other two." Jacqueline couldn't help herself—she caressed Cleopatra's cheek before she walked away.

But she didn't go far. She stayed in the dining room, talking with random family members, and didn't let Cleopatra out of her sight. They watched each other from across the way, averting their eyes when one caught the other staring. Jacqueline was beautiful as always. She had on a snug purple freakum dress that hugged her body so intimately that it made Cleopatra jealous.

Cleopatra was handsome, as usual. Jacqueline never could resist her in a tie, and tonight she wore a bow tie, a button down, an elbow-patched tweed blazer, wingtips, and her black-rimmed glasses. What was she trying to do to her? Jacqueline wondered. But tonight was no different; she could have worn a wife beater and her oversized basketball shorts, and Jacqueline couldn't have wanted her more.

"How's the food?" Jacqueline refilled her glass of lemonade. "Do you need anything else?" She placed her hand on Cleopatra's shoulder.

"It's amazing. The risotto and asparagus are melting in my mouth." Cleopatra winked at her. "You know you can do no wrong in the kitchen."

"You can have chocolate cake and grape and champagne sorbet for dessert if you're good."

"I'll be good." Cleopatra winked as she popped a seared scallop in her mouth.

"Baby, guess where my parents are."

"Somewhere banging?"

"Mm-hmm." Jacqueline smiled.

"I don't want to know where in this house they're getting it in. I might never go in that room again."

"You have to go in that room," Jacqueline warned her.

"La la la la. I can't hear you."

Jacqueline burst into laughter. "Ok. I won't tell you. Just don't go into the laundry room!"

Cleopatra's eyes bugged out. "Eww."

In that moment they both laughed at Jacqueline's parents' hyperactive sex life, just like it was old times. As if nothing had changed. They made each other laugh harder and more than anyone else in their lives, and they both needed that to break the tension.

Just as Jacqueline was about to tell Cleopatra how much she missed her, Cleopatra dropped her fork. "I know that's not your cousin Benny in this house?" She stood up from the table.

"Baby." Jacqueline motioned her to sit back down and relax. "It's ok, everyone is watching him."

The crooked family that didn't get invited to Thanksgiving at Jacqueline's parents' or to their wedding had crawled from the shadows to attend this anniversary party. The drunks, thieves, and hood rats had converged on their house, and Cleopatra wasn't happy about the cast of characters she had seen so far. They were equally unhappy with Jacqueline's 'no kids but mine' policy, and to see the prime cuts of beef and fish on the anniversary couple's and Cleopatra's plates, when Jacqueline had only made them a buffet of fried delights. Their plates overflowed with fried chicken livers, fried catfish, French fries, chicken wings, and fried pork chops. They fought over the deep-fried delicacies and fussed about Cleopatra's plate the whole time they were smacking their mouths, sucking their fingers, and accidentally biting their greasy lips.

But that was family. They were never happy, no matter what. And Cleopatra knew that families hid the ingrates during the courting years, but Jacqueline's family seemed to have an exponential number of people you just didn't want to fuck with. After they got married, they left the lock off the cage and let the freaks out.

"Your thieving cousin Benny. He's got to go." Cleopatra shook her head.

"I locked all the doors upstairs."

"It doesn't matter. He'll steal the toilet seat out of the bathrooms. I'm stopping and frisking him before he leaves this house." Cleopatra raised her voice. "I know you hear me, Benny."

Benny turned around and held up his cup acknowledging Cleopatra. He smiled and Cleopatra could see his mouth full of gold teeth from across the room.

"Who did he steal those teeth from, Jac? You know they're not his." Cleopatra sat back down. "You know I don't like all these people in the house. But that motherfucker? Damn."

"I know, baby, but I got behind making the arrangements and I couldn't find a decent venue in time. The planning kind of slipped through my fingers."

"Everything seems to be slipping through your fingers these days," Cleopatra said, annoyed.

Then Amir and Maya ran up to Cleopatra and hugged her, just in time to avert a major blowout between her and Jacqueline. They climbed up in two chairs next to her and sat with her as she ate the rest of her dinner. Jacqueline joined them. No one spoke; they just sat and stared at Cleopatra, marveling at her like they hadn't seen her just a couple of days before.

"Look, Mama," Amir whispered to Cleopatra. He pointed to his neck. He always wanted to dress just like Cleopatra, and had on his little plaid bow tie, but Jacqueline could never tie it perfectly like Cleopatra. "It's crooked," he said.

Cleopatra smiled as she took apart his tie and began to fix it for him right there at the table.

"I miss you," Jacqueline said to Cleopatra.

Cleopatra's eyes lit up. "You do?" She seemed genuinely surprised as she fixed Amir's collar.

The astonishment in her voice hurt Jacqueline, but it was overshadowed by Amir and Maya saying that they missed her too.

"I miss all of you too." Cleopatra smiled. "Especially you," she mouthed to Jacqueline.

A wide smile spread across Jacqueline's lips, and in an instant her eyes flooded with tears. She excused herself from the table.

Cleopatra followed her and caught her by her arm. "Hey."

Jacqueline came to a stop in the corner of the dining room, but Cleopatra didn't know what to say. She just wanted to stop her woman from crying and lighten the mood. She looked around the room.

"Um ... is she pregnant?"

"Who?" Jacqueline dabbed the corner of her eyes with a napkin.

"Her." Cleopatra tilted her head toward a group of Jacqueline's female cousins. "The one with no edges."

Jacqueline looked and paused. "Me, you, and my mama are the only women up in here with edges, so try again," she laughed.

"Ty-Te ... um..."

"Tyquelle?" Jacqueline asked.

"Yeah, her, she looks like she's about to pop."

Jacqueline studied her cousin, "No, she's not pregnant," And then, in her best Jamaican accent, she said, "She fat."

"I was about to say congratulations," Cleopatra laughed. "I didn't want to be rude and not mention it."

"It's good that you didn't. She would probably try to fight you," Jacqueline giggled. "She's not pregnant, but Levondia is."

Cleopatra shook with laughter. "Again? Every time she manages to get somebody to watch all those kids so she can go to the club, she ends up pregnant a few months later."

Jacqueline smacked Cleopatra's arm. "She's going to hear you."

"She already knows she stays pregnant. Does she know who the daddy is this time?"

"No. She's still trying to get on Maury Povich. She thinks she has a good chance to get on the show this time. They say third time's the charm."

"He needs to start testing for STDs on that show. As a matter of fact, throw out her glass and her silverware," Cleopatra said.

"Way ahead of you, baby. Everything she's putting in her mouth is marked with an L. I don't want a Levondia bump either," she laughed.

Levondia heard her name, looked up, and wobbled over to them. "Hey Jac, hey Cleo. Ya'll look so good together." She grabbed a plastic knife from the table and proceeded to strategically lift up the back of her curly auburn wig and scratch her scalp with it, moaning as she did it.

Cleopatra and Jacqueline stood there in shock as they watched Levondia dig into her scalp with her wig halfcocked on her head. It took so long that Cleopatra had time to look down at her watch.

"Hold me back, baby," Jacqueline whispered to Cleopatra. "I swear 'fore God if she puts that knife back on the table…"

Cleopatra laughed at Jacqueline. "Wait, you're serious? What's up with you?" She blocked Jacqueline from Levondia, just in case.

"Ah, that felt good." Levondia pulled her wig back into place and stuck the knife behind her ear, to Cleopatra's relief.

"Hey cuz," Levondia said. "So you gonna throw me another baby shower, right?"

Jacqueline struggled not to roll her eyes. "Vondia. You had two baby showers last year. Who the hell has two showers in one year? No, it's someone else's turn."

"Never mind, then. Don't nobody need you for nothing."

"Then why the hell did you ask me? I got an idea—how about we go to the drugstore and buy you some condoms, or go get you some birth control pills? I'm down for that."

"Whatever. You think you better than everybody." Levondia sucked her teeth.

"No. I'm just better than you."

"Damn." Cleopatra spit out her lemonade, but a good portion shot up into her nose as she laughed and pulled Jacqueline away from her cousin.

"Whatever, girl, bye." Vondia rubbed her belly as she switched away and turned her attention to the tray of chicken wings on the buffet table.

"What's going on with you?" Cleopatra asked Jacqueline.

"I'm just not in a good place right now. I'm sorry. I want to apologize for how I came out cursing at you earlier. I just had it in my head about how today was going to go. We were going to spend the day together, getting prepared for this party, and when it didn't happen I got furious. I miss you. I just want to be alone with you, and spend some time with my wife. And I can't. And it's getting to me, and people are starting to work my nerves."

"Jacqueline!" her mother called her from the kitchen.

"See what I mean? Don't go too far, baby." She caressed Cleopatra's hand as she walked away.

"I won't." Cleopatra watched Jacqueline switch her way to the kitchen in her tight purple dress.

"Hey, Cleo." Jacqueline's uncle Thomas slapped Cleopatra on the back.

"Hi, Thomas." She surveyed his powder blue leisure suit for the flask of alcohol she knew he had on him somewhere.

"It's in my sock." He lifted up his foot and patted his ankle.

"Don't worry, I'm gonna get into some Crown Royal in a minute." He started doing the electric slide by himself. "But first, I'm going to get some of those Swedish meatballs and..." He pulled Cleopatra to the side. "Where can I get into this? You know, in private? I'm not trying to share." He pulled a small bag of weed from his back pocket.

"Are you crazy?" Cleopatra yelled at him, drawing attention from everyone in the room. She yanked him by his arm. "Why did you bring that into my house? And my kids are here."

"It's medicinal. For my alcoholism."

"Wait ... what? Negro, please. You have a flask on your ankle! Take it outside, get it out of my house," she demanded. "And I saw that clear jug you put on the table. I don't even want to know what that is."

"Whewwww, shit. What the hell is that?" Someone yelled as he took a gulp from that same clear jug, which he must have mistaken for water.

"Too hot." Uncle Thomas's wife Roberta laughed. "Someone got into the shine. He made that in the tub last week. I had to wash in the kitchen sink for three days. He didn't rinse out the tub, though, it could be anything in there. Toenails, hair, part of my bunion." She laughed as she pulled a bottle of ranch dressing and a handful of chicken livers from her purse. She stood there and dipped the chicken livers down in to the bottle as she talked to Cleopatra.

This motherfucker is pulling chicken livers out of her purse!

"How you doing, Aunt Roberta?" Cleopatra asked with a raised eyebrow. There was something more off than usual with Roberta. She belched with her mouth open, showing Cleopatra the incinerated chicken carcass and her raw gums, undoubtedly infected by the teeth she chose not to wear for the special occasion.

Then it hit Cleopatra—what was off with her. Aunt Roberta had on a blue floral housecoat, but she seemed to think that the gold lame braided belt she'd strapped around it meant she could actually leave the house and hit the streets in it.

"I can't with this family … I can't," Cleopatra whispered to herself.

"Hey, Cleo." Cleopatra froze when she thought she saw something jump from Aunt Roberta's mouth to her own bottom lip. She poked her lip out to examine it and felt her way to the table for a napkin to wipe at her face. She didn't want a Roberta bump any more than she wanted a Levondia bump.

"I'm looking out for ya'll." Aunt Roberta slapped her own chest. Cleopatra saw Jacqueline's mother send the twins into another room. "Don't worry about what I do." Aunt Roberta slapped her chest again, harder this time. "I was a grown-ass woman before I could wipe myself, Cleo."

"You mean before *I* could wipe *myself*?" Cleopatra laughed.

Roberta looked up at the ceiling as if what she meant to say was written up there. "You know what the hell I mean."

"I didn't want to put words in your mouth or anything. Anything else, like teeth. Where are your teeth? You want me to help you find your teeth, Aunt Roberta?"

"They're in my coat pocket."

"Oh, ok. So aesthetically you don't think it's a good idea to have them in? Because honestly, your face collapses without them. It's like you have a roof and no house. Just dead. Dead."

"Why you messing with her, baby?" Jacqueline pulled Cleopatra away from her Aunt Roberta.

"She started messing with me," Cleopatra defended herself. "And I got bored," she laughed.

"Come with me. I want to talk to you. We need to disappear for a little bit." Jacqueline took Cleopatra's hand and led her out of the dining room.

But before they could vanish, Cleopatra saw Benny emerge from their library, looking suspect.

"What was Benny doing in there, Jac?"

Cleopatra went into the library and Jacqueline followed close behind her. They looked around, but everything seemed to be in place. Her laptop, flat screen, and headphones ... nothing immediately jumped out as missing.

"Well I know he didn't take a book," Cleopatra said.

"Um ... baby." Jacqueline stood looking at the wall behind Cleopatra's desk. "Look." She pointed.

On the wall was her undergraduate degree from Columbia, and right next to it was the empty spot where her MBA degree from NYU had been hanging.

"Wait." Cleopatra looked harder at the wall, as if it would appear if she focused more. "No way," she laughed.

Cleopatra walked through the house until she found Benny by the fireplace, having a drink. She slapped the red plastic Solo cup out of his hand and into the fire. She thought it strange, because Jacqueline hadn't bought any red Solo cups and he was the only person who had one. *Who rolls with their own Solo cup with their name written on it with a Sharpie?*

"Where is it?"

Jacqueline ran up behind Cleopatra and jumped in between her and Benny.

"Where is what?" he asked Cleopatra as he looked up at her.

He put as much bass in his voice as his wiry 5-foot-5 frame could muster.

"This motherfucker must think I'm stupid. Which makes absolutely no sense, since he took my degree!" Cleopatra looked down at the top of his head and laughed out loud as she talked to herself. She clapped as she uttered every syllable. "Just because you took my degree doesn't mean it applies to you. My name is on it, I earned it. Put my shit back."

"I don't know what you're talking about."

Pops jumped in between them, now, joining Jacqueline as he saw Cleopatra about to escalate.

"It's ok, Pops. It's going to be fine." Cleopatra pulled the assegai off the wall—an African spear that Mandisa had gifted her back when they were dating and she was trying to buy Cleopatra's affections.

"If you don't get my degree and have it back on the wall where you got it from in the next two minutes, I will stick you until I get tired. And I just woke up after sleeping for like twelve hours. I got all the energy in the world. Do you want to try me?" Cleopatra twirled the spear around in her hand. "And guest what? One minute is already gone."

Aunt Roberta sobered up enough to yell at her son. "Boy! If you took it, you better put it back with your ignorant ass."

Benny ran from behind Jacqueline and her father to the coat closet in the foyer, where he burrowed his body underneath the coats, to emerge a moment later with Cleopatra's degree in its oversized frame. He sprinted through the house and put it back up in the library where he found it.

Jacqueline pulled the spear from Cleopatra's hand and followed Benny into the library.

Cleopatra waited a few minutes until she saw him walk out, then shadowed him as he said his goodbyes and got his coat. She checked his pockets and shoved him out the front door.

When she looked for Jacqueline, she found her in the library with Robin. Jacqueline still had the spear in her hand and had Robin hemmed up in the corner. Cleopatra thought it strange that she hadn't seen the two sisters together at all that night, and equally strange that Robin hadn't even said hello to her.

Robin sighed when she saw Cleopatra. "Thank God." She slid from around Jacqueline, as Cleopatra had her sister's full attention when she walked into the room.

"Get out of here," Cleopatra told Robin when she saw the look in Jacqueline's eyes. She stopped her right before Robin left the room. "I'm sure Jac has already said this to you, but stay away from me and stay away from her until she tells you different. Keep my name and our business out of your mouth. Next time, there might not be anyone around to save you from her." Robin sucked her teeth and mumbled as she walked out of the library.

"Are you ok?" Cleopatra asked Jacqueline. "I thought you two were trying to work out your issues."

"We were, before the thing with her telling Alonzo our business. Why would she do that? You were right, baby. It's like she really hates me. I don't trust her anymore, especially not where you're concerned. I don't want her in the same room as you, I don't like the way she looks at you. I told her I can make sure that she doesn't look at you again if I poke her eyes out with this spear."

"Um. Ok. We aren't going to do that." Cleopatra took the spear from her and hid it behind her back.

"I want my hands wrapped around her throat so bad, you don't understand. If had a dick it would be hard right now."

"That bad?" Cleopatra twisted her lips.

A tear ran down Jacqueline's cheek and she wiped her face. "I will get her. Maybe not tonight, but we will have this out. Understand something." She pulled Cleopatra's face to hers. "Anyone tries to take you from me or fucks with our relationship, I will destroy them." She kissed Cleopatra softly and in an instant her tears stopped. "And no one will ever know it was me," she whispered in Cleopatra's ear before she walked out of the room.

Cleopatra was about to follow Jacqueline to ask her what she meant when she swore she smelled weed coming from the terrace off the library.

"No." She sniffed the air and looked through the window, but didn't see anything. She opened the French doors and was assaulted by a cloud of marijuana smoke.

"Are you crazy?" Cleopatra snatched the blunt from Uncle Thomas's hand and dumped it into his drink.

"You know how much I paid for that shit?!"

"My bad." Cleopatra pulled out her wallet and dumped a $5 bill in the same glass with his drink and the blunt. "I know cheap shit when I smell it."

"You said to take it outside."

"You know what? You're right. I guess I wasn't clear." Cleopatra rubbed her chin. "How about this? You ain't gotta go home, but you gotta get the hell out of here."

"What?"

"Get out of my house!" she yelled. "I already kicked your spawn of failure out. Now it's your turn. Out! Is that clear enough? And don't forget your shine, your wife, and her teeth. She's around here somewhere, stuffing damn chicken livers into a ranch dressing bottle." Cleopatra walked back into the party to find Jacqueline.

"Hey, Daddy. You seen Mom and the kids?" Jacqueline asked her father.

"Yeah." He took a sip of his brother's moonshine. "She took the kids upstairs to give them a bath and put them to bed. That's why she wanted your keys."

"She didn't have to do that." She laid her head on her father's shoulder.

"Yes, she did have to do that." Pops directed his attention to Cleopatra now. "She wants you two to spend some time together after the party without any interruptions. So that means you, Cleopatra, are staying for a while."

"But we aren't supposed…" Cleopatra was about to inform him of their attorney's warning to pretty much stay away from each other, but she just nodded her head reluctantly. "Yes, sir. I'll stay as long as Jac wants me to."

Cleopatra excused herself and walked over to the buffet table, where she picked a deviled egg up and popped it into her mouth. Uncle Cletus walked up to her, blasting Frankie Beverly and Maze's *Before I Let Go* from a small transistor radio. He wore a tight blue argyle sweater vest and matching cargo sweat pants, tucked into his tan work boots.

"Let me take you away from all this, Cleopatra," he said as he tried to freak her from behind and took a selfie with his flip phone. "I need a good, strong woman like you in my life."

Cleopatra nearly choked on her water. "You don't really seem to grasp this gay thing, huh? I'm with your niece. We're married, remember?"

He ignored her. "I got a good job. I been driving this bus like forty years now. I got a pension coming and I'm ready to settle down. Cleo and Cletus. Meant to be."

"Cletus. You do realize you have corns and washcloths older than me?" Cleopatra reminded him.

Jacqueline came over to save Cleopatra from her uncle, who had an embarrassing crush on her wife. "You ok, baby?" Jacqueline wrapped her arms around Cleopatra's waist. "Why can't you stay away from my wife, Uncle Cletus? You know if there was no me there would still be no you, right? You do understand this?"

"Ah, baby girl. She just needs a good man."

"Once again, there would still be no you."

Cleopatra felt her wife getting hot and pulled Jacqueline away from Cletus.

He immediately started singing. "Cleopatra and Cletus sitting in the tree…" Then that bathtub shine he'd been drinking all night made him forget the words, and he transitioned back to Frankie Beverly and Maze.

Cleopatra led Jacqueline into a far corner of the hallway. "You ok?" She slipped her arms around Jacqueline's waist. Jacqueline stood between her thighs, rested her head on her chest, and exhaled deeply. "I'm always better when I'm in your arms."

Cleopatra kissed her forehead softly and cupped her ass as she pressed into her. Jacqueline loosened the knot on her bow tie.

"You look beautiful tonight, baby. I've been thinking it all night, but I don't actually think I've told you," Cleopatra said.

"Thank you. I wore this dress just for you." She smiled shyly. "Have I told you I miss you tonight?"

"Yeah." Cleopatra nodded.

"Have I told you just how much?" Jacqueline's legs wouldn't stop trembling. "You're my whole world, baby. I can't live without you." She looked up at Cleopatra, wanting to kiss her.

Cleopatra saw the love and desire in Jacqueline's eyes, and everything they were going through was eclipsed by how her woman looked at her. Jacqueline inched in closer. Cleopatra breathed down the front of Jacqueline's dress, her lips brushed against her neck.

Jacqueline's heart raced; she was unsure whether Cleopatra could or would resist her. But those lips belonged to her and Jacqueline wanted to kiss them. She pressed her lips to Cleopatra's and Cleopatra sucked hungrily on her mouth. She ran her fingers through Cleopatra's locs and drew her in closer to her, pressing her breasts into hers. She wanted Cleopatra, but someone could discover them at any moment.

But this was her wife, they were in their house. If someone saw something, they just got a glimpse into what true passion looked like.

Cleopatra crouched down and ran the tip of her tongue down Jacqueline's cleavage, then grabbed Jacqueline's hips, holding her up when she saw her knees start to buckle.

"Baby ... I need you." Jacqueline moaned.

Cleopatra didn't hesitate. She reached for the bottom of her dress and began to pull it up. She was dying to touch Jacqueline's slickness and push her fingers inside of her.

"Wait." Jacqueline stopped her. As much as she wanted

Cleopatra's hands all over and inside of her, she knew they had to stop. "We don't do quickies, baby. You know that. You want to go upstairs and come back down four hours from now? I don't think that will go over well."

"Yeah." Cleopatra backed up from Jacqueline. "Guess we need to work on that." She lowered her mouth to Jacqueline's and whispered against her lips, "We can still make out, right? At least I can tell you what I want to do to you. Can't I?"

"You're killing me."

"I want to turn you around and press your face up against this wall, pull your hands up over your head. Take my tongue and lick the back of your neck as you push your ass back into me.

"I want to scream your name," Jacqueline whispered to her.

Jacqueline's mother walked up to them, then, with a frown on her face. "I'm ready for all these motherfuckers to get out of my house, and it looks like you are, too."

"Whoa. Whoa." Cleopatra burst into laughter. She and Jacqueline both pulled away from each other and straightened their clothes.

"Mommy! You never curse. And this is our house," Jacqueline said shocked.

"Whatever. I had a flashback, baby. I'm ready for them to go. Get to stepping, raise up. Whatever you kids say. Be out." She motioned for Pops to come to her. "These motherfuckers are making me itch. I can't," she told her husband. "Jac and Cleo need their house back. They need to spend some time together," she continued. "Make your speech so we can start tucking and rolling these nig—" She caught herself before she finished.

Jacqueline, Cleopatra, and Pops froze with their mouths open in anticipation of what was about to spill out of her mouth.

"Start tucking and rolling folks. I was going to say folks." She cut her eyes at them. "Just because we're related doesn't mean we're family. They need to go."

Pops scurried to fulfill his wife's requests. It was indicative of why they had stayed married so happily and for so long. He kept his woman happy. His wife asked, and he didn't argue, just did what she wanted immediately. Happy wife, happy life. Pops said a few words to everyone, thanking Moms for thirty-five beautiful years of marriage, and for loving him unconditionally and giving him two beautiful daughters.

It took another forty-five minutes for everyone to go their separate ways. With people scrambling for paper plates, aluminum foil, and Tupperware containers and arguing over who took home what leftovers, the departures took much longer than they should have. Then, finally, Cleopatra and Jacqueline were alone with the kids sound asleep upstairs and a big mess left in the kitchen.

"Where do you want to start?"

"I'll put the dishes in the dishwasher. Can you gather all of the garbage and take it out?"

"I can do that." Cleopatra grabbed a garbage bag and starting dumping everything in it.

"I miss that, you know." Jacqueline watched her. "Me cooking and you taking out the garbage. I miss you taking care of me and me taking care of you. I miss being your wife."

Cleopatra sat the bag down on the floor and dropped her hands to her sides.

Jacqueline walked up to her. "You really hurt me, baby. The things that ran through my mind when I thought you had betrayed me. I thought Supriti was having what's mine. It was the worse feeling in the world."

"I'm sorry. You know the last thing I ever want to do is hurt you."

"I'm sorry, too. And I'm sorry that I actually thought you would betray our vows."

"What happens now?" Cleopatra held out her hand and Jacqueline took hold of it.

"I don't know. I don't know how to live without you. I don't just want you. I need you. What am I supposed to do when I need my wife? What if I need her arms around me? What if I need to feel her body on mine? Her lips on mine? Feel her inside of me?"

"You're a grown woman. If you need something, you know how to get it." Cleopatra stood there, looking down at Jacqueline.

"I need you," Jacqueline whispered.

"You know how to get me." Cleopatra licked her lips. And before Cleopatra allowed her doubts to stop her, Jacqueline kissed her. They both wanted and needed each other. Jacqueline longed to scream in victory, but instead pressed her body closer to Cleopatra's, brushing her aching breasts against her chest. Erotic heat vibrated through her body, swirling low in her belly.

"I don't want to argue anymore," Jacqueline whispered in Cleopatra's ear.

"What do you want?" Cleopatra slid her hands up Jacqueline's dress and grabbed her ass. Jacqueline's moans in her ear drove her crazy.

Jacqueline gasped as Cleopatra put her weight on her. "I want you. All over me."

"You do?" Cleopatra stuck out her tongue and licked a trail across her lips. The passion in her eyes made Jacqueline's pussy throb and swell. Her body couldn't help responding. Beneath her dress, between her thighs, her lips puckered, goose bumps covering her arms and the tiny hairs on the back of her neck standing up on end. Her nipples hardened against the silk of her bra. She swallowed hard, and her heartbeat hastened. She had to make a conscious effort to breathe. Each inhale was full of Cleopatra's cologne, her natural body oils, and those pheromones that Jacqueline was convinced made her their bitch.

She kissed Cleopatra's neck, the soft, sensitive spot under her right ear—her spot. She used her tongue and licked in tiny circles, then cupped Cleopatra's pussy in her hands and rubbed her. "I want to feel you." Jacqueline gasped. "I miss you. Let me be your wife tonight."

✿✿✿

Jacqueline's body was hot and eager with anticipation as she spotted her wife at the foot of their bed. Cleopatra watched the way Jacqueline's hungry smile widened, and her eyes closed. Then her brown eyes opened again to stare up at Cleopatra as her cock slid into her and filled her up. Cleopatra bent her head down and took Jacqueline's lips in her mouth. Slowly, she moved in and out of Jacqueline, long stroking her with unbelievable control, until finally, she plunged deeper. Jacqueline trembled and squirmed underneath Cleopatra, needing to move, overcome by how good she felt inside of her.

She closed her eyes and moaned Cleopatra's name. The last time she remembered something feeling this good she was doing exactly this … taking all of her wife's cock, or some variation involving Cleopatra's mouth, tongue, or fingers.

Cleopatra's hands slid down Jacqueline's back and cupped her ass and thighs. She pulled her closer, grinding her dick deep.

For Jacqueline, the urge to rip her nails down Cleopatra's body was strong—so strong that she had to ball her hands up into fists to resist it.

"That's all yours baby." Jacqueline's lifted her legs up over Cleopatra's shoulders, tightening her grip on her cock. Cleopatra pulled out slowly, then slid back in as far as she could go.

Cleopatra drew her even closer, one hand resting on Jacqueline's plump ass, and groaned as Jacqueline arched her back to meet her thrusts. Nothing felt as good as sinking into Jacqueline's hot pussy. She pumped harder and faster as Jacqueline's orgasm ripped through her.

When Jacqueline finally exploded, she whispered, "I love you."

☼☼☼

Early the next morning, while Cleopatra showered, her cell phone vibrated on her nightstand.

"Baby, your phone!" Jacqueline yelled.

"Answer it, sweetheart."

Jacqueline saw Supriti's name on the screen. She looked at

the time—6AM—and punched the button to accept the call.

"Hello. Don't you dare hang up. I know who this is. I saw the caller ID."

"I'm sorry," Supriti said.

"For what? That the first thing you do when you wake up in the morning is call my wife? Or are you sorry that I picked up? Don't bother trying to explain yourself," Jacqueline continued. "Cleopatra is in the shower, but I'll be sure to tell her you called."

"Wait," Supriti said. "I have a message. Tell Cleopatra I just called to see how your parents' anniversary party went. Can you relay that message to her? Thanks." And Supriti hung up.

Jacqueline stormed into the bathroom and pulled the glass shower door open.

"Baby, you're letting cold air in." Cleopatra looked at her.

"That bitch just called your phone. It's 6 in the morning, Cleopatra. I should take this phone and flush it down the damn toilet." Jacqueline held up her cell phone.

"What bitch?" Cleopatra rolled her eyes, turned off the shower, pulled a towel off the rack, and covered herself.

"Oooh. You can't keep all of your bitches straight now? Supriti!"

"I don't know why. We aren't even speaking. You asked me to kill contact and I did. The same day. But why are you mad at me? She's the one who called me."

"Why the hell does she know about my parents' party? That was her message. She called to find out how *my* parents' party went! Are you fucking kidding me?"

"I probably mentioned it to her a while ago. I'm sorry."

"Do me a favor, when you're talking to that bitch, keep me

and my family's business out of your mouth. You got that?" Jacqueline stormed out of the bathroom.

"Loud and clear." Cleopatra followed behind her as she walked back in to the bedroom. She pulled out clothes from her drawer and started to get dressed as Jacqueline watched her.

"You are smarter than this, Jac. You don't think it's odd that she just out of the blue calls me early this morning, when she knows your parents' party was last night? She probably figured that we spent the night together, and that she would do what she had to just to separate us again. She knows calling now would make you hot."

"She was right. I guess her little plan worked."

"Why are you acting like this? You just said last night you wanted to be my wife again."

"You really don't get it." A tear ran down Jacqueline's cheek and she wiped it away with the back of her hand. She sighed. "All I fucking do is cry now. And I'm so tired of it. I'm your wife, but I'm threatened by her, Cleopatra. Why can't you understand that?"

"There's no reason to be. I love you."

Jacqueline shook her head. "Women may be attracted to you or want you, but they don't get up close and personal contact with you. They can't get to know you the way that you have allowed her to. You're confiding in her now. You used to confide in me. You aren't fucking her, but you have an intimacy that belongs to me. Or at least it used to. It just keeps building up, and it's just one thing after another with her. How much am I supposed to overlook and forgive? She's trying to replace me, and bit by bit, you're letting her."

Cleopatra started to speak and defend herself.

"I don't want to hear it. Just hurry up. You're moving too slow. I want you out now."

Cleopatra stopped. "What about the kids? I wanted to say good morning to them, maybe have breakfast."

"No. You're not supposed to be in this house anyway. They're still sleeping, so they'll never know you spent the night."

THIRTY THREE

....

A HOUSE IS NOT A HOME

"Why do you think there's always something wrong or that I need something when I call you?" Jacqueline asked angrily. "I just want to talk."

Though she was furious with Cleopatra for sharing family business with Supriti, Jacqueline had thought that their making love the night of her parents' anniversary party would restore their connection. But she was wrong; days went by before she was able to get Cleopatra on the phone again outside of the children's bedtime.

"You want to know why I don't want to talk? Because when we talk, we argue!" Cleopatra yelled into the phone.

"So you'd just rather not talk?"

"Basically."

"Fine." Jacqueline hung up.

Cleopatra didn't want to be on the phone with her wife; she just wanted to be with her wife. She was still reeling that Jacqueline planned to end their marriage like it wasn't a big deal. Cleopatra was going to go after Alonzo and hire a private investigator. But Jacqueline had refused her help, so she wouldn't get it. So where did that leave her?

Jacqueline became quick tempered and cranky with the children. She was sad, and anxious. The only way she got any rest was if she cried herself to sleep. And she was hornier than she had ever been in her life. She could feel Cleopatra slipping away from her, and she hated it. She didn't send her texts messages just to tell her how much she loved her, or her how beautiful she was. She didn't walk in the door with a present just because. Now when Cleopatra came to the house to see the kids they barely spoke and they never touched; sometimes she wouldn't even come inside the house. Their relationship was nearly non-existent and had dwindled to co-parenting.

Jacqueline needed to do something to get her woman back to her emotionally, before it was too late. She cooked one of Cleopatra's favorite meals—manicotti and peach cobbler—in an effort to get her to stay after she brought the twins home one day. Cleopatra was conflicted when she saw that look in Jacqueline's eyes. The symbolism of the meal wasn't lost on her; manicotti and peach cobbler was the first meal Jacqueline had ever cooked for her.

Jacqueline pleaded with her. "Please don't leave. You love my cooking. I made this just for you."

Cleopatra pulled out a chair and sat down at the dining room table to eat.

Jacqueline served her a heaping plate of manicotti and sat across from her. "I miss you so much," she whispered across the table. "I miss—"

"Have you heard anything about the court date yet?" Cleopatra cut her off.

"No." Jacqueline was taken aback by Cleopatra's question.

"Of course not. You'd be the first person to know."

"Why haven't I gotten separation or divorce papers yet? Or is that what this dinner is about? Do you have them? I can sign them right now."

"No. That's not what dinner was about. It was about spending some time with my wife." Jacqueline hesitated. "But there is something I need to tell you."

Cleopatra stopped eating and put her fork down. She waited for Jacqueline to continue. "They tested Alonzo, I don't know how, but his drug test came back clean. So no hope of just dismissing the case." Jacqueline picked at her manicotti. "And Vanessa also reminded me again that if Alonzo's attorney has someone watching the house it could ruin our chances. So we need to act like we're truly broken up. Remember, we really haven't been abiding by it. You can continue to pick up the kids for visits but spending time all together and spending the night ... we can't really do that right now." Jacqueline exhaled hard.

"Then why would you even—" Cleopatra interrupted.

"And I know that I cooked for you tonight and asked you to stay. I did that because I knew I wouldn't get any time with you after I told you," she admitted as she braced herself for Cleopatra's response.

"You asked me to stay so you could tell me I couldn't be here? That doesn't even make sense. It's my house." That was a turning point for Cleopatra. She was done. She felt her blood pressure rising and pushed her plate toward the middle of the table. She stood up as she felt the anger escalate inside of her. "You didn't answer me. Why haven't I received the papers?"

"Is that what you want? Why do you seem like you're in a

rush? You ready to be single again already?" Jacqueline got defensive.

Cleopatra shook her head. "Don't put this on me. It's not about me, remember? I don't want a divorce, but I do want this ridiculous situation to be over. This is yours and Vanessa's little scheme, not mine. I didn't agree to it, and I damn sure don't like it. I don't want anything to do with it. I'm tired of it hanging over my head. As a matter of fact, why don't we get an annulment, like this shit never even happened? I just want to move past this. Get on with my life, whatever that means."

"Fine. I'll have the papers drawn up as soon as possible."

✿✿✿

Nearly a month had passed since Cleopatra moved out of the house. She continued to slip away, and as time went on she became less and less accessible.

Then one night, things changed. They got worse.

"I need you to come over, now." Jacqueline sounded upset on the phone.

"What's wrong?"

"Amir won't eat. He's on a hunger strike and Maya won't stop crying. They miss you and it's really starting to affect them, baby."

"He's four. What does he know about a hunger strike?"

Jacqueline smiled. "A certain someone lets him watch Melissa Harris Perry with her. That's how he knows."

"I'm on my way."

With that, Cleopatra went back home, sneaking in the back

door of their townhouse on the off chance that they were being watched by Alonzo's associates. From the moment that Cleopatra walked through the door, the energy throughout the house changed. She sat down for dinner with Jacqueline and the kids. Amir got his appetite back and tried to eat as much as his Mama Cleo. She gave Jacqueline a break and helped the kids with their baths, then told them a bedtime story, just as she used to do every night.

"How come you have to leave?" Maya asked as she hugged Cleopatra goodnight.

Cleopatra looked at Jacqueline. "Are you going to answer that?"

"I want you here when I wake up in the morning." Amir tugged on Cleopatra's locs. "Last night I had a bad dream and I woke up and you weren't here."

"She'll be here when you wake up, baby, don't worry," Jacqueline said as she tucked him in.

Cleopatra looked at Jacqueline, surprised. "Sweet dreams," she said to both Maya and Amir as she turned out the light.

Then Jacqueline grabbed her by the hand and pulled her out into the hallway.

"Why did you lie to them?"

"It wasn't a lie. You will be here in the morning." She kissed Cleopatra and led her down the hall to their bedroom. "They aren't the only ones that need you, you know that right? Because I keep trying to tell you."

"I don't know that. It hasn't felt that way."

"I know, baby." Jacqueline unzipped Cleopatra's hoodie and slipped her arms around her waist. "I miss you. I can't take it." Jacqueline kissed her hard. "Spend the night with me,"

Jacqueline whispered in her ear.

"I shouldn't. You know I can't stay. What if someone saw me come in?"

"No one saw you come in through the back. I don't really care what the attorney or the judge say right now, or what they think. Plus, you just saw me promise the kids you'd be here when they woke up. I miss you. Don't you miss me? Waking up with me in your arms? Miss my breakfasts, my pancakes and biscuits? My Sunday dinners? Cuddling with me after dark? Kissing me?"

"I miss all of that. But I'm tired of going back and forth with you. You're divorcing me, but you love me, you want to cook me dinner and make love all night but then I can't be here outside of picking up the kids. I'm coming in the back door of my own home like a thief in the night. Don't use my love for you against me, because I'm over this entire situation. I'm sorry you made the kids a promise you couldn't keep, but you seem to be getting better at that every day."

✿✿✿

"When are you coming home? Don't you need some more clothes?" Jacqueline asked.

"Why would I go anywhere near there? You told me I had to stay away because someone might see me going into my own damn house, remember? Don't worry, I already bought a new wardrobe. And I wouldn't want to run into you or your kids."

"What did you just say? My kids? They're your kids too. *Our* kids. Are you out of your mind? Don't ever say some shit like that again. You think this is easy? Your being away from me? Away from us? Everything I did to be with you, and now this bullshit happened."

Cleopatra hung up the phone.

"Oh my God." Jacqueline hit redial on her cell phone.

Cleopatra picked up the phone.

"I know you didn't just hang the fucking phone up on me."

Cleopatra hung up again.

"Shit! Really?" Jacqueline called Cleopatra again. Cleopatra answered but didn't speak. "Why did you hang up on me, Cleopatra?"

"Don't curse at me, you know I don't fight that way. I've told you that on more than one occasion. My own mother never cursed at me, so if you think I'm going to tolerate it from my wife, you can continue to talk to the dial tone. You're one of the most intelligent women I know; you can express yourself with your vocabulary. Use your words." Cleopatra hung up again.

"Use my motherfucking words?" Jacqueline screamed. Then she struggled to calm herself down. She exhaled and called Cleopatra back. "I'm sorry for cursing. It's just killing me being away from you. The kids miss you like crazy. We have been crying ourselves to sleep every night. This is not what I want."

"So I still haven't received the divorce papers. I really would like to get this wrapped up. What's the hold up?"

"Don't say cruel shit you don't mean because you're hurting Cleopatra. Don't hang up, don't hang up." Jacqueline braced herself to hear a dial tone again.

"Who says I didn't mean it?"

"This separation, the divorce won't be forever. I'm still your wife, and I'm not giving up on us. That's the last thing I'm ever going to do."

"I'm tired," Cleopatra admitted.

"I'm tired of fighting too. I just want to be with you."

"No. I mean I'm tired of having this conversation." Cleopatra hung up.

THIRTY FOUR

....

PORN IN THE NYC

"Hey Cleopatra. I'm in town, want to have dinner?" Cassidy, the insatiable porn star and ex-fling, was back in New York and checking for her. She'd called just as Cleopatra was about to leave work for the day.

"I'm married. You know that."

"Everyone knows you're married, and some even care. It's just dinner, Papi."

"I know your just dinner, Cass."

"I'm serious—like in a restaurant, with clothes on. I won't even follow you into the ladies' room. I'm in a cab now. I'll be outside your office in like ten minutes."

"In that case, all right." Cleopatra packed up her bag and met Cassidy downstairs in front of her building. She had to walk through a group of men enamored by the adult entertainment star and wanting to take pictures with her. Cassidy was tall, voluptuous, oozed sex, and was immediately recognizable as she dressed every bit the role of the porn star, in a tight, low-cut red dress and matching stilettos. She ran over and embraced Cleopatra as soon as she saw her, and Cleopatra admonished her for grabbing her ass.

"You really should roll with security when you're on the East Coast. I'm going to need you to work on that." She pulled her away from the crowd of men, who yelled "Kiss her" as they walked away.

"That's so sweet that you still care." She pinched Cleopatra's cheek, then pulled her compact from her purse and checked her lipstick. "How do my lips look?" she puckered her mouth.

"Mmmm…" Cleopatra moaned. "Do you really want to know?"

"Excellent." She laid a big kiss on Cleopatra's cheek.

"Ewww…" Cleopatra grabbed her face.

Cassidy laughed, knowing Cleopatra hated lipstick. She took a handkerchief from her purse and took pleasure in wiping Cleopatra's face.

"I really like the brown." Cleopatra said as she played with Cassidy's hair. "It makes you look a little innocent. And that's a miracle."

"Such a smart ass." Cassidy sucked her teeth. "For your information, this is my Beyoncé hair. Someone hasn't been keeping up with my movies, I see. I have a routine that goes with this hair if you want to see it later." She winked. "All clean." She blew another kiss at Cleopatra as she looked at her freshly wiped cheek.

"Thank you."

They were walking down Broadway when Cleopatra felt someone's hands on her arm.

"Excuse me." Supriti pulled Cleopatra away from Cassidy.

"Who the hell is this?"

"Who the hell are you?" Cassidy stepped in front of Supriti and put her hands on her hips.

"She's a friend," Cleopatra said to Supriti. "You know, like you and I used to be. But I do know for a fact that her pussy hair is straight and usually shaved into a landing strip."

Cassidy laughed as she put her arm around Cleopatra's waist. "But one time she did shave a big old C into it. That was hot, too." Cleopatra winked at her. "Remember that? What did the C stand for?"

"Mmmm..." Cassidy pulled Cleopatra into her and pushed her double D's against her chest. "You remember, baby. It stood for Cleopatra's cunt." She stuck out her tongue.

"Oh yeah. I remember now."

"Yeah she's just a friend," Cassidy laughed at Supriti. "With an incredibly talented tongue. Come on, Papi." She yanked Cleopatra away from Supriti as a cab stopped for them at the corner.

"Have a good evening." Cleopatra nodded her head as they walked away.

Cleopatra enjoyed a platonic dinner and drinks with Cassidy that night at a cozy downtown Brooklyn restaurant. She was craving female attention that she couldn't get from Jacqueline, who did nothing but stress her out and was planning on divorcing her anyway. She liked how Cassidy looked at her, and Cassidy had no expectations outside the next few hours ... or so Cleopatra thought. Aside from some harmless flirting and reminiscing about the sleepless nights they used to share, they both behaved themselves.

But there was something different about Cassidy. She was

calmer, she was sweeter. It was a side that Cleopatra had never seen, and she liked it.

"What's different about you? Besides the 'Bey hair? You almost seem shy with me. It's cute."

"I'm turning thirty this year. And I've been thinking a lot about my life. My relationships. You know, you broke my heart when I asked you to be my girlfriend and you laughed at me. But I realize now that I wasn't ready for you then, not even close. I would have quit the business for you. All you had to do back then was say the word."

"I didn't know that. But you do realize why? I would never have been able to get past the hundreds of videos of you fucking numerous people with numerous holes in your body, sometimes at the same time."

"I know. That's why I wanted you to be the first to know that I'm retiring from the business. Well, at least from in front of the camera. I'm starting my own production company. There's just too much money in adult entertainment to leave it completely."

"Congratulations. About time you put that MBA to work." Cleopatra winked at her.

"You remembered?"

"I don't know a lot of adult entertainers who have their graduate degree in marketing. So yes, I remember. You've turned yourself and um … your skills into a brand. I have no doubt that you'll be successful. And since your career is ending soon, I'm going to need you to hook me up with your last few films. I'm a little behind."

"Anything for you. You know, it's too bad we never made a movie."

"Ha!" Cleopatra laughed. "That's probably for the best. I don't think the world would be ready for that."

"You're right. You would have been an incredible porn star." Cassidy licked her lips as she reflected on their time together. "We can still make one. Like tonight, like right now. You can have the only copy and you can watch it whenever your wife is acting up. Which I'm getting the feeling is right now since you haven't mentioned her once tonight." Cassidy raised an eyebrow. "What do you say, for old time's sake?"

Cassidy went into her purse and slid something across the table to her. Cleopatra looked down and saw a hotel card key with Soho Grand Hotel scrolled across the front of it.

"Aw shit..."

✿✿✿

Cleopatra rolled over in bed and turned on the lamp. It was just after midnight and her cell phone had woken her up.

"Who is that? She's all over you. And the picture of you helping her into a cab. Where were you going? And why the hell are you playing with her hair?" Jacqueline screamed into the phone.

Even though she was still half-asleep, Cleopatra wasn't surprised by the phone call. Her going around with someone as overtly sexual as Cassidy was bound to get back to Jacqueline. "That's a friend of mine, Cassidy. That was a hug hello."

Jacqueline texted Cleopatra the pictures that someone had snapped of her and Cassidy out on the street. "That's hello? What does goodbye look like?"

"A lot like the hello, but in reverse." Cleopatra put her on speakerphone as she looked at the pictures.

She studied the background of the photos, wondering if Supriti was the one who'd sent them. At this point, she wouldn't put anything past her. But the angles were all off; someone else had sent these pictures to Jacqueline.

"So you know her? You're friends? Why does this look a lot like that porn star?"

"Yeah, it is. I know her."

"So you've fucked her before? When? Why am I just now hearing about this?"

"When you and I were broken up before. Remember? You never wanted to discuss women I've dated."

"Yeah, but you got dozens of that bitch's movies up in our house. Did you fuck her tonight?"

"Seriously? No, I didn't. At the moment, I'm still married, and still committed to you. We had dinner. I don't believe you."

"Dated? What does that mean, to date a porn star? And a nasty-ass porn star. Because that bitch is nasty. You had an actual relationship back then, or did you just fuck her?"

"I fucked the shit out of her," Cleopatra said proudly.

"Wow. So did she pay you or what?"

"I'm sorry, what did you say? You have a lot of nerve to say some shit like that to me. Did she pay me for the sex?" Cleopatra laughed. "No, but as good as I used to fuck her, she probably should have."

"Is there anyone you haven't fucked?" Jacqueline yelled.

"Um ... let me think ... I haven't bent your sister over yet. You want to tell that ho to back up off of me?"

THIRTY FIVE

....

CLEOPATRA TO THE RESCUE

"Hello." Cleopatra answered her cell phone in the middle of the night.

"It's Supriti."

"I saw the caller ID. What do you want?" She strained her eyes to read the clock on her bedside table: 4:10AM. She'd had enough of these late-night phone calls.

"I'm sorry I woke you. I tried calling Mandisa and she didn't pick up. But I'm not surprised. It's my father. He had a heart attack."

"Is he...?" Cleopatra hesitated.

"No. He's still alive. But I don't want to see him."

"What if he...? You'll never forgive yourself."

"I would get over it."

"I think I know you a little better than that. You would regret it. Is that why you're calling me in the middle of the night? For validation not to go?"

"Would you?"

"I would." Cleopatra sat up in bed, reached over and turned

on the lamp. "My mother never wanted me to harbor any resentment toward my father. But at the same time, she said he would pay for everything he did with a slow death. And honestly I want to be there to see it. I guess that make me evil."

"It makes you human. He disowned me, Cleopatra. When I wouldn't enter an arranged marriage. And then the second I came out to him, he spit in my face. He took my mother away from me, forbade her to speak to me or he would kill us both. I haven't seen or spoken to her in over five years. He told me I was dead to him, that he wanted a son anyway. A daughter is a burden on her father's head. You know that's actually a Hindu saying? He said he would live his life like I never existed, and that if he ever saw me again he would kill me himself."

"Damn," Cleopatra mumbled under her breath.

"Why would I go see that person? Why would I care if he lived or died, if he didn't care if I did?"

"It's up to you. Just make sure you don't have any regrets. If he is on his deathbed, what can he do to you that he hasn't already done? I know you want me to, but I'm not going to tell you what to do, Supriti."

Later that morning, Cleopatra found herself over at Supriti's loft, booking her plane reservations for a flight home to San Francisco. She even packed a bag for her. She had only stopped by to check on her before going in to work, but Supriti was in tears and inconsolable when she answered her door. So Cleopatra did what Supriti wanted her to do from the start—she took control, told her what she was going to do, and how she was going to do it.

Cleopatra stayed with her until her car service to the airport arrived.

"You're strong, you can do this," Cleopatra reassured her.

Supriti held her tight, with tears in her eyes. "I told you…" She hesitated. "I told you before, you are such a good woman." She caressed Cleopatra's face. "I told you, but you didn't hear me. I love you so much."

Cleopatra ignored her confession. "Text me so I know you landed safely, and keep in touch."

But Supriti did much more than keep in touch. She stayed in constant contact with Cleopatra while she was in California. Her mother was nowhere to be found. No one in the extended family had seen or heard from her, and a good deal of her belongings were gone from their family home. This left Supriti alone and lonely, and Cleopatra as her only trusted support through her father's subsequent heart surgery and eventual death. They talked on the phone at all hours of the night, mended old wounds, and grew closer. And Supriti lost her battle to not fall deeper in love with Cleopatra.

THIRTY SIX

....

THE SET UP

{Jacqueline: I'm sorry we fought. I'm coming to your hotel later. Be ready for me.}

{Cleopatra: I'm always ready.}

{Jacqueline: Turn the lights off, get in the bed, and wait.}

{Cleopatra: I'm going to throw your back out.}

I'm going to throw your back out? Just the thought made Robin's body quiver. There was no turning back now. She was visiting Jacqueline, who was upstairs with the kids, when something had come over her. She saw the key card to Cleopatra's hotel room on the kitchen table, and she couldn't help but pick up Jacqueline's cell phone and text her sister-in-law.

Jacqueline hadn't told her why Cleopatra was out of the house again, and didn't dare tell her sister she was on the verge of divorce. She wasn't entirely sure what Robin knew or if Robin was still in contact with her ex-husband. She was just about to confront Robin about how Alonzo knew all of her and Cleopatra's personal business, and had decided that Robin must have been the one who sent her the picture of Cassidy and Cleopatra. She was furious, and it had the potential to get physical, but the kids saved Robin when they called for Jacqueline to go upstairs.

Robin put the key card in her back pocket and deleted the texts she'd just exchanged with Cleopatra. Then she gathered her purse and slipped out of the front door. But not before she went through Jacqueline's wallet. She fingered Jacqueline's name, imprinted across her black card, and ran her thumbnail across the numbers, but thought better of taking it. She grabbed five crisp one hundred dollar bills instead. Her sister would never miss them.

✿✿✿

Later that night, in the upstairs bedroom of Cleopatra's hotel suite, Jacqueline paced back and forth. "So you know what to do?"

"I got it," Cleopatra assured her.

Cleopatra couldn't stand to be in the same space and breathing the same air as Ratchet Robin. And Jacqueline wasn't exactly on the top of Cleopatra's list of favorite people at the moment—they were barely on speaking terms—but she'd decided to go along with Jacqueline's plan. What she and Jacqueline were going through would have to be temporarily suspended and put aside. For now, their mutual enemy in Robin needed to be dealt with. Robin was about to get what she deserved.

"Shh… I think I hear her," Jacqueline whispered.

Downstairs, Robin keyed into Cleopatra's suite with the key

card that she'd lifted from Jacqueline's purse. It was dark, just as she'd requested. But instead of waiting in the bed naked, Cleopatra had a surprise for her. She spotted Robin and called down to the lower level of the suite.

"Take off your clothes, come upstairs, get in the bed on your hands and knees, and throw your ass back until you feel me," Cleopatra yelled from her bedroom.

Robin turned on a table lamp and walked around the suite as she prepared to strip. She peeked out onto the outdoor terrace overlooking downtown Manhattan, and dropped her jacket and purse. She took a small bottle of Merlot out of the mini bar, kicked off her heels, and finished the wine in two chugs.

She took inventory like she was going to take up residence in the suite, surveying it to see if it was up to her standards. She ran her hands over everything, from the iMac to the flat screen television, where she pulled off her black dress and let it puddle at her feet. She fingered the ebonized hardwood, exposed concrete, Italian leather sofa, and marble surfaces. She dropped her bra and panties at the bottom of the steps by the silk draperies, and let the silk caress her thighs as she made her way up the stairs naked and ready to throw her ass like never before. Cleopatra waited, watching the silhouette of Robin walk into the bedroom and assume the position on the king size bed.

"Nice. Now," Cleopatra whispered to Jacqueline, who was standing next her.

"Come on, baby…" Robin moaned.

"Come on, throw that ass like you mean it," Cleopatra said. Robin pushed her ass up in the air, popping her hips back.

"Not like that," Cleopatra complained. "Do it harder, like

your sister." Cleopatra covered her mouth as she laughed, and Jacqueline punched Cleopatra hard in her arm.

"Owww." Cleopatra held her arm, thinking she was going to have a bruise later.

Meanwhile, the challenge had pissed Robin off, and she pumped her ass harder as she grunted.

Jacqueline couldn't hold it in anymore. Cleopatra saw her retreat to the corner and the next thing she knew, Jacqueline was leaping across the bedroom and landing on the bed like Spiderman. She proceeded to douse Robin with a bucket of ice water. Then all Cleopatra heard was the cracking of a leather belt against Robin's wet skin. And Robin screaming. It was all one big blur beating the shit out of another blur in the darkness. Robin's screams were B-movie worthy, and so jarring that for a split second Cleopatra almost felt sorry for her. Almost.

Initially, Robin thought it was Cleopatra taking a belt so aggressively to her ass, she moaned and laughed at the first few licks. But when she made out Jacqueline's face in the dim lighting and yelled out, "Jac what the fuck?" Her disappointment only infuriated Jacqueline more.

When Robin started to fight back, trying to grab the belt and come at Jacqueline, Jacqueline pinned her down and warned her. "Fight me back and you'll just make this worse. You want to talk shit and do dirty shit now to your own sister? You think you a woman now? You need to take this ass whipping like a woman."

Jacqueline repeatedly made contact with Robin's bare flesh, whipping her hard with the belt. Cleopatra cringed as she heard the leather hitting Robin's skin, sounding like a pot of popcorn on the stove, in between Jacqueline cursing her out and calling her sister a low-down dirty pussy-having bitch who fucked for peach Snapples and Little Debbie cakes.

Finally Cleopatra walked over to the nightstand and turned on the lamp.

Robin looked over and saw Cleopatra standing up to the side of her. But Jacqueline didn't like how Robin looked at Cleopatra. She pulled her by her hair and flung her back down on the bed.

"She wants some more?" And she started whipping Robin's naked ass and legs again with the belt.

"You better not be looking at her ass, Cleopatra!" Jacqueline yelled.

"Oh my God." Robin scurried across the bed and finally made it to her feet.

"Jac. You maybe want to stop?" Cleopatra asked her.

"It's cool, baby. She likes it rough. She's going to make me run after her, now."

Cleopatra let Jacqueline chase Robin around the bedroom, blocking the door and preventing Robin's escape.

"I warned you, I gave you a lot of chances!" Jacqueline yelled.

Robin glared at Jacqueline. "You set me up. Tricky bitch. How is that fair?"

"I would go to prison for you about now. I would leave the kids and Cleopatra and be well with it, just to watch you take your last breath." Jacqueline wrapped the belt tighter around her fist. "And the $500? Who steals from their sister? You broke bitch."

Instead of getting it out of her system, Cleopatra felt Jacqueline escalating, and pulled her back from Robin.

"Do me a favor, Robin, and just tell your sister that you hate her. You want to be her and have everything she has. That way she won't waste any more of her time trying to have a relationship with you, and you can stop hurting my wife. Jacqueline, you can have her. I don't want to witness this slaughter anymore."

Cleopatra left them and went downstairs to find Robin's purse. She dumped everything out onto the floor and found the five crisp $100 bills. A moment later Robin ran downstairs behind Cleopatra, fumbling around the apartment and picking up and putting on her clothes, with Jacqueline right on her tail, flicking the belt at her like she was fighting a bull.

Robin was death on her feet as she slipped on her heels and defiantly stumbled up to Cleopatra. "After I tried to fuck you the last time I decided I would leave it alone. I stopped going after you, but if it's laid out for me to take, yeah, I'm gonna take it."

Jacqueline mushed Robin in her head. "Get the hell away from my wife. What does she mean the last time?" she yelled at Cleopatra.

"Hurry up," Cleopatra said to Robin. "She came to my hotel in a trench coat the day after my birthday, when we had that fight about my working as an escort. I didn't tell you then because I didn't want to damage your relationship."

At that, Jacqueline dove for Robin, knocking her down on the couch. She choked her until Cleopatra was able to pull her off.

"That's enough," Cleopatra whispered to Jacqueline.

Jacqueline's plan was to teach Robin a lesson. It was meant to be payback for Robin tracking down Alonzo and offering him all the ammunition and information he would need to ruin their lives. But Jacqueline's rage had taken over her. The lies, the betrayal, the jealousy, and the constant attempts to sleep with her wife had caused her to snap, and no amount of pummeling Robin had managed to calm her down.

Cleopatra restrained Jacqueline. "Enough. All right?" she said.

Jacqueline nodded in agreement as tears streamed down her face. Then Robin stood up from the couch in an attempt to go after Jacqueline. But Robin was in so much pain and so slow that she broadcasted her intention to swing on her. Cleopatra stepped to her and mushed Robin, palming her entire face in her hand and pushing her down to the floor.

"You aren't serious?" Cleopatra looked down at Robin as she blocked Jacqueline's access to her sister. "All right. The ass whipping is over." She pointed to the door. "Get up and get out now, Robin."

Robin stumbled to her feet, darting hateful stares at both Cleopatra and Jacqueline. Cleopatra could see the red welts forming all over her body; she was going to be in a whole lot of pain for the foreseeable future. Hopefully she learned something, Cleopatra thought as she watched Robin leave. She hobbled to the door and when she opened it, ran smack into housekeeping. The woman was right on time to change Cleopatra's linens, as she had requested earlier in the day.

"Hello. You can go right on upstairs. Thank you so much," Cleopatra said. The woman excused herself to the bedroom to switch out the sheets. Cleopatra then turned to Jacqueline. "You can go now, too."

THIRTY SEVEN

··

PRIVATE EYES

{Pops: I'm disappointed in you, Cleopatra. I thought you loved my daughter unconditionally. But if you won't fight for her and your marriage, a divorce is probably best.}

That text message from Jacqueline's father both hurt and infuriated Cleopatra. But he was right. If she wasn't willing to fight for Jacqueline, she didn't deserve her. At the mere idea of Jacqueline divorcing her, Cleopatra had bailed on her and the possibility of saving their marriage. She'd stopped fighting for her woman and her family almost immediately. She hadn't even taken Pops advice when he told her to step up. She didn't seek out alternative ways to win the custody battle, and didn't enlist the assistance of the two most powerful women she knew—Alexis and Olivia—to help. All she was ready to do was pout, roll over, give up, and sign the divorce papers the moment she received them.

She and Jacqueline had grown apart. Cleopatra pretended like she didn't care anymore and didn't miss her wife, when it was the exact opposite. She couldn't fool herself into believing that she didn't love and need Jacqueline, because she did. She did love her wife unconditionally, and she needed to do the right thing, regardless of what happened to her and Jacqueline's marriage. And that was make sure that Jacqueline kept the kids. She finally took Pops' advice, swallowed her pride, ignored her pain, and put her wife first. Hopefully it wasn't too late.

✧✧✧

"Good to see you, Cleo." Detective Nia Humphrey raised up on her tip toes and kissed her softly on the cheek. They sat down at a corner table in the bar of Cleopatra's hotel. She had reached out to an old girlfriend of hers—an NYPD detective—to get a referral to a private investigator.

"I told you I would take care of this, that I would handle it for you. Didn't I?" Nia said.

"You did." Cleopatra smiled. She trusted her completely. "It's a good thing having a friend with big titties, a big gun, and a license to use both of them," she laughed.

"Same old Cleo," Nia laughed as she patted her perfect bun with the palm of her hand. Nia had gotten her and Jacqueline out of trouble before, and she was hoping she could do it again.

"Mr. Coleman should be here soon. He's coming straight from the airport." Nia looked at her watch.

A tall, heavy-set, dark-skinned gentleman with snow-white hair, dressed in a super snug burgundy Members Only jacket, suddenly walked over to their table.

"Nia, sweetheart good to see you." He hugged her and

shook Cleopatra's hand. "Good to finally place a face with the voice, Cleo." He said as he took a seat at the table. He handed Cleopatra a tattered brown leather briefcase.

"Thank you. I'm not going to go through all of this right now, but give me the highlights. How was your trip?"

"You ever been to Fresno?" He cracked his knuckles against his knee.

"No, sir."

"Good. Don't ever go." He waved his hand and motioned the waiter to come over. "Jack on the rocks, please," he said to the young brown-haired waiter. "Make that three of them," he huffed as he pointed to Nia's iced tea and Cleopatra's lemon water. "You ladies can't sit at a bar and not actually drink."

Then he got down to business. "He's broke as hell. I think that motherfucker might even owe me money," he chuckled. "He's over $200,000 in debt."

"How, student loans?" Nia asked.

"Nope."

"How do you do $200K in debt without student loans and you don't own anything?" Cleopatra asked.

"Credit card debt. You know those interest rates are a mother shut yo mouf." He laughed to himself and grabbed a handful of nuts from the bowl. "Pistachios? Where are the boiled peanuts?" he growled. "Anyway, my cholesterol is higher than his credit score."

Cleopatra tried not to laugh. "Where did you get him?" she asked Nia. "I love him."

"Let me remind you. One of NYPD's finest, retired. Leroy Coleman the Fifth at your service." He saluted Cleopatra as he took the drinks from the waiter. "He lives in a studio apartment

397

in this rundown neighborhood. He's a day laborer, does odd jobs, manual labor here and there. Gets paid in cash. I spoke to some of his associates and he told them that he was going to New York City to get rich."

"He said that to them?" Cleopatra asked as she sipped the Jack. "Ahhhh ...that's hot going down.

"He did say that. Dumbass, I know," Mr. Coleman continued. "There's a videotape and signed statements in that packet, of his associates saying that he said he was about to come into a whole lot of money, and that they probably wouldn't see his ass in Fresno anymore."

Cleopatra popped opened the briefcase and there was an actual VHS tape inside.

"You got them to say that on camera? How did you do that?" She studied the large tape in her hand.

"Don't worry, we have a VHS player down at the station," Nia laughed as she touched her hand.

"You gave me an unlimited expense account. That goes a long way in Fresno—slipped them $50 and they wouldn't shut up." He grinned, proud of himself. "And get this—nobody out there even knew he had kids."

"Wow." Cleopatra shook her head.

"Looks like you're dealing with a real scam artist, Cleo. He's shady, for sure." Nia said. "I wish you would just let me shoot him. I can make it happen."

Cleopatra looked at Nia and laughed, but Nia was serious.

"NYPD, you so crazy," Cleopatra laughed nervously.

"True, true," both Mr. Coleman and Nia said in unison. Still, only Cleopatra had broken a smile.

"The type of crazy Nia is talking about would be a little bit extra," Mr. Coleman said.

"Uh ... so does he have a record?" Cleopatra tried to change the subject. "Ever been in trouble with the law?"

"No. Not even a speeding ticket. But oh baby, the wife makes up for that." He took a sip of his Jack. "She has all of these aliases. She's a good time, and the best part—big bad mama did eight years upstate."

"Prison? Here?" Cleopatra asked. "As in New York State? Eight years for what?"

"Bank robbery."

"Get out of here." Cleopatra took another sip of her Jack Daniels.

"And even better than that? She skipped out on her parole. She got paroled about three years ago and never checked in with her P.O. There's still a warrant out for her."

"Find out where she is and I'll pick her up myself. End of custody case." Nia winked at Cleopatra.

"This is good." Cleopatra was hopeful that she and her family were about to be reunited.

"She had a pretty lengthy record before the bank robbery. Looks like she was just building up to it, but she got greedy and she got caught. It's all in there," Mr. Coleman said.

"This is exactly the dirt I needed, and a little more. Thank you so much." Cleopatra handed him an envelope with the rest of his fee. "There's a little bit extra in there for you, too."

He looked at the check and kissed it. "If you ever need anything else, just give me a call." He downed the rest of his drink and excused himself to the men's room.

"So what are you going to do now?" Nia asked her.

"I'm about to get my wife back."

✿✿✿

"Hi, baby," Jacqueline said when she picked up Cleopatra's call. "I was just about to call you. I have some news."

"I have some news, too." Cleopatra couldn't wait to tell Jacqueline everything that she'd found out about Alonzo and his wife from Leroy Coleman the Fifth.

"The attorney called with the court date," Jacqueline blurted out.

"When? I'll clear my schedule. You won't believe what—"

"No," Jacqueline interrupted her. You can't go, remember? I can't show up with you on my arm. I'm supposed to tell the judge that I'm ending the marriage and agree to go into counseling. We're moving forward with the plan."

"No. You don't have to do any of that. I'm trying to tell you, I hired a private investigator."

"For what? Why would you waste money on that? I told you I had it handled. Why can't you just listen, Cleopatra?"

"What are you talking about? Why don't you listen? Why don't you at least let me tell you what I found out?"

"What? That he's fucking broke? First of all," Jacqueline snapped and barked at her, "you can look at his bum ass and tell that. Second of all, the attorney and I have got this all figured out, right down to the last detail. Look, Cleopatra. It's going to work. I got this. What you need to understand is that I'm not taking any chances and I'm not losing my kids. Why do I have to keep fucking repeating myself to you? Damn."

Then Jacqueline hung up on her.

400

It was real now. Jacqueline was going before a judge to basically tell him she didn't love Cleopatra anymore. There would be no turning back from this. Jacqueline didn't need the information from the private investigator. She didn't even want it. Regardless of what Cleopatra had said in the heat of the moment, she'd been waiting for lightning to strike Jacqueline so she would wake the fuck up and say absolutely not, they were not ending this marriage, it wasn't an option and together they would figure out another way.

But that lightning strike had yet to come, and Cleopatra was doubtful that it would now. Jacqueline supposedly had it all figured out, and was going to fix it herself. If she was willing to divorce her to do it, Cleopatra would let her.

✪✪✪

"If I wanted your girl, I could have had her a dozen times, my own sister-in-law. And you wanted to fight me over her?" Cleopatra yelled at Shawn.

Cleopatra was confused by Shawn's unannounced visit to her hotel suite, and came to the conclusion that Shawn wanted to get her feelings hurt. You could only put Cleopatra through so much before she turned on you. She felt nothing for Shawn now. Once Cleopatra was really done with you, there was no coming back.

Shawn had come to visit her because she missed her friend. But having just gotten off the phone with Jacqueline minutes before and learning that a court date in the custody case had been set, Cleopatra was in no mood, and Shawn had caught her on the way to the gym. She felt the need to hit something, like the heavy bag, and Shawn was about to catch hell for her poor timing.

"I don't remember why we were fighting, why we were mad at each other, why we hurt each other." Shawn pulled a Snickers bar from the pocket of her hooded sweatshirt, sat down on the dark brown leather sofa in the living room, and began to make quick work of the roasted peanut, nougat, caramel, and milk chocolate bar.

"Let's see." Cleopatra paced back and forth in front of her. "You told your girlfriend something about me that I chose to keep in the past. She runs and tells my wife as soon as humanly possible, and enjoys that shit. That forces us to separate after we've been married only two months. And incidentally, her ex-husband, the same ex that you conveniently roughed up, magically appears and has that same information, and it's in the court papers. And let's not forget when Olivia threatened my family and you didn't give a fuck. If that isn't enough, I'm tired of your face, of your voice, the curve of your eternally broken jaw line, and the gaps between your teeth."

"I know you don't mean that. Deep down, you don't mean that." Shawn refused to believe that her lifelong friend, the one that taught her just about everything she knew of any value, was really done with her. "Look." She showed Cleopatra her surgically repaired cheek. "Can't even tell there was ever a scar there."

Cleopatra was unmoved.

"Anyway," Shawn continued. "Robin and I are going to work it out. She's moving back in with me."

Cleopatra sat down in an armchair across from her and

looked at Shawn like she didn't hear her, but she heard every word. "That is the dumbest shit I've heard you've say in a long time. And you say and do some stupid shit. Your street fight got like ten million views on YouTube because everybody wanted to see the glue trap, and you went back to that? Did she even tell you about her little stunt?"

"What are you talking about?"

"Never mind. It's not important." Of course Robin wouldn't tell Shawn that she went after her sister-in-law again and got caught. Cleopatra folded her arms across her chest. "It's probably all for the best that you two are back together. I wouldn't wish either of you on anyone else." She shook her head. "So congratulations."

"I've also been talking to this counselor about my anger, and I'm working on it. Robin believed me enough to take me back. I wish you had a little faith in me, too. Speaking of violence, in case you haven't heard, Jac whipped her ass. Like, it looks like she beat her until she got tired."

"Anything else on your mind?" The corner of Cleopatra's mouth curled in to a smile.

"I miss my friend. You're my family, like blood to me. You were always better to me than my blood."

"You know what? Stop." Cleopatra got up from her chair and waved her hands. "I don't have these emotional conversations with women I'm not fucking. There's really no reason for me to talk to you about feelings. So what motivation do I have to work this shit out with you? None."

THIRTY EIGHT

....

IS THIS THE END?

"You like these, baby?"

Jacqueline stood in the doorway to the sex room in nothing but her bare breasts and black lace panties. She turned around and stuck her butt out, displaying "Cleopatra's" across her ass.

"That's why you called me over?" Cleopatra was almost annoyed. "I thought this was important." They hadn't spoken since they fought over the phone and Jacqueline had hung up on her. Cleopatra still hadn't told her about the information that Leroy Coleman the Fifth had discovered in Fresno.

Jacqueline laid down on the bed. "This is important. Strip." She rolled around on the bed as she commanded Cleopatra to take off her clothes. Cleopatra hesitated before sitting down on the end of the bed; she had no intention of getting naked.

"We have a huge fight on the phone," she exhaled. "Then we don't talk, and the next thing I know you're telling me to get naked?"

"I know, baby. I'm sorry. And I'm going to make up for that. You know what I did today?" Jacqueline asked as she scooted up behind Cleopatra and wrapped her arms around her.

"What?"

"I went to my 'gay no more' counseling session. They tried to convince me that I don't want to wake up to this beautiful face every morning." Cleopatra frowned. "Sorry, I know you prefer handsome, but you are beautiful. And they tried to convince me that I don't want to feel this soft skin on this beautiful body. That I don't want to suck on those perfect breasts or lick that huge clit of yours. Trying to convince me that I should basically want dick."

"And do you?" Cleopatra turned toward Jacqueline.

"I only want your dick. So I guess it's working." She smiled. "But there is one thing I want even more."

"What's that?" Cleopatra asked.

"Your pussy." Jacqueline kissed her.

"I can't do this." Cleopatra stood up from the bed and covered her face with her hands. "It's been almost six weeks since I lived in my own house, we didn't even spend Mother's Day together. I can't be with my wife outside of these late night creeps, and I have to make an appointment to see the kids. I have a new routine now that doesn't include you or the children, and it's not ok. It's not."

"I know, baby." Jacqueline stood up and rubbed her back. "But it will be ok."

"You've done everything that Vanessa suggested so far—talked to the judge, gone to counseling now. When are you serving me with the papers? I keep asking and nothing happens. You never answer me." She stared Jacqueline in the face. "Are you really going to leave me? Are you going to divorce me?"

"Only on paper. It doesn't mean anything."

Cleopatra refused to make eye contact with Jacqueline now. "I guess this marriage doesn't mean anything, either. That's only on paper right now, too."

Jacqueline continued. "Baby, this is just until I'm granted full custody and we're free and clear. Then we'll get remarried, like it never happened. But nothing will keep us apart physically, not ever. I won't let it."

Cleopatra turned the knob on the bedroom door as she readied to leave. "Nothing will keep us apart?" Cleopatra looked at her in amazement. "A divorce will."

✵✵✵

The next day, Cleopatra met with Vanessa, who had never seen Cleopatra in such a state. She appeared to be in a trance.

"I don't want to be here, so I need you to follow me on this, and I'm only going to say what I'm going to say one time." She held up her index finger.

Vanessa scrambled for a pen and her yellow notepad.

"I don't know why Jacqueline is hesitating, so I'm doing it for her. File legal separation papers right now. I'll continue to pay all the household bills and her credit cards, and double her cash allowance to $20K a month in case they require anything in my absence. I own our home, but she can stay as long as she wishes, I don't really care. All I'm asking for is visitation with the twins—two weekends a month, assuming she wins the custody case." Cleopatra stood up and threw her messenger bag over her shoulder. "See that she gets the papers today. Any questions, text me. Send me the bill."

Vanessa wrote furiously on the canary legal pad and nodded her head.

Before she could look up, she heard her office door slam hard. Cleopatra had gone as quickly as she had appeared.

✿✿✿

Cleopatra shattered Jacqueline's world. She was inconsolable when she was served the separation papers at their home.

"You don't do shit like that to prove a point!" Jacqueline screamed into the phone. "Do you have any idea how much this hurts? Is that what you were trying to do? Hurt me?" She wouldn't let Cleopatra get a word in. She didn't want to hear anything she had to say. She needed to get across how hurt she was, and what this was doing to her. "Congratulations, you hurt me. You feel better now? You must not love me anymore. Why are you doing this? I don't believe you did this."

"Yeah, I do actually have an idea how much it hurts. Vanessa said you've been stalling on having any of the papers drawn up. So I'm giving you what you really want. But if you really want to divorce me, you have to file those papers your damn self."

THIRTY NINE

....

MAKING MOVES

"What do you want, Supriti?" Cleopatra asked as she stood blocking the doorway.

"I just felt the need to check on you." Supriti tried to peek inside of her suite, unsure as to why Cleopatra wasn't letting her in.

"You just felt the need? That's odd." Cleopatra studied her attire. "You felt the need to show up here naked under your coat?"

"I'm not naked under this coat," Supriti smirked. "See how much you know? I have on a thong, a purple one. Your favorite color. Want to take it off of me? Or do you just want to pull it to the side?"

It had been just a couple hours since Cleopatra had Jacqueline served with separation papers, and she was still trying to accept the fact that her marriage was coming to an end. Then Supriti showed up at her hotel suite. Cleopatra wasn't in the mood. She thought better of announcing the ending of her marriage, as she didn't want to discuss it with anyone. Especially not with Supriti, who would immediately think she was going to take Jacqueline's place.

She'd been dodging Supriti since her return from California. The empathy she showed during her father's illness and death had only strengthened Supriti's feelings for her, and now Supriti couldn't take being away from Cleopatra. So she started popping up more and more and inserting herself into her life. They had hung out on a few occasions and Supriti had behaved herself each time. She hadn't gotten butt naked, said anything inappropriately sexual, picked a fight with random chicks that flirted with Cleopatra, or even tried to kiss her.

Cleopatra had been getting more comfortable, and thinking that they could actually build a friendship. But she should have known that Supriti was bound to ruin it.

"Really? You want me to pull your thong to the side?" Cleopatra exhaled. "You don't get it. I really don't understand you. Every single time I think we may be able to salvage some type of friendship, you go and muck it up. You're impossible to deal with. You refuse to understand that it's not going to happen."

"I refuse to believe that," Supriti said defiantly. "Are you going to let me in or not."

"Absolutely not. You can leave or talk to me in the doorway. Your choice."

"Fine." Supriti unbuttoned her coat and Cleopatra saw the curve of her breasts.

"Do you think it's luck or just a coincidence that you're still walking around with teeth in your mouth?" Cleopatra asked her. "I'm telling you, you don't want Jacqueline to catch you. Especially not like this." She pointed to her thong.

"Remember how I got emotional right before I left for California and said a lot of things to you? I want you to know that

I meant every last word. I can't help what I feel. I only care about you. Your wife is not here. I don't care what she does, not anymore, because she's leaving you. Isn't she?" Supriti saw a sadness in Cleopatra's eyes, and knew she was right. She reached up to caress Cleopatra's face. "Never mind that. This is about you and me. You're living in this hotel all alone, and you don't have to. I'm here for you. Whatever you need. I can make it better if you only let me. Give me a chance."

"Is that right?" Cleopatra laughed.

"That's right," Supriti said confidently. "Can you deny that you feel something, Cleopatra? When I touch you? When we're together?" Cleopatra was silent. "You really have no idea how much I want you. Do you?" Supriti exhaled. "I'll wait as long as it takes for you to be honest with yourself, realize that you deserve to be happy, and understand that I'm the woman you should be with."

"I do know how much you want me. But you know life isn't fair. You don't always get everything you want. And I do feel something when we're together. Whenever you touch me."

"Yeah?" A smile spread across Supriti's lips.

"You make my dick hard. That's all. You're not in my head, and you are definitely not in my heart. The sooner you realize that, the better off you'll be. If there was no Jacqueline in my life or in my future, you would have already disqualified yourself from being any more than a jump off because you have no respect for me, my wife, my marriage, or even yourself. If there was no Jacqueline, honestly I would fuck the shit out of you. I would. But anything more? Forget it. Who wants to be in a relationship with such a disrespectful woman? If you think I do, you clearly don't know me as well as you claim to. You refuse to hear me when I tell you it's never going to happen."

"I hear you. And I hear you every single time you say you love your wife. But does she love you? You call me disrespectful? Does she respect you? If she does, then why have you been out of your own house for five, six weeks now? What are you going through? What happily married couple that loves each other lives like that? You can tell me. Tell me the truth. She's leaving you, isn't she?"

Supriti saw a pain and loneliness in Cleopatra's face that she'd never seen before, and as if she already knew the truth, she took Cleopatra by the hand.

Her mouth was waiting when Cleopatra turned her head. Instantly, Supriti captured her lips with her own, and she whimpered. She slipped her tongue into Cleopatra's mouth possessively and skillfully, urging hers to come out and play. Cleopatra's kiss was just as demanding and confident as she was, her soft lips driving the tempo, stealing Supriti's breath and sending vibrations straight down to her clit.

Imagine her lips down there... Supriti shifted her body, needing more contact. Wrapping her hands around Cleopatra's neck, she pulled her deeper, wanting to feel her in every part of her mouth. She imagined Cleopatra licking and stroking her, as Cleopatra's hands slid down to clutch her ass.

Supriti wanted all of Cleopatra. She needed her, and not only her tongue. She let her coat slide down past her shoulders and stood there in just her thong, rolling her hips against Cleopatra, begging for her to touch her down there, to ease the throb between her thighs. Cleopatra responded, moving her hands from her behind up to her shoulders.

Then she gently pushed Supriti away, breaking their kiss,

but leaving her hands on her arms as if trying to hold her at that distance. Supriti's mouth felt barren and cold as she struggled to calm her breathing. Cleopatra's breaths were equally labored.

"I have to know something," Cleopatra said when Supriti moved closer. "Wait. I can't." Cleopatra paused.

"What?" Supriti was inches from her face, and the lips she longed to suck on demanded her focus.

"Why me, Supriti? You could have anyone you want."

"I want you." She leaned in again, her mouth brushing Cleopatra's, her breath tickling her neck.

"Why?" Cleopatra pulled away. Not far, only far enough to look at her.

"I don't know. I just do." Supriti's words came out in a whisper. "From the moment I saw you..."

"What? The moment you saw me, what...?"

"It's hard to explain and understand. I just knew you were the woman for me."

Cleopatra looked at her and Supriti could see more hurt in her eyes. "No. I understand," Cleopatra said. "That's how I felt the first time I laid eyes on my wife."

"I'm sorry," Supriti apologized. "I'm sorry you're in so much pain." She took Cleopatra into her arms and held her. "You need to know, I would never hurt you the way she does Cleopatra. Never."

"No. I'm the one that should apologize." Cleopatra pulled away from her. "I just had a moment there, but I'm not going to cheat on my wife," she said.

"It's not cheating if you're not married, Cleopatra." Supriti moved in to kiss her again.

Then the elevator light lit up behind Supriti and the bell dinged. The doors opened and Jacqueline stepped off. "I knew that bitch was going to be here," she snarled.

Supriti yelled, "Shit!" and pushed passed Cleopatra, running into the suite and slamming the door behind her.

"Let me in, Cleopatra, before I pull this door off the hinges." Jacqueline banged on the door.

Cleopatra hesitated for a moment, but opened up and let Jacqueline in. Jacqueline ran past her; there was no hesitation, no moment of shock, no delay. She ran up to Supriti and grabbed her by the collar of her trench coat. Supriti couldn't break the grip that Jacqueline had on her, and before she knew it Jacqueline threw her down to the floor. Cleopatra was stunned to see Jacqueline had protected her hands with red boxing hand wrap. She ran over and picked Jacqueline up by her waist just as she was about to jump on top of Supriti, but not before she swung her leg and connected her red bottoms with Supriti's ribs.

"I want her." Jacqueline squirmed to break free, but Cleopatra was too strong. "What the fuck is she wearing under that coat? Is she naked?!"

"Get out of here, Supriti!" Cleopatra yelled at her.

But Supriti stared at Jacqueline like she wanted to fight her back, only infuriating her more.

"Let me go!" Jacqueline screamed as she reached out, swinging on Supriti.

Cleopatra pulled her back. "You don't want this. You really don't," Cleopatra warned Supriti. "Leave!" she yelled at her.

Supriti walked up to them, but stopped just out of Jacqueline's grasp. She looked at Jacqueline, and then at Cleopatra.

"What does she have that I don't?"

"Me. She's got me," Cleopatra said.

Supriti grabbed her purse and ran out of the suite. Cleopatra still wouldn't let Jacqueline go for fear that she would run after her. She kissed Jacqueline on the neck as she squirmed in her arms.

"Don't kiss on me."

"Mmmmm." Cleopatra kissed her on the crook of her neck again, and felt Jacqueline's body relax. She kissed on her earlobe and sucked it into her mouth. Jacqueline moaned as her body got heavy in Cleopatra's arms and she weakened. Cleopatra ran her tongue from her ear down to her neck.

Jacqueline pulled herself away. "Stop it. That's not why I came over here." She unwrapped the red tape from her hands.

"I'm sorry." Cleopatra said as she helped her free her hands. "Where did you get these?"

"From my boxing class a while back. I carry them in my purse now. See what loving you makes me do?"

"You're serious?"

"I'm very serious. I told you to handle that bitch, but you haven't. So I had to. So what do you want to do?" Jacqueline took off her jacket. She had on a white camisole and tight blue jeans with high-heeled boots. She saw how Cleopatra looked at her.

"You look beautiful."

"Don't get it confused. I could have beat her ass and still been sexy." Jacqueline pulled the separation papers out of her purse and threw them at Cleopatra. "Is this what you really want?" Her eyes filled with tears. "Do you want to be with her?"

"No, it's not what I want, and I don't want her. I want to be with you and the kids. She's a friend. This is what you wanted. Remember?"

"It's never been what I wanted." Jacqueline ripped up the papers and tossed them to the floor. "We'll just have to figure something else out. Because this is not happening, just the idea of it is already tearing us apart. I saw our names on those papers and I snapped." She looked up at Cleopatra and caressed the side of her face.

Those were the exact words that Cleopatra had been waiting to hear for weeks.

"You need to pick better 'friends.' Because someone is really going to get hurt. Pending custody case or not, I'm tired of being tested. I will come for her. Make her go away, or I will. I can't risk your falling for her. I'm not losing my family."

"That would never happen. You know that."

"No, I don't know that. Not anymore. We've been so disconnected. I know she's throwing it at you every chance she gets. I don't want you involved with her at all." She placed her hand on Cleopatra's heart. "Remember, this is mine."

"I remember."

"Then handle her. This is the last time I'm going to tell you. It's already been too much talk. Next time, I'll run up on her and no one will be around to save her. Then I'm coming for you."

"Ok," Cleopatra wrapped her arms around Jacqueline and pulled her to her lips. But suddenly Jacqueline pushed her away again.

"Don't touch me, Cleopatra. I knew I got a whiff of something." She scowled at her. "I don't know what I walked in on or what happened here tonight—if you kissed her, made out with her, or what, but I smell that bitch on you."

Cleopatra attempted to speak. "Don't even…" Jacqueline held her hand up to her face. "I'm so mad right now and so hurt. I just want to get out of here. I can't even look at you."

FORTY

....

THIS IS **NOT** A GAME

"Ms. G, your presence is requested by Ms. Alexis." A large gentleman in a black suit and thin necktie stood in the door way to Cleopatra's hotel room.

"What's up, Sam? She's back in town?" Cleopatra asked. Samuel had been Alexis's driver for years. He'd watched Cleopatra grow up, but rarely ever broke from formalities.

He handed Cleopatra his smartphone. Alexis was on video chat.

"I see you found me, huh? What's going on?" Cleopatra smiled at the phone.

"Of course. You know you can't hide from me. Are you alone?"

"Yeah. Jacqueline isn't really speaking to me right now."

"Please go with Samuel. He'll bring you to me. See you soon." She hung up.

Cleopatra slid into some Air Jordans, grabbed her cell phone and backpack, and went with Samuel. She thought about changing her clothes momentarily, as she liked to be a bit more presentable whenever she met with Alexis, but the summer heat called for the tank and shorts she had on. She sat comfortably in the back of the air conditioned Mercedes Benz G-Class SUV and picked up the *NY Post* that was rolled up on the seat. She knew Alexis didn't read the tabloid, and thought it strange that it was in her vehicle. When she scanned it, she was shocked to see Alexis's husband on page 6 with Mandisa.

"Damn it. Sam."

"Ma'am?"

"You put this back here on purpose, didn't you?"

He looked at Cleopatra through the rearview mirror and nodded his head.

"Why are you doing this to me? Why do I have to be the one to show this to Alexis?"

"Can I speak frankly?"

"Of course. Go ahead."

"If not you, than who? Who could this information come from and she not destroy the world?"

Cleopatra didn't respond. She pulled out her smartphone and checked TMZ. It was on their website, so she knew there was some truth to it. The picture spoke a thousand words. Mandisa and Alexis's husband emerging from a hotel in the wee hours of the morning, with Mandisa looking disheveled. Alexis wasn't on social media and didn't surf the web, so Cleopatra just might have to be the one to let her know.

"I've been meaning to call you!" Cleopatra said when she hugged Alexis. "Do you need to change into some clothes?" She looked at her black silk and lace negligée.

"No. I'm lounging around in this. It's quite comfortable. Besides it's nearly 90 degrees outside."

"Yeah but you're inside." Cleopatra side eyed her. "I've

never heard a woman say that she was comfortable in a garter belt, but ok." She smiled.

"If it's really making you uncomfortable, I can take it off right here, Cleopatra," Alexis laughed.

"I'm fine. Thanks."

"Would you like something to eat? The chef is preparing my dinner right now."

"What chef? Wait, there's a kitchen in here, too?" Cleopatra rolled her eyes as she looked around. "Is this suite big enough for you?" she asked as she sat on the couch across from her.

"Four bedrooms is cozy." Alexis took a sip of champagne. "The bedrooms have silk walls, the bathrooms have honey onyx walls."

"Ok. I don't even know what that is." Cleopatra raised her eyebrow.

"Me either, but it sounds rich, doesn't it? I just like saying it," she laughed. "Gourmet kitchen, that comes with a chef. There's a sofa and a sixty-inch flat screen in one of the bathrooms."

"I'll make sure to use that bathroom before I leave, then." Cleopatra smiled. "This suite is probably one of the most ridiculous things I've seen you do with your money, and you've done some foolishness. What's with the champagne?" Cleopatra asked.

"I took a long bath, slipped into this lingerie, looked in the mirror, and decided that I looked so damn good that it was cause for celebration. So I popped some Perrier-Jouet," Alexis said as she poured Cleopatra a glass of the champagne.

"Thank you." Cleopatra took the champagne from Alexis. "I wanted to tell you in person. Jacqueline knows all about my past now."

"You mean…"

"The business, and my having an extremely generous benefactor." She took a sip from her glass. "What the … damn!" Cleopatra held the glass up to the light. "That is delicious."

"Soothing, isn't it." Alexis winked at her.

"Do I want to know how much this is a bottle?"

"I don't think you do," Alexis chuckled. "I'll send you a case. Anyway, I'm glad you two have no more secrets." Alexis didn't feel the need to ask if Cleopatra had revealed Alexis's identity to her wife; she knew Cleopatra would take that to her grave.

"She says she wants to meet you," Cleopatra laughed.

"Ahh … that's cute," Alexis chuckled. "Never going to happen."

"That's what I said. So, you know Mandisa Botha?"

"I do." Alexis rolled her eyes. "Why do you ask?"

"She saw you coming out of my house. She's been on me asking about our relationship. Of course she got nothing. I saw the overtime you put in on her face. So you want to fill me in on that backstory?" Cleopatra took another sip of the champagne.

"We went to college together. Let me rephrase that—we went to the same college at the same damn time. Mandisa was the spoiled rich bitch that thought she was better than everyone else."

"So nothing has really changed?"

"She made my life hell. So I decided to take her man." Alexis smiled. "And I ended up marrying him."

"Old boy used to be her man? That's why she's so mad!"

Cleopatra realized this was way more involved than she thought. Mandisa hit it first.

"It's gotten physical more than once. Bricks through windshields, slashed tires, horse shit dumped on front lawns and set on fire, pig's head left on the pillow, dead rabbits delivered in a box of bloody tampons; you name it, it's gone down."

Cleopatra stared at Alexis. "Ugh ... tampons? That's disgusting." She sat her glass of champagne down. "You're serious? Where do you even get multiple bloody tampons? Never mind." She shook her head. "I'm not going to ask who did what. But really?"

"Yeah. But now she wants to be in my presence."

"So you two are cool?"

"No. I don't trust her. I have to keep her real close." Alexis leaned forward and whispered, "She's questioning my sexuality. She's convinced I'm gay, and you know I can't have that rumor. Deep down, I really wish I was as brave as you."

"You were raised differently. But you're one of the most fearless people I know," Cleopatra admitted.

"In every area but how I handle my personal life. I only need my husband for appearances. There's no passion there, no love, only civility. And I need him to live this life." She took a sip of champagne.

Alexis was terrified of being outed. She was the daughter of a devout southern Baptist minister who was popular throughout the South. When she was younger, she'd feared suffering the same fate as her older brother who, after coming out to their father, was beaten regularly until he was kicked out of their home at just fifteen.

Years later, college facilitated Alexis's escape out of the

small backwoods town, and marriage to a multimillionaire allowed her to go back for her brother, just as she had promised. The very weekend she returned, however, she arrived at her parents' home only to hear her father say, "They found your brother's body. He killed himself last week. Go and identify him, because we ain't going. He's better off dead."

Now, if she was outed, not only would she be hated and abandoned by her family at a time when she needed them most, she would be left penniless, and would get nothing from her divorce based on the prenuptial agreement she'd signed. Her first and last job was as a cashier at Piggly Wiggly her junior year of high school. She dropped out of college to be a full-time trophy wife. Where would she go? How would she support herself? Still, all these years later, she was conflicted and fighting her feelings.

"Alexis." Cleopatra waved her hand, pulling her out of her daydream. "Please tell me Mandisa is not threatening to out you. What are you going to do?"

"She's a formidable opponent. It won't be easy to get rid of her."

"Stop." Cleopatra covered her ears. "I don't want to hear this. The less I know the better."

Alexis laughed. "I'm only saying that this could get messy, that's all. So back to you, my dear, and the reason I summoned you. I've been waiting for you to ask for my help, but I see—as usual—you're not going to. How long do you plan to let this foolishness go on?"

"What are you talking about?"

"I guess you like staying in a hotel away from your wife and family. I'm talking about that moron of an ex-husband of hers.

I'll get rid of him. So what do you want to happen? I'm your genie in a bottle." Alexis pulled out a pen and a pad as if she was preparing to take dictation.

"I want my wife and kids back and for him to go far away, to like Guam or somewhere. I want my life back. That's what I want."

"I'll throw some money at him to make him go away. The question is, how much?" She rubbed her chin and scribbled some numbers down on the pad. "But I want to hurt him." She rubbed her hands together. "He needs to feel some pain."

"No." Cleopatra shook her head.

"At least let me make him disappear for good."

"What does for good mean? I have to be real specific with you."

"Can I do it my way?"

"When you do things your way, people go away for decades."

"For good. For decades. You're talking about Kenya? How much time did she get?"

"Twenty-five years," Cleopatra said. "But you already knew that."

Alexis nodded. "I just wanted to hear you say it. Still some of my finest work to date. I wonder if I can top that. She was crazy; she wasn't going to leave you alone. She was trying to ruin your life and needed to be stopped. So I stopped her."

"I remember, I was there." Cleopatra side eyed her.

"By the way, are there any new Kenyas that I need to worry about?" Alexis asked, with a raised eyebrow.

Cleopatra thought for a moment, then answered. "Nope."

"So you're saying there isn't a woman hanging around your

marriage that you need me to handle?"

"I didn't say that. I said there was nothing you needed to worry about."

"Ok. Um … hmmm." Alexis knew there was another woman in pursuit of Cleopatra from the information and surveillance her private investigators had gathered. She assumed that since Cleopatra had spent a good deal of time with the woman, she knew what she was doing. But Alexis didn't realize that the woman was Supriti; had she studied her pictures from the surveillance photos, she would probably have recognized Mandisa's best friend from college. If the woman became a problem and Cleopatra couldn't dissolve the situation, she wouldn't hesitate to do it for her.

"And for your information," Alexis continued, "I only send those who threaten your happiness off on long sabbaticals. I haven't killed for you … yet. So what's the big deal? Do you want your family back or not?"

"Where are you going to send him?"

"Were you serious about Guam?"

"I don't want to know."

"That's probably best. Of course you'll keep this between me and you. All your wife needs to know is that he'll show up to say goodbye. Now what about your sister-in-law?" Alexis inquired.

"What about her?" Cleopatra asked. "No." She shook her head frantically. "No, Alexis. Don't touch her. She's still family. Promise me you will not touch her," she demanded.

"Ok, I promise. I won't touch her."

"Thank you."

"But I will take care of the ex-husband, and you should go

and visit his new wife."

"What does she have to do with anything?"

"You don't know who she is, do you?"

"She's a bank robber. Obviously not a good one, as she did some serious time upstate. But I don't know her."

"Oh yes you do." Alexis smiled. "You know her quite well. You've slept with her before."

"Yeah, that really narrows it down for me." Cleopatra smirked. "I've seen her picture, I didn't recognize her."

"All that hard time probably jacked her face up." Alexis walked over to a writing desk in the corner of the room and pulled a sheet of paper out of a manila folder. She handed the sheet of hotel stationary to Cleopatra, who looked down to see a name and address on it. Cleopatra read the name. "Doesn't ring a bell. I still don't know who she is."

"That's because she's probably the only person I know with more aliases and disguises than me. This is her name right now. I don't know what she went by when you and your friend Shawn knew her. Go see her."

"Shawn? Queens? You want me to go all the way out to Queens? You have to tell me more than that."

"Secrets and lies. Lies and secrets. Do you really know anyone? She knows your friend Shawn very well. She knows her intimately. She also knows a lot of things that you don't, but that you probably should."

"This sounds messy. Should I be scared?" Cleopatra fingered the paper.

"No. She's a thief, but no killer."

✿✿✿

Alexis alerted Samuel to pull the car around and prepare to take Cleopatra back to her hotel. Cleopatra stood up, but she couldn't leave without telling Alexis what she had just read in the news. She pulled the folded newspapers from her backpack.

"Let me ask you a question. Do you read the Post?"

"You know I don't. I don't believe anything those rags say."

Cleopatra sighed. "I hate to do this, but I have to." She slid the paper onto the table and pushed it in front of Alexis, who looked down at the pictures of Mandisa with her husband as they left a Manhattan hotel. There was no look of anger, and no change in her facial expression. She only drummed her nails on the table as she sank deep into thought.

"Are you ok?" Cleopatra whispered.

"Yes, thank you." She was so calm that she scared Cleopatra.

"Seriously, I know you have a special arrangement, but this is different. This is Mandisa."

"Cleopatra. You're sweet to be concerned about me. And I love you for that. But trust me. I'm wonderful." Alexis smiled.

"Unless ... you already know about this. Of course you do. Shit." Cleopatra stared at Alexis as she walked backward toward the door of the suite.

Mandisa burst into the suite unannounced. "Alexis, the door was open so I just ... Cleopatra?"

"Oooh." Cleopatra covered her mouth and watched Alexis intently, not sure what she would do.

"Where is my damn security?" Alexis scowled.

"You gave him the rest of the night off. Remember?" Cleopatra reminded her.

"How romantic. You two do know each other. So this is where you've been hiding, because you certainly haven't been home lately. Does Mrs. Giovanni know that her wife is here?" Mandisa looked at Alexis with an accusatory glare. "Maybe I should go run and tell her." She smiled.

With that, she had sealed her fate. Alexis would have to deal with her immediately; not only was she an all-around nuisance, but posed too much of a threat now, on top of sleeping with her husband.

"Cleopatra. Thank you for stopping by. The car should be ready for you now." She stared at Cleopatra, waiting for her to leave.

Cleopatra cleared her throat, knowing that something was going to jump off. "Are you sure? I don't think—"

"Have a good night," Alexis growled at her.

The tension was thick and uncomfortable.

"Nice knowing you," Cleopatra whispered to Mandisa as she walked past her. Then she hesitated. "Actually, not really. But in a moment like this it just seemed the appropriate thing to say. Good luck. You're going to need it."

✿✿✿

"Extravagant enough for you? Isn't this the suite that sleeps eight?" Mandisa sat down on the sofa and made herself comfortable, all without an invitation.

"It is." Alexis bit her lip as she eyed Mandisa's scantily clad body.

"And it's just you in here? Alone?"

"Correct again." She nodded.

"So why exactly was Cleopatra here?" She studied Alexis's black lingerie as she covered herself with a sheer robe. "And what's with the garter belt?"

"You're full of questions tonight, aren't you? Not that it's any of your concern, but we are business associates."

"And what kind of business would that be? I saw the way you looked at her."

"My business. So is what I choose to wear around my own hotel suite. Now, what brings you by, so rudely unannounced?"

"You told me where you were staying and said I could stop by."

"Who drops by someone's hotel room unannounced? Have you no home training at all?"

"I ran into your husband recently on the Upper West Side. He tried to sleep with me again, but I told him no. That's why I came by. You asked me to stay away from him and I am. I'm proud to report," Mandisa lied.

"That can't be the reason you're here." Alexis refilled her glass of champagne and tossed the folded newspaper into the trash bin. Mandisa was never an accomplished liar anyway, and she knew her husband was a serial adulterer. It was the price she paid for her lavish lifestyle, but with Mandisa she knew it was more than sex. They were each other's first love, and college sweethearts. Alexis hadn't slept with her husband in so long she questioned if she even knew how anymore, but she had no desires or plans to do so. With no physical and emotional connections to him, how could she compete with Mandisa? She couldn't.

But she knew the old adage that if you can't beat them, get

rid of them always worked too. And she couldn't afford to let Disa take her husband and all that came with him away.

"You're a beautiful woman, Alexis." Mandisa crossed her legs. Her short canary yellow dress slid up, exposing her right thigh. "At one time, you did enough in bed to get him to marry you. So I wonder what changed. Did you even know he was in the city?"

"Excuse me, Ms. Alexis…" The chef appeared in the doorway. He had beady green eyes and straight, beige hair, with a broad-shouldered build. His china-white skin was harsh against his black chef jacket. "Dinner is ready. As requested, it's plated and covered. Ready for you to eat at any time."

"Thank you, Chef. You can have the rest of the evening off. I will see you in the morning for breakfast."

"Yes, ma'am. Good evening." He nodded his head and exited the suite.

"So why did you say Cleopatra was here again?" Mandisa's eyes settled on Cleopatra's leftover glass of champagne. Before Alexis could offer her a glass of her own, she picked up the champagne flute, licked the rim then sipped it. It was so erotic and inappropriate that Alexis couldn't resist.

"Excuse me. Do you want to be alone?"

"I'm sorry?"

"I saw that. You just licked Cleopatra's glass. You took your tongue and licked the entire rim of the glass. Who does that?"

"Anyway." Mandisa sat the glass down gently on the coffee table. "Why did you say she was here?"

"I didn't." Alexis studied Mandisa's legs, from her stilettos up to the thigh that peeked out from the little piece of yellow dress she had on. She wondered if Mandisa was on her way to see her husband, or if she'd worn the dress just for her.

"So you and Cleopatra were never in a relationship? She never once threw your back out?" Mandisa probed.

Alexis pulled her gaze from Mandisa's body. "You are so inappropriate. It's not very lady like." She remained calm, but knew she needed to make a move. "So what are you asking, exactly? Are you accusing me of being a lesbian?" She walked over to the couch and sat close to Mandisa, invading her personal space. She moved closer until she felt Mandisa get uncomfortable.

"I'm not saying you're ... gay," Mandisa stuttered. "I'm accusing you of sleeping with Cleopatra. Straight women would do her." Alexis sat so close that her bare thigh touched Mandisa's exposed one. She leaned over and put her hand on Mandisa's knee. Their lips nearly touching. And Mandisa couldn't hide her nerves.

"What's the problem?" Alexis caressed her cheek. "Are you getting turned on with me this close to you and touching you? Hmm? Nothing to say now, princess? You don't want to know about Cleopatra. You want to know all about me."

Mandisa had never been so close to Alexis. For the first time, she understood how easy it was to get lost in her hazel eyes.

"Why is it that you're so concerned about what I do with my pussy? Hmm?" Alexis whispered in her ear. "You want me, don't you?" Her eyes moved to Mandisa's lips.

Mandisa tingled at the heat coming from the body of such a cold woman. She was dizzy as she looked into Alexis's eyes.

"You really do want me to fuck you," Alexis laughed at her.

Mandisa pulled away from Alexis to the far side of the

couch. But Alexis moved with her. Her thigh still touching hers. She couldn't hold in the satisfaction she felt when Mandisa quivered next to her.

She slid on top of Mandisa and pinned her down on the couch. "Admit that you want me. Admit it."

Mandisa nodded her head as she pushed her hips up in to Alexis. "Yes," she gasped.

Alexis had her where she wanted her now. But she hesitated for a moment, not having fully thought her plan through. Mandisa watched her, praying Alexis wanted her too. She whimpered as she squirmed underneath her and arched her back, trembling in anticipation. Alexis was slow to react, so Mandisa would help her decide.

She slid from underneath Alexis, stood up, and slid her dress down over her hips to the floor. It lay in a silk puddle in front of the couch. She stepped out of her soaked black thong and abandoned her stilettoes as Alexis sat and watched her. Then she lay back down on the couch, butt-ass naked, her legs spread apart, inviting Alexis in. She moaned, and her breaths got shallow.

"Lexi," Mandisa called out for her. She grabbed Alexis's hand and pulled her close.

Mandisa had a pretty pussy; her clit was puffy as it peeked out from between her swollen lips and begged to be sucked. She took her fingers and spread her lips for Alexis, beckoning her to take a sip. Was she really about to do this? Were they really about to do this? They hated each other. No ... they despised each other.

Alexis stood up over her, looking down at her naked body, taking in every inch. Mandisa looked up at her. She studied

Alexis's body through her sheer robe, every curve just as she'd always imagined. She was perfect, her double D's begging for her attention.

Alexis bent down over Mandisa and whispered in her ear. "Bitch, I never said I wanted you too."

FORTY ONE

....

NEIGHBORS KNOW HER NAME

{*Cleopatra: Goodbye Supriti, I can't.*}

Supriti became even more desperate after Cleopatra sent her that text message. She wanted so much more than Cleopatra was willing to give, but now she had nothing at all because of Cleopatra's wife. She had to do something to make Cleopatra realize what they could have together.

She snuck her way into Cleopatra's hotel suite by telling a housekeeper she recognized that she was Cleopatra's wife and had left her cell phone inside. That and a $200 tip, and Supriti found herself alone in Cleopatra's temporary home. Somewhat certain beforehand that she wouldn't actually make it inside, however, she didn't have a strategy. She just decided to wait for Cleopatra to come back home and make her listen. She realized that this whole time she had been going about it all wrong. She was trying to seduce Cleopatra, but had never really poured her heart out or expressed just how deeply she felt. She'd yet to completely open up her heart and soul. She had tried several times, but hadn't gone all in. They had a moment when she told Cleopatra she loved her before leaving for California, and then both times that she kissed Cleopatra.

But maybe Cleopatra thought she was just caught up in her emotions, caught up in the moment and not thinking clearly. It was about time she sat her down and made her understand. She would do whatever it took to make her feelings crystal clear. No wonder Cleopatra hadn't taken her seriously; she'd been holding back.

Now she had to do whatever it took. Not having Cleopatra in her life was not an option.

She made herself comfortable in the bedroom, laying across the king size bed, and pushed her fingertips into the tufted leather headboard. If tonight went well, her face would be pressed up against that headboard one day soon.

The sound of the door slamming downstairs startled her almost snapping her sane again. She hadn't thought about the optics—how it would look when Cleopatra entered and found her there. She panicked and scurried into the closet, leaving it slightly ajar. The closet was warm, dark, and crowded, and smelled of rich Italian leathers and Cleopatra's cologne. She peaked through the closet door when she heard Cleopatra come into the bedroom and stared in anticipation as Cleopatra started to undress.

When she realized Cleopatra could open the closet door at any moment, she sank down into the corner and heard her short linen skirt rip as she sat on the floor. She couldn't resist the temptation to reach up and touch Cleopatra's clothes. She ran her hands along the bottoms of leather jackets, Bogosse button downs, tweed blazers, and cashmere and camel hair trench coats.

Supriti watched as Cleopatra stripped butt naked. *I should have taken her when I had the chance,* she scolded herself as she studied Cleopatra's naked body. For a split second she considered just bolting from the closet and making her presence known. But before she got the nerve, Cleopatra walked into the bathroom and jumped in the shower. No way Supriti could reveal herself now and surprise her. That would not end well. She hadn't thought this all the way through and realized that this impromptu plea for Cleopatra's heart would fail.

She had essentially broken into her hotel room. That was not the way to go about this.

She stood up in the closet and waited to make sure the coast was clear. She would make her escape and come back when she thought Cleopatra was dressed, and beg to sit down and talk to her.

The moment she stepped out of the closet, Cleopatra's cell phone rang on her nightstand. Supriti heard the water shut off and her heart dropped down into her stomach. She leapt back into the closet and quietly slid the bi-fold doors shut.

Cleopatra ran back into the bedroom, soapy and wet, and caught the call before her cell stopped ringing. Supriti cracked the closet door just slightly.

Damn. Now she's wet. She looked around the closet again, praying Cleopatra didn't need anything out of it and watched Cleopatra put on a fluffy white terry cloth robe from the bed. She thought she heard her say, "You're where?" and then she hung up the phone.

In less time than it took Supriti to blink, Cleopatra had run to the closet and put her hand on the knob. Supriti heard it jiggle. She swore she felt herself begin to pee and the next thing she knew the bedroom lights cut off. The room was now lit only by the light of the city skyline. Supriti struggled to see what was going on and adjust her eyes to the dimness. Cleopatra didn't open the closet door and to Supriti's relief, she walked away.

But before she had fully exhaled in celebration of escaping another close call, she saw a silhouette. And it wasn't Cleopatra's.

"Fuck." Supriti covered her mouth and slumped down in the closet. Another woman had walked into the bedroom. And straight into Cleopatra's arms. Supriti strained her ears to hear what they were saying, but couldn't make out a word. She couldn't see or hear the woman. The mere notion that it was any one but Jacqueline infuriated her. Could it have been Mandisa? Was it that half-naked porn star she caught Cleopatra with on the street? She couldn't imagine who it was, and just as she was about to emerge from the closet the bedroom lit up.

Outside the closet doors, Jacqueline stood in front of a naked and wet Cleopatra. She pulled Cleopatra's strap-on out of her handbag and threw it at her. Cleopatra wrapped the leather harness around her waist and thighs in what seemed like mere seconds.

"We've been through some bullshit these last couple of months. All I know is that we aren't separating," Jacqueline declared. "We aren't divorcing. You're mine. And I want you right now." She undid her single-button black wrap dress with one hand and let it drop down to the floor, then stood naked in front of Cleopatra, waiting for her wife to take her.

Cleopatra leaned back on the bed, stroking her dick as she watched her. She knew that drove Jacqueline crazy.

"Mmmm. You know what that does to me."

"I do." Cleopatra licked her lips. "You need to come closer." She held her arms out.

Jacqueline climbed on top of her and kissed her. "Let me show you how I feel. Let me prove to you tonight how much I love you."

"You know what I want." Cleopatra flipped her over, and pushed Jacqueline down onto the bed, and spread her legs wide.

Supriti was frantic as she watched from the closet, struggling to quiet her breathing and the pounding in her chest. She still couldn't hear what they were saying, but it was clear what was about to go down, and she would have a front row seat to it.

Cleopatra crawled between Jacqueline's legs and buried her face in her pussy. She licked her, slow and thorough. Jacqueline shuddered at the sensation. Another lick. A suck. And another. Then she plunged the full length of her tongue into Jacqueline's pussy as far as it would go.

"Ohhh, I've missed you so much baby," Jacqueline moaned as Cleopatra sucked on her clit with just the right pressure.

"Cleopatra..." she screamed as an orgasm crept up on her, the urge to fuck Cleopatra's mouth growing impossible to ignore. Cleopatra lapped up her cream, bringing her to climax, with a series of animated screams. Jacqueline's orgasm rolled through her. Again and again Cleopatra pushed her tongue inside of Jacqueline's pussy, licking and slurping her up. Cleopatra took her swollen clit into her mouth as she slid two fingers deep inside of her, cream covering her fingers as Jacqueline's pussy tightened down around them. Cleopatra teased and tortured her clit while she slid a third finger inside, and Jacqueline arched her back and moaned louder now, her pussy holding on to Cleopatra's fingers for dear life. Jacqueline pushed her pussy upward, allowing Cleopatra to taste more of her.

Jacqueline reached out for her wife as she came, her hands clenching her locs tight. She struggled not to slam her legs closed as her body convulsed. Cleopatra slowed her licking and pressed her tongue flush against her clit until Jacqueline groaned and squirmed underneath her. Then Cleopatra moved up her body, cupping her pussy in her hand before pushing two fingers inside of her again, making her moan and beg for more.

But Cleopatra wanted more than that. She pulled her fingers from Jacqueline's pussy and took them into her mouth, sucking her woman's essence from them. When Cleopatra lay down beside her, Jacqueline could see her wetness all over her mouth and chin. She touched her fingers to Cleopatra's lips, spreading her cream all around her face, and into her mouth. Cleopatra let out a moan as she watched her, then pulled Jacqueline to her face and kissed her, rolling her over on her back and laying on top of her. Cleopatra stopped for a moment to look at her wife, to look at Jacqueline in awe of how beautiful she was. Jacqueline moaned and squirmed underneath her, her eyes half closed, and her breath came faster. She reached down between Cleopatra's legs and grabbed her strap.

Supriti fell back, dizzy in the corner of the closet. Panting, her heart thumping in her chest. She couldn't stop herself from saying "Oh my God" over and over again. She got back up on her hands and knees again and pressed her face to the crack of the closet door.

"You put that dick on just to tease me with it?" Jacqueline asked Cleopatra "What are you going to do with it? Huh?"

Cleopatra tortured Jacqueline, holding her off until she begged her for it. She rubbed her dick against Jacqueline's clit, making it glisten in the moonlight.

"I want you, baby, take it." Jacqueline pulled Cleopatra on top of her, moaned, and arched her back as she spread her legs wider, begging Cleopatra to fuck her. "Baby, please."

Cleopatra slid into her as Jacqueline worked her hips, mimicking the circular motion that Cleopatra was moving her ass in. Cleopatra grabbed her hips tight, and slowed her pace.

Jacqueline scratched at Cleopatra's ass, begging her to come inside until Cleopatra finally raised up on both hands and thrust her dick into her, in long, hard strokes. Jacqueline screamed out at the power of it, and Cleopatra filled her up, Jacqueline's body trembling every time Cleopatra pulled out and pushed back inside, deeper every time. Jacqueline's pussy got tighter the more she stroked her, testing Cleopatra's stamina, until Jacqueline called out her name, her pussy vibrating in orgasm around Cleopatra's shaft.

Supriti, in that moment, didn't recall the last time she had taken a breath or even swallowed. She was consumed by what Cleopatra was doing to her wife. She used one hand to cover her mouth and the other to cup her pussy in the hopes that it would calm the throbbing.

Cleopatra pumped Jacqueline slow and soft, but Supriti could hear faint slapping sounds as she sped up her stroke. Jacqueline's moans and whimpers turned to louder and deeper gasps and grunts. "Fuck me" Supriti heard Jacqueline demand.

She knew she heard correctly, as their intensity built. Cleopatra wasn't making love to her anymore; she was pulling all the way out, long stroking Jacqueline and slamming into her.

Cleopatra pushed Jacqueline's legs up in the air, resting her ankles on her shoulders as she continued to work her pussy. Then she lifted Jacqueline's ass off the bed to push into her even deeper. Jacqueline was taking it, from cock to balls.

Supriti thought Cleopatra's stamina and control was incredible as she stroked her wife hard and slow. Supriti's clit pounded between her legs; no amount of squeezing sufficed.

Jacqueline moaned louder, and Cleopatra kissed her wife without breaking rhythm in her stroke. Jacqueline held her tight in her arms, receiving her long tongue and her long dick at the same time.

Supriti refused to blink for fear of missing something. She wanted to feel what Jacqueline was feeling, taste what she was tasting.

"Cleopatra," Jacqueline gasped as another orgasm took over her body. But Cleopatra continued her stroke until Jacqueline had no more fight left in her.

"I love you, baby," Cleopatra said, still inside of her.

"I love you more." Jacqueline took her face into her hands and kissed her.

Supriti could feel their connection, and she wanted it. She needed Cleopatra to want her, to make love to her, to look at her the way she looked at Jacqueline ... to need her just like she needed her wife. She watched as they kissed deeply and Cleopatra—still inside of Jacqueline—began to move her ass again. Their sweaty bodies glistened in the moonlight as they rocked back and forth and met each other's thrusts. Jacqueline slid up and down the length of Cleopatra's dick, burying her cock inside of her as far as it could go and curling her body around her wife, her arms and legs intertwined with Cleopatra's. The feel of her wife inside of her, so strong, so thick and long. Fucking her like she belonged to her, because she did.

"Baby. I'm gonna come all over your dick." Jacqueline sank her teeth into Cleopatra's neck as she went deeper and Cleopatra groaned, pumping deep inside of her wife, still grinding and banging, giving her every single inch. Jacqueline's body shuddered underneath her, her pussy throbbing and tight around her cock.

Supriti's body shivered as she listened to the tempered sound of Jacqueline's orgasm. She leaned all her weight against the closet wall, parted her legs as much as she could, and slid her fingers down into her panties. She moved her hand over the soft, wet hairs of her pussy, and started to rub her clit, spreading her legs some more, her panties still caught just at her thighs, as she leaned over and pressed her eyes to the crack between the closet doors to see better.

Now Cleopatra was coming, too. Supriti couldn't take it; her swollen clit throbbed and ached for relief. She came too as she watched Cleopatra thrust and grunt on top of Jacqueline. Supriti's pussy contracted so hard that she wanted to scream, but she bit her lip and held her breath to keep from making any sound as she shuddered and bucked against the closet wall. Not that Cleopatra or Jacqueline would have heard her over their own climaxes.

Jacqueline rolled over onto her stomach and clutched the pillow beneath her. She stuck her tongue out and threw her head back.

"Take my ass, Daddy. You know that's yours too."

Cleopatra pushed her face between Jacqueline's cheeks and tongued her ass. Jacqueline let out a sound that Cleopatra only heard when she had her tongue in her hole, then gasped when she felt Cleopatra pour the warm lube between her cheeks. Cleopatra gently slipped her finger inside of her ass. She moved it around, and then in and out as Jacqueline arched her back and moaned.

"Yes, baby. Give me some more."

Then Cleopatra pressed her cock around her ass and slowly pushed the head inside. Jacqueline yelped out in pain as the pressure intensified. Her ass tightened around the head of Cleopatra's dick and wouldn't immediately give way. A searing sensation shot through her ass, but she knew the pleasure that lay beyond the pain. She took a deep breath and met Cleopatra's gentle pushes as she inched deeper inside of her. Cleopatra's cock sliding into her ass tortured and pleasured her in the best ways.

Across the room and inside the closet, Supriti was stunned at first, almost appalled as she watched Cleopatra ease into Jacqueline in that forbidden place, so dark and sacred. She couldn't imagine letting someone do that to her. But that was Jacqueline's wife; their relationship was something beyond her comprehension. That was becoming clearer to her now.

Jacqueline called out Cleopatra's name as she moaned. "That's yours, baby."

Cleopatra grasped Jacqueline's hips tight, restricting her from moving, then pushed into her, burying her full length in Jacqueline.

Supriti slipped her hand into her panties again. Her pussy had been wet since Cleopatra emerged naked from the shower, but now it was swollen and throbbing. She parted her lips and rubbed her clit with her middle finger.

"Take it!" Jacqueline screamed. The words somehow thrilled and moistened Supriti even more, and so did Jacqueline's yelp when Cleopatra stroked her ass. Intently watching, Supriti leaned all of her body weight against the closet wall, squeezing her thighs tight together on her hand as hard as she could, in an attempt to quell the throbbing.

Cleopatra slapped Jacqueline's ass, her stroke slow and methodical, then went deeper, harder, and faster. Jacqueline bucked her body back, slamming into Cleopatra. Cleopatra took her, pushing into her as Jacqueline begged, Cleopatra's name oozing from her lips like the cum that streamed down her thighs.

Supriti's panties were already soaked all the way through. The heat from her pussy and the lack of air in the closet was suffocating her, and she gasped as she spread her pussy lips apart and circled her clit, longing for Cleopatra to fuck her. She rubbed her clit aggressively, now fully turned on by what she was witnessing, trying to imagine what it felt like to be stretched open in such a way.

Cleopatra's dick game made Supriti fragile with desire, and she imagined Cleopatra fucking her. She wanted to be her wife, needed to climb all 6 feet of her and slide her wet pussy down the entire length of her dick. She moved her hand back and forth, pushing her fingers deep into her pussy as she matched the rhythm of Cleopatra's stroke. She watched the muscles in Cleopatra's back and ass contract as she slid in and out of

Jacqueline. Cleopatra moaned and called Jacqueline's name. She pulled her dick almost all the way out of Jacqueline's ass, stopping just short of the head, and pumped her ass slowly.

She was coming, and struggling to control it.

Jacqueline had opened up and given her body to her wife. She was rewarded when Cleopatra pushed deeply into her, and the white cream slid from her pussy and onto her thighs. Cleopatra threw her head back, held Jacqueline's ass tight, and pounded into her, speeding up her strokes. Every muscle in Jacqueline's body tensed and locked up on her all at once; the tighter her ass clenched Cleopatra's dick, the more powerful the climax. She squeezed her ass around her wife's cock as each stroke brought her closer, and the orgasm finally shot its way through her body, first at her clit, then vibrating through her pussy, then to her ass around Cleopatra's dick. Her entire body convulsed until she could no longer hold herself up and fell to her stomach, still with Cleopatra inside of her. Cleopatra pulled out slowly before collapsing on the bed next to her.

Cleopatra and Jacqueline made love nonstop that night and Supriti witnessed every lick, every stroke, every orgasm. She hadn't seen anyone so capable of delivering such continuous delight as Cleopatra. She watched as waves of pleasure gushed relentlessly through Jacqueline. Cleopatra took her high, pushed her over the edge into wild climaxes, then eased off her, letting her recover, only to start building all over again with a stroke here, a finger or a kiss there.

And there was the connection. The energy and the chemistry between them could not be denied or severed. How they moaned "I love you" when they climaxed. How Jacqueline screamed Cleopatra's name when she exploded in orgasm.

Supriti understood now. She curled up into a tight ball in the corner of the closet and sobbed softly until she cried herself to sleep. She awoke the next morning sore and startled by laughter coming from the bedroom. She peaked out of the closet to investigate and watched Cleopatra chase a naked Jacqueline around the bed and into the bathroom.

Jacqueline prepared a bubble bath in the Jacuzzi while Cleopatra followed close behind her. And with her, she carried Leroy Coleman the Fifth's old brown leather briefcase.

⟡⟡⟡

Moments later, in the ladies' room of the hotel lobby, Supriti hunkered down in a handicapped stall and pulled her panties from under her skirt. They were soaked with her cum, her pussy still oozing and swollen from a night of unending sexual frustration. Her body trembled as she leaned against the stall wall, the memories of a lovemaking that she could never unsee leaving her broken and hopeless.

FORTY TWO

....

TRUE COLORS

"So you said on the phone you think we may be able to work this out somehow?" Jacqueline took a sip of masala chai and leaned back in her chair, waiting to be entertained by Alonzo's foolishness. Before she'd had a chance to call Vanessa's office with the information that Leroy Coleman the Fifth discovered, she got a frantic phone call from Alonzo, asking to meet at the coffee shop by their house.

"Go, baby," Cleopatra had encouraged her. "Just listen. Don't talk. He'll put his foot in his mouth. See what he has to say, but don't let on about what you know."

Now Jacqueline sat across the table from Alonzo in the crowded café, midmorning. The establishment was the newest hot spot in Greenwich Village with its dim lighting, dark leather furnishings, and monochromatic decor. Alonzo was nervous as he babysat a complimentary cup of tap water. He hadn't been prepared for Jacqueline to go into court and declare her intentions to divorce Cleopatra. That deal did nothing to line his pockets, but he didn't know that Jacqueline had changed her mind about breaking up her marriage, or that she

449

now had her hands on a packet full of information on him and his bank-robbing, parole-skipping wife.

Jacqueline was just excited that this nightmare was coming to an end.

"You've been gay all your life. Even I know that," Alonzo confessed. "So now you're telling me you aren't gay and you're leaving your wife? That's not what this is about. It's about that." He pointed to Jacqueline's wedding ring. "How much was that? Probably more money than I've made in the last five years. I mean, look at how you're dressed. What is that, Prada down to your toes? Now look at me." He rubbed his torn, stonewashed jeans and tugged at his dingy white t-shirt. "This is about you living the good life while I'm slumming in an apartment that's smaller than your foyer. How many floors is that house, anyway?"

"Cleopatra has made a beautiful home for me and the kids." She looked at him sideways. "What does that have to do with anything?"

"I don't necessarily want to know them. You know?"

"Say what?" Jacqueline cocked her head to the side as if she'd heard him wrong.

"I didn't come for the kids." He rubbed his hands together as if warming them by a fire. "Initially I was thinking I could get this money through child support, but then I would actually have to take care of them. That's a lot of work and responsibility that I don't want."

"You don't necessarily?" Jacqueline pushed her chair back from the table. She quickly estimated how much distance she needed in order to clear the table and land with her foot on his throat. "Do you realize the hell that you have put my family through these last couple of months?"

He took a piece of paper out of his pocket and slid it across the table. "If you can make that number happen—" He tapped it with his index finger. "—I promise you'll never see me again. Hold on." He took out a pen, crossed out the number and wrote a new number. "I forgot to add in my attorney's fee and travel expenses." He slid the paper back across the table.

Jacqueline's mouth dropped open. "Piece of shit." She looked around at the other patrons, considering whether she would make a scene or not, but took a deep breath and maintained her composure. "So that's what this is about?"

"I want to live how you're living. Set me up and I'm gone." He shot a fake gun in to the air.

"It's not my money. It's my wife's money, and even if it wasn't, I wouldn't pay your bum ass a dime. You really don't care about those babies."

He shrugged his shoulders and took the slip of paper back.

"I heard she gives you whatever you want. If you ask her for it, she'll give it to you."

"And who told you that?" Jacqueline asked. "My punk-ass sister?"

"Little sis told me a lot of things, she was full of details. She told me how good you were living, how happy and perfect your life was. She told me I needed to get back here quick and get me some of it."

Jacqueline balled up her fist and her heart pounded hard in her chest. She struggled not to jump across the table and tackle him. She visualized cracking a chair over his head and the satisfaction it would give her, but instead took a deep breath and exhaled.

451

"If I tell my wife about the number on that little slip of paper, your body will wash up somewhere off of Far Rockaway, and I honestly wouldn't be mad. I'm going to do you a favor by not telling her."

"She already knows." He smiled. "What? She didn't tell you? I thought you lesbians talked a lot. What do you call it? Processing?"

"Cleopatra said you would do this and I didn't believe her." Jacqueline shook her head. "I doubted her. That will never happen again."

"What you two do is none of my business. But you might want to seriously reconsider, because I have something else. Something new has just popped up." He rubbed his ashy sandpaper hands together. "There are more secrets, like you never even imagined. You crazy lesbians." He laughed. "That wife of yours and her family are shady as hell."

Jacqueline blew him off. "I know what you think you have on my wife, but it's not going to work. What you should do is stop digging yourself into a hole." She flipped her cell phone over and showed Alonzo that she'd been taping their conversation on her phone's voice recorder. "Just pack up your shit and go back to Fresno like a good little boy."

"You don't know anything, because your wife doesn't even know about this. So she can't even keep it from you or lie to you about it."

What the... Jacqueline leaned back in her chair, unable to hide the fear and uncertainty on her face.

"Right," Alonzo said. "I don't care what you recorded, because you know what? The judge wouldn't give custody to either one of us right now. Want your kids in foster care? Or better yet, how about with my parents? They're homophobic, so they can brainwash the kids and convince them that their mommy is going to hell just because she likes girls."

Jacqueline didn't know what to say, and stayed frozen in her chair.

"I didn't think so." Alonzo smiled. "People around your wife aren't safe. This goes way back, but looks like some things never change. Now, I don't want this to get any dirtier, but it can if you want to take it there. If I tell the judge what I know now, you'll lose this case for sure. Even if you didn't, there's no way this good ole boy, hee-haw of a judge will allow your wife visitation or to remain in the kids' lives at all. Even if you do go ahead with this divorce scheme of yours."

Jacqueline couldn't hide the surprise on her face.

"Yeah. Even I know you aren't trying to give her up for nothing." He winked at her. "But we can avoid all of that. Now what about this money?"

FORTY THREE

....

BLAST FROM THE PAST

"Long time, still fine," the woman said when she opened the door and saw Cleopatra standing there. While Jacqueline met with Alonzo, Cleopatra had gone to an extended stay hotel out in Queens to visit Alonzo's wife.

Although it looked like she had burdened her 5'2" frame with an extra fifty pounds since they were teenagers, and those prison years hadn't been kind, Cleopatra recognized Niecy as soon as she opened the door. Nasty Niecy, the girl who broke Shawn's heart and nearly tore the best friends apart forever. They were no more than eighteen or nineteen years old at the time, and Cleopatra had no idea that the girl she had spent a freaky weekend with was Shawn's new woman.

Shawn claimed to be in love with the girl, and wasn't giving her up for anyone. So she cut Cleopatra completely out of her life. It wasn't until six months later that Shawn came back around, after she had broken up with Niecy. Now, all these years later, the same girl stood in front of Cleopatra, probably just as much trouble as ever.

"Cleo." Niecy smiled when she saw her. "How did you find

me?" She scratched the scalp between her burgundy cornrows with her acrylic nails and stuck her head out the door to look around the parking lot suspiciously. Then she pulled Cleopatra into the room.

"I don't believe it." Cleopatra shook her head. "Jesse James. Three hots and a cot. Orange is the New Black. What are you doing back in New York?" she yelled over the loud rattling of the room's vintage air conditioner as she walked into the dark, damp space.

"I'm here with my new husband, who's here handling some business. How did you know I was here?" Niecy cracked her bubblegum nervously between her teeth.

"A friend told me you were in town and where I could find you." Cleopatra thought twice about sitting down. The brown microfiber couch had stains on it from something white that dried hard and crusty. "So you really got married? And to a guy? Does your husband have any idea how much you love pussy?" Cleopatra already knew the answer. "Does he know how long your arrest record is? Does he know that there's a warrant out for your arrest right now because you skipped out on your parole and left the state? How long ago was that?" Cleopatra counted on her fingers.

"No, he doesn't. And he doesn't need to know." Niecy twisted her lips at Cleopatra and grabbed a mini-croissant from a paper plate piled high with what looked like continental breakfast pastries she'd hoarded from that morning's complimentary buffet.

"Now that's where you're wrong. He just might need to know. Or should I just call NYPD now?"

A knocking on the wall got progressively louder and

quicker, and faint moans in rhythm with the knocking soon turned into screaming. Cleopatra pounded her fist on the wall three times. "Really?" she yelled. "Anyway. The business your husband is handling happens to be with my wife." Cleopatra paused and waited for the plane overhead to clear so that she didn't need to raise her voice. "Yeah Niecy. Let's stop playing games. I know you're married to Alonzo. That's why I'm here. Your husband has brought nothing to me and my family but problems since you two got into town. You and your man are shady as hell, and you know it." Cleopatra sniffed the air. "Why do I smell weed now?" She couldn't go back to work with her hair or clothes smelling like kush.

"That's them next door." Niecy tilted her head toward the room with the loud headboard.

"So what exactly is the plan?" Cleopatra cornered her. Niecy swallowed hard but didn't speak. "The NYPD knows you're back in town, they just don't know where, yet. One call from me and—"

"Money," Niecy blurted out. "He's tired of being broke. He found out his ex has money and he wants some of it. Give him enough and he'll go away. Simple as that."

"I already know that. I just wanted to hear you say it." Cleopatra glanced over at the small thirteen-inch black and white TV in the corner when she heard the theme song to *The Young and the Restless*. She made a mental note to catch up with the residents of Genoa City, who she'd watched religiously as a child.

Niecy exhaled. "He would kill me if he knew I told you. No, he didn't come back for the kids, not at all. He didn't even tell me he had kids until he came up with this plan a couple months ago. He doesn't care about them. Doesn't like kids. I don't like kids," she confessed as she sat down on the corner of the double bed.

Cleopatra swore she heard the old 1970s-style checkered bedspread crack under her weight. She wondered how many years of bodily fluid had contributed to the crispiness of that bedding.

"I knew that. All of a sudden he pops up and wants custody. And he's never once asked to meet them since he got back in the city. You come three thousand miles to get full custody and you don't ask to visit with them? To visit with kids you haven't seen in almost four years? Not once?"

"He'll regret this one day. When his ass is old and alone," Niecy professed.

"And that's the only reason he'll walk away from this in one piece. One day they'll want to know him, and I'm not taking that away from them. Every child should have the opportunity to find out on their own that their daddy ain't shit." Cleopatra readied herself to leave. "Wish I could say it's been a pleasure." She walked toward the door. "Damn. Ok, now what is that?"

Niecy sniffed the air. "Um…" She scrunched her face. "Smells like chitterlings. But it doesn't smell like they cleaned them good."

"Who the hell cooks chitterlings up in a motel room? I'm out." Cleopatra opened the door with her jacket sleeve to avoid touching the doorknob with her hand.

"Can you do me a favor, Cleo? And not tell my husband about my past and not call the police on me?"

"I have no interest in seeing you in prison, Niecy, or messing up your marriage. So don't worry about it."

"Thanks a lot. I appreciate that. How's Shawn?"

"Why?"

"We didn't break up on the best of terms, you know? Just wanted to know if she was ok."

"That was a long time ago. I'm sure she's over you."

"Three years isn't that long."

"You skipped out on parole about three years ago after you were in prison for eight. So that would have been about eleven years ago when you went away." Cleopatra added up the years in her head. "Correct?" she side eyed Niecy.

"She told you she broke up with me eleven years ago?"

"She said that if it moved you fucked it. And she was tired of you cheating on her."

"That's only half true. I cheated on her every chance I got, but she never broke up with me. I got sent upstate for bank robbery. She came to visit me every month for eight years and kept my commissary up. She came and got me on my release day and took me to dinner, where I had the best meal I'd eaten in eight years. Then I stole some money out of her backpack and caught a bus to California. We haven't spoken since." Niecy frowned. "It looks like your friend has been lying to you for a long time. Tell her I said hello and that I'm sorry."

"I'm not telling her anything."

"You know she was always super-jealous of you. She had this love/hate thing with you. I used to think she wanted to be you, then sometimes I thought she wanted to be with you. Especially after you and I spent that weekend together and I told her you were so much better in bed than she was."

"I tell you what." Cleopatra walked over to the coffee table, took a pen from her pocket, and wrote on a napkin. "Here's her cell." She handed her Shawn's number. "Don't forget, you're married. I believe your husband's exact words were that you are very straight." Cleopatra smiled. "He said you're in church five days a week. Is that true?"

"I am."

"So who is at church? Deacon or the minister?"

"Deacon, choir director. And the bible study teacher."

"Dic tac and no cock or clit is safe." Cleopatra walked toward the door. "By the way, your husband is going to be changing his mind fairly soon about pretty much everything, and he may or may not decide to keep you around. So you might want to plan for that. Whatever the case may be, stay away from me and my family."

"Speaking of family, you still don't know do you? You have no idea?"

"Know what?"

"Never mind. It's not important."

Cleopatra raised her left eyebrow and cocked her head. "What is it? What don't I know?"

Niecy exhaled hard. "About Shawn."

Cleopatra stared at her, waiting for her to say something. "Ok. What about her?"

Niecy still remained silent.

"I'm out of here. I don't have time for this Niecy." Cleopatra said.

"She has a son."

Cleopatra thought for a moment, then laughed out loud. "I almost forgot that you're a pathological liar."

"You don't have to believe me, but it's the truth."

Cleopatra laughed again. "Yeah, right. So when did she have

a baby? Where is he now? Who's the father? And why would she not tell me, of all people?" She smirked.

"All I know is he lives in Trinidad. He must be maybe sixteen or seventeen by now." Niecy hesitated. "Who's the father? That's the big secret."

"Do you realize how crazy this sounds? I don't believe you." Cleopatra shook her head. "There is no way. She would have had to hide a nine-month pregnancy. And giving birth."

"She's fat, she's always been fat." Niecy said. "It wouldn't be that hard to hide. And didn't she spend her summers in Trinidad back then?"

"Yeah she did," Cleopatra admitted. "I'm assuming Shawn's the one who told you all of this? How did she tell it to you, exactly?"

"She told me a long time ago. She said she came out to her parents when she was twelve and they kicked her out of the house. And she said she stayed with you and your family for a while."

"Yeah. All of that's true." Cleopatra nodded.

"Then she said that during that time her parents paid someone to take her virginity. Paid them to make her like men."

"What do you mean take? And make her like men?" Cleopatra asked disgusted. "That sounds like rape."

"It's crazy. I thought that too, at first. But it wasn't. Not really." Niecy shook her head. "So the dude came to Shawn like, 'Yo, look what your parents gave me. They gave me $1,000 to pop your cherry because you don't like dudes.' He came at her from a place of trying to help her out. Like look how fucked up your folks are. You know? But Shawn told me she had a crush on old dude, she always thought he was cute and

461

all the girls in the neighborhood were constantly running around trying to get with him. So she told him she would do it with him, if he bought her a pair of new sneakers with some of the money. The same kind he had just bought his little sister."

"What?" Cleopatra was dumbfounded. "So she did it for sneakers? She lost her virginity for a pair of sneakers?"

"And she liked it. She told me she liked it," Niecy said. "A lot."

"I don't believe this shit."

"She liked it so much that she kept doing it with the dude. She basically had an affair with him for like two years or something. But she messed around and got pregnant calling herself trying to trap him. She told me she went to Trinidad and had the baby during the summer. When she came back in the fall, no one knew anything. But her parents were furious at the guy because he wouldn't give them any money to help with the baby. Then Shawn got mad because she wanted him all to herself, but she always saw him with other older and prettier girls. So as payback some stupid time later, after he had taken her virginity and she'd had the baby, like years later, she went to the cops and told them he raped her and got her pregnant. He got arrested and no one has heard from him since."

Cleopatra was shocked silent. Pathological liar or not, she believed every word that Niecy said.

"But there's something else," Niecy continued. "Alonzo was looking for something else on you guys to get money out of you. Something he could hold over your head in the custody case. And his attorney found it."

"What? I need a minute to digest what you just told me

about Shawn. You're going back and forth here. You're confusing me." Cleopatra waved her hand. "What does one thing have to do with the other?"

"You still don't get it. You don't get what I'm trying to tell you. The man that had an affair with Shawn, took her virginity, impregnated her as a teenager, and went to prison for it…" Niecy hesitated. "Everyone knows who he is accept you. Your parents really never told you, Cleo? It was your brother."

FORTY FOUR

··

WE DON'T HANG NO MORE

"You still work here, huh?" Cleopatra asked Shawn, who was sorting packages in the back of the brightly lit, cramped basement mailroom. It hadn't even been two days since Cleopatra visited Niecy. She had no intention of confronting Shawn about what had gone on between her and her brother back in the day; she wasn't sure she ever would. She hadn't completely wrapped her head around Shawn being the reason that her brother wasn't in her life anymore. She hadn't even told Jacqueline yet. She struggled to push it out of her head—how different her life would have been had she'd had him to lean on, and had her mother had her first-born around in her final years. At this point she couldn't despise Shawn and her family any more than she already did. Confirming with Shawn wasn't going to help anything or anyone. It surely wasn't going to change the past.

But still, Cleopatra struggled to contain her anger as she thought that Shawn's past actions could have an effect on the custody case. Shawn's little bastard was the last thing the judge needed to find out about. She imagined the homophobic judge

465

deeming her entire family full of sexual deviants, with her past as an escort and her brother having committed statutory rape that resulted in a child. He'd proclaim no children safe around Cleopatra, even though she hadn't seen her brother in over fifteen years and had absolutely nothing to do with him. But she wouldn't be able to prove lack of contact since Vanessa had found that unbeknownst to her, her brother had listed her as his emergency contact on a recent job application for a dishwasher at a restaurant somewhere in the city.

"I'm still working here for the moment." Shawn walked up to the window. "I got demoted back down to clerk, lost my office, and I'm on my feet all day with this blue polo shirt. I look like I work at Best Buy and I'm not even getting that Best Buy discount. I won't have this shit much longer." She popped a handful of Swedish Fish into her mouth.

"A package just came in for me?" Cleopatra looked down and brushed her suit jacket free of the dust and dirt she had to walk through to get to the mailroom. And probably for the first time in her life, she saw the contrast between her and Shawn. Her former best friend in a blue polo shirt and khakis, and her in a Dior suit. That's when it hit her, and a calm came over her. Life was about choices. They'd made different ones, and Shawn's wellbeing was no longer her burden to carry.

"Yeah. You have a package," Shawn said, "I could have had it sent up immediately if it was a rush. Where's Racquel?" She searched through the packages due to the executive floors.

"Racquel did some spring cleaning this weekend and came across some of her old jelly shoes from back and the day."

"Don't tell me she…"

"Yup. She decided to wear them out on Saturday night. Her

466

feet swelled up and that plastic cut into her like crazy. She hasn't moved all day. She might be soaking her feet in a trash can under her desk—I'm just too scared to look."

"That's hilarious." Shawn handed her an express envelope and a blue Bic to sign the delivery log. "So, you gave Niecy my cell number?"

Shawn had reunited with Niecy in between the sheets in the hotel room she shared with Alonzo, just as Cleopatra knew they would. And as usual with Shawn, the ensuing aftermath was predictable, but never ceased to be entertaining.

Cleopatra initialed and printed her name on the log. "I sure did. She asked about you. I thought you would want to catch up with your first love."

"We hooked up."

"Is that why you smell like Afro Sheen and chicken noodle soup?" Shawn frowned at her. "I'm serious. It's coming out of your pores." Cleopatra shrugged her shoulders.

Shawn smelled her arms. "Anyway. Her husband caught us. Walked into the room right after we had banged it out. I was in the bathroom and had to jump out of the damn window."

Cleopatra wondered how Shawn fit her big ass through a hot sheets hotel window. She would have paid to see that, she smiled to herself.

"He was so hot," Shawn continued. "That fool tried to chase me."

Cleopatra leaned in close and lowered her voice. "You were fucking his wife. Yeah, he was mad." She neglected to say who Niecy's husband was. She wondered how many people Shawn had fought recently if she didn't realize that Niecy's husband was the same fool she had run up on a few weeks before at her house.

"So since their marriage was over, we got back together."

"Wait. What?" Cleopatra thought she heard her wrong.

"I'm not done." Shawn raised her hand. "I was about to break up with Robin, move her out, so I could move Niecy in. I had it all planned. I was going to take Niecy home, like walk through the door with her and tell Robin to get out, all at the same time. That shit was going to be efficient as hell. So we're packing up Niecy's hotel room and we hear all of this commotion outside. The next thing we know, we hear 'Deneicia Jenkins, come out with your hands up' on a big-ass megaphone. I opened the door with my hands up and it's like ten police cars in the parking lot, guns drawn and everything. Her husband called and reported her, violated her. Now she's back upstate to do the rest of her original sentence. She's trying to get transferred to Georgia because her family just moved down there."

Cleopatra remained silent. She looked at Shawn and wondered how someone so stupid had managed to live as long as she had.

"And there's something else."

Cleopatra held her breath, waiting for Shawn to say something else stupid that she didn't care about, and that had no effect on her or her family.

"So I go home from leaving Niecy at the police station and catch Robin tangled up in the sheets with somebody else. Caught her cheating on me," Shawn confessed.

"You're surprised?" Cleopatra offered nothing in the form of a sympathetic look.

"Yeah I am." Shawn pulled a half-eaten honey bun from her back pocket and took a bite.

"So you were going to take Niecy home and kick Robin out? But Niecy got busted and sent back to prison, so you stroll home dejected and find Robin getting done by somebody else in your bed?" Cleopatra smiled. "That's ratchet. That's more ratchet than the time you smoked so much weed that you couldn't order for yourself at KFC. So you called me and asked me to text you your usual order so you could show the text to the girl behind the counter."

"Why you bringing up old shit?"

"That was six months ago!" Cleopatra laughed. And for a moment it almost felt like old times, when they talked about stupid shit they had done and thought it was the funniest shit in the world. But Cleopatra quickly snapped out of it. She hated Shawn and there was no coming back from that.

"Let me finish telling you about Robin. So I walked in and there she was fucking a dude in my bed." She paused. "Ok, the bed you bought me. But in my house, man."

Cleopatra's eyes widened. She covered her mouth and tried not to laugh. "I'm sorry."

"No. You don't understand." Shawn shook her head. "I don't believe I'm telling you this. When I say she was fucking a dude, I mean just that. She had a strap on and had this dude bent the fuck over. Dick, balls all on my pillow."

"Stop it!" Cleopatra hollered. "So what did you do?"

"I kicked his pretty ass out."

"He was pretty? His name wasn't ... um, Jose, Joseph ... or Javier, was it?"

"How did you know?"

"That's her boyfriend, or used to be. She was dating him when Jacqueline and I first met. Maybe she never stopped. He

469

does gay porn, a lot of gay porn. Oh … sorry." Cleopatra caught herself.

"That motherfucker does porn? Shit."

"Gay, gang bang porn. He's a bottom like you wouldn't believe. He started from the bottom and he's staying there! You do remember she's bi-sexual right? She never claimed to be strictly clitly, all women all the time, anyway." Cleopatra still wasn't trying to soften the blow. "Why do lesbians get with bi women and then get mad when they go back to dick? I never understood that."

"It gets worse. She was using my strap." Shawn nodded her head when Cleopatra's mouth dropped open.

"So she's been using it on him, you use it on her, then go down on her? You two are some messy motherfuckers. I'm gonna go throw up now."

Shawn shook her head. "They were doing some SST shit when I walked in on them."

"What?"

"Sissy slut training."

"I know what it is. He doesn't need it. Wait." Cleopatra covered her face with her hand. "So tell me exactly what he was wearing."

"A nurse's uniform and a blond wig."

Cleopatra grabbed her stomach and shook with laughter.

"I don't even want to think about that part. Point is, she was cheating on me."

"Seriously, that's the part you're upset about? You've cheated on her dozens of times—more than she even knows about. You were just about to kick her out on the street two minutes before for Niecy."

"Yeah. Yeah. It's different. I wouldn't let her top me; that's why she did that shit. She wanted to use the strap on me."

"Eww. She wanted to fuck you, fuck you?"

"You know I ain't with that."

"Actually I don't know that. But whatever." Cleopatra nodded. "So you two broke up again?"

"Nope." Shawn smirked. "And Robin doesn't know anything about Niecy. She doesn't know she was an hour away from being out on the street again. So don't say anything to her."

Cleopatra laughed. "We no longer have any allegiance to each other. I don't know, maybe I will tell her. You two seem to love to tell all of my business." She smiled. "And I never see Robin anymore. My wife doesn't speak to her since she tried to fuck me again." A shocked look spread across Shawn's face and she cut her eyes at Cleopatra. "Like I said before, I'm good. I don't want anything to do with either of you."

"What happened to you, man?" Shawn asked. "You think you grown or something, now? What do you expect, me to be just like you?"

Cleopatra laughed. "Yes and not at all. Yes I am grown and no I don't expect you to be just like me. I don't expect anything of you anymore, Shawn. But it's sad because you shouldn't be doing the same shit you were doing ten, fifteen years ago. Grow up. Just a little." Cleopatra pinched her thumb and index finger together. "What about a career, going back to school? What's your purpose? What's your passion? Learn a trade or a skill. Why do you wake up in the morning? I sold my ass so I could go to school and get an education, but you ... what the hell are you doing?" Shawn was quiet.

"If you were to say I'm going to be an escort, I'm going to be the best ho in NYC I would have to respect that," Cleopatra admitted. "But you do every single thing half-assed. The only thing you don't do half-assed is act half-assed. Your supervisor is calling me because I brought you into this company how many years ago? And he's pulling out the three shaky strands of hair he has left in his head because he wants to fire you but he's afraid of what I might say or do."

"Did you have anything to do with them letting me take a leave of absence a few weeks ago?"

Cleopatra nodded. "I asked them not to fire you then. But Olivia is calling me because your clients aren't happy, either. She's thinking about squashing the rest of your debt, breaking both of your legs, and running your ass out of New York."

"So what did you tell everyone?"

"I told them to leave me out of it. And that you can handle your own affairs."

"What the fuck happened to you, man?"

"Just because you came up *with* me, doesn't mean you're coming *with* me."

FORTY FIVE

···

IT AIN'T OVER 'TIL IT'S OVER

"I don't understand, Alonzo. All of a sudden?" Jacqueline asked, surprised. "Just two days ago you were hell-bent on taking the kids from me, then on getting money, and blackmailing me with some deep dark secret. Now you're giving up your parental rights?" Jacqueline looked down at a copy of his court petition to terminate his ties to the children.

She studied Alonzo. Something didn't sit right with her. All this time he looked like he had been living on the street. But now he looked like a new man, with a fresh haircut, clean-shaven face, and crisp new tailor-made suit. She thought this change of heart was particularly strange, since she had just the day before turned all of Leroy Coleman's findings over to Vanessa. The attorney had just begun to build a case for dismissal when Alonzo showed up to say goodbye. So this had nothing to do with him gracefully bowing out.

"I thought about what was best for everyone involved." Alonzo said. "I figured your wife might want to adopt the kids one day. So yeah, take care of yourself, Jacqueline." He bent down to wipe a speck of dirt off his new Bruno Magli loafers, then threw up his hand as he hopped down the steps toward his chauffeured sedan.

"So where are you going? What is all that? The car, the suit?" Jacqueline asked. "You even looked like you bathed."

"Actually, I don't know where I'm going. Somewhere pretty far away, though. I'll find out when I get there." He looked down at his new Gucci watch. "But I have an 11AM flight to catch.

"Don't you mean *we* have a flight to catch? What about your wife?" Jacqueline asked.

"Oh. Her. Actually, it's not going to work out. I found her in the middle of an extracurricular activity. So I decided to leave her here, and let the state take care of her. Anyway, my attorney will call your attorney, tie up any loose ends, and wrap up the termination. So we will most likely never see each other again."

"Promise?" Jacqueline smiled.

"Promise."

✪✪✪

"Thank you for everything." Jacqueline said, excited. "Hopefully we'll never cross paths again."

Jacqueline had received a phone call from Vanessa, who told her that the custody case had been dismissed. But she still couldn't stop herself from crying. The nightmare of the last couple of months was finally coming to an end.

She was anxious to get her wife back home so they could

pick up where they left off when they returned from their honeymoon. She went to Cleopatra's hotel, expecting to bring her wife home.

"Baby, tell me the truth. Did you pay him? Did you give him money to go away?"

"Hell no. I didn't give him a dime," Cleopatra swore. Jacqueline was alarmed that Cleopatra wasn't more excited, and didn't understand her hesitation. She didn't seem at all happy. She was cold, she was unemotional. She didn't smile, laugh, raise her fist in victory, or anything. She was just deadpan and deep in thought. All Cleopatra could think of was how much Alexis must have paid Alonzo for him to give up his parental rights and what remote part of the world she had banished him to.

"I need some time before I make a decision about coming home." Cleopatra said.

"What the hell do you mean? There's no decision to be made. You're coming home! I'm here to help you pack."

"I'm tired of going back and forth. I actually feel somewhat settled here right now. I almost feel stable. So I need a minute. Do you realize that since we've been married I've been out of the house more than I've been in it?"

"I know. But it's over baby. He never had a chance with what your P.I. found. A bank-robbing wife? Come on. I should have listened to you, and I'm so sorry. I should have trusted you and let you handle it from the beginning. I'll never doubt what you can do ever again. I promise you."

"Yeah, you should have trusted me."

"It's over now. If only I had let you take charge from the start! I've been meaning to ask. When did you find all of that stuff anyway?"

"I don't know. A few weeks ago." Cleopatra admitted.

"What? A few weeks ago? You had proof and you sat on it?"

"Yeah."

"What the hell, you should have been on the phone calling me the second you got it. What the hell is wrong with you? This could have been over."

"I did get on the phone the second I had the evidence in my hand. And you know what you said? You had a court date and that my dumb ass shouldn't show up because you were going to tell the judge you were divorcing me. That's what you said. You had it handled. Then you hung up on me. You remember that? I thought you knew what you were doing, Jac? Hmm?"

"I was never going to abandon you. Never. Baby, please. I'm asking you to come home, now. Stop trying to drive me away because you're still hurting. I was never going anywhere; you have to know that I'm yours. You own me, all of me. And if it takes the rest of my life to prove that to you, I'll do it."

"Like I said. I need some time before I move back home. A lot has happened these last couple of months. We have both done and said some rotten things to each other. And it wasn't ok. It's still not ok. There are things that you need to forgive me for and things that I need to forgive you for. And honestly I'm not there yet."

Cleopatra opened the door to her suite, patted her pockets for her wallet and cell phone, and crossed over the threshold into the hallway. "I'm starving. I'm going to get something to eat. Maybe I'll come by the house later."

FORTY SIX

....

I NEED TO FUCK YOU

"I need to fuck you," Cleopatra whispered into her cell phone. Jacqueline rolled over in bed, sat up, and turned on the bedroom lamp. The alarm clock read 1AM.

"Where are you?"

"Standing outside the bedroom door."

Jacqueline hung up the phone and tried to catch her breath. She stood at the end of the bed, waiting. She wore only a t-shirt and no panties. She tried to calm her desire when Cleopatra walked into the room. She needed her badly. But she also needed to teach her a lesson. Who did she think she was, refusing to come home with her but showing up hours later saying she needed to fuck her?

Jacqueline held her breath as she walked in. Her eyes moved up Cleopatra's body. Cleopatra's eyes were bright with anticipation; the look in her eyes that Jacqueline longed for was back. She slid her fingertips up Jacqueline's arms, then massaged her breasts through the thin cotton. She pinched at her nipples as Jacqueline moaned.

Jacqueline moved her hand down between Cleopatra's legs,

477

cupping the massive bulge stuffed into her jeans. She squeezed it in her hand, massaging her through the denim.

Cleopatra licked her lips as she watched how excited Jacqueline was getting. She took both of Jacqueline's arms and raised them up over her head, then pressed her thickness against her body and kissed her. She picked Jacqueline up and threw her on the bed. They could barely speak to each other without arguing, but now Cleopatra was manhandling her on their bed—the bed in which Jacqueline had been sleeping alone for weeks.

She was furious, but she couldn't harness her desire to have her wife's body all over hers.

Cleopatra stood at the end of the bed, unbuckling her jeans as she watched Jacqueline pull off her t-shirt. Jacqueline licked her lips when Cleopatra pulled her large cock from her black briefs. A wave of desire flushed through her veins and her nerves melted into an inexplicable need. She laid down across the bed and called Cleopatra's name.

Cleopatra slid on top of her, grinding the dildo against her thigh, and Jacqueline dug her nails into her back. She pushed her pussy up against Cleopatra's hardness. Her cream flooded her, prepping her for Cleopatra.

Cleopatra kissed Jacqueline and sucked her tongue. Jacqueline's thighs shook as she smiled against Cleopatra's lips, and Cleopatra started to lick her way from Jacqueline's mouth down to her neck.

"Wait." Jacqueline pushed Cleopatra off her. "You think you can just come in here and have your way with me? You think you can just take it?" Jacqueline teased her.

Cleopatra looked in her wife's eyes and nodded her head

yes. She held her hips up and lifted her pussy toward her, and plunged into Jacqueline with unexpected and shocking force. Jacqueline gasped as Cleopatra gave her the entire length of her in one stroke. The magnitude and the sensation of her cock felt better than Jacqueline remembered. Making love to her wife stirred up emotions she hadn't felt since that night they made love in Cleopatra's hotel room. Jacqueline squeezed herself around Cleopatra's dick, moaning and begging for more as she ran her fingertips up Cleopatra's neck and into her locs.

The sounds that came out of Jacqueline's throat were low, aching, and erotic as Cleopatra moved inside of her. Sweat dripped from her body as Cleopatra stroked her tightness until they both lost control.

Jacqueline whispered "I love you" in Cleopatra's ear.

Cleopatra stood up and put her clothes back on. Before she walked out of the bedroom, she looked back at her wife.

"I love you, more."

FORTY SEVEN

....

WALK OF NO SHAME

"Hey, Lexi. Rough night, huh?" Cleopatra made loud kissing sounds from across the street. "I've never seen a walk of shame look so ... well, shameful." She laughed. Alexis looked back at Mandisa's front door to make sure she wasn't spying on her and motioned for her bodyguard to stay put. She walked quickly across the street and approached Cleopatra.

It had been several days since the custody case had been dismissed, and Cleopatra and Jacqueline still hadn't patched things up to where she was ready to move back home; if they weren't making love they would start to argue. There were still too many hurt feelings from the things they had both said and done, and too many things that needed to be said before they moved forward.

Early that summer morning, Cleopatra was leaving the house again, after spending the night.

Then she saw Alexis tip out of Mandisa's house across the street.

Alexis had toyed with Mandisa that night in her hotel suite out of desperation. But it all fell into divine order. She needed to buy herself some time to figure out what to do to keep her secret from coming out, and decided to keep her enemy as close as possible without actually sleeping with her. Truth be told, leading Mandisa on tickled Alexis; most of her revenge plots were a lot more rigorous and involved. Mandisa was as simple as they came.

"Don't draw attention to me like that." Alexis kissed Cleopatra on the cheek and walked her down the block, out of sight of both Cleopatra and Mandisa's houses.

"Draw attention to you? You have on a red halter dress and the widest brim on a sun hat that I've ever seen," Cleopatra teased her. "I hope you and Mandisa know what you're doing, Alexis, because you are both rabies-carrying, bat-shit crazy," Cleopatra warned her.

"This is true. But I'm crazier."

"Don't mess around and catch feelings for your enemy."

"That would never happen, so don't worry," she smirked. "If I told her to light her own ass on fire and walk in front of a subway train at this point, she would. I have her wrapped around my pussy and she hasn't even had it. None of these lips, as a matter of fact. Can you imagine if I let her actually have some of this?"

Cleopatra shook her head. "Yeah. You really are crazy." She backed away from Alexis. "I have to admit, when you said it was going to get messy, this is not what I was expecting. So what happens now?"

"My dear, it's best that you don't know about part two of this episode."

"I'm going to take your word for it," Cleopatra concurred. "So Alonzo is gone?"

"That he is." Alexis smiled.

"So..." Cleopatra was deep in thought until Alexis interrupted her.

"All you need to know is that he's far away, and not dead. He'll be well taken care of in his current location—which, I might add, is absolutely breathtaking—until all of the termination business is wrapped up. Then life will become significantly harder and he'll be relocated to a ... shall we say, a more primitive locale."

"Primitive? Why do I think Flintstones and Bedrock when you say that?"

"Ha! Close." Alexis burst into laughter. "Let's put it this way: You've heard of Third World countries?"

"Of course."

"Did you know there was such a thing as Fourth World?"

"Damn."

"I say all that, to say this: You won't see him again—that you can be sure of."

When Alexis put her mind to something, she was an unstoppable force. She left Cleopatra with the assurance that Alonzo would never bother her family again. And now she could direct her focus back to Mandisa. Alexis had wined and dined her, showered her with lavish gifts even Mandisa couldn't afford for herself, and mindfucked her into submission so much that she no longer responded when Alexis's husband beckoned her. Cleopatra joked that she had worked some voodoo and put a root on Mandisa, but stopped kidding when Alexis laughed a deep, guttural, uncontrollable laugh and failed to deny Cleopatra's claim.

So when Mandisa broke off her relationship with Alexis's

husband a few weeks later to enter into a committed relationship with Alexis, Cleopatra wasn't surprised.

ΦΦΦ

"Stay with me tonight," Mandisa begged Alexis. "I just want to talk."

Cleopatra had been right when she warned Alexis about the enemies becoming closer. Mandisa had caught feelings for Alexis in record time.

Alexis was not one to talk about her emotions, and not having been in a relationship with a woman outside of the sexual relationship she had with Cleopatra, had no idea that "I want to talk" was code for processing emotions.

They sat and talked on Mandisa's couch for a while, with Alexis doing most of the listening in between dozing off, waking back up, and pretending that she was paying attention.

But her ears perked up when Mandisa mentioned a former friend that had tried to break up Cleopatra's marriage.

"Supriti was infatuated from the moment she laid eyes on Cleopatra," Mandisa said. "I don't know how many times I told her to leave her alone. Cleopatra hasn't told me everything she's done, but what I've seen for myself is enough for a major beating. I don't know why her wife put up with it."

Because she was fighting for custody of her children, you silly wench, Alexis thought to herself. She had no idea that the woman Cleopatra had been spending so much time with was Supriti. She remembered her and Mandisa being attached at the hip in college, which made her a nemesis by association. This was the bitch that had inserted herself into Cleopatra's life? And Cleo-patra didn't appear to be shutting it down? She really did need the assistance that Alexis had offered her before, although Jacqueline was no longer under the court's microscope and free to lay hands on Supriti. But Cleopatra's wife need not worry about her.

Alexis was well versed at revenge, and would handle Supriti if no one else could. She preferred to teach lessons herself, ac-tually; no one was as thorough as she. Whatever she did always stuck.

Alexis was furious that things had gone so far and gotten that out of control, and she couldn't hide her emotions, or fix the rage on her face or how quickly her heart thumped in her chest. Her multiple follow-up questions annoyed Mandisa until she finally snapped.

"It's obvious that Supriti is not the only one that is obsessed with Cleopatra." Mandisa was furious that she had developed feelings for Alexis. Alexis had managed to make a fool out of her and she refused to just let her get away with hurting her. She was determined to get her questions answered and her sus-picions confirmed. "So you may not be fucking her now, but you've fucked her before. How long ago was it, Alexis?"

Mandisa would press her again and again about Cleopatra. And the more she pushed Alexis, the more she sealed her fate. Now Alexis realized that she would be forced to act swiftly. And not only did she need to shut Mandisa down; Supriti was more of a problem than Cleopatra had led her to believe.

Alexis would protect Cleopatra's interest at all costs, but now it was becoming a full-time job. Still, if anyone was up to the task, it was her.

It had taken what felt like forever, but Mandisa finally found a way to terminate Supriti's contract and fire her. She used a generically worded morality clause in her contract as the grounds for her dismissal, accusing Supriti of openly pursuing a married colleague, multiple counts of sexual harassment, and creating a hostile work environment. She threw a small severance package at her and enjoyed dismissing her former friend. She advised her to move back to the other side of the country if she was smart.

"Because I want you out of New York City." Mandisa and everyone on the executive floor watched as security escorted Supriti out of the building.

But it wasn't long before Mandisa realized that Supriti had no intention of leaving the city, or leaving Cleopatra alone. There was only so much abuse and bullying, so much backing up into a corner that Supriti would take before she snapped.

✿✿✿

"Cleopatra. What are you doing here?" Supriti asked as she stood outside her door.

"Teresa called me from the shelter. She said you tried to get a bed there. But she turned you away and you got belligerent with her. What's going on with you? Eww … you look terrible."

Supriti tried to brush her hair back and straighten out her sweats. She pulled Cleopatra into the loft by her arm. "You saw

486

Mandisa fire me and have me kicked out of the building, right?"

"Everyone saw it." Cleopatra shrugged her shoulders. "There's videos of it on YouTube. Nikki took video of it, even put it on her Facebook page with commentary. It's hilarious, actually. You should watch it … never mind … sorry."

"Well, that wasn't enough for her. She contacted all the top firms in the city to blackball me. I can't even get an interview, much less get hired somewhere. I'm so tired of her bullying people just because she has money. Well, I have more than she has now."

"What do you mean?" Cleopatra side eyed her.

"Sit down." Supriti patted a spot next to her on the white sofa. "I've been waiting for the right time to tell you. To thank you. Remember when you made me go home to see my father on his deathbed? He put a clause in his will that if I did go home while he was sick, and attended his funeral, I got his fortune."

"Fortune?"

Supriti nodded. "He left me—"

"No. No. I don't want to know the number. And this was on top of your trust fund, which had already pretty much set you up for life anyway?" Cleopatra shook her head. "Rich, or wealthy?"

"Wealthy." Supriti smiled.

"Who was your daddy, again? Never mind. What I don't understand is why the hell you're trying to live in a shelter."

"My landlord and Mandisa are friends. It's how I found the loft in the first place. She told him that I don't have a job or any way to pay my rent. He's threatening to void my lease and kick me out."

Cleopatra stared at Supriti, still waiting to hear the reason why she was trying to move into a woman's shelter. But Supriti had stopped talking.

"So he obviously hasn't kicked you out," Cleopatra prodded.

"No." Supriti shook her head.

"So he's just threatening you. Don't you know anything about real estate law? He can't do that. He's trying to scare you into moving out so he can rent your place for more money. And Mandisa's helping him. Wait. Why the hell are we even talking about rent? You just fell into all this money. Can't you buy this bitch now? Or any other place you want?"

Cleopatra saw a light bulb go off in Supriti's eyes.

"Actually, yeah I can." She smiled.

"Then why the hell were you trying to get into a shelter?" Cleopatra snapped at her, annoyed. "You're quick to play the victim when you have no plight."

Supriti shook her head. "Yeah. I don't know why I didn't think about that before. I haven't been thinking straight with everything that's going on."

"You've been through a lot recently, I understand. We tend not to think clearly when we're attacked. But this is not cute."

"Is that how you see this?" Supriti asked.

"It's obvious. Mandisa used the word 'ruin' on more than one occasion when she and I spoke of you. She was determined to get you. She's turned into an ugly person."

"Yeah, she has. Makes me think I need to get ugly myself. Someone needs to put her in her place for once. I would love to see that." Supriti gazed off into space.

"Are you just going to go back and forth like you're in middle school, trying to get back at each other until someone gets hurt for real? You weren't exactly innocent; she didn't start fucking with you for no reason."

"I need to take responsibility for my part in this, I realize that."

"You're a grown woman. You made some horrible decisions, and got fired, but life goes on. Now you were trying to take the bed from a woman that needs help. These women have no Soho loft, or a dime in the bank, or damn, even a bank account. You have no dilemma and you know that. You've even worked with these women. This self-absorbed, pitying shit is tolerable for about five minutes. You need to cut it out."

"You're right. I do." Supriti hung her head.

She would heed Cleopatra's advice, she thought. She'd dust herself off and work on rebuilding her life. But Cleopatra's warning to put a stop to the childish back-and-forth games of revenge with Mandisa would be a bit harder for her to heed.

"Are you ok?" Cleopatra asked her. "I mean, is there anything else going on with you?"

Supriti thought for a moment and hesitated before she answered. "No. I mean yeah. Everything is fine."

FORTY EIGHT

....

WHO DO I TURN TO?

{*Found a lump getting a biopsy today at Memorial Sloan.*}

When Cleopatra came up out of the subway at 42nd Street on her way to work, her cell phone alerted her to a missed text message. She was stunned by the cryptic message.

She hopped into a cab to East 66th and 2nd Avenue. She called her cell phone, but it went straight to voicemail. When she entered the cancer center waiting room, and didn't see her there, she got worried. Then the door to the ladies' room swung open.

"You came." Supriti's eyes filled with tears as she embraced her and rested her head on Cleopatra's shoulder.

"Of course. Tell me what's going on." She patted Supriti's back to calm her down.

"They found a lump in my breast and I'm getting a biopsy today."

"You're just telling me this now?"

Supriti pulled away from Cleopatra and looked in her eyes. "I thought I could handle it alone. But I can't. I'm so scared.

And I don't have anyone. I met with the psychiatrist and social worker, and they tried to prepare me. But I just really need you with me." She grabbed and hugged Cleopatra again.

"You're going to be ok, no matter what. This is one of the best hospitals in the country. I'll stay as long as you need me."

"Thank you."

"Supriti Khan," a nurse called from the front receiving area.

"Here." Cleopatra raised her hand and held Supriti up around her waist, but Supriti didn't move.

"She can come with you if you like," the nurse said as she walked over to them and touched Supriti lightly on the shoulder, attempting to comfort her.

Supriti looked up at Cleopatra, who nodded and said, "Ok." Cleopatra had again found herself in another situation that she probably shouldn't have been in. The common denominator was always Supriti. She and Jacqueline hadn't fully reconciled, and she was still living at the Soho Grand, and if Jacqueline knew where she was, she would try to knock Cleopatra's head off. But like it or not, Cleopatra had always been a good friend to people—loyal to a fault, deserving or not. She had yet to leave someone in a true time of need, and she didn't plan to start with Supriti.

Cleopatra walked with Supriti back into one of the private treatment suites.

Supriti froze and drew a blank when the doctor asked if she had any questions. So Cleopatra asked, since Supriti was too distraught to speak, what type of biopsy had been decided on. Would Supriti be awake? Would the doctor do it by feel or ultrasound? How many times would they go in? Would there be any scarring? And so on.

Supriti loved how Cleopatra could take control of any given situation at a moment's notice. She made her feel safe. She trusted Cleopatra with her life, and there was no one else she'd rather have by her side during this ordeal. She was convinced now that Cleopatra loved her. She wouldn't have come if she didn't. She would have just deleted her text message and gone on with her life. But she didn't; she dropped everything and sat by her side. Sensitive, patient, gentle, and in control. In this moment, she couldn't have loved Cleopatra more.

Supriti kept staring at her, and all she could muster up was, "Thank you."

Cleopatra stayed with Supriti during the biopsy and held her hand the entire time. She wiped her tears when she cried out in pain and kept her laughing at the most inappropriate times.

"So you can't feel anything, right?" Cleopatra blew on her nipple. Supriti was under local anesthesia and they had numbed her breasts.

"Are you seriously blowing on my titties?" Supriti laughed. "This is not how I wanted to be naked with you the first time."

"Those really are some nice tits you got there, though. You should be proud." Cleopatra winked at her.

"There's a needle in one of them right now, Cleopatra, don't make me laugh." Supriti gritted her teeth. "You need help. You need Jesus."

"You mean Ganesh don't you? Or Shiva? I don't know. You all have a lot of gods. I like Saraswati myself."

"What do you know about Saraswati? Oh, I forgot all your little Indian girlfriends."

"The Indian women I dated taught me a lot of lessons. Trust me, none of them were religious. Besides, I read!"

"Thank you, Cleopatra." Supriti couldn't stop thanking her.

Cleopatra saw her home that evening and made sure she was comfortable and fed. "If I had known this was all I had to do to get you to spend some time with me, I would have done this a long time ago." Supriti smiled.

"Someone is getting their sense of humor back, I see. That's what friends are supposed to do. Where else would I be?"

"Is that what we are? Friends?"

"You know what I mean. I know what it's like to feel and be alone. It's not fun."

Cleopatra offering her support did nothing to put out the longing Supriti still felt for her. She was there for her through her father's death and now a cancer scare. They weren't lovers, they weren't friends, and they weren't even supposed to be speaking, and yet Cleopatra gave her the emotional support she needed that no one else was offering. She didn't flinch no matter what mood Supriti was in. She'd be anxious, she'd be sad, scared, or angry, and Cleopatra let her cry whenever and however much she needed to.

Supriti thought back on the last several months and realized how insane she'd been acting. And she knew it would be equally insane if she didn't do everything in her power to keep a woman like Cleopatra in her life. She couldn't have her as a lover—that had been made clear—but Supriti could hold a place in Cleopatra's heart as a friend. And who knew; maybe one day it could turn into something more. But for now, she was satisfied. A little bit of Cleopatra was so much better than none of her at all.

Cleopatra went back with Supriti when the doctor called her in to hear the results a few days later. The biopsy results were negative, tumors were benign, and she was cancer free.

Supriti naturally hadn't wanted to do much while she awaited her results. She'd put her life on hold. She had barely eaten or set foot outside in the sun over those last few days, but she agreed to Cleopatra taking her out for a celebratory dinner. Only because Cleopatra promised her a surprise that would change her life.

It took Leroy Coleman the Fifth to help pull it off, but he'd found her in a battered women's shelter in East Oakland. When Cleopatra and Supriti walked into the restaurant, Supriti was greeted by her mother.

FORTY NINE

....

BITCHES GET STITCHES

"Hey. I got a message that you wanted to speak with me." Mandisa walked into Cleopatra's office. "Thanks for stopping by. This won't take but a minute. I just wondered if you had any idea what's been going on with Supriti recently."

"This is about her?" Mandisa rolled her eyes and bit her lip.

"You two have been friends a very long time."

"Well, that's over. We aren't friends anymore." Mandisa rubbed her hands together briskly to warm them. Cleopatra was blasting the air conditioner and Mandisa was freezing.

"I understand that. I understand your reasons—she made a play for me and you had a problem with that. Realistically, the only person who should have a real beef with her is my wife. I'm not sure that what she did was grounds to end a ten-year friendship, but that's your business."

"So why am I here?" Mandisa sat down in front of Cleopatra's desk, smoothing out her white floor-length skirt.

"Usually, no matter what the state of the relationship is, if somebody you were that close to is going through something like what she's gone through recently, you kind of suspend that

497

shit and find a way to show up for them."

Mandisa was appalled. "Do you know who I am? I am a princess in my country. One day I will be queen."

"And what country in Africa is that, Mandisa? Zumunda?" Cleopatra slammed her hand down on her desk. "Because nobody knows where the hell you're from. You tell everyone South Africa. South Africa isn't a monarchy. You do realize that we laugh at you, right? There's an office poll. The consensus pick was New Orleans. People think you're from NOLA. Even if you were royalty, that means nothing in New York City. I'm so tired of 'I was a princess in my country.' Yeah, that's nice. You know what people say to you under their breath? Do my laundry, walk my dog, watch my kid, deliver my food. Nobody gives a shit here. And what happened to the British accent you used to have? It used to come and go, and now it's just gone. *Bitch*," Cleopatra whispered under her breath. "Like I was saying, in instances like this, you try to be there for your friend, be the bigger person, even if just for a little while."

"I guess I'm not that big of a person, then."

"Well, I guess not. I'm not going to tell her business, but you do know what I'm talking about, don't you?"

"What, her father dying? And that cancer shit. She emailed and texted me, but I didn't respond. I wasn't interested. People die every day, people get sick every day. Circle of fucking life."

"Ok. Get out." Cleopatra pointed to her door.

"You know—" Mandisa started to speak and didn't hear Cleopatra command her to leave.

"Thanks for your time. Now get out of my office," Cleopatra said louder, standing up and pointing to the door.

"I was just going to say, speaking of your wife, that I don't see you around the house anymore. Hardly ever. Trouble in paradise?" She smiled. "Maybe I'll go over and knock on the door and see what Mrs. Jacqueline Giovanni has to say. Or maybe I'll ask her if she knows Alexis and knows that Alexis was sneaking out of there in just a bra and some panties a few months ago. Oh, and how I walked in and found you in a hotel room with Alexis half-naked in a garter belt. You think your wife would be interested in hearing any of those stories?"

"Did Alexis knock the sense out of you? I mean, when she beat your ass a few months back? Oh wait, that's the same night you said you saw her creep down my steps, right?" Cleopatra for the first time insinuated that she knew much more about Mandisa's interactions with Alexis than she had initially let on. "Seriously, did she literally beat you out of your mind? Because that's the only reason for my wife's name to be coming out of your mouth. You must be crazy. You do realize that I let it slide when you went and snitched on me and told Jacqueline I was in Supriti's bed. I know you were mad that I wasn't in yours. Everyone knows that. But get over it. And stay away from Jacqueline," Cleopatra warned her. "I'd be very careful if I were you."

"What?"

"Fuck with me and my family, and I'll fuck with you and yours."

Supriti took up the hobby of harassing Mandisa with angry

emails and voicemails. Mandisa brushed them off as juvenile until they got progressively angrier and more aggressive.

It all came to a head when Supriti showed up at a board meeting at Midtown Properties and proceeded to scream at Mandisa about her being jealous of her relationship with Cleopatra. And how she would never get away with firing her and trying to destroy her career, and how now with her new inheritance Supriti was by far the richer of the two of them.

When Supriti was confronted by security, she snapped. She spat on one of the security guards, flailed her arms like a windmill, and landed blow after blow on the three male guards that tried to subdue her. She continued to curse out Mandisa, going back and forth from Hindi to English. Cleopatra stepped in to keep them from tazing her, and walked with security as they escorted Supriti out of the building, passing by just about everyone employed by Midtown Properties, who all saw her second ceremonial removal.

Nikki caught Supriti's attention as they marched her out through the crowd of enthralled onlookers.

"I told you, girl. I told you don't. But you don't listen." She shook her head.

"You're making a real ass of yourself. Cursing her out in Hindi? Really?" Cleopatra asked.

"You understood what I said?" Supriti smiled.

"I have a good idea what you said. Look, Mandisa is done with you, and you have no business here. You have to move on, this is not a good look. How do you go up to someone's job, a place of business, and threaten them? And in front of everyone. Do you realize who was in there? The president, the CEO, the CFO. You really won't work in this city again, now.

You're smarter than this. Seriously, just get your shit together." Cleopatra walked away.

"You're right, and I'm sorry. I didn't mean to embarrass you or hurt you," Supriti called out to her.

Cleopatra was confused. "You haven't done either. I know that your feelings have probably gotten stronger, and you think we're cool now because I was there for you when you needed me, but nothing has changed. What you do doesn't affect me, Supriti. I don't love you, I don't want you, and I don't need you. Like I said, get your life together. And please leave me out of it."

❁❁❁

From there on, the wrath appeared to come down on Mandisa from all directions. She was robbed at gunpoint right on her front steps in broad daylight, and no one saw a thing. Days later, a pigeon shit-covered brick came burrowing through her living room window, just missing her head, and no one saw a thing. The Visine eye drops that she kept in her purse were switched with Crazy Glue. Her right eye was glued shut for three days and she lost all of her eyelashes. The final straw was Mandisa's father being run down by a black SUV while he was out for his evening stroll along Central Park West. They broke his leg and killed the family dog. And no one saw a thing.

With all the upheaval in her life, Mandisa ran back to Alexis's husband Christopher. She didn't know where else to turn, and knew at least that he would protect her. But she wouldn't dare tell him that she thought Alexis might be behind her recent misfortune. She couldn't even prove it. The police had no suspects in any of the cases, and Alexis was three thousand miles away, in California. Then again, Alexis didn't usually do her own dirty work. But getting Mandisa would have been so personal that she wouldn't have been able to resist being actively involved.

Then there was Supriti. She had been gunning for her, and appeared to have gone off the deep end. So much so that Mandisa had gotten a restraining order against her. Even Cleopatra had all out threatened her and her family at the mere idea of her speaking to Jacqueline. And then there was Jacqueline herself, who had professed regret in not dealing with Mandisa earlier, and vowed that she would get what was coming to her.

Mandisa showed up at Alexis's hotel the moment she arrived back in New York City. She had convinced herself that all of the crimes were entirely of Alexis's doing.

"I love it!" Alexis clapped her hands. She laughed so hard tears streamed down her face. "But seriously. You've had a bad couple of weeks, huh? I actually don't know whether to be insulted or not. You really think I did all of that? What happened to you is like … ahh…" She snapped her fingers as she closed her eyes. "It's like robbing a credit union in the ghetto. It's far too much work for too little pay off. I would've just had you killed."

Mandisa was stunned by Alexis's candor and terrified at the possibility that she didn't have anything to do with the incidents. If not Alexis, then who?

Alexis laughed as she pinched a ridiculously large diamond pendant between her fingers. "Do you like this? Present from my husband." Alexis winked at her. "Anyway, I'm kind of un-comfortable being this close to you. You've had some bad luck recently and I don't want it to rub off on me. I think you should go. But be careful out there—my husband can't protect you from everything. And have you heard? Those streets are mur-der."

Sadly, Mandisa mistook Alexis's husband letting her back into his bed as much more than it was, so when she learned that he had no intention of ever leaving Alexis for her she was heartbroken. A divorce would cost him half of his fortune, and he wasn't giving that up for anyone. Mandisa already knew that he and Alexis had an understanding—they could both satisfy their needs outside of the marriage with discretion. But he did admit to Mandisa that sensing Alexis's sexual fluidity, he'd added a clause to their prenup. If Alexis were to be caught in a lesbian affair he could divorce her and retain all of his wealth. Proof that Alexis was gay would be the only way he would ever divorce her.

And that was dangerous information for Mandisa to have.

Mandisa racked her brain to come up with a plan to put an end to Alexis and destroy her sham of a marriage. She went back to the drawing board and thought back to months before, when she first became convinced that Alexis was gay. It was the moment she spotted Alexis sneaking out of Cleopatra's townhouse practically naked under that chinchilla fur. She knew there was something suspect going on then, but Christo-pher and Supriti had kept her distracted from investigating any further and getting solid proof. She would never get any infor-mation out of Cleopatra—that would be a dead end. There was nothing for her in outing Alexis. She didn't need anything, so

Mandisa couldn't bribe her with money, and her loyalty to Alexis would ultimately prevail.

Worst of all, she didn't need Cleopatra alerting Alexis that she was trying to dig up dirt on her. Maybe if Mandisa could find someone who had known Cleopatra well, and for a long time, they would know details about her relationship with Alexis. But it had to be someone who had nothing and even less than that to lose. That's when it hit her.

Mandisa wasn't sure why she hadn't thought of it before. The person who could tell her all she needed to know was literally right under her nose. First thing the next morning, she headed into Midtown Properties and, instead of taking the executive elevators up to the top floor, entered through the service entrance and followed the ramp down into the basement, where a maintenance worker directed her to the mailroom.

"You must be lost or slumming. Which is it?" Shawn asked when she looked up and saw Mandisa standing at the front desk of the mailroom. "Can I help you with something?"

Mandisa hadn't had too much contact with Shawn while she dated Cleopatra, or since. But she never really liked her; she remembered Shawn as lazy, ghetto, mundane, and a hanger-on of a best friend. In other words, the perfect ally.

"Oh, you can definitely help me, Shawn. You have no idea." Mandisa smiled so hard that her face began to hurt. "I'm about to change your life."

✿✿✿

With all of the information that she had in her hot little

hands, Mandisa couldn't wait to make a move. But she was giving Alexis one last chance to come clean on her own. She sent Alexis dozens of text messages, threatening to out her if she didn't tell her husband, and do it immediately.

Alexis didn't fall for the bait by texting her back; instead, she just showed up outside of Mandisa's townhouse.

"I was trying to be the bigger person and let you tell Christopher." Mandisa smiled. "But you're obviously not taking me seriously. If you don't tell him your deepest, darkest secret by midnight tomorrow, I will. Not only will I tell him, I'll show him evidence," Mandisa threatened as she sat across from her in the backseat of Alexis's Mercedes truck.

Alexis sat back unfazed, most of her face concealed by the large Jackie O sunglasses she wore. "You don't have any proof." She licked her lips confidently.

"Oh, I have enough."

"What are you going to do? Lie and tell him you were fucking me? If you do that, you'll never have him either."

"I have nothing to do with this. I'll come out of this totally unscathed—not a spec of dirt on me—and probably with your man and all that money of his."

Alexis gazed out the window at Cleopatra's front stoop, unimpressed by Mandisa's threats and more annoyed than concerned by her yammering.

"You should really be more worried about what I have on you," Mandisa interrupted Alexis's daydream. "You're not going to win this time. To see you with nothing would set my life on fire. Mmm ... my pussy is wet just thinking about it. You want to see?" She hiked up her black maxi dress, spread her legs, and winked at Alexis.

Alexis extended her high-heeled foot to push Mandisa's thighs back together. "Setting you on fire can be arranged. I do like my bitches hot and spicy," she laughed.

"You'll be on the first mule back to Mississippi. You have thirty-six hours." Mandisa placed a large manila envelope on the seat. "There's a present in there for you, too. I thought I'd get you a parting gift, since you're about to be, you know, *poor.*"

Alexis waited for Mandisa to leave the truck and go into her house before she opened the envelope. Inside was a large head-shot of a young Cleopatra, and paper clipped to it was a business card with Love Unlimited Escorts embossed on it, with the name Olivia Devereaux, Founder and CEO of Pleasure. Alexis felt hot and beads of sweat began to form on her forehead as she pulled out a copy of the property deed transfer. She'd signed it many years before, when she gifted her Greenwich Village townhouse to Cleopatra. And stapled to that was a copy of the actual deed in Cleopatra's name. Her stomach clenched as she felt pressure in her bladder start to build.

Alexis exhaled as she looked back down at the envelope. There was something else stuck inside. She dumped it onto the seat, and out fell a Greyhound bus ticket, one-way, from New York Port Authority to Jackson, Mississippi.

She tapped the partition and Sam rolled down the divider.

"Everything all right, ma'am?"

"What do you do when you have roaches, Samuel?"

"Ma'am?" Samuel asked for clarification.

"What do you do? Do you call the exterminator or do you stomp them out yourself?"

"No time for all that, ma'am. Stomp them out myself."

"Exactly."

....

FIFTY

THE ROOF, THE ROOF, THE ROOF IS ON FIRE!

"I can't hear you over the sirens, Jac," Cleopatra yelled into the phone. "Where are you?"

"There was a fire."

"Where? At the house? Are you ok?"

"No, Mandisa's house. The whole townhouse went up in flames, baby."

"Where are you and the kids?"

"The kids are in Jersey with my parents. I'm at the end of the block—they evacuated the whole street. But I'm fine. I'm ok."

Cleopatra ran out of her hotel and held a cab. "I'm close, baby, I'll be there in five minutes. You sure you're ok?"

"I'm fine and our home is ok, but ... Mandisa was in the house, baby. She's gone."

"Do you really think Supriti burned Mandisa's house down?" Cleopatra had just left Mandisa's memorial service and gone to Alexis's suite to confront her.

"She's in jail, isn't she?"

"That's not what I asked you." Cleopatra made herself comfortable on the sofa. "Some things just don't seem right. You know what I found to be odd? She was alone, with no chef, no housekeeper, no butler, no one in the house but her. And she never lifted a finger to do anything for herself. Someone is always there, except, when you two had your little play dates."

"Your point?" Alexis rolled her eyes.

"It's an enormous coincidence that she was by herself in that house, like it was arranged beforehand. Maybe it was calculated by someone evil, but not so evil as to take out anyone they saw as an innocent bystander."

Alexis stared at Cleopatra. "Interesting. I read in the newspaper that Supriti was the last person to see and be seen with her. They even have the 911 recording of Mandisa calling to report her for trespassing and sitting on her steps. She had a restraining order against her. Dozens of people heard Supriti threaten her."

"That's true. I saw it for myself. Guess you're right." Cleopatra nodded her head. Maybe she was wrong, thinking that this fire had Alexis written all over it.

"Anyway ... Supriti won't go to prison."

"Why would you say that?" Cleopatra asked.

"It looks bad on the surface, but there's no physical evidence against her," Alexis said confidently. "At least that's what the newspaper said." She shrugged her shoulders. "She wasn't stupid enough to leave a trail. I remember her from college—smart girl. She's emotional, entitled, and a bit obsessive, but not crazy … at least not like Kenya crazy." Cleopatra perked up in her chair. "Kenya needed to be off the street. Supriti just needed some sense knocked into her head. Sometimes you can't have everything you want."

Cleopatra knew if she kept talking to Alexis that the truth would reveal itself.

"Mandisa told you Supriti came after me hard, didn't she? You know she tried to break up my marriage?"

"Why don't you just come on out and ask me if I had anything to do with Mandisa's death? Ask me if I set that fire, Cleopatra. I'll tell you the truth. I promise." Alexis sipped from a highball glass of freshly squeezed lychee lemonade.

Cleopatra thought about it for a moment. "You know, I would. But I'm not sure I want to know."

"Have it your way. So, have you gone to see Supriti in jail?"

"You're joking, right? I've managed to keep my wife from killing me because of her so far. Why would I do something like go and see her? I actually want to save my marriage."

"That's very smart. I think I like this Jacqueline." Alexis smiled.

"All right," Cleopatra said. She was thoroughly confused, and not sure what to believe.

"You know…" Alexis stared off into space. "My mother used to clip coupons when I was a kid. If we didn't have a coupon for it, we didn't get it. And we saved a lot of money. So I do appreciate a good deal now that I'm an adult, even if I don't need to clip coupons anymore, and honestly haven't even seen one in over a decade." She laughed.

"What the hell are you talking about?" Cleopatra shook her head, confused.

"Both Supriti and Mandisa are out of the way. Buy one, get one free." Alexis rubbed her hands together. "Two for the price of one, the best deal ever," she laughed. "By the way—" She slipped her hand under the couch cushion and appeared to fish around for something. "—This belonged to Mandisa. Take a look at it." She handed a manila envelope to Cleopatra.

Cleopatra pulled out the Love Unlimited business card and an old picture of her with the name Taylor DuBois, a.k.a. Hot Rod scrolled across the back. The hair on the back of her neck stood up on end, and a chill left goose bumps on her skin. She clenched her fist and scrunched her own picture into a ball, then shuffled through the photocopies of the deed and the deed transfer to her house.

"So ... she pulled me into your shit, Alexis?"

"Still feel sorry for her?" Alexis whispered, and put an arm around Cleopatra, her sarcasm her way of offering her comfort. Cleopatra jolted away from her, silent and cold, then stood, facing Alexis with her eyes closed.

Alexis asked again. "Well, do you?"

"What?" Cleopatra asked, still with her eyes shut.

"Still feel sorry for her?"

Cleopatra opened her eyes and focused on Alexis. Then, in a low voice, said, "No. I don't feel sorry for Mandisa." She cleared her throat and raised her voice. "Or for the person that gave her this information." She held up the envelope.

"You don't?" Alexis asked, surprised.

Cleopatra shook her head. "Nope."

Alexis smiled as she nodded her head. "Good to know."

FIFTY ONE

....

LONG WAY HOME

"Cleopatra had gone home to her hotel suite to find Jacqueline there waiting for her.

"I've been busy packing up your things." Jacqueline pointed to her luggage. She'd packed up all of her clothes and placed them by the door.

"Remember you told me that our living apart wasn't an option, that if we were going to be mad at each other we were going to be mad at each other and be all up in each other's face? Well, that's what is about to happen." She pulled on Cleopatra's shirt and pulled her to her lips.

"When was the last time we kissed?"

"I don't remember." Cleopatra looked in her eyes.

"That's a shame." Jacqueline took Cleopatra's fingers, draped them across her lips, and sucked them into her mouth. Cleopatra pulled them out and kissed her.

"No." Jacqueline pushed her away. "When you called me that night and said you needed to fuck me, I won't lie. It was hot. And I wanted you bad. We finally had our version of a quickie. But I'm not a jump off or a booty call. Never was, and never will be. I'm your wife. I am so weak when it comes to you. But we are not … We are not making love again, you will not touch me again until your ass is back at home. The house is empty tonight; it will be just you and me. You can have me wherever, however, all over that house tonight if you want me. For the last time, Cleopatra, I want my wife back. So what's it going to be?"

✿✿✿

A short time later, Jacqueline saw someone who looked like Supriti standing down the block from their house. She was standing under the light of the street lamp, watching Cleopatra unload her luggage from the taxi and take it into the house.

Jacqueline couldn't resist; she jogged down the block in the darkness, toward Supriti.

"Somehow I knew that I would see you before the sun went down, and here you are, right on time. I believe this belongs to you." Jacqueline pulled a familiar box out of her shoulder bag. "Thanks, but my woman doesn't need this anymore. She's home now, so I can keep her neck warm."

Supriti pulled the Burberry scarf from the box, put it to her nose, and inhaled.

"Pathetic. I had it dry cleaned, so all traces of my wife are gone. You lose. Why are you even here? Just out on bail, and you come to the scene of the crime?"

"I had nothing to do with that fire," Supriti said emphatically. She looked across the street at Mandisa's townhouse. Prime Greenwich Village real estate didn't stay vacant long. It had already been gutted, and the new owner had started renovations.

"I was almost in there. Mandisa texted me to come by, that she wanted to be friends again. But I got there and she started screaming on me and called the cops, saying that I violated the restraining order. So I just ran off down the block. I could have been in that fire, too." Supriti drifted off in thought. "The police checked her cell records, and she never sent me any texts. They traced it to a smartphone app."

"You're boring me." Jacqueline faked a yawn. "What does any of this have to do with my wife?" She looked Supriti up and down. "You still got it bad for her, don't you?"

"I was just checking up on her. I guess you accumulate a lot of stuff when you stay in a hotel for months, locked out of your own home."

"I can take care of my wife. There's no need to check on her."

"Can you really take care of her? Your wife and I were just friends. She needed one these last few months. Kills me to admit it, but that's all she wanted from me, and that's what she'll get from me until she wants otherwise. Keep taking her for granted and I will succeed in taking her away from you next time. Keep her out of your bed and I promise she'll find her way to mine ... again. I assure you, next time I won't hold back. I'll always want Cleopatra. The moment she realizes she wants me too, she can have me however she wants me."

Jacqueline exhaled deeply and backed Supriti up against the wrought iron gate. The spikes of the gate dug into the middle of Supriti's back, but she couldn't push Jacqueline forward for the fear that would set her off.

"When you told my wife you wanted her, what was her re-action? Did she throw you over her shoulder, whisk you away, and make love to you for hours at a time?"

"No." Supriti cowered.

"Hmmm … that's what she does when I tell her that I want her. And yet you think you can have her. Why, because she has a thing for Indian women? Yeah, I know about that. I know about all of her fantasies and fetishes, because I fulfill all of them. And I'll continue to. So you see, whatever you think you can offer her, she doesn't need it. I give her everything she needs, and I do mean everything."

"Ultimately I want Cleopatra to be happy. I know it's dis-tracting, but you need to focus your energy on her and not all the women that want her. If you want my advice."

"I don't," Jacqueline interrupted.

"You know what? I've been through a lot in these last few months. I moved across the country to a city where I had only one friend, I lost that friend, I lost my job, my father died, and I had a cancer scare. But I'm still here. And I feel great. I feel strong. Because you know who was there with me through it all? Who made me realize that I could make it through any-thing? Your wife. She even found my mother, she gave me my mother back. She's an amazing woman, who only wants to be loved, and you need to remind yourself of that every day. I don't know, put a Post-It on your mirror and your refrigerator. What you need to do is go in the house and fuck your wife real good, because if things go back to the way they have been, I'm going to be the one fucking her real good. And once I get her, I won't give her back. Please mess up."

514

Jacqueline pushed her right index finger into Supriti's temple. "I told you before to let it go. You will never have her, over your dead body," Jacqueline whispered in her ear.

Supriti pushed Jacqueline off of her and moved to stand in front of a parked car, away from the iron gates. "Just so you know, Mrs. Giovanni," she smirked, "I won't ever let Cleopatra go. We could never lay eyes on each other again … and I will still never let her go. I'm not scared of you."

"I see. Wanting my wife's dick helped you grow some balls?" Jacqueline laughed. "Since you brought it up, why don't you go home so you can think about me fucking my wife?" She pushed Supriti so hard that she fell across the hood of the parked car, and bent down over her. "I'm sure you can conjure up a picture in your head of what it looks like when my wife and I make love. It's not like you've never had a front row seat to it."

Supriti was stunned as she lay on the car. She realized Jacqueline must have known she was in their hotel room watching her and Cleopatra that night.

"You never saw someone make love that good, long, and hard before have you? I hope you remember it, because you will never experience it for yourself. My wife and I are back together for good. Forever. Don't come for her again. If you do, you'll die screaming. Just like Mandisa."

FIFTY TWO

....

GUESS WHO'S COMING TO BREAKFAST?

"We're leaving," Shawn said proudly, with her chest poked out. It was just after sunrise on a warm Saturday in July, and she and Robin both stood on Cleopatra and Jacqueline's front steps. But Robin stood behind Shawn, out of fear that Jacqueline would sock her in the face.

Cleopatra stared at them both for a moment in confusion. "Rocks, bitch, kick 'em." She slammed the door in their faces and proceeded to walk back upstairs.

"Baby!" Jacqueline yelled at Cleopatra. She flung the door open. "Going where?" Jacqueline raised her eyebrows.

"Atlanta. We're going to start a new life, get out of both of your shadows, try and be our own people." Shawn pointed to the U-Haul they had double-parked down at the end of the block.

"You're moving to a new state? Together?" Cleopatra asked. "As a couple?" At this point, she didn't believe a word that came out of Shawn's mouth.

"Yeah. We're together." Shawn looked back at Robin. "Here you go." She handed Cleopatra four Whole Foods bags. Cleopatra opened one and found that it was full of $100 bills. "We're all even now. Paid in full."

Cleopatra paused as she looked at the money, knowing that Shawn had gotten it from Mandisa for blabbing about her past with Alexis. She wanted to ask Shawn if it was all worth it, but stayed silent.

Shawn didn't wait for a thank you or any other response from Cleopatra. She just moved to the side of the steps so Robin couldn't hide from her sister anymore. Cleopatra and Shawn both stared at the sisters, waiting for one of them to say something.

"Mom and Dad know?" Jacqueline asked Robin.

"Yeah. They understand that I need to do this."

"Don't call me for anything, but take care of yourself," Jacqueline said.

"I will." Robin nodded her head.

"Take care of my sister, Shawn. If I fucked her up, and we aren't even cool, just imagine what I'd do to you."

"I got it." Shawn tapped Cleopatra on the arm. "I want to apologize, man." Everyone turned and looked at her, waiting for her to continue and possibly say something heartfelt or profound. But Shawn went radio silent, then looked to be deep in thought. "Um ... for everything. I'm really sorry. I will call you. But I won't need anything."

Cleopatra smirked as all three of them looked at her, waiting for a reaction, assuming she and Shawn would have a sentimental moment. Jacqueline held her breath; she knew her woman well, and knew that what was coming would cut deep.

She was undecided about whether she wanted stay to get blood, flesh, and bone marrow splattered on her white La Perla robe, and pivoted, turning her right foot toward the foyer.

Meanwhile, Shawn anticipated that their twenty-plus-year relationship would endure, that Cleopatra would say goodbye on a high note, that all beefs would be squashed. Robin wasn't sure what Cleopatra would say, but was more concerned with whether her sister would sucker punch her as a farewell gift.

"That sounded almost genuine," Cleopatra laughed. "I'm lying. No, it didn't. It was half-ass, just like everything else you do. At least you're consistent, right? Why are you even here? You think I care that you're leaving and taking this crumb-snatching leech with you? Sorry, baby." Cleopatra looked at Jacqueline.

"Truth." Jacqueline nodded.

"You've known me longer than anybody else in my life," Cleopatra continued. "And you know if someone crosses me, I'm done with you. And I'm done with you, I've been done with you."

Shawn's body froze and sweat formed on her forehead.

"You are a hateful, envious, lazy, and ignorant mother-fucker," Cleopatra spewed at her. "And I don't have the en-ergy, the time, or the desire to breastfeed meaningless friendships and unnecessary conversations. And what is this? An unnecessary conversation. You're chipping away at my wife's time right now. So, as you so sympathetically mentioned that night in Prospect Park, about how everyone leaves me, you're right. They're gone and they are all dead to me, and that night you added yourself to that list. You've been gone, in my eyes for months. As I said at the beginning of this unnecessary conversation. Rocks." And she slammed the door.

"So what do you make of that, baby?" Jacqueline pulled on Cleopatra's black t-shirt to stop her. "Atlanta, just out of the blue?"

"I don't care. But if you really want to know, they lied to us and to each other. Let's say Shawn is leaving for health reasons, and Robin ... well, Robin is broke and is probably just hitching a ride. But I'm sure she's up to no good. They both have different plans for ATL, and it's going to be ugly when it jumps off."

✿✿✿

"What the...?" Cleopatra and Jacqueline had just slammed the door in Shawn and Robin's face, and hadn't yet gone back upstairs yet when the doorbell rang again.

"Sam?" Cleopatra said when she opened the door. She looked behind him and saw the black Mercedes Benz truck parked in front of the house.

"Hello, Ms. G. I have Alexis for you." Sam trotted down the steps to the back of the truck and opened the door.

Jacqueline joined Cleopatra in the doorway. "Who is that, baby?"

Alexis emerged from the truck in a white sundress, sunhat, and a pair of oversized sunglasses. She floated up the steps.

"Cleopatra. I know your wife wanted to meet me, so I figured no time was like the present. She can thank me for getting rid of that poor excuse of a baby daddy, and let's not forget Ms. Kenya. Bravo, bravo!" She clapped her hands.

Cleopatra introduced them. "Alexis Scarborough, meet the love of my life, Jacqueline Giovanni."

Alexis extended her hand. "It's a pleasure."

"Pleasure's all mine." Jacqueline shook her hand.

"I've heard so much about you," Alexis continued. "I know you can't say the same. Anyway, I'm starving and Cleopatra always raves about your cooking. I believe your Belgian waffles are her favorite. What's for breakfast? Do I smell Belgian waffles? *Could* I smell Belgian waffles?" she laughed, then turned and motioned to her chauffeur. "Samuel."

Samuel pulled a case of Perrier-Jouet from the back of the truck, skipped up the steps, and delivered the box to the foyer.

"Ahh." Alexis pinched Cleopatra's cheek. "And you thought I forgot that I promised you a case. Didn't you?"

Alexis turned her attention back to Jacqueline, and looked her up and down. "La Perla. Hmm," she said, referring to Jacqueline's silk and lace robe. "Yes, dear. We are going to get along just fine." She walked into the house, made herself comfortable on the living room couch, and instructed Samuel to pop open a bottle of the champagne.

Jacqueline stood there frozen, stunned, then turned to Cleopatra. "Do you know who that is?"

"That's Alexis."

"I mean, who she's married to?"

"Yeah, I do." Cleopatra smiled.

"Baby, can I ask you…" Jacqueline took her by the hand. "Do I know everything that I need to know, now?"

"Nope." Cleopatra bent down and took a bottle of champagne from the case and handed it to her. "Take this, you're going to need it."

EPILOGUE ONE

....

AND THEN ... THERE WAS THIS

"Somewhat dejected, both Robin and Shawn were silent as they left Cleopatra and Jacqueline. Neither of them was sure what their expectations were of their final goodbyes in the first place, but they were grateful that it was all over. They were walking down the block toward the double-parked U-Haul that would lead them to their new life in Atlanta when Robin's cell phone rang.

"Go ahead." Robin waved for Shawn to continue walking toward the truck.

Shawn jogged ahead and jumped in on the driver's side. Meanwhile, Robin stood on the corner and picked up the incoming call.

"I just got to Port Authority." Robin's ex-boyfriend and part-time lover, Javier, squealed into the phone, excited. "My bus leaves in an hour. Yaas ... bitch. I'll see you in the ATL in a couple days, baby!"

"Ok. Can't really talk now," Robin whispered into the phone, even though Shawn was already inside the truck.

"You found a place for us to stay, right?" Javier asked.

"Yeah ... Yeah, I got it all handled. Just wait at the bus station until I come for you."

Meanwhile, in the truck, Shawn's cell phone vibrated on her hip.

"You have a collect call from Arrendale State Prison Inmate 0001228410, Deneicia 'Niecy' Jenkins."

"Hi, baby," Shawn whispered into the phone as she watched Robin through the steering wheel from the driver's side seat. "I'm about to get on the road and head down there."

"Ok. I miss you, I just wanted to hear your voice."

"Miss you too. I put some more money on your commissary. I'll see you in a couple of days."

Operator: "You have thirty seconds."

"Ok, good. Drive safe. Love you." Niecy hung up.

Shawn honked the horn. "Come on!" she yelled, waving to Robin from the truck.

"Hold on." Robin held her hand up. She'd just received a text message on her cell.

{Jasmine: Hey baby, was called out of town on business, I told the doorman to expect my woman some time tomorrow, so he'll have your keys when you arrive. Bought out Vicky Secret, going to wear what you like as soon as I get back. Can't wait to spend our first night together. Welcome to Atlanta! Love u.}

{Robin: Love you, beautiful, I can't wait either!}

"Damn, come on. It's gonna take forever to drive down there. Ready now?" Shawn complained when Robin finally hopped into the truck.

"Let's go," Robin said. "I'm so ready to get the hell up out of New York."

"Me too. Give me a kiss." Shawn leaned over and puckered her lips.

Robin laid a kiss on her and slid her tongue into her mouth. "I love you, baby." She winked at Shawn.

"Love you too." Shawn's cell phone vibrated again, alerting her to a text message, and she looked down at it quickly.

{*Olivia: You were given 3 days to get out of NYC. If it were up to me you'd be at the bottom of the East River. Like I said, I gave you 3 days and 3 of them are already gone.*}

Then her phone vibrated again, there was a series of incoming texts from a blocked number.

{*Blocked number: The only reason you aren't dead is because Cleopatra saved your life at the last minute. Her exact words, "Death is too kind, let that piece of shit live."*}
{*Blocked number: Stop reading your text messages, and get the fuck out of this city.*}

A cold chill swept over Shawn's body. She had no idea who sent the texts. But whoever it was must have been watching them.

{*Blocked number: If you don't start the fucking engine of that fucking U-Haul truck I'm going to blow it the fuck up. Get the fuck out of this city.*}

Shawn panicked. She dropped her phone and started the

engine to the truck. Her phone vibrated again, and she picked it up and read the text message.

{Blocked number: Dumbass! How do you know we didn't plant a bomb on the truck while you were down the block giving Cleopatra that pathetic half-ass apology? Stupid!}

Shawn dropped the phone again, exhaled, and pulled the truck out into traffic. Her phone vibrated again, and she picked it up and read the text message while still trying to focus on the road.

{Blocked number: Thank you! Now, Don't text and drive!}

She wiped the sweat from her brow with the collar of her t-shirt. "So, do you think Jac and Cleo believed us? What we said to them back there?" she asked Robin.

"Why would they believe anything we told them? Anyway, forget them. This is going to be amazing. You, me, ATL, no Jac, no Cleo. We can just relax and focus on making each other happy finally." Robin caressed Shawn's cheek as she struggled to hold back her laughter.

"Finally, just you and me," Shawn snorted as she held in her own chuckle.

EPILOGUE TOO

....

...THEN THIS

Supriti,

If you're reading this, I must be dead. Fuck. If I'm dead, Alexis Scarborough killed me. You know her from college as Alexis Harris. She's in the closet and I threatened to out her. Now you must do it. You have to make her pay. Everything you need to destroy her—pictures, documents, who to contact—are on the enclosed iPad.

I know this is asking way too much of you given how our friendship ended but if you really do want to be with Cleopatra, if you are truly in love with her like I think you are, you will use what I'm about to tell you. Cleopatra used to be an escort, and Alexis was her sugar mama. I can't be entirely sure, but I don't think Cleopatra's wife knows about her past. Can you imagine the fallout? I know if Jacqueline were to ever find out, she would leave Cleopatra for sure and Alexis's husband would divorce her and send her packing on the first chicken truck back down south. Just think about what you're willing to do, and how far you're willing to go for Cleopatra.

I shouldn't have to say this, but be careful—Alexis is dangerous, obviously. And she watches over Cleopatra like a hawk. You don't want to get on her hit list, if you aren't already, and if I were alive and a betting woman, I would bet that you are.

If you do decide to go after her … be ready.

ABOUT THE AUTHOR

Tasha C. Miller is a self-taught, self-represented artist of both impactful images and wondrous words. Born in Brooklyn and raised in Detroit, her literary and art journey began when she was just a child. Tasha returned to her hometown to attend Pratt Institute and studied architecture. She then received her B.A. in Literature and Creative Writing from Harvard University. Tasha currently lives, loves, works, and plays in Brooklyn, New York.

Tasha is what most would call a serenely introverted and karmically indifferent writer. From a young age, she was fascinated by the tragic and felt compelled to write about it. She blames daytime soap operas for supplying her with that first taste of infinite despair. Since that time, she has written to experience a sort of high that caresses all of the senses and the soul itself.

Tasha's short fiction has appeared in the anthology *Longing, Lust, and Love: Black Lesbian Stories* and *Saints & Sinners 2011: New Fiction from the Festival.* Her debut novel, *She Wants Her* was a finalist for The Saints and Sinners Emerging Writer Award. *She Wants Her Too* is its sequel. To find out more about Tasha and what she's up to these days, visit her website: www.tashac-miller.com